Praise for Novels by

COURTNEY WALSH

IF FOR ANY REASON

"Warm and inviting, *If for Any Reason* is a delightful read. I fell in love with these characters and with my time in Nantucket. Don't miss this one."

ROBIN LEE HATCHER, AWARD-WINNING AUTHOR OF *WHO I AM WITH YOU*

"*If for Any Reason* took me and my romance-loving heart on a poignant journey of hurt, hope, and second chances. . . . From tender moments to family drama to plenty of sparks, this is a story to be savored. Plus, that Nantucket setting—I need to plan a trip pronto!"

MELISSA TAGG, AWARD-WINNING AUTHOR OF *NOW AND THEN AND ALWAYS*

JUST LET GO

"Walsh's charming narrative is an enjoyable blend of slice-of-life and small-town Americana that will please Christian readers looking for a sweet story of forgiveness."

PUBLISHERS WEEKLY

"Original, romantic, and emotional. Walsh doesn't just write the typical romance novel. . . . She makes you feel for all the characters, sometimes laughing and sometimes crying along with them."

ROMANTIC TIMES

"A charming story about discovering joy amid life's disappointments, *Just Let Go* is a delightful treat for Courtney Walsh's growing audience."

RACHEL HAUCK, *NEW YORK TIMES* BESTSELLING AUTHOR

"*Just Let Go* matches a winsome heroine with an unlikely hero in a romantic tale where opposites attract. . . . This is a page-turning, charming story about learning when to love and when to let go."

DENISE HUNTER, BESTSELLING AUTHOR OF
HONEYSUCKLE DREAMS

"Just the kind of story I love! Small town, hunky skier, a woman with a dream, and love that triumphs through hardship. A sweet story of reconciliation and romance by a talented writer."

SUSAN MAY WARREN, *USA TODAY* BESTSELLING AUTHOR

JUST LOOK UP

"[A] sweet, well-paced story. . . . Likable characters and the strong message of discovering what truly matters carry the story to a satisfying conclusion."

PUBLISHERS WEEKLY

"*Just Look Up* by Courtney Walsh is a compelling and consistently entertaining romance novel by a master of the genre."

MIDWEST BOOK REVIEW

"This novel features a deeply emotional journey, packaged in a sweet romance with a gentle faith thread that adds an organic richness to the story and its characters."

SERENA CHASE, *USA TODAY* HAPPY EVER AFTER BLOG

"In this beautiful story of disillusionment turned to healing, Walsh brings about a true transformation of restored friendships and love."

CHRISTIAN MARKET MAGAZINE

CHANGE OF HEART

"Walsh has penned another endearing novel set in Loves Park, Colo. The emotions are occasionally raw but always truly real."
ROMANTIC TIMES

"*Change of Heart* is a beautifully written, enlightening, and tragic story. . . . A must-read for lovers of contemporary romance."
RADIANT LIT

PAPER HEARTS

"Walsh pens a quaint, small-town love story . . . [with] enough plot twists to make this enjoyable to the end."
PUBLISHERS WEEKLY

"Be prepared to be swept away by this delightful romance about healing the heart, forgiveness, [and] following your dreams."
FRESH FICTION

"Courtney Walsh's . . . stories have never failed to delight me, with characters who become friends and charming settings that beckon as if you've lived there all your life."
DEBORAH RANEY, AUTHOR OF THE CHICORY INN NOVELS SERIES

"Delightfully romantic with a lovable cast of quirky characters, *Paper Hearts* will have readers smiling from ear to ear! Courtney Walsh has penned a winner!"
KATIE GANSHERT, AWARD-WINNING AUTHOR OF A BROKEN KIND OF BEAUTIFUL

"*Paper Hearts* is as much a treat as the delicious coffee the heroine serves in her bookshop. . . . A poignant, wry, sweet, and utterly charming read."
BECKY WADE, AUTHOR OF MEANT TO BE MINE

Courtney Walsh

If for Any Reason

Tyndale House Publishers, Inc.
Carol Stream, Illinois

Visit Tyndale online at www.tyndale.com.

Visit Courtney Walsh's website at www.courtneywalshwrites.com.

TYNDALE and Tyndale's quill logo are registered trademarks of Tyndale House Publishers, Inc.

If for Any Reason

Designed by Eva M. Winters

Edited by Danika King

Published in association with the literary agency of Natasha Kern Literary Agency, Inc., P.O. Box 1069, White Salmon, WA 98672.

For information about special discounts for bulk purchases, please contact Tyndale House Publishers at csresponse@tyndale.com or call 1-800-323-9400.

Library of Congress Cataloging-in-Publication Data
Names: Walsh, Courtney, date- author.
Title: If for any reason / Courtney Walsh.
Description: Carol Stream, Illinois : Tyndale House Publishers, Inc.,
   [2019]
Identifiers: LCCN 2019023540 (print) | LCCN 2019023541 (ebook) |
   ISBN 9781496434395 (trade paperback) | ISBN 9781496434401 (kindle edition) |
   ISBN 9781496434418 (epub) | ISBN 9781496434425 (epub)
Subjects: LCSH: Life change events—Fiction. | GSAFD: Christian fiction. |
   Love stories.
Classification: LCC PS3623.A4455 I3 2019 (print) | LCC PS3623.A4455 (ebook) |
   DDC 813/.6—dc23
LC record available at https://lccn.loc.gov/2019023540
LC ebook record available at https://lccn.loc.gov/2019023541

Printed in the United States of America

25	24	23	22	21	20	19
7	6	5	4	3	2	1

For my daughter, Sophia—
one of the strongest people I know

PROLOGUE

Dear Emily,

As I write this, you are approximately six days, three hours, and thirty-two minutes old. We've been home from the hospital for four days, and I haven't been able to stop looking at you the entire time. You sleep in a bassinet next to my bed, and I lie awake at night, listening to you breathe.

To be honest, listening to you breathe is all I do. I feel like it's my sole responsibility to make sure that continues. It's a little scary, if I'm honest. And I'm always honest. You see, you came as a bit of a surprise to me, and I guess that's why I've been so nervous lately, in the days leading up to your birth. Because I don't want to mess anything up.

I don't want to mess you up.

People always talk about how wonderful it is to have a baby, but no one ever talks about how terrifying it is too. You see, I'm a little bit terrified, and I'm not sure who else to tell. I'm pretty sure my mother would use that fear against me somehow, so I'll only share it with you, my little girl.

I'll share it because I want you to know that sometimes we have to do things that are scary in order to get to something good. Sometimes the hardest things we're faced with bring us the best results. It's strange how that works, but it's true.

1

You're probably wondering why I'm writing you a letter when I could just pick you up and tell you this in person.

Well, I've always wondered about my own childhood. I remember once sitting on the floor of my friend Samantha's bedroom, looking at her baby book. It was a scrapbook, I guess, and her mom had written all kinds of funny stories about Samantha from the time she was a baby and stuck them down next to photos of her at every stage of life. My mom isn't the sentimental type, so I never had a book of stories. I don't know what she was thinking about anything, and I wish I did. Maybe then I wouldn't feel so alone.

I'm not the crafty type, so I decided letters were more the way to go. Lessons I've learned along the way and want to pass on to you. Love letters to my little girl. I'll put them all together in a book and keep it for you. And if for any reason I can't tell you these important lessons in person, you'll still have my words, so you'll never have to wonder what I would say.

I won't waste time on silly or frivolous lessons, only the ones that mean the most to me, so if this book falls into your hands, I hope you'll give it the attention it deserves.

I'm not a wise woman. Most people wouldn't call me a woman at all, not yet anyway . . . but I'm learning so many things about myself, and bringing another person into the world has made me grow up fast. I want to be the best mom I can for you, Emily. It's you and me against the world.

And you know what? I'm terrified. But I'm going to do the very best job I can. I know I'll make mistakes, but hopefully you'll forgive me. I never knew how much love I had to give until I held you in my arms.

And PS—I'll do my best to keep Alan and Eliza off your back . . . mostly I'm guessing they'll want to stay on mine!

Love you so much,
Mom (It's so weird to write that!)

CHAPTER 1

~~~

EMILY ACKERMAN HUMMED WHEN SHE WAS NERVOUS. No particular song, just whatever melody popped into her head. At that moment, it was the Harry Connick Jr. version of "It Had to Be You," the one in the old movie *When Harry Met Sally*. Her mom's favorite.

The bouncy melody danced around her mind as she closed her eyes and pretended she was anywhere but on the ferry from Hyannis to Nantucket. She made her living pretending, and she'd traveled the globe for the last ten years—why was this so hard?

She leaned her head back, thinking only of the song—of Harry's smooth, sultry voice—but instead of going blank, her mind wrapped itself around a memory. Her mother, dancing on "their" beach, singing "It Had to Be You" at the top of her lungs while Emily dug her feet in the cool sand and giggled at her silliness.

Emily opened her eyes and found a little boy with dark hair and big brown eyes staring at her.

"You're loud," he said.

"Andrew, that's not polite." The boy's mother wrapped an arm

3

around him and pulled him closer. "I'm so sorry. We're working on manners."

Emily smiled at him. "Sorry. Sometimes I get lost in my own world."

"Me too," Andrew said. "I have an imaginary friend named Kenton."

Emily widened her eyes. "I had an imaginary friend when I was little!" She tried to sound more excited than she felt. She was an actress. It wasn't that hard.

And yet, for some reason, it left her feeling hollow.

"Mom says people will think I'm out of my mind if I keep talking to myself."

Andrew's mother gave him a squeeze. "Andrew, let's leave the nice lady alone."

Lady? Emily knew the other side of thirty was a downhill slope, but when people started calling you "lady," you might as well sign up for AARP.

"I'm Andrew," the boy said. Then he looked at his mother and blinked. "See? That's manners." Then back to Emily. "Now you tell me your name."

"I'm Emily."

"Mom says I'm not supposed to call grown-ups by their first name."

"Oh." Emily glanced at the boy's mother, whose expression was a cross between amused and apologetic. "I guess you can call me Miss Ackerman."

"Miss Ackerman," Andrew said. "Nice to meet you."

Emily decided she liked this boy. She hoped he didn't lose his charm as he got older, and she hoped even more that he remained genuine. So many men she'd known were the exact opposite. Not a single one worth holding on to.

Especially not Max, who, she was convinced, had never told her one honest thing the entire time they were together. Not that it mattered really. Emily's rules were set up to protect her from getting too attached. She'd never stick around long enough to find out if a man's motives were impure—three months and she was off. Max had taken their breakup harder than she'd expected. He'd actually cried.

Ugh. The memory of it made her feel like such a jerk.

Emily exhaled. She'd been doing so well. Why did she have to go and think about Max?

The regret wound its way back in, and she could feel her cheeks flush at the memory of him. Maybe he'd actually loved her? Maybe she should've given him more of a chance?

But no. She'd taken Mom's advice to heart, as she did in all things, but especially about this. Her mother knew something about heartache, after all.

Be passionate in other areas, but in matters of the heart, be mindful to use caution. Your heart isn't something to give freely and without thought. It should be protected at all costs so you can ensure your whole world doesn't come crashing down around you. Hear me on this, Emily. I know what I'm talking about.

Without thinking, Emily slid her hand inside her bag until it found the soft, worn cover of the book of letters. In all her travels, it was the one thing she always made sure to keep close.

While Emily didn't know all the details, she knew that Isabelle Ackerman had suffered a great heartache. She only wished her mother had gotten a bit of closure before she died.

The letters were unspecific about so many things, but this was not one of them. This was not an area where she had to wonder what her mom would say—Isabelle had found a way to get her message to her only daughter, and Emily had fully embraced it.

She'd kept her heart safe. When someone got too close—and they did sometimes—she knew it was time to run. Also time to run when she could feel herself liking someone too much, which was what had happened with Max. He was charming and handsome and wealthy, and Emily knew if she hadn't been careful, she could've convinced herself he was worth a little rule breaking.

Thank goodness she wised up before there was permanent damage to her heart.

She had enough damage to deal with, and sadly, none of that could be blamed on Max or anyone else. It had been her own stupid mistakes that had landed her here—penniless and reeling. She hated the way this felt.

An utter failure. That's what she was.

When she'd finished writing her play, she'd been so confident in it. She'd seen so much potential, and nothing could've dissuaded her—not even the rejections from several big-name directors who wanted nothing to do with the project. They'd left her no choice but to produce and direct it on her own.

She should've listened. She should've started small. She didn't. Instead, she sank everything she had into the show.

She'd given all her blood, sweat, and tears to her work—and yes, most of what was left of her trust fund. So when the play opened to terrible reviews (*"A meandering disaster that doesn't know what it's trying to be"*) and folded in two weeks' time, she was left with nothing but people to pay and a humiliating professional failure.

She'd bet on the wrong horse, so to speak. The show had so much promise—she'd been so sure it would be a huge hit. She'd been so wrong.

Worse, everyone in the theatre world now knew that she was a failure—there was a huge article about it in *Backstage* magazine. A cautionary tale of sorts.

"Former Child Star's Directorial Debut Is This Year's Worst."

At least she could take comfort in the fact that her grandparents didn't read *Backstage*.

She supposed it was the one blessing in GrandPop's dying when he did. He never found out she'd lost everything with her poor business decisions or her short-lived creative endeavors. He'd never known just how incompetent his granddaughter was, even after years of watching him make millions with his savvy business sense.

But that was over now. Now, sitting on the ferry next to her new best friend, Andrew, Emily screwed her eyes shut and willed herself to stop thinking about Max, her failures, her grandparents, and her empty bank account.

She wasn't sure which of those things would be most difficult to put out of her head. All of them seemed to have her attention at any given point of the day. She supposed that's what happened when you hit rock bottom. You wasted a lot of time replaying your mistakes, trying to figure out if there was any way to undo them in order to right your own ship.

So far, she'd found no indication such a solution existed. She only knew that when you found yourself at rock bottom, it would be nice to see a hand offering to pull you up.

For her, there was no hand, and that was maybe the worst part of all.

"You're humming again." It was Andrew. Earnest Andrew and his big brown eyes.

"Don't grow up to be a jerk, okay, Andrew?" Emily said absently. Andrew's mother frowned.

"Sorry," Emily said. "Sometimes I say inappropriate things."

"Kenton does that too. One time he spent the whole day talking about poo." Andrew's face was so serious Emily couldn't help but laugh.

He smiled at her. "What's your imaginary friend's name?"

"I don't see much of her anymore," Emily said. "But her name was Kellen."

"Kellen," Andrew said. "Kellen and Kenton. I bet they're friends."

"You ask him the next time you see him, okay?" Emily smiled. She'd been having such a lovely time with Andrew she didn't even notice the ferry had slowed and was now docking in Nantucket.

If she closed her eyes tightly enough, Emily could almost imagine she was just another Nantucket tourist. If she stopped her mind from wandering, she could almost believe it was her first time on the island, her first time seeing in real life what she'd only seen in photos—the cobblestone streets, the gray Shaker homes with big bushes of purplish-blue hydrangeas out front, the rows of brightly colored Vespas for rent, the lighthouses that beckoned weary travelers to come and rest here.

Nantucket made promises, but in her experience, the island didn't make good on them.

What she wouldn't give for this to be her first time.

But it wasn't, was it?

She glanced into her big, floppy bag, the one where she'd stuffed all the necessities, including the haphazardly assembled book of letters, worn with years of handling. Sometimes just touching it was enough to make her mother feel close, almost like she had a magic lamp she could rub and see her wishes come true.

But as she placed her hand on the tattered, hand-decorated cover, even her mom felt far away.

It was as if her presence had been pulled out of the book the second the island came into view. As if even her mother's memory wanted to forget.

All around her, other passengers were gathering their things, anxious to get the season started on the island. But Emily stayed in her seat, dazed and maybe kind of motion sick. Or perhaps the nausea had nothing to do with the boat ride at all.

If she were smart, she would've approached Nantucket the way she would a two-day-old Band-Aid.

One quick rip and it would all be over.

If only . . .

"You're getting off, aren't you?" Andrew stood in front of her now, his red-and-yellow tiny-person backpack wrapped around both of his shoulders, a red baseball cap doing its best to tame his unruly chocolate-colored hair.

"I'm thinking about it," Emily said with a smile.

"You like it here, don't you?"

Ooh. A trick question. What was she going to tell the kid? That this island had stolen everything from her and she was only back here because she had absolutely no other option? His mother would probably call the police.

"Yes, it's very lovely," she finally said. It wasn't a lie, not really. Nantucket *was* lovely. At least it was for other people.

"I love this place," Andrew said. "Here." He held out his fist and gave it a shake.

She held her hand out underneath his and he dropped a smooth white rock into it.

"I found this on the beach last summer." Andrew grinned and she could tell his front tooth was about to fall out. "You can have it."

Before she could protest, Andrew's mom gave his hand a tug.

He looked back at her and waved, and for the briefest second Emily's heart ached.

His mom was, quite possibly, younger than Emily. And she had that beautiful little boy and probably a devoted husband waiting for her somewhere. That life had never appealed to Emily, but in that moment—and it was a fleeting one—something tugged at her insides.

But Emily didn't have time for heartache when she was about to get off the ferry. She grabbed her suitcase, her purse, and the large bag she'd stuffed with toiletries, Kind bars (to keep from eating junk), dark chocolate–covered blueberries (because sometimes it was okay to eat junk), two books, and anything else that hadn't fit in her suitcase.

She made her way to the door of the ferry and drew in a deep, deep breath.

I can do hard things.

She'd tossed the mantra around in her head for so many months, the words were meaningless by now. Well, they were pretty much already meaningless because once a phrase caught on and became popular, it lost its value. Every fitness expert in America probably shouted those words out as they reached the fourteenth rep of a particularly challenging exercise.

But she *could* do hard things. She'd been doing hard things since she was eleven years old.

Emily stood at the edge of the island and took another salt-tinged breath, the faint smell of fish reminding her that not everything near the ocean was lovely. Certainly not.

She pinched the bridge of her nose and willed herself to press onward. She hadn't come this far to chicken out now, and besides, what other choice did she have?

Sometimes she wished Nantucket hadn't been ruined for her. Just another complaint to add to the pile, she supposed. If she wasn't careful, she'd rack up so many she'd become one of those cranky old women whose mouths were permanently frowning, like that cartoon character, Maxine, on the Hallmark cards.

Or her own grandmother.

But no, that would never be her. Not Emily Ackerman. Not the girl who looked for fun wherever she went (and usually found it). Not the free-spirited wanderer who'd worked acting jobs all over the world, had more friends than she could keep track of, and knew exactly how to turn every trip into an adventure.

This was just another trip, right? Never mind that this trip had a purpose other than fun. This trip was her second chance—and she could not screw it up.

That certainly put a damper on any plans for a good time.

She dragged her single suitcase behind her, aware how pathetic it was that at the age of thirty-one, she could fit nearly everything important to her in one suitcase—and it wasn't even the largest one in the set her grandmother had sent when she graduated from college nine years ago.

She heaved a sigh and moved with the flow of foot traffic as tourists flooded off the ferry and onto the street. When she was a girl, this was the moment she looked forward to all year long—the moment her flip-flops hit the cobblestones, the moment she and her mom arrived in Nantucket.

So much had changed.

As she watched Andrew's red-and-yellow backpack disappear into the crowd, she said a quick prayer that his days in Nantucket were filled with nothing but good things—lobster boils and fish fries, giant ice cream cones from the Juice Bar and long, sun-kissed days at Jetties Beach.

She wished for him all the things she would've held on to if Nantucket hadn't been ruined for her all those years ago.

And suddenly, she wasn't so sure she actually could do hard things.

But she was about to find out.

CHAPTER 2

~~~

Hollis McGuire watched the summer crowd get off the ferry and flood the street in front of him, wishing he could slow his pulse.

It hadn't been that long since he'd seen Jolie, but what if he didn't recognize her right away? He'd give her a complex, send her to therapy for years. But wasn't that usually what parents did to their kids?

Last night on the phone, he'd told Jana exactly where he'd be standing, but what if she hadn't relayed the message to their twelve-year-old daughter? What if Jolie was lost in that crowd somewhere? His eyes scanned the people exiting the ferry and for a moment he felt like he was thirteen again, a kid who didn't fit in with this crowd, a kid only good enough to clean their pools, pull their weeds, or carry their golf clubs.

He watched as an old couple, Rich and Helen Delancey, filed off the ferry. They'd been living every summer in Nantucket for decades. They were old money, and Rich was a decent guy—he was the one who'd taught Hollis's father about the stock market, and without that, his dad might still be working as a sailing instructor at the

12

Nantucket Yacht Club, which was what had brought them to the island in the first place all those years ago.

Jeffrey McGuire was something of a sailing legend, but he didn't come from money, and even though they did okay, they were poor by Nantucket standards, which had always carved a deep chasm between Hollis and the rest of the Nantucket kids.

It seemed like the perfect place to bring Jolie for a few weeks—after all, they hadn't spent more than a couple nights together in . . . well, ever. Hollis wasn't proud of it, but it was reality.

But now? Well, what else did he have to do? It's not like his calendar was exactly full.

He watched the crowd slim down and still saw no sign of Jolie. He started to get nervous. He pulled his phone from his pocket to see if she'd called or texted him that she'd arrived, but his phone was blank, except for his lock screen—a photo of his daughter.

He'd changed it that morning, horrified to find the most recent photo he had of her was two years old.

He could've done without that reminder—he regretted so much as it was.

He glanced up as a woman appeared at the top of the ramp. He didn't recognize her, but she was vaguely familiar. Hollis watched as she put her sunglasses on and tossed a hand through her long, wavy blonde hair. She wore a thin white T-shirt that dipped to a V, leading his eyes straight to a place they shouldn't go. She was on the tall side of average height with narrow hips and long, slender legs, and even if nothing about her was familiar, he still would've noticed her. She had a sort of effortless beauty, the kind that didn't require heavy makeup or fake nails.

After several seconds, the woman started off the ferry, but she quickly stopped. As she did, she pinched the bridge of her nose, holding it tightly for a moment.

In a flash, he was a kid again, standing on the beach next to Emily Ackerman—the girl who'd stolen his preteen heart—holding a freshly picked bouquet of wildflowers and marveling at her beauty.

"Emily?" Hollis straightened, squinting to get a better look at the woman as she came down the ramp.

"Dad, I'm right here."

Hollis startled at the sound of a girl's voice. He turned to face her. "JoJo, you made it!"

"Yep." Her expression told him she was less than thrilled.

Jolie was twelve going on twenty-five, probably a result of Jana's loose parenting. Jana was a good mom, but she treated Jolie like one of her friends half the time. Not that Hollis had any right to an opinion on the matter. It wasn't like he'd been around.

Regret twisted in his belly again.

He looked up, but the woman who'd reminded him of Emily was gone. It had been so many years since he'd seen her, he was foolish to think he'd recognize her even if she was standing right in front of him.

But the way that woman had pinched her nose . . . Emily had always done that, usually when she was deep in thought or worried about something.

Emily Ackerman. How many years had it been? And why did his pulse quicken at the thought of her? He'd been a kid the last time he'd seen her, not even old enough to call his little crush "first love."

But Emily had stuck with him. How many times had he wondered what had happened to her after that awful night?

And when had he stopped wondering . . . ?

"Earth to Dad?" Jolie dropped her backpack on the ground at her feet.

Hollis picked the bag up. He needed to stay focused. This summer was about redeeming himself. He'd already lost so much time—he knew he didn't have much left. After all, his only daughter wasn't getting any younger.

"Sorry, kiddo," he said. "Did your mom and Rick get out okay after the wedding?"

She shrugged. "I guess."

"Your mom said you'd have pictures from the big day."

"You really want to see them?"

"'Course I do."

After a pause, she pulled her phone out of her back pocket.

Hollis flashed her a smile. "Just show me the ones of you."

She swiped around on her phone, then finally turned it so he could see an image of his daughter, wearing a yellow bridesmaid's dress, holding a small bouquet of orange roses.

He grabbed the phone out of her hand. "This cannot be you." Her hair was swept up, a few loose curls around her face, like a high schooler heading off to the prom. How had they gotten here?

How had he let himself miss so much of it?

She tried to hide her smile, but clearly his response was just what she was hoping for. She knew she looked gorgeous in this photo— she must've felt like a princess. He wished he could have seen her for himself. Not that he'd been invited to the wedding. Not that he would've gone anyway.

"Yellow isn't really my color." She tossed a strawberry curl over her shoulder.

"That's not even true," Hollis said. He swiped the screen, hoping to see another photo of Jolie, but was met with the image of Jana and her new husband, Rick, arms wrapped around his daughter and looking more like a real family than Hollis and Jana ever had.

His expression must've changed because she quickly snatched the phone out of his hand and clicked it off, the image of the happy trio disappearing.

"Looks like it was a great day," Hollis said.

"It was fine," Jolie said. "And now they're off in Hawaii and I'm here." She raised her eyebrows and let out a quiet sigh.

"I'm glad you're here," he said. And he meant it.

"I'm glad you're here too," she said. "My bags were getting heavy." She half smiled, and he knew that while he wasn't her favorite person, he hadn't completely fallen out of her good graces—not yet.

In spite of his many attempts to screw things up, Jolie had turned out to be a pretty great kid. At least he thought she had. He'd find out for himself over the next few weeks.

"Your mom looks happy." He picked up her bags and led her toward his car.

"She is," Jolie said. "Rick's good for her. Helped her settle down. Makes her feel pretty. You know, all the stuff she needs."

He studied Jolie and wondered how she'd gotten so wise in her long twelve years on this earth.

"Does it upset you?" she asked.

For a second, he thought maybe she hoped that it did—after all, she was their daughter and she'd probably had visions of the three of them one day—finally—becoming a family, no matter how many times he and Jana both told her they were sorry, but that wasn't going to happen.

"No, I'm happy for your mom."

Hollis wanted Jana to be happy. He wanted her to fall in love with someone who would treat her well and take good care of her (and make her feel pretty, he guessed), but he didn't want that someone to take his place as Jolie's dad.

Not that he'd done much to secure that place over the last twelve years.

"Are you hungry?" Hollis asked as he tossed Jolie's bags in the back of his Jeep.

"Starving, but I can't have anything with gluten."

Hollis tried not to roll his eyes. He wanted to be supportive of his daughter, but really?

"Or dairy."

"No, that's where I draw the line," he said. "We're going to the Juice Bar—like every day this summer."

She stared at him. "No other species consumes cow's milk into adulthood, Dad. Do you know how hard it is to digest?"

"I don't, but I know how good it tastes." They got in the car and ventured out into the narrow, crowded streets. Driving in Nantucket was typically more of a bother than it was worth, but Hollis didn't know how much luggage a tweenager would have when he left the cottage that morning.

Jolie sat quietly, staring out her side of his Wrangler. A group of boys about her age came bounding out of the Black Dog, laughing. Hollis thought they looked like they were up to no good. His daughter seemed to have a different opinion.

Jolie craned her neck to watch them walk down the street, and one of the boys lifted a hand to wave at her. She giggled and turned back around.

"Nantucket boys are off-limits," Hollis said.

"Oh, please, Dad," she said. "You were a Nantucket boy."

No, he wasn't. Not really. His family spent the summers here because an old college buddy got Dad a job at the yacht club. The money had been good enough to come back summer after summer, to bring Hollis's mom and eventually their family. The rental cottage was part of the deal, so how could Jeffrey refuse? It was like a gift, a working vacation that gave his kids summers they never would've had otherwise.

Those summers became a family tradition, and now, thanks to a few very wise investments, Jeffrey McGuire owned that little rental cottage.

So, yes, Hollis had spent his summers here, but no, he wasn't a "Nantucket boy." Growing up, he didn't know how it felt to have a disposable income. He didn't have people picking up after him or clearing the path so every one of his dreams would come true. The McGuires earned their money. And he'd made something of himself.

Now money was the least of his problems. Now he fit in. And yet, he still didn't.

He'd always be more comfortable in his Nike running shorts than a suit and tie. And he knew at his core he was still the same kid, sitting on the outside looking in on a life he didn't really want.

Maybe that's why he felt so displaced.

Maybe that's why it had been a year since his dream died and he'd yet to figure out what his next step was.

"You're doing it again," Jolie said, waving her hand in front of his face. "Are you this upset over Mom getting married?"

"No, not at all," he said.

He gently accelerated as he caught a glimpse of the woman he'd seen getting off the ferry. She pulled a suitcase down the busy street, and while she sort of looked like a tourist, she also sort of looked like she knew the lay of the land.

"Who's she?" Jolie followed his gaze to the sidewalk.

"Maybe nobody," Hollis said. "Probably nobody."

"Or maybe somebody?" Jolie waggled her eyebrows.

Yeah. Maybe somebody.

Hollis gave the woman one last glance as he stepped on the gas and drove away.

CHAPTER 3

EMILY SUPPOSED SHE SHOULD FEEL THANKFUL that Nantucket hadn't really changed. It was still the same charming island it had always been. Nobody would ever wonder why people chose to vacation here or, in many cases, spend their summers here.

If circumstances were different, Emily might do the same.

But circumstances being what they were, it was hard to feel that rush of sweet nostalgia. Even as she walked the cobblestone streets. Even as she window-shopped in the boutiques. Even as she remembered the way she and her mother would zip through town on their preferred method of transportation—the old bikes they buried in the shed behind the house.

She could practically hear the ding of the bell on her mother's robin's-egg-blue bike as they pedaled their way up and down the narrow, crowded roads.

Emily and her mom loved to ride all over the island. They'd search for seashells, dig up clams, collect rocks on the beach. Led by passion and not by common sense, Isabelle Ackerman had been the most carefree person Emily had ever known, which was perhaps what made her untimely death an even greater tragedy. All that zeal for life snuffed out in an instant, leaving only memories that played on a continuous loop for Isabelle's daughter.

Her mother's death had awakened something inside her. It made her keenly aware of the passage of time, the way it cruelly walked out, without a word of warning.

Somewhere around her sophomore year of high school, Emily had stopped living cautiously. She began to buck her grandmother's rules, to carve her own path.

She'd been carving ever since. Living her life the way her mother had dreamed she would.

No, nostalgia wasn't so sweet these days—not where Nantucket was concerned.

Emily stopped at an intersection, and when she looked up, she realized she stood on the corner of Water Street, where the arts center was situated, right in the center of a block.

Unhurried, she walked down the block, still dragging that suitcase behind her.

How many days had she spent in that very building? It had been the place where she'd first discovered a love of theatre, the first time she'd felt truly passionate about something. The first time she learned how it felt to make her mother proud.

She made her way over to the back entrance, which would lead her in to where all the rehearsal rooms were. She could still picture each room, decorated in a different theme. Photos from past shows had lined the walls of the hallways, a sort of "hall of fame," the kids said. Once upon a time, her face had been on that wall.

When she was a girl, the arts center had bustled with activity. Rehearsals went on at the same time as costume sewing and prop designing. Every classroom was occupied as music and blocking and dance were all taught on a rotation.

The children's productions put on at the arts center were summer events the entire island supported. Looking back on it now, she didn't know if it was because their shows were actually good or because the adults on the island simply loved seeing their kids onstage.

It didn't matter. It was about so much more than that. It was about making friends and having fun, sure, but Emily learned a lot too. She learned how it felt to be a part of something—to belong somewhere.

Now, as she walked down the hallway, she was struck by the quiet. The walls echoed with laughter left over from years gone by, but how long had it been since anyone filled the space with that same kinetic energy she'd known? The building seemed a shell of its former self, perfectly tended yet drained of all life. A remnant of what once had been.

She walked through the empty rehearsal rooms, down a long hall-way that ran parallel to the theatre. It led her straight out to the lobby, where there was a podium outside two doors leading to each side of the auditorium.

Emily inhaled the lingering smell of popcorn in the lobby, thankful that after all this time at least that hadn't changed.

Slowly she opened the house-left theatre door and walked into the space. The stage was bare and the theatre empty, lit only by work lights. She resisted the urge to get up on the stage and recite a favorite monologue—one of Helena's speeches from *A Midsummer Night's Dream* or Mabel Chiltern's monologue from *An Ideal Husband*.

An empty stage always had this effect on her. It made her want to jump up there and feel the lights on her face, to try on someone else's skin for a while. She'd found such comfort in shedding her own when it got too heavy.

Today her skin felt too heavy.

She walked out of the auditorium and into the lobby. Across from the box office was a large bulletin board with posters advertising all kinds of events happening at the arts center and around town—a book chat and signing with a local bestselling author, a culinary demonstration by a world-renowned chef, a French film festival, a concert series. The arts center was alive and well—but where were all the children's programs?

"May I help you?" A voice disrupted the silence in the empty lobby.

Emily turned and found an older woman with a pouf of white hair staring at her. She wore a pair of oversize black glasses, and though her skin had its share of wrinkles, it was still milky white.

Emily's skin would not look like that when she was this woman's age—far too much time in the sun.

"I hope so," Emily said. "I was wondering where I could find information on your children's programs."

The woman removed the glasses and let them hang by a chain around her neck. "Unfortunately, we don't have much to offer for children these days."

Emily studied her for a moment. "I thought the arts center had a big show every summer performed by the local kids?"

"It's been many years since we've been able to put one of those productions together, but we have so many other events happening here. Maybe something else might appeal to your little ones? Every other Saturday morning we do a cartoon movie festival. Let me get you a flyer." The woman started off toward the bulletin board.

"No." Emily's forceful tone stopped the woman, whose expression turned annoyed.

"Sorry." Emily gathered herself. "Can you tell me who's in charge of the arts center?"

"Well, I am," the old woman said. "I'm the director of operations."

"And your name is . . . ?"

The woman straightened as if she weren't used to being questioned. "Gladys Middlebury."

"Mrs. Middlebury, my name is Emily Ackerman." She might've emphasized her last name. Just a bit. After all, it was on the sign above the arts center's door.

The woman's eyebrows shot up. "Emily Ackerman? Isabelle's daughter?"

Emily willed herself not to collapse in a pile of tears. Why did it suddenly feel impossible to talk about her mother? She jutted her chin out. "Yes."

Gladys softened slightly. "I was so sorry to hear about your mother. I never got the chance to say that to you—or to your grandparents. I know their relationship with Isabelle had always been rocky, which maybe made her passing that much more devastating."

Emily frowned. What was she talking about? Sure, her mom and her grandparents had their ups and downs, but she wouldn't have classified their relationship as "rocky."

"What brings you back to Nantucket?" Gladys asked before Emily could demand an explanation. "You haven't been back since the accident, have you?"

Emily decided she did not like this woman. Too nosy. Too blunt. Too presumptuous.

"My grandfather passed away, and as we got his affairs in order, I learned he's still giving a substantial amount of money to the arts center annually, but he earmarked the majority of it for children's programming."

The woman opened her mouth as if she was going to say something but quickly closed it again. What could she say, really? It was fairly clear to Emily that they'd been taking her grandfather's money and using it as they saw fit. Was that even legal?

"There are a number of factors at play here, Miss Ackerman." Gladys shifted where she stood. "Maybe you could come back when more of our staff is here and we could explain it to you? Or perhaps a member of the board?"

"What is there to explain?" Emily hated the fact that her grandfather's wishes weren't being carried out, but more than that, she hated that for probably years now, the children who spent their summers on the island had no access to theatre.

For years, kids hadn't known the feeling of having their family cheering them on from the front row.

"I'm taking over where my grandfather left off, and I expect to see

23

documentation of where his money has been going." (That sounded like someone who was in control, right?)

"That's not going to be easy, Miss Ackerman."

Emily eyed Gladys. "No, I wouldn't expect that it would be." She rummaged through her purse and scribbled her number on a piece of scratch paper, then handed it to the older woman.

"I'll see what I can do."

"I'll look forward to your call." Emily walked out of the theatre and exhaled a long, hot stream. Being assertive sent adrenaline rushing through her veins. It wasn't like her. She liked to go with the flow, not cause waves. And while she felt confident most of the time, she also avoided conflict the way she avoided long-term relationships—with great fervor.

~

When you find something worth fighting for, fight.

Dear Emily,

It's so tempting to go with the flow. Even now, there are days I don't want to stand up for anything because it can be so exhausting to put yourself out there. Plus, you open yourself up to ridicule. You ruffle feathers. You make enemies or at least step into possible confrontation.

But nothing will ever change—nothing will ever get done—unless we're willing to fight for the things we feel are worth fighting for.

Now, I don't advise becoming a person who fights only for the sake of fighting, but every once in a while, there will be something that ignites your passion—something the world needs but isn't getting, something so important to you that it will be worth putting yourself on the line to try and make it happen.

Sometimes you'll be successful. Other times, maybe not so much.

But knowing you did all you could to push for something that really matters—that's a good feeling. You can lay your head on your pillow knowing you've contributed a sparkly piece of gold to the world.

And the world needs a little more sparkle.

Love,
Mom

CHAPTER 4

AFTER EMILY LEFT THE ARTS CENTER, she found a cab and forced herself to stop getting sidetracked. She wasn't here to save the children's theatre. She was here to renovate the old cottage, sell it, and start her life over.

Now, she sat in the cab in front of the old beach house for the first time in eighteen years, and the only thing she felt was numb. What was she doing here?

This was a bad idea.

She'd dragged her suitcase through town, then stopped at the arts center mostly in an attempt to avoid this exact moment—the moment she arrived at the cottage. The cottage that haunted her dreams.

Staring at the house now, she tried to keep the memories where she'd safely stored them—in the corners of her mind—but all around her, there were reminders of a life gone by. Reminders of her mother. Carefree days. Her grandfather—his fingerprints everywhere she looked.

She still couldn't believe it. If she was honest, she hadn't given herself time to process his death. Her grandparents were the only family she had, and now one of them was gone.

The thought gnawed at her. How long until she was completely alone?

She'd held herself together remarkably well after her grandmother gave her the news and all the way through the funeral, but she could feel it there, bubbling just below the surface, another reminder that life was fragile, that time was short, that her days, too, were numbered.

And what did she have to show for it?

"You getting out?" The cabdriver met her eyes in the rearview mirror. She hadn't realized how long she'd been sitting there. It was just as well that he pulled her away from memory lane.

It wasn't a good place to park.

She paid the man and got out, then trudged up the sidewalk, seashells crunching underneath her feet, and dropped her suitcase on the front porch. She was intent on not glamorizing Nantucket or the life she'd lived here. Intent on staying focused.

Renovate. Sell. Leave.

But how could she not relive that night? Panic gripped her. In a flash she was eleven again, awakened by the sound of angry voices filtering up the stairs to her bedroom.

Mom arguing with her parents. Grandma and GrandPop begging her to keep her voice down. The memory was hazy, and it made her heart race. What were they fighting about? Nobody had ever told her, and now she might never know.

"I can do hard things," she muttered to herself, though her voice carried an edge of sarcasm.

The house looked terrible. How had her grandparents let it go like this? They should've sold it that same summer, but something stopped them. Of course something stopped them—it was the last place they'd seen their daughter alive. The last place they were all a family.

As far as Emily knew, they hadn't rented it out, but why hadn't they hired a property manager to take care of it? Surely there had been interest in it over the years—it was in a desirable location with the ocean for a backyard. It wasn't like her grandparents not to pay attention to appearances—and the appearance of their summer home was far below their usual standards.

The gray shingles on the sides of the house were weathered, with several missing. She ran a hand over the chipped white paint on the trim around the window. She turned in a half circle to face the yard and shook her head at the overgrowth, the mess left from a harsh winter. Her grandmother would be horrified if she saw what had become of this place.

Her heart ached for what had become of their beloved summer home. Should she have gotten over her fear and done more to help? She'd never seen her grandparents cry over her mother's death—not once—but had their suffering been deeper than they let on?

Emily fished the book from her bag but didn't let her eyes linger on her mother's handwriting. She opened to the center, where she'd put the key for safekeeping, pulled it out, and did her best not to think about the moment after GrandPop's funeral when Grandma had sprung it on her that they were giving her the Nantucket house.

"He wanted you to have it, Emily," she'd said, pressing the key into Emily's sweaty palm.

"No," she'd protested. "You know I can't go back there." *And also, apparently I'm not good with money. I don't deserve it.*

"That house, that island, it meant the world to your grandfather, and he made it very clear he wanted you to decide what to do with the house. We've done a terrible job keeping up with it, so I'm sure it's in bad shape, but there's money for repairs and renovations. Just go look at it and then decide. Please? It would mean so much to him." She was still holding Emily's hand, a rare intimate moment between them. "To me."

What was Emily supposed to do? Truth be told, a ticket to a new life couldn't have been more timely, what with her old life in a humiliating shambles.

Grandma knew Emily's play had been a critical failure. She did not know Emily was broke, and it was important to keep it that way.

Emily tucked the key in her pocket and set her purse down next to her suitcase. She was here, and that was enough. She couldn't go inside—not yet.

She walked around to the back of the house, taking in the landscape. As she came around the side of the house, the view stopped her. She'd seen the ocean from the ferry, and yet seeing it here—that same view, that same dock, that same beach—it was different. It held her captive as the seconds ticked by.

She inhaled the salt air and took her shoes off, walking around the empty, dirty pool, the patio, the screened-in porch, and straight to the place she'd always called hers.

The red- and white-striped beach hut was long gone, but if she closed her eyes, she could remember every detail of the tent GrandPop had set up for her on the shore. How many hours had she spent in that very spot, running to the water and back, building sand castles, hunting for starfish and seashells?

She reached the sand and felt the heat as it radiated through her feet. The wind kicked up, blowing her hair in front of her face. She pulled it back, securing it in a loose side ponytail with the elastic she always wore around her wrist.

She stood still for several seconds, staring out at the sea, wondering what Mom would say about Emily being back after all this time. She'd stayed away because it was too painful to relive any of the memories but also because it brought up too many questions.

What were her grandparents and her mother arguing about that was so bad her mom had to leave in the middle of the night? Nobody had ever answered that question, and not because she hadn't asked.

Then there was the knowledge that her mother had met her father right here on Nantucket, so there was always the chance when meeting Bob the grocer or Sid the landscaper that she was actually meeting a man whose DNA she shared.

"Hey, Bob, thanks for bagging my groceries, and by the way, I think I have your eyes."

Emily shook the thoughts away. It didn't matter who her father was. It didn't matter if he was here on this island. Why should she waste a single second thinking about a man who'd never wanted her in the first place? He'd made his choice long ago, and there was no place in his life for a daughter. She wouldn't romanticize the idea now.

A dog barking in the distance pulled her attention down the beach a few yards to her right. The waves lapped the shore and a black Lab raced out of the brush toward the ocean, followed by a young girl wearing a cute red tankini with white polka dots.

The girl was probably about eleven, maybe twelve, about the same age Emily had been her last summer on the island. She remembered how it felt to be on the cusp of the next stage of life. She'd been so excited at the thought of becoming a teenager, and her mom must've known it. Why else would she write about it in the book?

On the day you turn thirteen

Dear Emily,
*   While it's hard for me to believe it now, there will come a day when you're going to feel more grown-up than you are. I call this age "the in-between." I hope you don't rush through it too quickly. When you're thirteen, you're a teenager, so you'll feel like you should be treated like an adult, but I guess as someone who had to grow up really quickly, what I pray for you is that you can enjoy being young as long as possible.*
*   It's okay if you still like dancing in the ocean under the stars. It's okay if you sing yourself to sleep or tell yourself stories to keep from feeling lonely. It's even okay to talk to your imaginary friend. Because thirteen might feel grown-up, but it's not quite, and that's okay.*

The girl turned and looked at her, and Emily realized she was staring. She didn't really want to make friends with anyone new right now. She wanted to wallow and be moody and have a little pity party for herself. In fact, she'd already made plans to find one of the old bikes in the shed and ride into town for a pint of Häagen-Dazs and turn it into dinner. She was an expert wallower.

But she was also the adult, and this was her neighbor, and she should be neighborly and kind and at least ask the dog's name.

She walked toward the girl, whose hair was the loveliest shade of strawberry Emily had ever seen.

Emily lifted a hand to wave at her as the wind pulled several strands of hair from her elastic. "Hi there."

The girl dropped her beach bag at her feet and waved back at Emily. "Hey."

"Beautiful dog," Emily said. "What's his name?"

"She's a girl. Tilly."

"Do you live here?" Emily pointed toward the cottage next to her grandparents' house—her house now, she supposed. The neighboring cottage had always been a rental property and nearly every year Emily spent on Nantucket, it was rented by the same family.

She hadn't thought about her lazy summer days with Hollis McGuire for a lot of years, but she couldn't help but remember them now. She might have been young, but even then she knew there was something special about the boy next door.

"I *live* in Boston," the girl said. "I'm *staying* here for a month."

"Lucky girl." Emily smiled. She could sense the girl's disappointment with her current situation. Her poor parents probably thought they were giving her the summer of a lifetime—and they likely were—but this young beauty didn't know it yet. She'd yet to discover the magic of Nantucket.

"Doesn't feel so lucky," the girl said.

"Doesn't feel so lucky for me either," Emily replied absently.

The girl squinted up at her, lifting a hand to shield her eyes from the sun. "Really?"

Emily was doing a terrible job of encouraging her young neighbor. She should be ashamed. "No," she said. "It's an amazing place to spend your summer. When I was your age, it was my favorite place in the world."

"Do you live in that run-down house next door?"

The way she said it made Emily realize how different things would be for her this summer than they had been all those years ago. They were a family of means. Her grandfather was well-respected. He'd single-handedly saved the arts center, not to mention his substantial gifts to the hospital and who knew how many other charities.

They fit in with Nantucket society—even as a girl, Emily had known that.

Now she was the single woman living in the run-down house that had become an embarrassing eyesore. The fact that no one had fined her grandparents or taken some kind of legal action was astonishing. Or maybe they had and Grandma had just failed to mention that.

"I'm just visiting," Emily finally said. "I'm here to fix it up so I can sell it."

"Why would you sell it if it's so great here?"

Emily laughed. This girl was smart. Emily bet her parents didn't get away with anything—not on this girl's watch.

"It's a long story," Emily said. And not one she was going to get into with a child.

"JoJo!" A man's voice broke through the brief silence and the girl rolled her eyes.

"I have a feeling he's not going to leave me alone for a second this whole month."

What I wouldn't give for a dad like that . . .

A man wearing a pair of long khaki shorts and a faded-red T-shirt emerged onto the beach from the yard next door. His distressed baseball cap was pulled low over his eyes, which were covered with a pair of aviator sunglasses.

Emily took a very brief moment to notice his well-built torso. And then another very brief moment to appreciate it.

The dog raced back from the water and sniffed his hand.

"Tilly, be good," he said.

As he strode toward them, Emily felt her shoulders straighten. It was almost as if he were moving in slow motion, as if her past were unraveling right in front of her. Her heart quickened. She hadn't counted on this—on him.

Hollis.

"Dad, this is our neighbor," the girl said. "She says it's nice here but she's selling her house, so . . ." She shrugged.

But Hollis didn't seem to hear or see his daughter. He'd stopped moving and was now staring. At Emily.

Her pulse quickened. Her stomach roiled. Her mind spun.

What was he doing here? Why did he look *like that*? Did he recognize her? After all these years?

She must've had a dopey expression on her face because the girl huffed (loudly) and said, "Oh, please. Are you, like, one of his fans?"

Hollis still didn't seem to hear the girl.

"Emily?" He studied her with eyes that were too intent. "It *is* you."

She wanted to pull her gaze from his, but it was as if they'd been tied together by an invisible force and she couldn't sever the connection.

"Hollis." His name on her lips caught at the back of her throat, a slight whisper that held so much weight.

He looked as stunned as she felt as he moved toward her, then opened his arms to pull her into what was likely meant to be a friendly long-time-no-see hug but felt like so much more.

She stepped into his arms and for a fleeting moment inhaled the safety of his embrace. She could get lost here. Time could stop and the past could fall away.

And yet it couldn't.

She inched back, despising the betrayal of her own emotions.

"I thought I saw you at the ferry," he said. "It's been—what? Eighteen years?"

Emily wasn't sure she could speak. Being here, on this beach, on the island, at this house, and now with Hollis—she hadn't planned to have to *feel* any of it. She didn't want to remember the good things about Nantucket. Those memories had been swept away the day her mother died.

There was nothing dark or sad or tragic about the Hollis McGuire she'd known. If she let herself, she would've remembered him only as good and wonderful and kind.

But she'd lumped him in with the rest of her Nantucket memories and thrown them out to sea. How did she reconcile standing here in front of him now?

"Do you remember me?" he asked.

Emily nodded, willing herself not to cry. She wasn't a crier—what was happening to her on the inside?

"Wait, you two know each other?" the girl asked.

"We did," Emily said, still connected to Hollis as if by an imaginary string. "A long time ago."

Hollis pulled his sunglasses off and looked at her with those bright-hazel eyes. Were they greener now than when they were kids? He'd always had that special something, the thing that drew people to him like pieces of metal to a high-powered magnet. Mom had called it "the 'it' factor."

"Watch out for that one, Emily Elizabeth," Mom had said. "He's one part trouble and two parts charm."

She hadn't understood then, but she understood now. At least about the trouble part. She could practically hear warning bells blaring in the back of her mind, like the sound of a European ambulance racing through the streets of London.

People might've made him feel like he never belonged in the Nantucket world back then, but nobody could say that anymore.

"I can't believe you remember me." Emily felt suddenly—and uncharacteristically—shy.

"Are you kidding?" Hollis gave her arm a shove, putting her squarely in the friend zone. Of course he did—he was standing there with his daughter. What was she thinking fantasizing about this man who was clearly taken? She shook the thoughts away, forced herself back to reality.

"Summer was never the same after you left," he said.

Emily looked away. How would she survive being back here? How would she revisit all the unanswered questions she'd been burying all these years?

"Glad you guys are catching up and all, but I'm starving, Dad. You said burgers on the grill. Can we make that happen?" She called out for Tilly to follow her and disappeared in the sea grass.

"That's Jolie," Hollis said. "She's my daughter."

"I guessed that much when she called you Dad." Emily smiled. "She's beautiful."

"She's a pistol." He laughed, then looked away. "Honestly, I have no idea what I'm doing with her."

A gentle lull fell between them.

How did he do that? Instantly put her at ease? How did he, in a matter of seconds, make Emily, the girl who trusted no one, feel like he was safe?

She reminded herself that he wasn't that boy she'd known before her life turned upside down. He'd grown up. And all sweet boys, when they grew up, became men. And she didn't need a man in her life any more than she needed the old Nantucket cottage.

"Kids are tricky," she said because it was something she'd heard people say, not because she knew it to be true.

"Do you have any?"

"No." She looked away. "Kids don't really fit into my life plan."

His eyebrows rose. "Is that right?"

"I travel a lot," she said. It was an understatement. She traveled. It's what she did, almost exclusively, or what she had done before settling in to produce a play that apparently wasn't ready for an audience.

"Yeah, I know a little something about life on the road," he said. "It's hard with kids for sure."

She didn't respond. The conversation had turned, making her long for things she absolutely did not want.

"Approach love with caution. Always guard your heart."

She clung to that truth her mother had imparted all those years ago. So far, it had served her well.

"You seem to manage a kid, even with your big career." She forced herself to stop daydreaming.

"You know about my career?" He looked pleased.

She found her most incredulous look and aimed it at him. "You're kidding, right?"

He shrugged. "Didn't know if you followed baseball."

She didn't, but she did follow Hollis at least a bit—much to her embarrassment in that moment, it turned out.

"You should come eat with us," he said. "We can catch up."

How could she bear it? Sitting at the same table as Hollis and his wife and daughter (and more kids)? The fact that he had a family and she hadn't known about it proved how far back into her past she'd pushed her childhood friend. Best to keep him there.

"I couldn't intrude," she said.

"You just got in today," Hollis said. "There's no way there's food in that house."

He was right. There wasn't. She needed to get to town or she wouldn't even have coffee in the morning.

"I insist."

"Won't your wife be annoyed you're bringing in a stray?" She looked up at him and realized he was disastrously good-looking. Whoever his wife was, she was one lucky girl.

"My wife?"

"Jolie's mom," Emily said.

"Jolie's mom is on her honeymoon with a doctor named Rick," Hollis said.

"Oh," Emily laughed. "And how do you feel about that?"

"We were never married." He looked away, and it occurred to Emily that even superstar baseball players had their demons.

And just like that she heard herself agree to dinner. With Hollis McGuire. Boy next door–turned–baseball phenom and quite possibly the most beautiful human being Emily had ever seen.

"One part trouble, two parts charm."

Uh-oh.

CHAPTER 5

~~~

HOLLIS WASN'T EMBARRASSED by the small Nantucket cottage until Emily walked through the front door. Yes, her grandparents' cottage currently looked like a "before" picture on one of those HGTV home improvement shows, but she came from money, just like everyone else in Nantucket.

And seeing her in the doorway reminded him that he didn't.

Never mind how much he had in the bank now. Part of him would always be that kid who refused to wear plaid shorts or comb his hair, the one who didn't fit in.

Though, he had to admit, Emily didn't really look like someone who fit in here either—there was something decidedly unstuffy about her, like a person who couldn't put on airs if she tried.

Maybe that's why she'd captivated him even back at the ferry.

"So your dad bought this place?" Emily asked, looking around. "It's amazing."

"Yeah, he did pretty well for himself." Hollis motioned for her to have a seat at the island in the center of the kitchen. It unnerved him, her being there. Set his senses on high alert. "They always loved it here, so it was the first major purchase he made."

"No kidding?" Emily sat and he grabbed the hamburger patties from the fridge, willing himself to talk to her like a human and not admire her dumbly like she was a stone statue in a museum. It was hard, though—with her porcelain skin and that wavy blonde hair. He wondered if the freckles that used to spill across the top of her nose onto her cheeks would return in the sunshine. He'd like to find out.

"They'll be here later." Hollis unwrapped the patties and put them on a platter, then flicked on the faucet to wash his hands. "In time for dinner, I think."

"They will?"

"It's a family affair." Truth be told, he was thankful he'd have some help with Jolie. He didn't know what to do with a preteen girl all day, especially one who, despite being somewhat cordial, didn't like him all that much.

"That'll be so nice for you guys, to all be together."

He glanced up from the sink and shut off the water. "Don't think you're getting out of it."

She found his eyes. "What?"

He studied her, his pulse slowing just enough to let himself be amused. "You think you're going to escape the McGuire family craziness, but you're as much a part of this as I am."

She looked puzzled. "Did you get hit in the head with a baseball?"

He laughed, and some of his nerves began to dissipate. How long had it been since a woman had made him nervous? Her big blue almond-shaped eyes could've made any man forget his own name, but Hollis found himself mostly trying not to stare at her full lips and the tiny gold necklace hanging perfectly in between her prominent collarbones.

Get a grip, McGuire. It's just Emily.

Emily, who'd also felt to him like a bottle that had been tossed out to sea. Even if he could've seen her, he couldn't have gotten to her, not after the way her grandparents whisked her off the island right after the accident.

It was like they'd vanished into thin air after that, leaving him sitting in a pile of confusion nursing a broken heart.

His mother said it would just take time to get over the loss of his friend, that they needed to give the Ackerman family space just now—they could reach out once the dust settled.

The dust must've never settled because no one ever reached out.

But Hollis didn't care about any of that—he only cared about the girl who'd looked past everything he wasn't straight to what he could be. She'd seen something in him when all everyone else saw was a poor kid who was out of place.

He turned toward her, thankful she wasn't a mind reader. "Family dinners, picnics on the beach, backyard baseball games—your presence is expected. You know Nan McGuire would be crushed if you didn't show."

Emily swiped a stray hair away from her face.

Man, she was pretty.

She'd always been in a league all her own, and yet for some reason, she happily spent her Nantucket days hanging out with Hollis and his little brother, Hayes. Their sister, Harper, was too young for most of their crazy Nantucket adventures, but he had no doubt if things had been different, the four of them would've made some pretty wild memories.

But things weren't different, and he'd be smart to remember that. He thought he might've picked up on a little bit of sadness at the mention of his family, but what if all Emily wanted was to be left alone? He didn't know her anymore, after all. It wasn't like they could carry on from right where they left off. There was a lot of life between them now.

"I don't want to get in the way." She cleared her throat. "Can I have a glass of water?"

"Oh yeah, of course." He walked over to the fridge and pulled out a bottle of water. He held it out to her, but before he let go of it, he forced her gaze. "And you could never be in the way."

She looked down, taking the bottle from him and turning a sweet shade of pink. He reminded himself that Emily wasn't like the girls who followed the team around or the ones he met in bars after games. He'd tired of women like that a long time ago, but he'd always known how to win them over. If he wasn't careful, he'd fall into that same pattern and he had a feeling Emily Ackerman would call him out on it quicker than an unexpected fastball.

Friends. That's what they would be. It was the smartest thing for everyone.

Besides, Emily might not have kids, but that didn't mean she wasn't involved with someone—or even married.

He glanced at her bare left hand.

Or maybe not.

The front door flung open and Tilly barked. Hayes walked in carrying two duffel bags, which he dropped in the entryway to give the dog his full attention.

"Oh, my gosh," Emily said quietly. "Is that Hayes?"

"He's never going to believe it's you." Hollis walked over to his brother, who people used to think was his twin. Nobody would make that mistake now. Hayes's once-blond hair had darkened and he was a few inches shorter than Hollis, though a little sturdier these days. Hollis made a mental note to get back to the gym. His baseball career might be over, but that didn't mean he should let himself go.

"Big Bro," Hayes said, pulling Hollis into one of those friendly guy hugs. "Am I the first one here?"

"Well, you and JoJo," Hollis said. "And Tilly."

Hayes looked past Hollis and into the kitchen, where Emily sat, watching them. She looked like she might burst.

"Who's the looker?" Hayes asked quietly.

Hollis took a few steps toward the kitchen. "Hayes, you remember Emily from next door," he said.

Hayes's eyes widened. "Emily?"

Emily stood as Hayes moved toward her, his arms open. He pulled her into a giant bear hug and Hollis thought it was strange that Emily, someone they'd known so well all those years ago, didn't know Hayes had become famously kind and philanthropic. She didn't know Harper had turned into an elite runner. She didn't know anything about any of them, and they didn't know anything about her.

He could still remember chasing her car all the way to the end of her driveway the day her grandparents took her away. When he found out about the accident, he'd gone to the hospital, but they wouldn't let him in. They said he was too young and he wasn't family.

But he *was* family, wasn't he? At least he felt like family. Emily had always felt like family.

And somehow he wondered if things would ever feel that way again.

"Hayes, I cannot believe this is you." Emily pulled out of his hug and looked him over. "An actual grown-up."

"Believe it, young lady." Hayes was still holding on to her hands. Hollis was keenly aware of it. "What are you doing back here? Haven't seen you in years."

"It's been too long," she said.

Hayes finally (finally!) let go of her hands and moved around the kitchen island to the bowl of grapes sitting on the counter. He popped one in his mouth and smiled. "You look incredible, by the way."

Hayes was such a flirt. Hollis actually envied his brother—the way he interacted with people so easily. It wasn't a trait they shared. Hollis had a much different way of charming people.

"Thanks, Hayes." She smiled.

"You staying next door?" he asked.

She nodded.

"Place is looking kinda rough. We can help you whip it into shape."

Emily glanced at Hollis. "I think it's a bigger job than that. I'm going to have to hire someone."

41

"Well, we're offering our services," Hayes said. "If you change your mind."

Hollis nodded dumbly, like he couldn't find the words to be kind.

"Thanks." She spoke the word quietly, and in a flash he could see there was a whole world behind her eyes—pain and hurt and anger and so much more that he wanted to know.

Jolie descended from upstairs as the front door opened again and Hollis's parents walked in. Dressed in lightweight white linen pants and a pink button-down shirt, his mom looked like someone who belonged on Nantucket. His dad wore a pair of plaid shorts and a yellow polo shirt. A sun visor wrapped around his balding head.

"JoJo!"

Jolie walked straight into his mother's arms, like there was a Jolie-shaped hole there. Hollis hoped his wince went unnoticed. Sometimes it was still hard to watch everyone else getting along so easily with his daughter when he seemed to struggle for even the slightest connection.

He glanced at Emily and found her gaze had drifted over to him. Had she seen the shame behind his eyes?

"Hey, GrandNan," Jolie said with a smile.

Hollis's dad propped their suitcases next to Hayes's bags and opened his arms toward his only granddaughter. "Good to see you, kiddo. I hope you're ready for a Nantucket summer."

Jolie pulled away. "There's no Wi-Fi in this house."

Dad's gasp was purposely over-the-top. "Hollis, how could you bring her out here under these conditions?"

Jolie's eyes brightened. Poor kid didn't catch his father's sarcasm. "Does that mean we can get it?"

Dad tweaked her nose. "Not on your life."

Jolie huffed away and Mom swooped in to console her. "You're going to be so busy, you're not going to need Wi-Fi, JoJo. We'll have picnics on the beach and we'll bake cookies and go swimming and—"

"Fishing and sailing and yeah, yeah, yeah. Dad told me all that." Jolie harrumphed onto the sofa in the living room and Tilly hopped up next to her.

"Tilly." Dad's tone was stern. "Get off that sofa!"

Tilly's ears perked up and she cocked her head to one side, looking at Dad like she didn't understand. Hollis knew full well his dog understood.

"Oh, fine, just stay there, you big mutt." Dad rubbed her ears, then turned toward the kitchen. "What's going on in here?"

"Oh, how rude of us," Mom said, making her way toward the rest of them. "I didn't know you had a guest. Hayes, is this a friend of yours?"

"It's Emily, Mom," Hollis said, noticing how Emily's ears matched her bright-red cheeks. "Emily Ackerman."

Both of his parents now wore a dumbfounded expression that didn't become either one of them.

"Emily." The word escaped from his mother as a whisper, as if it had slipped out without her permission. It was like being catapulted through time, he supposed. He'd had a similar reaction when he'd first seen her.

In fact, he still wasn't sure he'd recovered.

"Emily!" Dad walked over to her and pulled her into a tight hug, so tight, in fact, Hollis was concerned he might crush her.

Then he took a step back and looked her straight in the eye. "You are absolutely gorgeous, young lady, and you're the spitting image of your mom."

Emily's face fell, but she uttered a quiet "Thank you." Dad mistook her response for shyness and barreled on. "We weren't sure we'd ever see you again. What brings you back to the island?"

Emily shifted. Hollis wished he could take her out back for a deep cleansing breath and maybe a shot of whiskey, though he had a feeling she wasn't a whiskey kind of girl. Still, she needed something to take the edge off, he could tell.

"My grandfather passed away," she said.

The room hushed. Hollis hadn't heard. He remembered Alan and Eliza Ackerman as the king and queen of Nantucket. When their daughter died, the whole island was in shock. Suddenly everyone was on edge. If something so terrible could happen to the Ackerman family, it could happen to anyone. Even the wealthiest and most prominent members of society weren't exempt.

"I'm sorry to hear that," Dad said. "He was a good man."

Hollis thought that was mostly true, but he also thought Emily's grandfather was a jerk for taking her away the way he did.

"Are you back for the summer?" Mom asked.

"He left me the house," Emily said.

"Whoa." Hayes popped another grape in his mouth. "That house is on prime real estate. You could make a fortune."

Emily met Hollis's eyes. Even after all this time, he knew she didn't want to make a fortune on that old house. She wanted something she could never have—she wanted things to go back to the way they'd been before that terrible night.

He knew how that felt. He'd spent the whole last year wishing for things to be different. But time was funny that way. It marched on whether you wanted it to or not.

"Are you going to sell it?" Hayes had their father's boisterous personality. He asked whatever question came to mind whether it was his business or not.

"Definitely," Emily said. "But it needs a ton of work."

Definitely? Why was she so matter-of-fact? Had she considered that she could keep it? Spend her summers here like old times?

"How's the inside look?" Hollis asked.

She looked away. "I don't know."

"You haven't been inside?" Hayes stopped chewing.

"Not yet." Her smile looked weak. "I ran into Jolie and Hollis on the beach just a few minutes after I got here, and then Hollis invited me over, so I haven't gone in yet."

An awkward silence fell on the room.

"Can we eat?" Jolie called out from her spot on the sofa.

Hollis's gaze lingered on Emily for a few long seconds, and while he wasn't satisfied that she was okay, he knew it wasn't a conversation they could have now, in front of everyone else. Not that he'd know how to have that conversation even if they were the only two people in the room.

"I'll get the burgers going," he called out, finally breaking eye contact with her.

"All right." Mom moved to the other side of the island and washed her hands. "Let's get to work. Emily, you can help me cut the vegetables and tell me all your latest news. We've seen you on a few television shows over the years, and of course there's all those reruns of *Dottie's World*. Do people still recognize you from that?"

Hollis stole a glimpse of their guest, whose blush softened into that same sweet smile he remembered from all those years ago, though there was something different about her now.

It was funny how you could miss something so much and not know you missed it until it was back in your life again.

~

When you don't feel like you belong

Dear Emily,

I can't lie—I've never really felt like I fit in with Alan and Eliza. One day you'll discover they view life in a very specific way, and I'm not sure how my views became so different, but they did. I don't think I'm owed anything. I don't think people are better or worse depending on what clothes they wear or what car they drive.

Because of that, I don't always feel like I belong.

For a long time, that really bothered me. I tried to blend into this world I was a part of, but so often I just seemed like a square peg in a round hole.

It's taken me a very long time, but I'm finally okay with it. I'm okay figuring out who I am, and I'm okay being that person, whether it meets someone else's expectations or not.

I hope you're confident enough in who you are that when you feel like you don't fit in, you're able to realize that it's okay, that you won't fit in everywhere, that not everyone you meet will instantly understand or respect or admire you.

Still, it can be lonely, this state of not belonging. You can feel like you're floundering a little. I hope you find a place where you're loved and accepted, but on the days you feel neither of those things, I hope you remember that you are in fact loved and accepted, not just by me, but by God. Yeah, I'm going to go there—I'm going to be that mom, talking to you about Jesus.

You can roll your eyes—go ahead.

But it's true. I've learned it the hard way.

Your grandparents are people of tradition, and while I can appreciate tradition, and I actually find it quite beautiful, the truth is, I feel God best when I'm not closed in by four walls and a ceiling. In a meadow or on a beach. And while I love the church and see so many reasons to go every Sunday, I also don't think you have to leave God in the pew when you walk out the door.

The way I see it, God is everywhere, which means you can find him everywhere (and I really hope you do). The thing I want you to know about God, if for any reason I'm ever not here to tell you myself, is that he's ready and willing, whenever you are, to meet you where you're at. No matter what.

Keep in mind that I've made some pretty big mistakes in my life, and still I've felt God off the shores of Nantucket or even just looking at your smile. You don't have to go through puzzles or mazes or riddles to find him—he's right there, hand extended in your direction, anytime you're ready.

It'll be worth it, Em. I promise. Everyone else in this world will let you down, but he never will.

Whenever you feel lonely, he's there. And he loves you so much. More than I do, though I find that hard to believe considering I love you more than anything. You'll always belong with me, Emily Elizabeth, and you'll always belong with him. No matter what.

Love,
Mom

CHAPTER 6

MEMORIAL DAY WEEKEND, 1989

Isabelle Ackerman bypassed the cottage's front porch and ran straight to the backyard. She stripped down to her bathing suit on her way to the ocean, dropping her shirt and shorts in the sand beside her sandals and hat.

She'd been dreaming of the water as she slogged her way through junior year, anxious to get back to the island. It was the only time she felt like a true adventurer. With her parents' proclivity for rules and order, some days Isabelle felt like she was wearing a straitjacket or struggling for a good, deep breath.

Here, that all went away.

They loosened their hold on her ever so slightly, and Isabelle began to feel alive.

The weight of the upcoming year loomed in the distance, and she pushed away the idea of growing up and moving on in favor of Nantucket skies, trips to Brant Point lighthouse, bike rides all over the island, lazy days on the water, and whatever other adventures the summer held.

She dove into the waves, marking the moment in her mind—it was the moment she'd been craving since she left Nantucket at the end of the previous summer.

The water glistened as the sun cast a diamond-like shimmer over the ocean. She swam out farther, imagining she was in Australia or Thailand or some remote island ripe for exploration.

She'd already created a mental map of all the beaches she wanted to visit the year after she graduated high school, but she was fairly certain her parents would have something to say about her taking a gap year. Namely, *You're not allowed to take a gap year.*

But how blissful would it be to wake up every morning right on the beach? To visit different countries and inhale different cultures? To eat their food and study their ways? It was a dream, but the kind she kept to herself. Telling anyone else felt too risky, and she didn't want to jinx it.

She stayed in the water long enough to fill her soul, but not so long she'd end up in trouble for missing lunch. She swam toward the shore just as a trio of guys walked out of the beach grass and onto the sand. They wore swim trunks and carried surfboards.

The closer she got, the clearer they became, and that's when she saw that one of the guys was holding her clothes.

If she showed up back at the house without them, her mother would have a fit.

She reached the shore, aware of three pairs of eyes on her as she emerged from the water. She'd never seen any of the boys before—they weren't locals, which meant they were probably here for summer work at the golf club or one of the restaurants. That meant they were probably in college, which suddenly made them more attractive than scary.

"These yours?"

She shielded her eyes from the sun, trying not to look like a dorky high schooler and also trying not to look panicked that this guy was about to play some kind of trick that would leave her clothesless.

"Yeah," she said. "I guess I was pretty happy to see the ocean."

"Come on, JD," one of the other guys said. "We've only got an hour."

They raced off toward the water, jumping face-first onto their surfboards, but the guy who had her clothes—JD—didn't follow.

"You live here?" he asked.

"Only for the summer," she said. "My family's cottage is right up there."

He tossed a glance over his shoulder, but his eyes quickly returned to hers. "I'm staying at my aunt's place, but it's not right on the beach like this."

She nodded, unsure how to respond.

"I'm working at the country club," he said. "Do you ever go there?"

"My dad does," she said.

"Maybe I'll see him, then."

But he won't see you.

She hated how pretentious her parents could be. Ever since she'd first noticed it last summer, it had grated on her, how they seemed to believe they were better than other people just because they had money. It had been the cause of several arguments over the last nine months.

"I'm JD," he said.

"I heard." She smoothed her hair back, aware that while women in movies came out of the ocean looking hot and sexy, she likely looked awkward and disheveled.

"Are you going to tell me your name?"

She grinned. "If you want to know it badly enough, you'll have to find out for yourself."

He laughed. "Is that right?"

She held out her hand. "My clothes?"

He narrowed his gaze as if trying to decide whether or not to give them back to her. "I would say I'd trade you—your clothes in exchange for you telling me your name—but I have a better idea."

"Oh, really?" She was flirting now. She'd seen her friends do it plenty of times, but truthfully, she'd never met a boy worth flirting with. The boys at school all seemed so juvenile, and while Isabelle didn't have an overly high opinion of herself, she wasn't about to waste her time.

"I figure out your name, and you go out with me," he said, an endearing cockiness coming over him.

It wouldn't be difficult for him to figure out her name—her parents were well-known in the community—so agreeing to this was essentially agreeing to go out with a perfect stranger.

A perfectly handsome stranger. Unlike his friends, JD looked like he'd seen sunlight in the last month, his skin a deep-bronze shade, his hair sandy-colored and overgrown in a way that made looking good seem effortless.

Finally she reached out and took her clothes from him, holding them in front of her as if that could keep her from feeling self-conscious about her body.

"So it's a deal, then?" He extended a hand for her to shake.

Slowly, as if making up her mind, she shook his hand and hid her smile. "Deal."

He held her hand for several seconds and didn't seem to have any intention of letting it go.

"So do you like seafood, *Isabelle*?" The expression on his face turned mischievous, and she pulled her hand away.

She eyed him accusingly. "Do you know my parents?"

Maybe he wasn't summer help—maybe he'd only pretended to be.

"No, your license fell out of the pocket of your shorts when I picked them up."

She forced herself not to smile.

"But hey, a deal's a deal, right? I get off at five, so I'll pick you up then." He started off, surfboard under his arm.

"Wait," she called after him.

He turned.

"Meet me in town," she said. "Children's Beach?"

"Ashamed to be seen with the help?"

"Something like that," she said with a smile.

"I'll see you tonight, Bella."

"No one calls me Bella!" she called out after him, but he was already in the water, the whoops and hollers of his buddies drowning out everything else.

Nobody had ever called her Bella, but with eyes like that and muscles like those, she decided JD could call her whatever he wanted.

CHAPTER 7

EMILY LISTENED TO THE FAMILIAL BANTER of Hollis, his brother, their parents, and even Jolie, who seemed to be more familiar with her grandparents than with her own father.

What was the story there?

Nan put her to work in the kitchen, and even though Emily wasn't much of a cook, it was nice to be included. She chopped vegetables, sliced French bread, put ice in the cups. She did the things a mother would have her daughter do.

Occasionally she found herself staring at Nan, wondering if she was the kind of mother her own mom would've become if she'd had as many years to figure out who she was.

She sat quietly through most of dinner, doing her best to piece together the last eighteen years of the McGuire family's lives and forget about the last eighteen years of her own.

So far, she knew Hayes was a travel writer, recently split from a good friend–turned–girlfriend he'd met right here on the island the summer he turned eighteen. It seemed like a sore subject, and one he changed quickly.

Harper, who would arrive in the morning, ran marathons for fun. For fun! Who did that?

Hollis's parents said very little about their own life, though she gathered they were still the same happy couple they'd always been. At one point, she glanced over and saw they were holding hands.

They'd been together over thirty years and they still held hands?

Grandma and GrandPop weren't affectionate with each other. Or with Emily. Even after the accident, they still remained on the luke-warm side.

Another reason Emily had practically covered her own heart in bubble wrap and written *STAY OUT* in permanent marker on the outside of it.

Nan and Jeffrey McGuire were the exact opposite of Emily's grandparents. They used to love embarrassing their children by kiss-ing under the beach umbrella and sometimes, late at night, Emily had seen them slow dancing in the backyard from her bedroom window.

Did they still slow dance?

She hoped so.

The whole conversation was light and easy, and each of the McGuires found ways to make Emily feel included. She wondered if someone had taught them the fine art of drawing people into their family or if they just came by it naturally.

By the time Nan pulled a fresh fruit torte from the refrigerator, Emily felt like she'd been adopted.

She wouldn't lie—it was nice.

"Is that from . . . ?" Emily's voice trailed off as her mouth watered.

"Nantucket Bake Shop," Hollis said. "Mom sent me over this morning."

Emily had forgotten about the bake shop. She'd forgotten about a lot of things.

"We've been talking this whole time, Emily," Nan said, setting the dessert at the center of the table. "Tell us about you."

She preferred to listen. At least in this setting. Emily was used to being the center of attention—she came by it naturally, which was maybe why acting was an easy fit for her. She'd never found it difficult to pretend to be someone else.

Being herself was much harder, and lately, she'd lost the desire to pretend.

"Oh." Emily took a drink of water. "Well, I'm not sure where to start."

"You're still acting?" Nan asked.

"You were on Broadway, right?" Hayes reminded Emily of a golden retriever, happy and energetic and so darn cute. Hollis, by comparison, was more thoughtful and not nearly as talkative.

But he watched her with such intensity it sent her insides swirling.

How easily she could get lost in his eyes if she let herself, which she most certainly would not.

"You were on Broadway?" Jolie's eyes widened.

"I was," Emily admitted. "I was in a Broadway revival of a play called *The Importance of Being Earnest*. You've probably never heard of it." After all, how many people knew classic plays that closed after only a few weeks? Her cheeks flushed with embarrassment. It wasn't as impressive as it sounded.

"I have," Hayes said. "I saw it in London."

"Uncle Hayes has been everywhere." Jolie took a drink of her water and grinned. "But he's never been on Broadway."

Hayes tousled her hair playfully. "I've still got time, JoJo."

"What kind of costume did you wear?" Jolie looked at Emily with a new kind of admiration. She was probably too young to have ever seen *Dottie's World*, the children's show that had turned Emily into a star for, it turned out, a rather short time. To Jolie, being on Broadway was a huge accomplishment. Emily wished she'd seen it that way. As it was, the play felt like something of a step down after having a hit TV show—at least, that's what gossip rags had said.

Emily set her fork down thoughtfully, letting her mind wander back to her nine-week run on Broadway. "I wore the most beautiful costume," she said. "And a corset. The gown was so intricate—I'd never seen anything like it. It should be in a museum somewhere."

"Right next to your Dottie costume," Hayes quipped.

Jolie looked up from her plate. "Who's Dottie?"

Emily waved her off. "No one."

"Come on, Em," Hayes teased from across the table. "Don't be modest." He jumped up. "What was that pose you did?" He stood with one fist on his hip and the other fist punched out in front of him, affecting the all-too-familiar "Dottie pose."

The others chuckled and Emily buried her face in her hands.

"Emily was a child star," Nan said. "A big one."

"Dottie Do-Right, sweet girl next door with a secret world in her backyard," Hayes said.

"It was an adorable show," Nan said. "How old were you when that started?"

"Ten," Emily said. "I was ten when it started."

"People on the island used to stop her for autographs." Hayes sat back down.

"So embarrassing," Emily said.

"You shouldn't be embarrassed, Emily," Jeffrey said. "It was a great accomplishment, and I know your mother was very proud of you."

Emily shifted uncomfortably. How did he know that? He sounded so sure.

Would her mother be proud of the mediocre review of her Broadway debut or her director's criticism that she seemed "creatively blocked," that there was more in her past she could tap into and when she did, she could be truly brilliant?

"There's something inauthentic about your performance, Emily," he'd said. "Something is holding you back. If you want people to think of you as anything other than Dottie Do-Right, you have to give them a reason to."

His words stung. And she was just entitled enough to reject them. So she'd chosen next to take a job on the road—a touring performance of a new musical called *Cool Rider* that tanked after three months. From there, she traveled to Tokyo, London, a cruise ship, and finally back to New York, which was where she'd been the past twelve months, the last six of which she'd spent throwing everything into the show that had eventually landed her back on the theatre critic's radar—and not in his good graces.

Ackerman's turn in *The Importance of Being Earnest* should've been enough to keep the child star out of the New York theatre scene, but here she is again, this time in a production of her own, which has left many wondering why Dottie didn't find another world to visit instead of filling our world with her pointless drivel. This actress should stick to fluffy children's television and leave the real theatre to the professionals.

"Do you have pictures?" Jolie had set her fork down and now gave Emily her undivided attention. "Of the play you did?"

"I probably do—somewhere. I didn't do a very good job of keeping mementos."

Emily prided herself on not being sentimental.

"Broadway." Jolie sighed. "That's amazing. I'd love to be on Broadway someday."

"You would?" Hollis swallowed and glanced at his daughter.

"I've been in three plays already." Jolie's tone suggested he should know that.

How did Hollis not know?

"Wow, that's quite a résumé." Emily hoped she could lighten the mood—she could see by Hollis's face he felt embarrassed.

"Will you tell me about Broadway sometime?" Jolie asked, her attention wholly fixed on Emily. "And the other shows you've done?"

It was bittersweet to think about any small success she might've had after *Dottie's World* ended, now that her life was such a disaster.

"Sure," Emily said.

"I tried to get my mom to send me to theatre camp this month." Jolie pushed food around on her plate. "She said no."

Emily glanced at Hollis and saw the fresh wound his daughter's words inflicted.

She cleared her throat. "Do you know where I got my start?"

Jolie's wide eyes met hers.

"Right here at the arts center downtown."

The girl sat up straighter. "For real?"

"We used to do a big show every summer. That's where I first fell in love with the stage. I stopped at the arts center earlier today. I'm hoping they'll put something on the schedule this year too."

"Really?" Jolie's eyes lit with excitement.

"Really," Emily said, praying she wasn't overstepping. She didn't actually know if Gladys would come through—Emily wasn't nearly as threatening or powerful as her grandfather had been. "If you give it a chance, you might discover this island is the best place in the world to spend a summer."

Jolie smiled at her, and it was lovely, but it was Hollis's thankful expression that pricked her heart.

"It's been years since there's been a show there," Nan said.

Emily tried not to let it bother her—how nobody cared enough to make sure the children's productions went on.

"When you find something worth fighting for, fight."

Her mom's words tumbled through her mind. Was this a cause worth fighting for? A children's show? Shouldn't she be marching at some political rally or doing something . . . *bigger*?

Maybe, but back in the day, those shows mattered to a lot of people. Sure, it wasn't global-level influence, but it made a difference here. Emily would never forget the day she was finally old enough to participate. Four consecutive summers she'd lived on that stage—and she loved every second.

"Hopefully this is the year they bring it back," Emily said. "If it's anything like it was when I was a kid, Jolie, you're going to love it."

The girl smiled again.

"Well, I'm beat," Jeffrey said. "I'm going to bed. You kids stay up as late as you want to." He stood and took his plate to the sink, rinsed it off, and put it in the dishwasher.

In all her years of living with Grandma and GrandPop, she'd never once seen the man take his dishes to the sink. Something about it made her love Mr. McGuire, if only for Nan's sake.

But not only for Nan's sake.

"I should go," Emily said. She followed Jeffrey's lead and filed her plate in the dishwasher.

"Don't rush off," Nan said.

But prolonging the inevitable seemed a little silly.

Still, Emily dreaded walking back to the cottage. She dreaded opening the door. She dreaded turning on the lights and not hearing her mother's laugh filling the empty hallways.

"I really should check on the house," Emily said. "Thank you so much for dinner."

"Well," Nan said, "we better see you tomorrow night too. Harper will be home, and she'll want to say hello. It'll be just like old times."

And as much as she wished that were true, Emily knew it wasn't. In all of the last eighteen years, nothing had ever felt like old times.

"I'll walk you." Hollis stood.

"You don't have to," Emily said, but secretly the thought of spending a few minutes alone with the man had her insides quivering—and not in an unpleasant way.

CHAPTER 8

EMILY STEPPED OUT ONTO THE PORCH with Hollis close behind her. The night air was warm, but not hot, as if summer had decided to take its time. She drew in a deep breath and let it out, wishing she could slow time. She reached into her pocket and turned the key to the cottage over in her palm. The old house, filled with memories, beckoned to her, daring her to open its doors. Daring her to let the light in.

"Was that as awful as I think it was?" Hollis asked, breaking through her silence.

She glanced at him. "No, it was actually pretty wonderful. It's been so long since I've had a meal like that." Meals with her grandparents were much more . . . formal.

"No family dinners on Broadway?"

She laughed, hoping it covered her sadness. *No family dinners anywhere.*

They walked through the backyard, and she could hear the ocean waves chasing the shore.

"Do you mind if we take the long way?" she asked. "I'm not in much of a hurry to get back."

"Fine with me." Hollis turned toward the water, and soon they were on the beach. She removed her shoes and let the cool sand squish through her toes.

"Thanks for what you said in there," Hollis said. "About Nantucket. Jolie's been hard to convince."

She fixed her eyes in front of her. "I thought so. But I meant what I said—those shows are the reason I'm still an actor."

"Those shows? Not *Dottie's World*?"

Emily laughed. "No. I never saw my mom and grandparents in the front row at *Dottie's World*. But they were always there for every performance at the arts center. The curtain call was my favorite part because that's when my family would jump up and cheer—that's when I knew I'd made them proud." She'd tucked that memory in her pocket to save for a rainy day.

She would never forget the way it felt to know that they were there *for her*. Her grandfather had taken over the arts center the following year, donating enough money that they renamed it in his honor.

He'd done that for her too—she realized that now. It was meant to be something she could love every summer, as if there weren't enough things to love about Nantucket.

She thought she'd be doing shows there for many, many years, but things hadn't worked out that way, had they?

A quiet pause fell between them, and Emily cleared her throat in an effort to fill it. She hadn't meant to get so serious—she hadn't even meant to have that memory at all.

But that was the one, wasn't it? The one that kept her onstage all these years?

"Did you miss it here?" Hollis asked.

She shrugged, though she doubted he could see her in the darkness. "Maybe a little."

"I think Nantucket missed you."

This was no good—the way he made her feel. Like he cared about these unwanted memories. Like she was special, like she was the only person in the world. She didn't want to feel that way, not because it wasn't nice but because it wasn't genuine. It couldn't possibly be, and she knew it.

So why did she still let it warm her from her toes up?

"Nobody in your family brought up baseball," she said. In fact, Hollis was the only one who had escaped the life recap. Did his parents assume she knew more than she did? She didn't even know he had a daughter. Websites called him "notoriously private," and maybe now she understood why. She'd seen a spark of shame behind his eyes when he told her he and Jolie's mom had never married, as if that would shape her opinion of him.

It would never. But he didn't know that. He didn't know her.

"They know better." Hollis bent over and picked up a rock, then faced the water and threw it in, sidearm.

"Sore subject?" She slowed.

"You could say that."

They walked in silence across the beach, the memory of simpler times ringing in the air above them. So many summers they'd spent together in this very spot, though in those days, Emily never would've imagined sweet little Hollis would grow up to be, well, *Hollis McGuire.*

"So you're kind of famous." She grinned at him.

"Nah, I'm just a ballplayer."

She ran her shoulder into his. "Whatever, Mr. Modest."

"Well, I haven't been on *Broadway,*" he said, pushing her back.

"No, but you do have a daughter." She glanced at him.

He grew quiet. "That I do."

"What's the story there?" She knew she had no right to his personal information, but why pretend she wasn't curious? They were beyond pleasantries after spending the evening together—and she wanted to know. Besides, tact had never been her strong suit. He knew that as well as anybody.

"It's not really a story," he said. "I was young and stupid and making a lot of money. I made some poor choices. Forgot who I am."

"Forgot who you are?"

"Yeah," he said. "I'm not the kind of guy who hooks up with someone he's just met."

A slightly uncomfortable silence followed.

"So, you and Jolie's mom?"

"Just friends," he said, practically cutting her off.

"And Jolie?"

"What about Jolie?"

"Seems tense."

He raised an eyebrow. "You've been back here about five hours and already you're digging for my dirty laundry?"

"Just doing my job as your oldest and dearest friend."

He laughed. "Same old Emily."

She gave him a soft shrug.

"What about you? Got any skeletons in your closet?"

She smiled flirtatiously. "More than you can count."

It was only partly true, because while she'd made her fair share of poor relationship choices, she was also mostly talk. Truth was, most days she battled insecurity just like every other woman on the planet. And never having let herself get close to anyone only fed into those insecurities.

But she'd created a certain image for herself—confident, aloof, life of the party. The persona she wore when she didn't feel like wearing the truth, which, now that she thought about it, was pretty much all the time.

Truth was messy. This was easier.

And Emily liked easier. Or she had. These days, she wasn't so sure she had the energy for pretense.

They were in her backyard now, and the thought of what was in front of her tied her stomach into a tight knot. The sight of the patio, even in the darkness, broke her heart. Once upon a time, it had been filled with giant pots of vibrant flowers. Now it was covered with weeds.

Hollis must've sensed her concern because he slowed his pace and said, "We'll be over to help with the yard."

She shook her head. "You don't have to do that. It's not your responsibility."

"McGuires take care of their own." A grin crept across his face.

She didn't bother correcting him. If he wanted to treat her like family, who was she to stop him? And she knew to keep him at arm's length.

Don't get too attached.

Emily started off toward the front of the house. She reached the porch and saw her suitcase waiting for her. She slipped her hand in her pocket and pulled out the key, rubbing her forefinger and thumb on either side of it.

She felt Hollis watching her and quickly ordered herself to get it together. "Okay, here goes." Did her voice sound as shaky as it felt?

She met his eyes and quickly smiled, then turned back to the door. Why was this so difficult?

"Want me to go in with you?"

His kindness caught her off guard. She could hear her heart responding without her permission. *Yes, please, come in with me. I don't think I can do this alone.* But before she could make another huge mistake, she heard herself say, "No thanks. I'll be okay."

He gave her a nod but said nothing else.

"Really, thank you." It would be easier without him watching her.

"No problem. I'll see you tomorrow." He started to walk away but quickly turned back around. "And, Emily?"

She met his eyes.

"I'm glad you're back."

Hollis returned home to find Jolie waiting on the porch. She sat on the steps, Tilly at her side, and even in the darkness he could tell her mood was sour.

"Hey, kid," he said. "What are you doing out here?"

"You're not going to date her, are you?" Jolie snapped. Jana told him he might have some attitude to deal with. He'd had it in his mind that somehow he could win her over if she'd just give him a chance.

But all his charms were lost on his daughter. He found himself feeling awkward and tongue-tied around her.

Losing baseball had resulted in the loss of so much, including, it seemed, his ability to go with the flow—and being around Jolie only emphasized his shortcomings.

She'd fixed her face in what appeared to be a permanent scowl, and he realized she expected an answer to her question.

"What are you talking about?" He laughed as if to communicate something much more lighthearted than her expression conveyed.

"Emily," Jolie said. "You walked her home. Did you kiss her?"

"JoJo, I think you're confused." He sat down next to her, and she scooted over. "Besides, do you really care who I date?"

"I care if you date Emily." She crossed her arms in front of her chest.

Hollis frowned. "Why?"

"Because I like her." She glowered now, making it obvious that as much as Hollis didn't understand grown women, he understood preteen girls even less.

"I like her too, Jolie," Hollis said. "She's a very old friend."

"But she's pretty."

"Sure, she's pretty." *So pretty. Take-your-breath-away pretty.* Throughout dinner, while Hayes rambled on about his escapades all over the globe, Hollis stole glimpses of her, two words flitting through his mind in utter disbelief: *Emily Ackerman.*

He thought he'd never see her again after that summer. He hoped—every year, he hoped—but the house next door remained empty. The Ackerman family was wealthy enough to hold on to a property they never used, but it still seemed crazy to him.

For years, the house had suffered. His family always mowed the lawn and pulled the weeds. His mother planted new hydrangeas when the old ones stopped blooming, and they would've done the same this summer if Emily hadn't returned. But nothing about the Ackerman cottage was ever the same.

It was as if it were frozen in time, as if Emily's grandparents were afraid to change anything for fear of ruining whatever good memories they had of the place.

But how often did anyone think of the good memories when the bad ones were so very bad?

"Dad?"

"Sorry, what?" Had Jolie asked him a question he didn't hear?

"This is how I know you like her," Jolie said with a pout.

"How?"

"You look all dopey and you zone out. Mom did that all the time, every time she started dating a new guy." Jolie wrapped her arms around her knees and pulled them close.

"What's wrong with me liking Emily?"

"You ruin things, Dad. You'll like her for a little while and then you won't like her and she'll never come around again. Just look at you and Mom."

"Is that what you think?" Did Jana give her these ideas?

She looked at him pointedly. "Let's be honest, Dad. You don't have the best track record when it comes to relationships."

"I've been kind of busy, Jolie."

"Lots of other guys on your team had wives and kids."

Her words hung there between them. It was the unspoken truth he didn't have the courage to confront.

"Just don't date Emily," Jolie said. "She's too nice for you." His daughter stood up and looked at him. "Promise."

The memory of Emily's sweet smile raced through his mind. He looked at his daughter. Jolie's being here this summer was his second chance, and he wouldn't do anything to jeopardize it. He couldn't— he knew he wouldn't get another shot. "I have no plans to date Emily, JoJo."

"Promise, Dad."

"Fine, kid. I promise."

She spun around on her heel and walked back inside the house, leaving Hollis on the porch with too many unwanted thoughts.

CHAPTER 9

MEMORIAL DAY WEEKEND, 1989

JD's workday slogged on. He caddied for a first-class blowhard named Rich Heard, which meant most of his afternoon was spent listening to the guy talk about how great he was, how much money he had, and why everyone else was an idiot.

JD wasn't sure he'd last the entire summer carrying golf clubs for guys who were perfectly capable of carrying their own.

Mostly, he spent the afternoon thinking about the girl he'd met on the beach that morning. He knew the Ackerman name (who didn't?) and he'd already been warned by two different people not to even attempt to date Isabelle, but he didn't like being told what to do. If he was honest, it only made him want to date her more.

After he came off the course, he went straight to the staff locker room and cleaned up, wishing he had time for a shower. Wishing he had time to perfect his look before picking her up.

He hurried into a pair of khaki shorts—the same kind so many guys wore to the club, only without the designer label—and a striped polo shirt, which made him feel like an impostor.

Who was he trying to fool? He hardly had enough money to buy her a burger—it wasn't like he could pretend more money into his wallet. One last glance in the mirror, and he figured this was as good as it was going to get.

As he left the club, Alan Ackerman strolled toward the pro shop with an older man.

Isabelle's dad didn't give JD a second glance. Typical.

He made his way down the sidewalk toward Children's Beach, arguing with himself the whole way. He could just not show up—save himself the heartache of falling for a girl he had no business asking out in the first place.

And he was pretty sure if either of them were in danger of falling, it was him.

But no matter how much he tried to reason with himself, he couldn't convince himself to go back.

He turned down the road and spotted her, sitting on a bench looking out across the water.

He stopped for a second. Let himself stare.

Her long, dark hair was pulled back into a loose braid, and she wore a flowy floral top with a pair of white shorts. Her skin was already slightly tanned, as if today hadn't been her first day on the beach.

The sun lit her from behind, wrapping her in the perfect yellow-ish hue, and that's when JD knew there was no going back.

Yes, he'd likely get his heart broken, but Isabelle was worth the risk.

He made his way across the grass toward the bench where she sat, eyes glued to her the entire time.

He felt completely unworthy.

He walked up behind the bench and drew in a deep, shaky breath. *Last chance to get out of here.*

"Bella?"

She turned and faced him, and her big blue eyes nearly knocked the wind out of him.

"You're late," she said.

He glanced at his watch. "Only three minutes."

She raised an eyebrow.

"I was working up the courage to come over here."

She held his gaze for a long moment, then looked away, doing a poor job of hiding her smile.

"Have you eaten?" he asked.

She shook her head.

He'd managed to scrounge enough money together to take her somewhere nice—at least, he'd have enough if he limited what he ate.

"There's a place down on the beach where you can get hot dogs and fries," she said.

He glanced at her. "You don't have to do that."

Her forehead puckered. "Do what?"

"I have money to take you to a real restaurant." He didn't like feeling this way, like he wasn't good enough. Maybe this was a bad idea.

She groaned. "Maybe I'm tired of 'real' restaurants," she said.

He watched her as she looked away.

"I don't want to be a stuffy little rich girl anymore, okay?"

He slid onto the bench next to her.

She steeled her jaw as she stared out in front of her. A toddler ran by, naked, his mom chasing him, waving a tiny bathing suit over her head.

"Sorry," she said. "I didn't have a great day."

He tried not to stare at her, but she had him in a sort of trance. Her jaw twitched, only slightly and barely noticeable, and in that moment he realized that just because a person had money, that didn't automatically mean their life was easy.

"You know what?" he said. "If you're looking to escape your world for the night, I think I can help."

He reached over and took one of her folded hands in his. She stared at his hand wrapped around hers but didn't pull away. He decided he liked the way her skin felt and hoped he could hold on to her hand for the rest of the night.

He stood, tugged her to her feet, and planted himself directly in front of her, forcing her eyes to meet his. "Whatever it is that's bothering you, do you think you can forget about it for a couple of hours?"

She shrugged softly. "You don't know my mother." The wind pulled a strand of hair from her braid, and without thinking, he reached out and tucked it behind her ear. She didn't shrink under his touch, but her breath caught and she looked away.

In that moment, he knew Isabelle was special. She was precious—untouched. He'd be surprised if she'd ever had a boyfriend or even kissed anyone. He wouldn't take advantage of that. He was more experienced, sure, but that meant he knew the difference between a fling and something real.

He didn't need another moment with her to know this could be something real.

And as they walked away from Children's Beach, excitement welled up inside him at the prospect of discovering Isabelle for himself.

~

When JD didn't let go of her hand, Isabelle felt her stomach flip-flop, and she wondered if this was what it felt like to have a boyfriend. No wonder her friends acted so goofy about boys they liked. Isabelle had never understood before because she'd never found a boy who looked at her the way JD did.

The fight with her mother that afternoon might as well have been her life stuck on repeat. She never seemed to live up to her mom's standards. Why it still bothered her so much was something of a mystery.

Mom wanted her to be the perfect high society daughter, and Isabelle wanted to be herself. She didn't like the way her parents and their friends treated people, and she didn't want to put on an Eliza-approved dress and go to a luncheon the following day. Her mother didn't understand why not.

And Isabelle hadn't figured out how to explain herself without everything turning into a giant argument, which was exactly what had happened on the way out the door to meet JD.

The effects of that still hung around now. She hadn't meant to blurt out anything about her family, but it was out, and he didn't seem to mind.

"Where are we going?" she asked.

He met her eyes and grinned, looking a bit like a kid with a secret.

They walked down Beach Street, over to Water Street, and finally landed on Main, then turned to find themselves standing in front of Nantucket Pharmacy, an old-school soda fountain with sandwiches, hot dogs, milk shakes, and everything her mother forbade her to eat.

"You ever been here?" he asked.

She grinned. "Once, for an egg cream."

"And?"

"It was amazing."

"Then let's get that."

"And a grilled cheese?" she asked.

"Definitely."

They went inside and stood in the line leading to the counter, still holding hands like two people who'd known each other for months, not hours.

They stepped forward and JD ordered, leaving Isabelle to glance around the space, suddenly aware that at any moment she could be spotted by someone who knew her parents. She pulled her hand from JD's, and he stopped midsentence to look at her.

"You okay?" he asked.

She nodded and smiled.

The girl behind the counter looked at him, clearly annoyed that he was taking longer than he should.

He finished the order and glanced back at Isabelle, who avoided his eyes. He'd see right through her, and she knew it. How did she explain without hurting his feelings that her family situation meant they couldn't be seen in public together?

Maybe this first date should also be their last.

Never mind the somersaulting stomach or her inability to stop inhaling the scent of him. That was all infatuation. He was showing her a lot of attention and he was really, *really* good-looking. But Isabelle was smarter than those vapid girls who giggled their way through conversations with cute boys. She needed to stay focused on what was important—getting through high school so she could announce to her parents she was taking a gap year to travel the world, and then maybe, if she felt like it, she'd go back to school and figure out what career she wanted.

That plan wouldn't have their blessing, and neither would dating JD—so if she had to choose, which of those two was more important?

But as they walked out to Brant Point, the lighthouse ahead, and behind it, a stretch of beautiful ocean, JD took her hand as if it were his to take, and the hair on the back of her neck stood up.

They sat on the beach and ate their sandwiches, and they talked. For hours. He told her about college and how he was working his way through, determined to have a life different from the one his parents had.

"I don't want to live paycheck to paycheck," he said. "I don't want my kids going to school in ripped jeans and holey shoes. I want to make something of myself, and I think I can. I just have to work a little harder than most people."

She saw a fire behind his eyes—the need to prove himself to everyone else, to people like her parents. Did her situation only make that feeling of inadequacy that much worse?

The sun set, and the beach grew quiet and bare, leaving just the two of them, their empty food bags, and a night sky full of stars.

He lay back on the beach and peered up into the dark sky. "You ever wish on the stars?"

She lay next to him, her face warming into a soft smile. "Every single night. I always wish on the first one I see."

"Even tonight?"

She couldn't say it out loud—what she'd wished when she spotted that first bright star off in the distance.

He rested his head on his fist, elbow holding him steady, and grinned at her. "You did—what did you wish?"

She shook her head, eyes still focused on the sky above her. "Nothing."

"I'll tell you what I wished for," he said.

Isabelle glanced at him. "Okay."

The corners of his mouth drew into a smile. "I wished that this wouldn't be the last time I got to take you out."

"Oh, really?" she asked, trying to keep her heart rate steady.

"Yeah," he said, then dreamily—"You're the most beautiful girl I've ever seen."

She looked away, certain her cheeks had flushed bright pink and wishing for a quick escape. He made her feel a way she'd never felt before, but as much as it scared her, it also excited her—she'd never met anyone who said exactly what they thought the way JD did with such ease.

She propped herself up on her elbows, drinking in the sounds and smells of the ocean.

"You know this is a bad idea, right?" she asked.

She could practically feel his frown as he sat up and stared at her. "Why?"

She looked at him. He was older, more mature, more experienced. He was handsome and real and honest. He didn't deserve to be put in a category simply because he wasn't "one of them," but she knew that's exactly what her parents would do if they ever heard she'd gone out with him.

"Because of your parents?" he asked.

She nodded. "We're awfully different."

"Different can be good," he said. "You'll show me a world I don't know, and I'll do the same for you."

She pushed herself up the rest of the way and looked at him. "It's a bad idea."

"It's a bad idea, so you think we shouldn't see each other, or it's a bad idea, but let's see each other anyway?"

Isabelle shook her head. She didn't know. She was out of her depth. He shifted her sideways on the inside.

"You've got to feel this between us, Bella," he said. "It can't just be me."

She drew in a deep breath. "But my parents . . ."

"Aren't here right now."

"But there's no future for us, JD—you have to know that. Isn't it better to end it now, before it begins?"

He reached out and touched her cheek. "It's already begun. There's no way I'm gonna be able to get you out of my head now."

Her heart sputtered. She wanted to believe him. She wanted to hold on to him because he was more genuine than anyone else she knew. She liked the realness of him—and she liked his lips. They were soft and full, and when his eyes dipped down and drank her in, she imagined what it would be like to kiss him.

"Maybe we don't think about the future," he said. "Maybe let's just think about this moment, right now, and let the rest of it figure itself out—later."

That sounded good. It sounded better than good. It sounded brilliant. And Isabelle was tired of being practical. For once, she wanted to make a decision based on her own thoughts and feelings and not on something her parents instructed (or ordered) her to do.

"What do you think?" he asked.

"Just this moment right now?"

"Yeah."

"Okay," she said. "Can you convince me it's worth ignoring what comes next?"

He smiled. "I'd like to try."

Her stomach butterflies were back, and as he inched toward her, he didn't take his eyes off of her for a second. He reached up and took her face in his hands, studying her with such intent it made her insides quiver.

"Can I kiss you, Bella?" he whispered.

She nodded, holding on to his gaze, then begged her breath to steady as his lips met hers. She was right—they were soft and full. His kiss was tender to start but quickly grew more hurried as he drew her closer. It occurred to her that perhaps up until this point she'd been kissing the wrong boys. She'd never much cared for kissing—but in that moment, she thought it might be her new favorite thing.

His hands moved down her back, and Isabelle marveled at the way he felt like someone she'd known for years—or maybe like someone she'd been waiting to know.

He pulled away and searched her eyes. "Sorry, I gotta calm down."

She could practically feel his restraint and how difficult it was for him to exercise it. Something about that endeared him to her, made her feel safe.

And she felt herself falling for a boy she'd only just met and wondering how to keep his very existence a secret from parents who would most certainly not approve.

Because she understood what JD meant—there was no way she would get him out of her head now.

CHAPTER 10

EMILY FELT THE WET TONGUE OF AN ANIMAL licking her hand, rousing her from sleep. She squinted in the morning light after a very long, very uncomfortable night.

"Emily?"

She forced her eyes open and found Hollis and Jolie staring at her.

A part of her had been aware she was outside on the patio—every time she shifted positions throughout the night—but she couldn't bring herself to face the inside of the house.

Now she felt completely exposed.

Being back in Nantucket, in this house, forced her to revisit so many feelings she'd put in the background of her life. It was like digging up a time capsule and being transported back decades in an instant.

Why had she agreed to this?

"Sorry," Emily finally said, straightening her disheveled clothing. "I must've been really tired." It wasn't all that different from waking up on the beach after a late night out with friends. And yet it was completely different.

As she shifted, Mom's book of letters fell on the ground. Hollis grabbed it before she could, glancing at it long enough to read the words her mother had painted on the cover.

If for Any Reason

His eyes found hers, and judging by his expression, he had questions. And concerns.

She held out a hand and he gave her the book, which she tucked neatly under her arm, avoiding his watchful eye. She'd forgotten how it felt to be looked after, fussed over.

She wasn't sure if she liked it.

Emily had carved out a life of adventure, and her fearlessness had started at a young age. It drove Hollis nuts when she'd jump straight in the surf or dive headfirst into the pool or go hunting for crabs—which he refused to touch.

By contrast, Hollis had always been serious and practical. One summer, Emily learned what the word *somber* meant and decided it described him perfectly. If she were collecting words to describe him, *somber* and *magnetic* would top the list. He was like a walking oxymoron. Hollis had always been concerned about everyone else, but especially about Emily, as if he had the burden of being her protector. Clearly he hadn't outgrown that.

"You guys are up early," Emily said, trying to keep her tone light and truthfully oblivious to how early it was or wasn't.

"We came over to invite you down to the beach for a picnic later and also out on this big, fancy boat my dad is renting this weekend with his baseball money," Jolie said.

"Jolie—it belongs to a friend." Hollis sounded embarrassed. "Em, what are you doing out here?"

Emily ignored his question and smiled at Jolie. "A big, fancy boat, huh?"

The girl shrugged. "I mean, I'm scared of the sharks, but I'll go if you go. Maybe we can talk about Broadway and all the other acting jobs you've done?"

The light in Jolie's eyes was so familiar. She remembered when she'd first discovered a love for the stage—she was a couple of years younger than Jolie was now.

Emily wasn't great at it—not at first. Her grandfather threatened to step in when she was cast in the chorus that first year, but his "Don't they know who we are?" attitude was exactly what Emily's mother despised, and Isabelle demanded that he stay out of it.

"Let her be a kid who doesn't have everything handed to her," she'd said. "Let her be normal."

It had been important to Isabelle that Emily didn't turn out to be a spoiled brat, and Emily had learned a lot being in the chorus of those shows.

The summer she was ten, she had her first speaking role. She played a lady of the court in a production of *Cinderella* down at the arts center. She would never forget how it felt to dance across the stage with the prince—to feel the stage lights on her face, to look out across the dark theatre and see an audience of people watching her. It was exhilarating.

The joy of performing hadn't died with her mother, though it had changed the few years she was on television. She'd gotten the title role in the kids' show not long after the summer she was ten and spent three years being Dottie.

She'd been so passionate about theatre in those days—but lately, performing had lost its luster. Theatre had taken a cruel turn.

Seeing how excited Jolie was at the whole idea of Broadway stirred something inside her. She'd felt it yesterday at the arts center and she felt it now, the reminder that she still had the ability to feel that kind of passion. She'd missed it, the passion for something—anything—but especially for theatre. Hollis might've been her first crush, but theatre had been her first love.

"I'd love to talk to you about Broadway," Emily finally said, forcing herself out of her own mind. She had a feeling her memories would be interrupting her a lot this summer.

"Really?" Jolie grinned a big, toothy grin. "Awesome!"

Was that all it took to make a preteen girl happy? "Yes, but unfortunately, I don't think I can come to the beach today."

Jolie groaned. "Let me guess, you have work. Grown-ups always have work."

"Jolie—" Hollis shot her a look, but a second later his eyes were back on Emily.

"I do, actually." Emily motioned with her head to the house behind her. "This old place isn't going to fix itself. I have a contractor coming over this morning." She pulled her phone out and looked at the time. "Oh, wow. He'll be here any minute."

"This early?" Jolie twisted her face.

She thought about her conversation with the investment banker who was looking to "stay busy" this summer. He'd answered her ad the day before she left for Nantucket, and he'd set the time for their meeting. She would've definitely picked something a little more in the 10 a.m. range. Or maybe noon.

"Who is it?" Hollis asked.

Emily found Hollis's eyes intently fixed on hers. "You won't know him."

"I know a lot of people."

"His name is Jack Walker," Emily said. "He hasn't been on the island in a few years."

"And you're just going to let him in the house?"

Emily shifted. "Is that a big deal?"

"We don't know anything about this guy, Emily."

Already she felt like she was doing this wrong. She just wanted someone to come in and fix the house so she didn't have to think about it.

"I'll stay." He had that protective stance again.

"That's really not necessary." Emily tried to be kind but firm. Mostly, she thought she just sounded annoyed. Did he know the number of people she'd met over the years? She knew how to take care of herself.

"Jolie, run home," Hollis said. "Eat your breakfast, and I'll be back just as soon as I make sure this guy checks out."

Jolie shot Emily a look of solidarity, as if to say *See what I mean?* and Emily did her best not to roll her eyes at the girl's father.

"Maybe when you're all finished, you can come eat pancakes?" Jolie asked. The girl had obviously taken to Emily, more so than her *somber but magnetic* father had seemed to, anyway.

"Oh, I shouldn't," Emily said. "I already barged in on your meal last night."

"Dad, tell her she should come eat pancakes." Jolie glanced at Hollis, who shifted uncomfortably.

"You should come eat pancakes," he said unenthusiastically.

Emily shot him a look. "I don't think I have time. Hollis, really, I'm fine here. You can even watch from a distance to make sure he doesn't murder me, wrap my body in a sheet, and toss it in the back of his work truck."

"Ew." Jolie grimaced.

"Sorry," Emily said, realizing her commentary was a little gruesome for a kid.

"Aunt Harper is coming," Jolie said, unfazed.

Hollis didn't move—he was still stewing about the contractor, Emily could tell.

"I'd love to see her," Emily said, turning her attention toward her younger visitor. "Maybe you could text me when it would be a good time to stop over later?" She directed that last part to Hollis.

"Sure, if you give me your number." Hollis met her eyes and Emily hung on to his gaze for too long.

"Give *me* your number," Jolie said. "I promise I won't spam text you." She reached in her back pocket, pulled out the latest iPhone, and handed it to Emily.

"Oh," Emily said. "You have a phone."

"Everyone has a phone." Jolie sat down in one of the chairs across from Emily.

Emily's eyes darted to Hollis, who only shrugged. She punched her number into Jolie's phone and handed it back to the girl.

"Okay, now let's take a picture." Jolie tapped around on her device, then pointed it at Emily.

Instinctively, Emily put her hands in front of her face. "I just woke up."

Jolie snapped. "Too late." She tapped around again, then grinned. "Done." She turned the phone around and showed the photo to Emily. "I think you look beautiful."

There was something sweet about the way she said it—something genuine—that made Emily pause.

"I'll text you after Aunt Harper gets here!" Jolie hopped off the chair and walked over to Tilly, tossing Hollis a quick look over her shoulder. "Ready?"

Emily could still feel Hollis's attention on her—concerned, protective. When would he learn she didn't need anyone protecting her?

Emily found her brave face and stood up, doing her best to reassure Hollis that everything was absolutely fine.

"Are you gonna be okay?" Hollis asked, eyes drilling a hole straight through her.

Emily didn't like this. She didn't like that even after all these years, he seemed to sense things about her that she wanted to keep to herself.

"I'm fine, Hollis." Her tone was colder, shorter than she'd intended, but she couldn't have Hollis hovering over her like this. She was a grown-up. She'd figure this out her own way.

"I'm not talking about the contractor," he said.

She pretended not to understand. "Then what are you talking about?"

"You slept outside."

"I like the stars."

He knew she was lying—it was clear on his face. "Em."

She met his eyes—earnest and kind—and softened, just slightly. "I'm fine," she said again, this time with more kindness.

He watched her for a few seconds, then finally gave her a nod and started off toward Jolie.

"Bye, Emily!" the girl called out.

Emily lifted her hand lamely and waved at them as they strolled off. She groaned, running her hands over her face. *I'm such a jerk.*

Her phone buzzed in her pocket. She glanced down and saw a text from a number not in her contacts.

Hi, Emily. It's Jolie. I wanted you to have my number. And here's a photo you can use for my contact. Do you think it would make a good headshot?

Emily smiled. Jolie might be the best person she knew. Would it be weird to befriend a twelve-year-old? Adults were so untrustworthy.

She turned her attention back to the house and drew in a breath. "All right," she said to herself. "Let's really get this over with."

CHAPTER 11

EMILY TRUDGED BACK to the front porch, all the time reciting the same phrase to herself: *I can do hard things.*

She stood there, holding the small book of letters. The words in her mother's "For When You Want to Give Up" letter raced through her mind—she practically had this one memorized.

My dear Emily,
People will tell you God will never give you more than
you can handle. I disagree. God allows us more than we can
handle so we have to rely on him. After all, if we could handle
everything life throws at us, why would we need God at all?

Her mother was right. God had certainly given Emily more than she could handle. He'd allowed the accident that claimed her mom's life. How could her mom expect her to trust God for anything after that?

And let's be honest, after the way Emily had lived her life, she was pretty sure she'd run him off a long time ago.

Emily stood on the porch, staring at the door for the third time when suddenly it all felt ridiculous. She was putting so much weight on this house. It was only a house. And at the moment, not even a nice house.

She needed to jump in the deep end and get this over with. It was why she was here, after all.

Before she could muster the nerve, she heard the sound of a vehicle approaching. She turned and saw a red pickup ambling up the driveway.

Jack Walker was a punctual man. Normally this would be a tremendous asset, but on a day when Emily had woken up on the patio, it read more like a shortcoming.

She whispered a quick "Please don't let him murder me" prayer and did her best to unruffle herself as she watched him park, turn off the engine, and get out.

First impressions were important—her grandmother had taught her that. First impressions of Jack Walker (aside from his punctuality): Tall. Handsome. Chiseled features. Wave of sandy-colored hair with some gray sprinkled in around his temples.

Does not appear to be a serial killer.

He took one look at her and smiled. "It's early."

"I overslept," she admitted, wondering what she actually looked like after her open-air sleep. She did her best to smooth her hair, but she could feel a bump in the back that probably made her look like the female version of Alfalfa. "I'm sorry."

Jack held up his hands in front of him. "No need to apologize."

She stuck out her right hand intending to redeem herself with a firm, good-enough-for-GrandPop kind of handshake, but Jack took her hand in both of his and squeezed it gently.

"It's nice to meet you."

She pulled her hand away and silently prayed again. "I'm Emily."

"Jack Walker." He gave her a quick once-over. "So you're an Ackerman?"

"I am," she said. "You're not a murderer or anything, are you?" Emily's body blocked the front door, and she realized if the answer to her question was yes, she'd be helpless to stop him.

He laughed. "I'm not."

She sized him up.

"But I can find a reference letter that says so if you need me to."

She stuck the key in the lock. "It's okay. I don't have time for that. Come on in. I'll show you around." She pushed the door open and stepped inside, the musty smell of neglect instantly hitting her nostrils.

She turned and found Jack still standing on the porch. "Do you want me to bring this inside?" He pointed to her suitcase, which she promptly grabbed and dragged into the entryway.

"Sorry," she said.

There was a quizzical look on his face, but he didn't say anything. Grandma would not be proud of the first impression she was making.

He stepped inside and she closed the door.

The house didn't feel as big as she remembered. Straight ahead was the great room, with one whole wall of windows giving a perfect view of the backyard, the swimming pool, the cracked concrete patio. Off to the left was the kitchen, a true chef's kitchen that—once upon a time—had been outfitted with the very best of everything.

"To be honest, I haven't really had a chance to assess everything that needs to be done in here," she said. "I just got in yesterday."

Jack's eyes crinkled at the corners as he smiled and said, "That's what I'm here for."

She took a step to her right, and she could practically see GrandPop sitting behind his big desk, the smell of tobacco and peppermint filling his study.

"Maybe we can just walk through together and make some notes?" Jack asked.

"Sounds like a good idea." Was it completely obvious she had no idea what she was doing?

She turned toward the stairway, and for the briefest moment she was twelve again, traipsing down those very stairs in her nightgown in the middle of the night, clinging to her mother's hand.

She closed her eyes and let herself remember, just for a fleeting second.

You can't dwell here, Emily. Assess the damage to the house. Make a list of what needs to go. Arrange for a Dumpster ASAP.

Emily opened her eyes, took out her phone, and began a list, which Jack also seemed to be doing on a clipboard. His list was probably a bit more comprehensive considering she'd never renovated a house before.

She typed:

- Refinish floors.
- Paint walls.
- Get Dumpster.

They walked into the kitchen, and Emily nearly gasped at what it had become. "Wow."

"How long since you've been in the house?"

"Eighteen years."

Jack's eyes widened. "That explains a few things."

Yes. It did. Like the shabby floral café curtain partially covering the window over the sink. She pulled it down, wadded it into a ball, and threw it on the counter.

- New window coverings
- New windows?

"Let's get some air in here," Jack said. He leaned over the sink and fought with the glass pane until eventually it gave way, sending a warm breeze through the space. "What's your plan with the house?" He set the clipboard down on the counter and looked at her.

"I'm going to fix it up so I can sell it."

His eyebrows rose. "You don't want to fix it up and live in it?"

Her laugh lacked amusement, and it sounded phony even to her. "Definitely not."

"Then I think this room will need a lot of work." He scribbled something on the clipboard. "The kitchen being the heart of the home and all. Buyers love a beautiful kitchen."

She nodded, though it occurred to her that the kitchen had never been the heart of this home. That honor had gone to the living room. With a wall of windows facing the backyard and an opposite wall covered in floor-to-ceiling bookshelves, the living room had always been the gathering place for the Ackerman family.

She walked into the space and knelt down to study the bottom two shelves, where all her books were stored.

Trixie Belden. *Anne of Green Gables. Pippi Longstocking.* They were still here as if they'd been waiting all this time for someone to open them up again.

It was here where her love of story had begun—and her love of adventure. Her mom read to her out loud more nights than not, even after she was perfectly capable of reading chapter books on her own. It was their special time.

Grandma didn't approve. "Don't fill her mind with all that nonsense, Isabelle," she'd say with a shake of her head. "We don't want her head up in the clouds like yours always was."

Her mother would lean in close then so Grandma couldn't hear. "I think there's no better place for a head than up in the clouds."

Emily would laugh and they'd go back to reading, taking turns making up voices for the different characters.

She ran her hand along the spines of the old books and felt, for a moment, like she'd just been reunited with her dearest friends.

But this mental detour wasn't why she was here.

- New furniture
- New rugs
- New fixtures
- New everything!

"Why didn't you sell the house sooner?" Jack asked, standing in the doorway of the living room. "Eighteen years is a long time for a place like this to sit empty."

She stood. "It wasn't mine to sell. My grandfather passed away, and he left it to me."

"I'm sorry to hear that," he said.

She pretended it hurt less than it did, swatting his apology away before it had a chance to drill a hole in her perfectly placed facade.

"I haven't been back in a long time either," Jack said as if sensing her inward struggle.

"Did you spend a lot of time on the island when you were younger?"

"I did." He inspected the trim around the sliding-glass door that led to the backyard. "I picked up some odd jobs here and there before and during college."

She smiled. "I bet that was pretty fun, being here when you were that age."

Finally he looked at her again. "Some of the best times of my life."

"Did you know my mother? Isabelle Ackerman?" Emily had no idea why she'd asked that.

But Jack smiled at her question. "Everyone knew your mother."

His answer surprised her.

"All the guys at the country club—" his eyes practically twinkled—"well, we admired her from a distance."

"She was beautiful, wasn't she?" Emily stilled.

"She was that," he said.

After a brief pause, she started toward the stairs.

This might hurt a little. Actually, this might hurt a lot. This was a Band-Aid she wasn't ready to rip off, a wound that needed to stay covered.

She heard herself filling the silence as she pressed forward, giving herself what was quickly becoming a very tired (and annoying) pep talk: *I can do hard things.*

"If memory serves, my grandmother was a fan of wallpaper, so that'll have to come down. It's really ugly wallpaper."

Jack laughed, following her up the stairs, and she opened the door to the room that used to be hers. She stood in the hallway while he went in and looked around.

"This room looks pretty good." Jack pulled back the rug, which covered most of the floor. "Might not need to do much but paint in here." He stood next to the bulletin board hanging over the bed.

"Is this you?" He pointed to a photo of Emily and her mom down at the beach. She didn't need to get any closer to know which photo it was or from which day. A happy memory Emily had pushed out of her mind.

"Yes, a long time ago."

Jack touched the photo, then glanced at her. "Cute."

"There are three other bedrooms. You can look at them later—they're all about the same as this one." Only she didn't know that for certain—not really. It wasn't like she'd inspected them herself.

Dusty old memories didn't need unearthing.

He stuck his hands in the pockets of his cargo pants with a stern nod. "Sounds good."

As soon as he stepped back into the hallway, she closed the door behind them and exhaled. She didn't want to think about what other memories were pinned to the bulletin board or tucked in the drawers.

She hurried back toward the stairs and started down. "Then there is some work in the yard." That much she knew for sure.

She showed Jack the patio area, the torn screens on the porch, the rotting wood, the cracked cement. "It's probably obvious, but I don't know the first thing about renovating a home."

He tucked his clipboard under his arm. "We'll muddle through it together."

"Yeah?" *Does that mean you'll take the job?*

"I think we can handle most of what you need," Jack said. "I can hire some local help—might take a bit of time, but there are always young guys who need work. Why don't I put together an estimate and bring it by tomorrow?" Jack looked at her now, his eyes kind, fans of well-worn wrinkles at their corners.

89

"That would work," Emily said. "I know my budget, so I'll tell you what we can and can't do."

Her grandmother had sent her the information for a bank account with funds set aside for renovations—the point being to prevent the house from becoming a financial burden for Emily. She'd dipped into the account twice—once to buy her ferry ticket and once for a sandwich on her way over.

Looking at the cottage now, she wondered if she had enough money to cover the cost of the renovations. Did her grandmother know the shape this place was in?

"I'll give you a fair price." Jack smiled. He had a nice smile and looked nothing like an investment banker in his cargo pants, light-blue T-shirt, and work boots.

"I appreciate that." Emily pulled her sleeves down over her hands.

Jack watched her for a few seconds, then finally looked away. "Grateful for the opportunity, Miss Ackerman."

She gave him a nod. "I'll look forward to your estimate."

He pulled out a pair of sunglasses, stuck them on his face, and disappeared around the side of the house.

Her phone vibrated in her pocket. Jolie again: Aunt Harper just got here! GrandNan wants to know what kind of sandwiches are your favorite? She's going to bring you one even if you can't come to the beach.

The text was accompanied by a photo of the girl, her strawberry locks pulled up in a messy ponytail. She was making a peace sign with her partially painted fingernails and her dad was in the background, looking pensive.

Emily zoomed in on Hollis, who looked less like the baseball hero and more like a man with too much on his mind.

But still so very handsome.

She texted back: She doesn't have to do that!

But she's going to, so it might as well be something you like. ;)

I like everything! Turkey and cheese, ham and cheese, chicken salad. I'm not a picky eater.

Very quickly, her phone buzzed again. Dad said he'll make you cheese and mayonnaise sandwiches.

Emily laughed out loud at the memory.

She—in all her nine-year-old wisdom—mistakenly proclaimed that she'd invented the best sandwich ever: a slice of white bread, doused with spreadable cheese, then balled up in her fist. The final touch? Mayonnaise—on the outside of the bread ball.

Emily was bossy at that age, so she forced Hollis and Hayes to try her culinary masterpiece, which ended in groans and a dash for something to "wash down the grossness."

She couldn't believe he remembered—she'd forgotten all about that.

She quickly typed back: Whoever invented that is a genius! ☺

I think it sounds disgusting.

Emily laughed as another text came in.

I hope you change your mind about the beach. I can't wait to hear more about Broadway!

Broadway, right.

Emily couldn't bring Broadway to Jolie, but she could at least follow through at the arts center—do whatever it took to get the children's show up and running again for the girl's sake.

And maybe for her own sake too.

CHAPTER 12

Isabelle's summers had always been the same. Days on the beach or in the water, followed by parties and dinners with her parents and their friends. Somehow Eliza and Alan Ackerman loved to show her off, as if she were meant to be paraded around, a symbol of their good parenting, a symbol of their excellent life.

But what her parents didn't know was that their daughter spent those dinners thinking about the handsome golf caddie she would later sneak out to see. Her parents didn't know about the late-night picnics when she said she was with her friends. They didn't know about all the times she'd skip the beach to meet JD at the Juice Bar. And they certainly didn't know about the kissing—so much kissing.

Isabelle didn't expect to be good at hiding her relationship with JD, but it turned out she was a wizard at it. Almost everyone in town knew her parents, so this was no small feat, but she knew where to go so as to not run into any of those people.

Still, they were careful—she didn't want anything to jeopardize her time with the college boy who had most definitely stolen her heart.

JD said things to her that nobody had ever said before. He paid her compliments that had nothing to do with money or even beauty (though he often commented on that too). Mostly he seemed in awe of her spunk, her fire, her intelligence. And that made her feel like a person who could do anything.

It was a powerful thing, to feel invincible, like nothing could touch you. She had a feeling she made JD feel that way too, because he often came to her with new ideas and plans for their future—*their* future, not just his.

"I want to make sure you have the life you deserve," he'd say.

"The only life I need is one with you."

Now, sitting on their picnic blanket on Ladies Beach, a more secluded location than their first date, Isabelle laid her head in JD's lap, gazing up at him as he stared out across the water.

"What are you thinking about?" she asked quietly, seeing a pensiveness behind his eyes.

"Same thing I'm always thinking about," he said. "You."

She reached up and touched the bottom of his chin, his slight stubble rough underneath her fingers. The tentativeness of their initial meeting was gone, and in its place was a quiet familiarity between them, as kisses were more frequent and hands were often interlaced.

"What about me?"

He brought his eyes to hers and smiled. "That I love you, Isabelle Ackerman."

She fought the urge to look away. Surely he'd gone mad. Love was something you experienced when you were much older and had known a person for months, maybe even years.

"Sorry." He shifted, and she sat up. "I shouldn't have said that."

She could see hurt on his face. "No, I'm sorry—you just took me by surprise. Can you say it again?"

He glanced in her direction and she willed him not to look away.

"Please?"

He drew in a tight breath. "I've been thinking about it a lot, Isabelle, and I know it sounds crazy, but . . . I love you."

She smiled, and his face turned shy.

"What are you thinking?" he asked.

"I'm thinking that I love you too."

"Yeah?"

She nodded. "When you know, you know."

She couldn't explain it. It was crazy to think she was in love with someone she'd met just a month ago, especially when she was only seventeen, and yet everything inside of her believed that this was love. This was how love felt. And who could argue with that?

They didn't talk about what would happen at the end of the summer, focusing instead on the moments they were together. Maybe that's why it all felt so intense—it was as if they were living only one moment at a time, as if that were all they had.

JD kissed her, not like a person who'd kissed her a hundred times before, but like a person who might never get to kiss her again.

And she got lost in every single kiss.

But sometimes there was the lingering concern of what would come next. Every once in a while, there was that question—how would they last once they left the bubble of Nantucket?

"Don't think about it now," he said as if reading her mind. He wrapped his arms around her, pulling her close and letting her melt into him.

"I can't help it," she said. "What am I going to do without you?"

"You'll never have to know."

And even though she mostly knew it wasn't true, a sliver of hope seeped in through her seams, and that's what she decided to cling to.

CHAPTER 13

HOLLIS WATCHED FROM A DISTANCE as Jolie gingerly made her way out toward the water. The tide raced up, and as soon as the water hit her feet, she turned and ran the other way, Tilly following close behind.

Jolie had been in Nantucket four days now, and every day she got a little braver. Sort of.

Dad sat in the beach chair next to him wearing a goofy sun visor and sunblock that he hadn't fully rubbed in on his nose. "That's quite a kid you've got."

"She's something," Hollis agreed.

"This summer will be good for you two."

"I only have her for a month," Hollis said.

His mind ticked off the hours like a metronome. *It's already been four days.*

"That's all? Why? Jana has had her for twelve years—isn't it your turn?"

Hollis sighed. "I don't think Jolie wants to stay any longer than she has to."

Dad glanced at Hollis. "Well, a few weeks on the island will change her mind."

"Will it change her mind about me?" Hollis regretted saying it as soon as the words were out. He didn't want to talk about his shortcomings as a parent, especially not with his father, who somehow had managed to do everything right.

"I think only you can do that, Son," Dad said.

Hollis knew that. He knew it was up to him to mend what was broken between himself and Jolie, and yet where did he begin? She was like a foreign language to him—mysterious and nonsensical. Too much time had passed, and he'd made too many mistakes.

When Jana had asked him if Jolie could spend a few weeks with him this summer, he'd actually gotten nervous—over spending time with his own daughter. If his family weren't here, he wasn't sure what he would do. So far, his efforts to connect with her had been fruitless.

The worst part? He didn't blame her. If he were Jolie, he'd hate him too.

"Maybe I wasn't cut out to be a father," Hollis said quietly.

Dad snapped his book shut. "Well, Son, you don't get to make that choice now, do you?"

Hollis hated it when his father was firm. It didn't happen often—mostly Jeffrey McGuire was fun-loving and playful—but when it did, Hollis knew he better listen.

The trouble was, as much as he hated to admit it, Dad had never steered him wrong. Why did some people seem to get a double dose of wisdom when he felt like he hadn't even gotten his fair share? At least not when it came to Jolie.

So far, every decision he'd made about the girl had been wrong. Giving her space. Moving away. Not insisting he should be more than just a checkbook to her and Jana. So many mistakes . . .

"Don't lecture me, Pop," Hollis said.

"The way I see it, you've got a choice," his dad said. "You can sit here and dwell on how you wish things were different, or you can move forward and make things right."

"Yeah, I know." And he did know. He knew he'd failed as a father, and he knew his parents weren't proud of that. He didn't like to think about how his parents made time for Jolie, how they saw her school plays and dance recitals and band concerts and he'd missed nearly all of those things. And maybe he would've done better if it weren't for the accident, but maybe he wouldn't have. Maybe the accident had become an excuse to do a bad job raising his daughter. Maybe he was just a terrible father. "I screwed up, Dad. I screwed up, and I think it's too late to make it right."

"It's never too late," Dad said. "Not as long as there's air in your lungs."

Hollis sighed. Easy for him to say. "I don't even know where to start." Hollis hated that he didn't. He didn't like it when things didn't come easily to him—and Jolie definitely didn't come easily to him. If she were into sports, at least they could go play catch or he could pass on what he knew about the game, but she wasn't. She was a soon-to-be teenage girl with interests that made absolutely no sense to him.

"Start with her," Dad said. "Figure out what she likes and then force yourself to care about that."

Hollis frowned.

"You think your mother cares about baseball?"

"She loves baseball," Hollis said. He glanced over at his mom, sitting under an umbrella next to Harper. Mom wore a giant sun hat and was still fully clothed like a woman allergic to the sun.

"No, Hollis," Dad said. "She loves *you*."

"She loves the game."

Dad eyed Hollis for too many seconds.

"She doesn't love the game?"

"She loved how happy it made you to play," Dad said. "Think of how well she knew you because she took an interest in what you loved."

He paused. "I don't even know what Jolie loves." And as much as he wished he could, he was pretty sure he wouldn't be able to take an interest in something like hair or makeup or clothes.

"Well, we know one thing she loves," Dad said.

Hollis followed his father's gaze out to the ocean, where Jolie was now waist-deep, laughing with her uncle. "Theatre."

"Right," Dad said. "You can get that children's production back on at the arts center."

"It's not that easy."

"For you, it will be. You're on the board."

"I also voted to get rid of the children's programs, remember?"

Jolie raced out of the surf to the shore with a shout followed by a loud laugh. Even Hayes had found a way to connect with her. It didn't matter how difficult it was, Hollis needed to try, because he had a feeling if she left Nantucket at the end of the month feeling no differently about him than she'd felt when she came, it was over.

Something about that had him reeling. It was time to step up—past time to step up. And he prayed he wasn't too late.

~

Hollis spent the next couple of days chewing on his dad's advice, which was probably why he now found himself inside the arts center and on the way up the stairs to Gladys Middlebury's office. The old biddy was likely going to have a few choice words for him.

It had been nearly twenty years—no one would've guessed Emily would ever return.

He bypassed the receptionist's desk—the last thing he wanted to do was spend an hour talking to Hillary Schweitzer about her cats—and went directly to Gladys's office.

She was on the phone, sitting behind the large mahogany desk she'd inherited from her predecessor, a burly man everyone called Teddy. The desk didn't suit Gladys—she was a lot smaller than Teddy and kind of prissy. Why she hadn't replaced the giant desk was unclear.

Gladys's family was one of the richest on the island. She didn't take a salary for her work at the arts center—she didn't need it. She only did it because she was bored and wanted to "contribute." She never would've spoken to Hollis before he became a professional athlete. She wouldn't have even noticed him on the street except to turn up her nose at him. That's the kind of woman Gladys Middlebury was.

Which made speaking to her in a polite tone just on the edge of difficult for Hollis.

Gladys hung up the phone and glared at him. "Didn't I tell you something like this would happen?"

Hollis closed the door behind him.

"You insisted they would never be back in Nantucket." She stood. "You were so certain."

"I don't know what to say, Gladys," he said. "I'm as surprised as you are."

"Maybe we should discuss that eyesore of a house while she's here." Gladys walked over to a plant in a red pot that was sitting on the windowsill. She picked up a spray bottle and squirted it three times. "Maybe that would put her in her place."

"I think I have a better idea," Hollis said, hoping to distract Gladys away from the petition he knew she'd stuffed in one of those big desk drawers. Signed by at least one hundred people, it stated that something needed to be done about the Ackerman cottage. That petition was the only reason Hollis ever gave in to the vote about the children's program and the redistribution of funds.

If he hadn't, it would've gotten personal for Emily's family, and in his mind, that was the last thing any of them would've wanted. Sacrificing the children's programs seemed like a small price to pay.

Had he gotten it all backward?

Gladys spun around. "I don't trust your ideas, Mr. McGuire. And I won't listen to another word until you take that ball cap off in my office."

Hollis sat in one of the black chairs opposite the desk, swiped his hat off, and folded it between his hands but didn't respond.

"Fine," she finally said. "Tell me."

He planted his elbows on his knees and leveled a gaze at her. "We bring back the children's show."

Gladys waved him off. "You know we can't do that. The whole problem was lack of personnel. Lack of interest from the kids. Nobody wants to spend their summer wrangling children—even their parents don't want to do it."

"Gladys, if Emily wanted to, she could probably take legal action against the arts center." Hollis leaned forward in his chair. "I don't think you have a choice but to give her what she wants."

"She wants a detailed outline of where her grandfather's money has been going."

"She *wants* a children's production," Hollis said.

Gladys sighed and slumped back down in the chair, which she'd also inherited from Teddy and which completely engulfed her five-foot frame. "It would create a shortfall in other areas. You know we reworked the budget, and we used that money to keep the film festival and the concert series and—"

"You might have to rework the budget again," Hollis said. "Or do some fund-raising?" *Or chip in a little of your own money,* he thought.

She scoffed. "Fund-raising?"

"A charity event in support of the arts center? People would go crazy for it."

Gladys's eyes glimmered. She did love a good charity event. But the cynicism quickly returned. "Even if I wanted to bring back the children's show this summer, we don't have anyone to run it. You remember what happened with the last lady."

He'd heard the stories, and he didn't want to get Gladys wound up over their last children's director, a woman who'd touted herself as a professional but who had made up 95 percent of her résumé. "Professional theatre in Chicago" actually meant "middle school production in the very (very) distant suburbs." Gladys had been furious when she'd found out the truth, most likely because she'd been the one who'd hired the woman. In other words, she'd been the one who hadn't done her homework.

"I think I have the perfect person to take it on," Hollis said.

Gladys peered at him over her thick-framed glasses. "Is that right?"

Hollis shrugged again, this time as if to suggest, *What can I say? I'm a well-connected man.*

"Well, are you going to tell me or are you just going to sit there with that goofy smirk on your face?" Gladys's mouth took on the shape of a rainbow. "People your age do everything halfway—even your smile is lazy."

"I'm here to help you, Gladys," Hollis teased. "You're not being very appreciative."

"Considering that you had a vote in all of this, I'd say it's not only me you're helping, Mr. McGuire." She eyed him for a long moment. "Hurry up and tell me before I lose interest."

"You should hire Emily."

"Emily, the girl who stormed out of here the other day like she owned the place?"

"Yep." And he wasn't at all surprised she'd gotten fired up with Gladys. Emily had never been the kind of person to keep her opinions to herself.

Hollis explained Emily's unique qualifications for this position, but Gladys remained unconvinced.

"She's obviously passionate about this place, and she's worked in theatre most of her life—she was even on Broadway. It's like a divine appointment."

"Don't go bringing God into this, mister." She adjusted her glasses and let out a sigh. "You said she was on Broadway?"

"She's the real deal, Gladdy."

She wagged a pointed finger in his face. "I told you not to call me that."

He grinned. "Will you talk to her?"

"Why don't *you* talk to her? You seem to know an awful lot about her." She raised a single, knowing brow.

"I think it would be better coming from you," Hollis said.

"She doesn't like you, does she?" Gladys folded her hands on her desk. "What did you do to her?"

"I didn't do anything to her," Hollis said.

The old woman scowled. "You professional athletes are all the same."

"Yeah, you've got us all figured out." Hollis stood. "So you'll talk to her."

She glowered. "I suppose I don't have much of a choice."

"Good. Keep me posted."

Gladys watched him for a long, unnerving moment. "Why the sudden interest in the children's programming, Mr. McGuire?"

Great. Just what he needed—the third degree from Gladys Middlebury.

"I'm invested in the well-being of this island. You know that."

"And that's all this is?" She waved her hand when she said *this* as if it were something hanging in the room between them.

"Don't know what you're implying, Mrs. Middlebury, but the only ulterior motive I have here is doing what's best for the community."

He didn't stick around long enough to let her say anything else. The last thing he wanted was to land under Gladys Middlebury's watchful eye—or to confront the full scope of his reasons for wanting Emily to take over the children's programming for the summer.

CHAPTER 14

EMILY SCROLLED THROUGH TWITTER as she rounded the corner toward the main entrance of the arts center. She'd given Gladys a full week, and now Emily was going to follow up with her.

She looked up for a brief second to avoid running into a young family walking three deep on the sidewalk when she spotted Hollis heading toward her.

He had that easygoing, I'm-too-handsome-for-my-own-good thing going on, as if he'd just rolled out of bed looking like someone on a billboard.

It both delighted and irritated her at the same time.

"Hey." He smiled as the gap between them closed.

They stood on the street staring at each other for what felt like a solid minute but was probably more like three seconds.

Had it really only been a few days since she'd seen him? It felt much longer. Maybe because she'd been hiding herself away in that old house, watching his family from the second-story window and making up excuses why she couldn't join them on the beach.

"What are you doing here?" Hollis finally asked.

Emily exhaled her held breath and thought it probably wasn't good for her to keep holding on to air. "I was going to follow up with the director of operations. This old woman named Gladys. No way she's going to actually do anything unless I apply some pressure. I wanted to make sure Jolie gets her show."

His expression changed. "You do?"

"Yeah, I have to make good on my promise. Better than theatre camp, remember?"

He smiled.

"Is that why you're here too?"

He looked toward the building, then back at Emily. "Uh . . . yeah. My dad says it would be good to take an interest in something she's into."

"Isn't that what fathers do?"

Hollis looked away. "I don't really know."

Emily watched as he refused her eyes. Had he become a completely different person from the one she knew all those years ago? She shook away the thought—it didn't matter. He wasn't a part of her life. What he did or didn't do was none of her business.

"You think this Gladys will be open to your pressure?" Hollis asked.

She shrugged. "After everything my grandfather gave to this arts center, they cut the one thing that mattered to him most. I'm not going to just let them get away with that."

Hollis started to say something, then stopped.

"What?"

"You seem upset."

"I am upset—you know how much this place meant to me."

"But it's been a lot of years, Em. Things change."

Did that mean it should matter less? This was *her* place. This was the place where one of her very best memories had been made, but the way he was looking at her now—it made her feel like she was overreacting.

Was she overreacting? She wasn't sure how to tell anymore.

"Hey, you wanna go to the Juice Bar?" Hollis hitched a thumb over his shoulder as if to point Emily in the direction of their favorite Nantucket ice cream shop.

Emily crossed her arms over her chest. "No, I want to pretend I have some pull and strong-arm this old lady."

"For Jolie."

"Yes, of course for Jolie. Who else would I be doing this for?"

Hollis shrugged. "You stopped by here before you even met Jolie, so maybe you've got your own reasons?"

He watched her for several unnerving seconds, and she decided she didn't like it. His eyes saw too much of what she wasn't willing to share.

"What are you doing here anyway?" she asked, turning the tables.

"I already told you. I was coming to check things out for Jolie—"

"No, I mean *here*, in Nantucket?"

He looked away. "My family comes every summer."

"Yeah, but you don't."

His jaw twitched. He didn't like her prodding him, she could tell. Too bad that only made her want to keep going.

"You play baseball and do baseball things in the summer," she said.

"In case you haven't noticed, Emily, I don't anymore." He stuffed his hands in his pockets.

"I googled you," she said.

"Great." His expression took a miserable turn.

"I read that you were offered two different jobs commentating this summer—you could've been the voice of Major League Baseball."

"I don't want to be the *voice*," he said. "I wanna play." The words seemed to surprise him, as if they'd escaped without his permission.

She held his gaze for several seconds, and then he finally looked away. "Forget it."

In her head, she counted to three as if it were enough time for him to relax. "You seem lost, Hollis."

"You can't come back here after twenty years and act like you know anything about me."

"No, you're right," she said.

But oh, how she wanted to know everything about him.

His shoulders relaxed, but only slightly.

"But I can see you're hiding out here with a daughter you hardly seem to know." She wished she could just shut up, but she realized in that moment a wall of questions had been forming at the back of her mind, and she couldn't *not* ask them.

"I'm not hiding out—" He shook his head.

Her bluntness sometimes upset people. Why couldn't she mind her own business?

"I'll talk to you later." He started off in the opposite direction from where her bike was parked, leaving her standing on the sidewalk, wishing she'd never run into Hollis at all.

It was true: she didn't know Hollis McGuire anymore. Didn't know the pain he'd suffered from his accident or how hard it had been coming back from that. They called him "Miracle Man McGuire"— but even after the comeback of the decade, it was all over four years later.

She'd been so focused on her own pain, she hadn't even stopped to think for a single second that maybe she wasn't the only one suffering, but the chances of him talking about it with her after that conversation were slim.

Me and my big mouth.

After a brief, unproductive conversation with Gladys, who seemed intent on stalling, Emily went back to the cottage, fretting over her conversation with Hollis. She should go find him and apologize. It's what a good friend would do. But smoothing things over with Hollis would mean making him feel like she didn't have questions—and that wasn't honest.

She had lots of questions.

Mostly—*What happened to you?*

She parked her mother's bike near the old shed just as a mail truck pulled to the end of the driveway. The small truck honked and the driver waved as she stopped at Emily's mailbox.

That was odd. Nobody besides her grandma knew she was here, and while Grandma was a fan of old-school traditions, she was the least sentimental person Emily knew. The odds of her sending anything to Nantucket were slim.

She traipsed down the driveway to the box, waving as the carrier pulled away.

Inside the mailbox, she found one envelope, addressed to her. Her eyes darted to the return address: *Blakely and Shore, Attorneys-at-Law.*

She tore open the envelope and found two sheets of paper inside. On top, a typed letter from Solomon Blakely, one of GrandPop's lawyers.

Dear Ms. Ackerman,

I had the pleasure of serving as your grandfather's attorney for the past thirty years. The man was as brilliant as he was generous, and we were grieved to hear of his passing. Eliza tells me you've received the keys to the Nantucket cottage and that you'll be spending the summer there. That would've made your grandfather very happy.

I was honored to handle his will for him, and one of his requests was that I send you this letter after his passing.

You meant the world to him, Emily, and I know he loved you very much.

If you have any questions, please don't hesitate to give me a call.

Sincerely,
Solomon Blakely
Attorney-at-Law

Emily flipped the paper back to reveal a handwritten letter on a plain sheet of cream-colored stationery. She stared at the page as the sight of her grandfather's familiar scrawl clouded her eyes.

She thought she'd heard the last of his advice. She thought he was out of her reach now that he was gone, but here he was, giving her one last bit of wisdom, after his death.

Emily moved toward the front porch of the cottage and sat down on the top step. The sound of the ocean in the distance slightly calmed her racing heart.

She drew in a deep breath, knowing that this was truly the last she'd hear from her grandfather, wanting every word to mean something, maybe even more than it did.

Dearest Emily,

If you're reading this letter, then I've taken my final bow. Perhaps that makes you terribly sad, or maybe you know that I'm in a better place and you can take comfort in that. Either way, I do hope you miss me a little when I'm gone.

I'll miss you, of that I'm sure. I'll especially miss watching you do what you love—perform. It has always brought me so much joy.

I've watched you grow into a strong, confident, and impressive young woman, and I'm thrilled to leave the Nantucket cottage in such capable hands. It may seem a daunting task, renovating a house like this one, but I hope that it may turn out to be a bit of fun for you. And I suppose I'm also hoping that you'll do what I couldn't do and revisit old memories—good memories.

We were always afraid to go back, knowing it would dredge up so much pain and so much sorrow, but I realize now there was good there too—and your mother loved the island, almost as much as she loved you.

So while it may feel difficult and sad at first, I hope you can use this time to heal, to really heal. And maybe even to let her go a bit.

Now remember: the cottage is yours—no strings. I've made that very clear, and while your grandmother may not completely realize it yet, she knows this is what's best. We won't be offended if you decide to fix it up and sell it. But if you decide to keep it, that's fine too. It's your choice.

I do have two requests:

1. Get rid of Grandma's ugly wallpaper.

2. Bring back the rose garden. I always loved that.

Maybe in being there, you'll rediscover Nantucket and all of its charms. Maybe you'll fall a little in love with the island again. And maybe, just maybe, it'll help you move forward to the next chapter of your life.

Just remember, Emily, everything we did—everything we've ever done—we did because we loved you.

All my love,
GrandPop

Emily reread the letter, swiping away the tears that slid down her cheeks.

Her grandfather was a businessman, but he always had a soft spot for Emily. Why had she been so afraid to tell him about her failures? Maybe he would've surprised her. Maybe he would've understood.

She scanned the words again. He was a good man, despite his shortcomings, and she'd loved him. He'd loved her. She supposed in some ways, she was still mourning his death, grieving as one more person she loved disappeared.

"And maybe, just maybe, it'll help you move forward to the next chapter of your life."

Would it? Could it? And if so, how? Why hadn't he explained how the "moving on" worked?

Maybe he couldn't. Maybe he didn't know.

She hadn't seen him or Grandma move on—not where the island

was concerned. It was as if every good thing had died here and Nantucket had become a permanent burial ground for their happiness.

"Just remember, Emily, everything we did—everything we've ever done—we did because we loved you."

She paused. Reread the last line again.

"Everything we did"?

She felt her brow furrow. What had they done? Did he mean taking her in after her mom died? It was a given that they'd done that because they loved her. It didn't need explanation.

"Everything we've ever done."

The words stared at her. If they were on a computer screen, they would've been flashing red.

What was he talking about?

She folded the letter and pressed it to her chest, looking off in the distance, drinking in the view of the ocean.

"What don't I know, GrandPop?" she whispered.

A gentle breeze sent a coolness over her skin, and a wave of goose bumps appeared on her arms.

And Emily wondered if whatever it was would be better off left buried right here on the island.

CHAPTER 15

Workdays dragged on for JD, whose only real desire was to spend as much time with Isabelle as he could.

The morning of the Fourth, he stood on the course with a bag of golf clubs, waiting to caddie for one of the uppity rich guys who would most likely treat him like he was invisible and tip him far less than he deserved.

He tried not to think about it. He and Isabelle had a big night planned. She'd agreed to meet him at his aunt's cottage for a cookout with his friends and then they were all heading down to the beach to watch the fireworks.

It was a big deal because it was the first time they'd be around other people, and while it was his people and not hers, it was a step—and he couldn't wait to feel like they were an actual couple.

He stood in the hot July sun, wearing his one pair of nice khakis, a navy-blue golf club polo, and a white Titleist cap, his caddying uniform. His roommate, Jeb, stood a few feet away, polishing a nine iron from the bag in his charge.

When two older men started up the hill toward the first tee, JD's stomach dropped.

Alan Ackerman and one of his hoity-toity friends were heading right for them.

As soon as the pair of older men reached the tee, Jeb took a step toward them and extended a hand toward Isabelle's dad. "Morning, sir. I'm Jeb."

Alan shook Jeb's hand. "Good to meet you, Jeb, but it looks like you've got my friend's clubs." He turned to JD. "Your name, son?"

"JD."

"Prefer my caddies not to give advice," Alan said. "Just give me the clubs I ask for, and we'll get along fine."

"Works for me, sir," JD said.

Alan nodded.

What followed was the tensest four-and-a-half-hour round of golf JD had ever caddied for—and it had nothing to do with the actual game.

When they reached the fourteenth hole, JD wanted to correct Alan on his club choice but stayed silent. (Alan landed in the sand.) At the sixteenth hole, the other man asked Alan about his daughter, Isabelle, and Jeb's eyes shot to JD with all the subtlety of a freight train.

JD remained nonchalant, in spite of his racing heart.

"She's heading into her senior year," Alan said. "She'll no doubt end up at one of the Ivies—we're thinking she might study law."

Again, JD wanted to correct Alan. He wanted to tell the man that his daughter had no interest in an Ivy League school or in becoming a lawyer. She wanted to travel the world and explore new cultures, maybe work with underprivileged kids. Mostly he wanted to tell Alan not to put his daughter in a box because Isabelle could do anything she wanted to do—but she needed time to figure out what that was.

And he wanted to tell the man that he was in love with his daughter, that he would make her happy—he knew he would—if they could get past the fact that he was a golf caddie working his way through university.

But he didn't say any of those things.

Instead, he walked behind Alan all the way to the end of the eighteenth hole, accepted a decent tip from the man, then made his way to the locker room to change for his date with Isabelle.

But the whole day had shone a light on what the two of them were up against—years of tradition and money and expectations.

He met Isabelle later on that evening, struck once again by her beauty and her goodness. How she'd managed to turn into the person she had living with someone as privileged as Alan Ackerman, he didn't know.

But it made him love her even more.

She stepped into his embrace and he held her as the seconds ticked by, wishing they could escape every prying eye from the outside world, wishing there was nothing to live up to but love. But the world didn't work like that.

He kissed her, then led her out back, where several of his friends had already gathered, most of them having gotten the holiday off of work. JD needed the extra money, so he chose to spend his morning at the club, though now he almost wished he hadn't.

"Are you sure these people won't say anything?" Isabelle asked, pulling her hand from his.

"They're good people," he said. "But if it makes you feel better, we can keep our distance."

Her eyes scanned the crowd—not a single face she knew.

"Or we can leave," he suggested. "I don't mind going to our beach and watching the fireworks from there."

She shook her head. "No, I want to meet your friends."

He smiled. "Good, because I want to show you off a little."

She laughed, smoothing the line of concern on her forehead and settling his own worries, at least for the moment.

They ate burgers off the grill and drank wine coolers and he introduced her to everyone he knew. Oddly, Isabelle blended right into his world, as if the whole idea that money should separate them had never occurred to her.

But then, maybe money mattered more to people who didn't have it.

By nightfall, the whole group had made their way to the beach, and they now found themselves on a plaid blanket with Jeb and a girl named Michelle. At one point, Jeb leaned over and said, "You were right, man. She is cool."

He couldn't be sure, but he thought Isabelle might've overheard.

As the fireworks started, Isabelle sat in front of him, leaning into his chest as he wrapped his arms around her, inhaling the scent of her and wishing he could stop time.

They stayed like that throughout most of the fireworks, neither one of them feeling the need to move, and JD began to think he was the luckiest guy in the world.

Until he heard a voice behind them. A familiar voice. A voice he'd heard on the golf course earlier that day.

"Isabelle?"

She shot up straight, every muscle in her body tense, and spun around to face her father, who stood on the beach with Eliza. The pair of them looked self-righteous, shocked, and irate—not a good combination.

"You're supposed to be with Lydia," Eliza said. "Who are these people?"

Isabelle stood, and JD followed. "They're my friends, Mom."

Eliza looked JD up and down. "Your friends?"

"Yes," Isabelle said. "My friends."

"Where's Lydia?"

Isabelle shifted.

"Aren't you that caddie from the club?" Alan's glare drilled a hole into JD.

"Yes, sir."

"Isabelle, what is going on here?"

Slowly she slipped her hand into JD's—maybe not the best move in the moment, but he wasn't about to pull away, not when she needed him most.

"Mom, Dad," Isabelle said, "this is JD. He's my boyfriend."

Eliza's eyes widened, and Alan looked like he might explode.

"Let's go, Isabelle," Eliza said through clenched teeth.

"Go where?"

"Home," she said. "We are taking you home."

"Mom, you're being unfair," Isabelle said. "I'm seventeen—that's practically an adult."

"'Practically' doesn't cut it. You lied to us, young lady. Now let's go."

Isabelle turned to JD, eyes filled with tears. He squeezed her hand as if to silently let her know he wasn't going anywhere—no matter how scary her parents were.

She walked toward them, shoulders slumped, sadness oozing from the inside out.

He wondered if this was the last time he'd ever get to see or touch Isabelle Ackerman.

And the thought of it turned his insides out.

CHAPTER 16

~~~

THE LAST TIME EMILY had seen Harper McGuire, Hollis's sister was a seven-year-old girl with long dark pigtails, big brown eyes, and a sprinkling of freckles.

Now, Harper stood in front of her looking like someone who'd stepped out of the pages of an Eddie Bauer catalog—the kind of girl-next-door pretty that felt less intimidating than runway models who graced the covers of fashion magazines.

It seemed beauty ran in the McGuire family. Even goofy Hayes, who would always feel like a little brother to Emily, had grown into a man women would go out of their way to meet.

Emily didn't feel like she fit in with any of them, which was funny considering that years ago it was Hollis's family that stood out in Nantucket for all the wrong reasons. Not anymore—with a dilapidated cottage on a piece of prime real estate, now it was Emily who didn't belong.

Still, the second she saw Harper standing on the front porch of the McGuires' cottage, Hollis's beautiful sister pulled her into a giant hug, as if they were twins who'd been separated at birth and were finally reunited.

"I can't believe you're back!" Harper said. "You do remember me, don't you?"

"Of course I do," Emily said. "But you look a lot different than the last time I saw you."

Harper laughed. "I can't wait to catch up. Hollis told me you were on Broadway."

Emily's eyes panned the yard until she found Hollis, packing up his Jeep with coolers and beach bags and whatever else his mother was dumping at his feet.

"Mom, we're going on the boat for one day," Hayes said, joining them. "You packed like we're never coming back."

Nan patted Hayes's arm. "You never know when you're going to get stranded somewhere, kiddo," Nan said.

"You think we're going to get stranded?"

She waved him off and started back toward the house, giving Emily that sweet smile and a squeeze of the arm as she walked by.

Emily had almost forgotten about the McGuires' invitation to go out on the boat this weekend, but she welcomed the change of pace, in spite of the cool encounter she'd had with Hollis only days before.

The truth was, she was bored in the house alone. The only exciting thing that had happened all week was getting the estimate back from Jack Walker and hiring him on the spot. Not that she had much choice—not a single other person she'd called had any openings for a project as big as hers.

Jack asked for a few days to assemble a crew, and he hoped to be working by Monday.

It was a good thing. Emily couldn't spend another day holed up in that house or making excuses not to go fishing/picnicking/hiking with Hollis and his family.

She knew she could have easily spent those days with people she genuinely liked, and they would've welcomed her, but she wasn't a part of the McGuire family, and no amount of wishing would make it so.

Best to remember that from the beginning.

But she'd told Jolie she'd go boating with them today, and breaking promises to children had to be among the world's worst offenses.

"Emily?"

"Sorry." She realized she'd been daydreaming again. "Yes, I was on Broadway. Only once."

"Don't downplay it." Harper gave her a playful push. "How many people can say they've been on Broadway at all?"

Maybe she should be proud, but with circumstances what they were, all the good things she'd lived seemed like another life.

"So you run marathons?" Emily remembered hearing that at dinner on her first night back.

Harper laughed. "Is that what they told you?"

"Yeah. Is it not true?"

"No, it's true," Harper said. "I just think it's funny that no matter what I do, my family thinks *that* is the most impressive thing about me. Yes, I run. It helps me clear my head. You should try it sometime."

"You think I need to clear my head?" Emily asked, thinking that she definitely needed to clear her head, though she'd rather do it by watching Netflix and eating a pint of Häagen-Dazs than running even one mile, let alone twenty-six.

Before Harper could respond, Jolie burst through the front door. "Emily! You're here!"

Harper backed up. "Whoa. I didn't get that kind of greeting when I showed up, JoJo."

Jolie flung her arms around Harper and squeezed her aunt. "Sorry, Aunt Harper. Here's an extra hug to make up for that."

"You have all summer to make it up to me, kid," Harper said.

"Not the whole summer," Jolie said. "Just a month."

Harper tousled the girl's hair. "Why not the whole summer?"

"Didn't Dad tell you?"

"No," Harper said. "Why wouldn't you stay the whole summer?"

Jolie shrugged. "Dad probably didn't want me here that long."

Harper looked at Emily, whose eyes darted to Jolie, then over to Hollis.

But before either of them could respond, the girl grinned. "Emily, what did you think of the headshot I sent you? I've got so many questions!"

Emily had questions for Jolie too—namely, why wouldn't Hollis want her there for the whole summer?

Jolie slipped her hand inside Emily's and squeezed. "Do you like the ocean? I do, but only from a distance. Uncle Hayes is helping me conquer my fear that a wave is going to pull me down and carry me out to sea." They started walking toward Hollis's Jeep. "I'm kind of scared to be out on a boat. I think my dad is a good swimmer, though. At least I hope so—you know, in case one of us goes overboard."

"Jolie, run and grab the sunscreen," Hollis said. "I left it on the counter."

Jolie let go of Emily's hand, all the warmth draining from it.

Emily stood awkwardly beside Hollis's Jeep as he played Tetris with their boat-trip supplies.

"How's the house?" he asked.

They hadn't spoken since their unfortunate meeting on the sidewalk outside the arts center. She didn't like being at odds with Hollis—it felt like something in her world was broken. But then, lately it felt like everything was broken.

She folded her arms and looked away, a gentle wind riffling her hair. She tucked it behind her ear and nodded with complete indifference. "Needs a lot of work."

"What are you going to do about that?"

Emily shrugged. "I hired a guy."

"The guy from last week? What do you know about him?" Hollis had abandoned his task and now gave Emily his undivided attention, which, coincidentally, Emily did not want.

"Well, I met him," Emily said. "I interviewed him. He didn't murder me."

"Did you interview anyone else? You should've called me before making a final decision."

"I wasn't sure you would've wanted to talk to me, you know, after . . ."

He looked away as her voice trailed off. "I'm sorry about the other day."

She shifted. "No, I'm the one who's sorry. I shouldn't have been so nosy."

His face warmed into a familiar smile. "You wouldn't be you if you weren't nosy."

"Ha-ha." She rolled her eyes, but secretly, she was thankful for the ease of tension between them.

"So is this guy a contractor?" Hollis had probably been stalking her house with a pair of binoculars the entire time Jack was there.

"He's an investment banker," Emily said.

Hollis only stared.

"Look, he's nice. He said he gets bored easily and needs a summer project." Emily was losing confidence. "And he was the only one who called me back."

"Emily—" Hollis was about to say something sensible; Emily could hear it in his tone.

She cut him off before he could go on. "The goal is to get it on the market and sell it as quickly as possible." *The sooner I can get out of here and put this all behind me, the better.*

Hollis looked away. "Maybe you'll want to keep it."

"I would never keep it," she said. "It's not practical."

"Why?"

"Because I don't want a house, Hollis." Was the third degree payback for bringing up baseball?

"It's a summer home," he said. "You wouldn't have to live there year-round."

"I don't want a home here at all," she said quickly. *Not that I could afford it.*

Seconds ticked by and Hollis held on to her gaze, and for a moment, it was as if every fear she'd buried were on her face—and Hollis could see it all.

"So glad you could join us today, Emily." Nan had reemerged from the cottage with another armload. "You've been hiding away over there all week—it'll be good for you to get out in the sunshine." She smiled.

"Thanks for inviting me," Emily said.

Hollis finally released her from his eye prison and took the stack of towels his mother was holding, then loaded them into the car without a word as Nan raced off to fuss over something in the other car. Emily tried not to notice the muscles in his arms—even his forearms were well-defined. Who had muscles in their forearms? Baseball players, that's who. Emily found it terribly distracting.

So far, retirement had done nothing to harm his physique.

"I can help," Hollis said without looking at her.

Emily frowned. "With what?"

"The house."

"Not this again." Was his goal to keep her under his watchful eye until she was ready to leave the island for good?

"Why not?"

"It's a silly idea." She looked away.

"Why?"

She searched her mind for any practical-sounding reason and came up empty until she heard Jolie chatting in the house behind her. "You should spend the summer with your daughter."

"I *am* spending the summer with my daughter." There was an edge to his voice. "But I'm guessing she wants to do more than hang around with me for the next three weeks."

Did she? Maybe all she really wanted to do was get to know her dad. Couldn't he understand that?

"Besides, I hate to break it to you, but putting a crew together this late in the season isn't going to be easy."

"Late?" Emily felt her pulse quicken. "It's barely summer."

"People line up their summer help months in advance. Most of the really good workers are already booked—are you sure this guy is legit?"

Emily screwed her eyes shut and pinched the bridge of her nose. No, she wasn't sure. She'd been moderately concerned about Jack Walker being a serial killer, but she'd never considered he might not actually be able to get the job done.

But Hollis had her mind spinning.

Emily inhaled a deep breath and gathered herself. "Jack was going to make some calls. He's supposed to start Monday. If he doesn't have enough help, then we can talk about me hiring your family."

"Hiring us? Emily—"

But Jolie cut him off. "Found it!" she called out, handing the bottle to her dad, then turning to face Emily. "You're riding with us. There's no room in the other car."

Emily turned her full attention to the girl. "Sounds great to me."

But it didn't sound great. So far, nearly every interaction she'd had with Hollis had been filled with tension. How was she supposed to hold it together when he seemed able to slice through her pretense with a single glance?

They all loaded into two vehicles and made their way from the house to the Town Pier, where Hollis said a guy he knew would be picking them up in a Boston Whaler.

"That's a nice boat," Emily said.

Hollis quirked an eyebrow as if to challenge her—did she really know what a Boston Whaler was?

"I've spent a lot of years by the ocean," she said.

"So you're not scared of the water?" Jolie asked.

Emily released herself from Hollis's gaze. "Not a bit."

"You surf?" he asked.

"Surf. Paddleboard. Swim. Sail." She fixed her gaze forward. "I love the water."

"Maybe you *haven't* changed," Hollis said with a gentle smirk.

They arrived at Town Pier and walked toward the dock. Hollis pointed them in the direction of a large, sleek white boat with a red bottom and the name *Edna* painted on the side in red.

"That's us," he said.

"Will we all fit?" Jolie asked.

"It's a 420 Outrage," Emily said.

"What's that mean?"

"It fits twenty." Emily glanced at Hollis, pleased she'd effectively impressed him with her knowledge. "Your friend owns this boat?"

"It's like his baby." Hollis shook his head, but his face read amused.

Jolie took off in the direction of the boat, followed by the rest of the McGuire family. Harper was teasing Hayes about something that sounded like an inside joke while their parents walked hand in hand toward the water.

Emily tried not to fall into sync with Hollis, but it happened, the way it always had when they were kids. She was a year between the two brothers, so she could've just as easily had the best friendship with the younger McGuire. But it was the man at her side with whom she'd made a blood pact of lifelong friendship, not to mention the countless spit-shakes, pinkie swears, and even a first kiss, if you could call it that.

She certainly didn't. She still credited Tommy Wayfair from the ninth grade with that honor. Or the horror, as it were.

She and Hollis were so young it couldn't be counted—even if she did remember everything about that night in stark detail.

It was late one night after a full day at the beach. They'd had dinner outside in the McGuires' backyard and Nan had made them a huge pitcher of fresh-squeezed lemonade to quench their thirst after hours in the sun. All four of the kids ate burgers off the grill, laughed, played in the yard, ran back down to the beach, and now, at the end of it all, Hollis and Emily were the only two left outside.

Hayes and Harper had both been called in—Harper went willingly; Hayes protested. "I'm practically as old as Hollis, Ma," he'd whined.

"Practically as old means not quite as old, young man," Nan said with a wink. "Hollis, a few more minutes, okay?"

Nan took her reluctant son inside, and Hollis plopped down in the sand, staring out over the ocean, the moon full and bright.

Emily sat down next to him. "Secret, secret."

Hollis groaned. He hated most of the games she made up, but especially this one. The rules said that once a week, one of them could call "Secret, secret," and the other had to share something about themselves that nobody knew or answer whatever question the asker wanted to know. They took turns, and that week, Emily got to be the asker.

Hollis hated the game because he hated anything that required him to share feelings. "Boys aren't into all that talking stuff," he'd told her the year before when she first explained the rules.

"Then how am I ever going to really know you, Hollis McGuire?" she'd asked.

"You already know plenty," he'd said, but they both knew it was pointless for him to protest. When Emily made up her mind, she didn't stop until she got what she wanted.

The night had gone quiet, and Emily thought of all the things they'd shared thanks to this game and its "silly rules" as her friend called them. It's how she'd learned he didn't like coming to Nantucket for a long time because the kids on the beach called him "white trash" and "Holly Hobbie." He didn't bother to tell them Hollis was a family name and one he was proud to have.

It's how he learned that sometimes, late at night, she wondered if her mother would ever tell her who her father was, that she was afraid of never knowing him, of never having a real family. It's how they both learned they didn't have many friends once they left Nantucket.

They might have been from two different worlds, but in those moments, Emily Ackerman and Hollis McGuire weren't that different at all.

"I don't have a secret," Hollis had told her after she announced it was time to play again.

"Everyone has secrets," Emily said.

"You already know all of mine." Hollis pulled his knees closer to his chest. "You even know about the time I shoplifted that package of Skittles and my dad made me take it back and apologize. Nobody knows about that—not even Hayes."

"Secret, secret," Emily said as if to remind him she didn't want to hear his lame excuses—the rules were the rules.

He sat quietly for a long time as if running through a list of things he might tell her. The water chased the shore only a few feet in front of them as they sat in silence. Sometimes it took him a while to come up with something. He was a pensive kid to begin with, and Emily appreciated that he took the game seriously enough to consider his options before finally sharing.

After several minutes of silence, Hollis groaned again. "I don't want to play tonight, Em."

"You have one, I can tell." She spun toward him. "I can always tell when you think of something to share. Spill it."

Then, with his eyes fixed on the ink-black ocean in front of them, he finally blurted the secret as if it were a shaken bottle of soda whose lid had just been unscrewed. "Sometimes I wonder what it would be like to kiss you."

Emily was taken aback. "You do?"

Hollis still refused her eyes. "Yeah." He picked up a rock and threw it in the ocean.

She paused. "Well, then, why don't you kiss me so you can stop wondering?"

He looked at her. "Seriously?"

Emily shrugged. "Why not?"

"Because we're friends."

"So?"

"Friends don't kiss."

"Yeah, that's true." She turned away and sat for a few long seconds without speaking. "But maybe we're the kind of friends who do?"

Hollis stared at her, those bright-hazel eyes flickering, as if he wondered if she was trying to trick him. "I've never kissed anyone before."

Emily turned to face him square on and folded her legs underneath her. "Me neither."

Slowly Hollis mirrored her position, legs crossed underneath him, facing her. He looked serious and maybe a little nervous, but Emily didn't feel nervous at all . . . until he scooted closer.

"You sure?" he asked.

She nodded. She hadn't thought about kissing Hollis before, but now she was curious.

She could hear distant voices down the beach, and if she listened closely enough, she bet she could also hear her heart pounding.

He sat up on his knees, leaning in close, and Emily closed her eyes as he pressed his lips on hers. Hollis's lips were soft, and they tasted like cherry Popsicles. After a few seconds, he pulled away, just as his mom rang the bell that meant it was time for him to come inside.

"I gotta go," he said.

"Okay, see ya."

He ran off, leaving her sitting on the beach wondering why kissing was such a big deal. And also wondering when she'd get to do it again.

~

Dear Emily,

Let's talk about kissing for a minute. I really hope we get to have this conversation face-to-face, mostly because it will be so fun to get your thoughts on kissing. After my first kiss (which I did NOT tell my mom about) I remember thinking, "This is super weird." I mean, who invented kissing? It was wet and sloppy and not pleasant at all. The movies had it all wrong, I can tell you that. . . . There was nothing romantic about that kiss.

But then I had my second kiss and I wanted to find whoever invented kissing and personally thank them for their contribution to society. I hope your first kiss is sweet and innocent. I hope there's no pressure (and no unwanted saliva!). I hope you wait until you find someone you really like before letting him kiss you.

And I hope, afterward, you run inside and tell me all about it.

Love,
Mom

CHAPTER 17

IT WASN'T LIKE HOLLIS to call in favors. Especially not from former teammates. Maybe someday it would feel perfectly normal, but his retirement was still so fresh it was hard to associate with anything about baseball, including his old friends.

They were a couple of months into the season, and he'd found ways to keep himself occupied, at least enough not to think about everything he was missing.

But Jimmy Williams somehow felt less like a "baseball buddy" and more like an old friend.

More than once, the two had bonded over their summers in Nantucket—neither of them really fit in. Hollis's family came to work, not to rest, and Jimmy was a poor kid who first discovered the island through an outreach program with his church. Even after Jimmy was traded to Philadelphia, he and Hollis stayed in touch. A power hitter and womanizer, Jimmy "The Crank" Williams was all brawn and had always been known for partying. But he'd found Jesus somewhere along the way and his whole lifestyle had changed.

The rest of the guys, including Hollis, all said it would never last, this religion thing, but as far he knew, Jimmy and Jesus were still going strong.

It had been Jimmy who'd shown up at Hollis's bedside after the accident. Jimmy was the one who sat there for hours, telling stories, reliving glory days, reassuring Hollis that he'd come back from this. It was his old friend who'd listened quietly while Hollis worked through his anger—at himself, at God, at the whole world.

And it was Jimmy who'd mentored him out of that anger, who'd shown him what grace and forgiveness looked like.

After all, the man had handled getting traded with more grace and forgiveness than anyone else Hollis had ever known. "God's got a plan, Mack," he'd said. "I'm trusting that."

And it had worked out. Hollis hadn't liked it, but Jimmy thrived— and he finished his career on a high note. Later, Jimmy had said, "Told you God knew what he was doing. He's got my back—and he's got yours too."

Some days Hollis believed that. Other days, like when he was faced with his greatest obstacle—winning over his daughter—he wasn't so sure.

Hollis walked the length of the dock, Jolie in front of him, the rest of the family behind him, and Emily at his side. As soon as Jimmy spotted them, the man lifted a beefy arm and hollered a long, drawn-out "My man, my miracle man!"

Hollis reached the end of the dock and walked into his old friend's waiting bear hug. Jimmy squeezed him (hard), then pulled back. Hollis patted Jimmy's stomach, which, he had to admit, had grown since they'd both played the game. "Still looking good, Crank."

"You don't look too shabby yourself, Mack." Jimmy's hands were on Hollis's shoulders, his eyes bright. Even if the man hadn't said a word, Hollis would've known he was genuinely happy. There was something different about him—had been for a while. Jimmy said it was "the Jesus," and Hollis believed it. When it came to his faith, Jimmy approached things his own way. God wasn't something far-off in the sky that couldn't be grasped or understood—to Jimmy, he was as real as Hollis and the other guys he called friends. Hollis now aspired to that level of faith—a real, tangible relationship with God. Sometimes it felt attainable. But often it felt like his mistakes firmly placed a wedge between him and "the Jesus" that made it impossible.

"How's the hip?"

Hollis glanced at Emily, aware they had her full attention, and quickly changed the subject. "I'm doing great, Crank. I want to introduce you to some people."

"Your people," Jimmy said.

"Right, my people."

Jimmy finally released Hollis from his grasp and faced the others. Hollis started on the introductions, pausing for a moment on Jolie. "And this is my daughter, JoJo."

Jimmy's grin widened. "Finally we meet."

Jolie blinked in surprise. "You've heard of me?"

"You kidding? Your dad used to show your baby pictures all around the locker room."

For the briefest moment, Jolie beamed, but as soon as she met Hollis's eyes, she went cold again.

Jimmy must not have sensed the tension between the two of them because he gave Jolie's pigtail a tug and said, "Good thing you got your looks from your mama."

JoJo smiled. "You haven't met Emily."

"Ah," Jimmy said. "You must be Hollis's new love."

Emily's eyes widened. "Guess again."

Jimmy arched one eyebrow upward.

"This is one of my oldest friends, Emily Ackerman."

"Ackerman? Like the arts center?"

"You know it?" Emily asked.

"Everyone knows it. Used to be one of my favorite places to go on the weekends. They always had something going on. My wife took a pottery class there. Bought her a kiln that she's used twice." Jimmy laughed a hearty laugh. "Probably better they stopped doing all those classes. At least for my wallet."

Confusion spread across Emily's tightly knit brow.

"It's a great day to be on the water," Hollis interjected. "Thanks for the favor, man."

"Are you kidding? We should've done this years ago." Jimmy stepped down into the boat, then helped Jolie in. She immediately raced toward the bow. One by one, Hollis's family got in, leaving him standing on the dock with Emily.

"Where's the steering wheel?" Jolie called from the front of the boat.

"Hang on. I'll show you!" Jimmy rushed off and Hollis took his spot, then lifted his hand in Emily's direction.

She hesitated for a moment, then finally slipped her hand in his. The second their skin touched, he felt it in his toes. Their eyes met and his breath hitched in his throat.

What was it about this woman that captivated him so wholly?

He quickly summoned his most nonchalant self. "You're not afraid, are you?"

She stepped into the boat and got her footing, then straightened and looked him square in the eye. "Of course not, Hollis. Don't you remember me at all?"

He did remember. He remembered everything about Emily, including the time she refused to leave the beach during a tropical storm. Hollis and Hayes knew their mom would be furious if they didn't come home, but Emily insisted on surfing "one last wave." She seemed to have no concept of danger.

But looking at her now, he saw no trace of that girl, only one with a knack for pretending. He didn't buy this act for a second. She wanted them all to believe she was still that same girl, unafraid and confident, but he saw the truth she tried to hide.

What happened to you, Emily Ackerman?

He followed her eyes to his hand, which was still wrapped around hers. He let it go and instantly felt the coolness of her absence on his skin.

She slung her bag over her shoulder and walked toward the rest of the group, seemingly unfazed, as Jimmy reappeared at his side. "She's a looker, Mack. She could be the one."

Hollis shook his head. "No, she's not."

"What? Why? If *she's* not good enough for you, who will be?"

"Nah, Crank, you've got it backward," he said. "*I'm* not good enough for *her*."

Jimmy laughed. "Well, maybe she'll take pity on you." He made his way to the front of the boat to ready the rest of them for their day on the water, and Hollis watched Jolie sit so close to Emily, he wondered if his old friend was annoyed.

Judging by the look on her face, though, she was anything but. Jolie pulled her phone out and scrolled through photos—maybe from the wedding?—and Emily asked questions and kept his daughter utterly engaged in a way he had never been able to do.

His mom stopped trying to get everyone situated and made her way over to Hollis. She followed his gaze to Jolie and Emily, then put a hand on his arm. "She's awfully good with JoJo."

"Yeah," Hollis said quietly. "She is."

"You're doing just fine, kiddo," his mom said as if sensing his frustration over his inability to connect with his daughter.

Mom was kind to take pity on him, but he'd made almost no progress and they were already a week into their month together. He was running out of time.

Jolie erupted into giggles, and Hollis glanced over to find Emily's eyes drilling straight into him. Maybe she could see right through him the same way he could see through her. Maybe she was thinking the man in those wedding pictures was far better suited to be Jolie's dad. Maybe she was thinking Hollis was a first-rate jerk for letting his daughter practically grow up fatherless, the same way Emily had grown up.

And maybe she would be right.

But Hollis wasn't a quitter, and the thought of another man stepping in as Jolie's dad set his bones on fire.

He had to do better. Keep every promise. Do more than expected. He was going to have to be SuperDad if he had any hope of winning back his little girl.

He only hoped it wasn't too late.

CHAPTER 18

"I WAS IN A WEDDING right before I came here," Jolie had said. "Wanna see pictures?"

The girl curled right up next to Emily and pulled out her phone.

The conversation had started off innocently enough. Meaning, Emily wasn't trying to pry. She was curious, though, about so many things, not the least of which was why Hollis and Jolie's relationship seemed so stunted and why Jolie thought her dad didn't want her to stay the entire summer.

"Of course," Emily said. Because who wouldn't want to see pictures of a wedding? And also because she secretly wanted to see what the girl's mother looked like.

The wedding was beautiful. Jolie's mother, Jana, wore the most exquisite strapless dress with a beaded bodice and the perfect amount of pouf to the skirt. She looked stunning. And Jolie, in her yellow bridesmaid's dress, the epitome of adorable.

"I love her dress," Emily said. "So many details."

"Yeah, it was really pretty," Jolie said. "You think you'll want a dress like that? When you get married?"

Emily laughed. "I don't think I have to worry about that, at least not for a very long time."

"Really? Aren't most people your age married?"

Emily shifted. *Yes. They are.* "I don't think marriage is for me."

"I thought everyone wanted to get married."

"Not everyone, I guess." If she were honest with herself, maybe Emily would've had a different answer. But some days being honest was too hard.

"I was the only bridesmaid," Jolie said. "Because I'm Mom's favorite person. She wanted me to know that even though she's got Rick now, it's still me and her, just like always."

Emily had glanced at Hollis, who, unfortunately, looked very much like someone she would want to be more than friends with. He was wearing a plain gray T-shirt that looked like it had been worn a thousand times and a pair of navy board shorts. She couldn't imagine he wore flip-flops very often, but today he pulled it off. Then there were the trademark aviators and baseball cap—not his team, she noticed.

"How often do you see your dad?" Emily asked.

Jolie swiped the photos until another one appeared. "Oh, hardly ever. He's a baseball star. We used to see him more—well, I did. He never wanted to marry my mom. She says they might've been a mistake but I sure wasn't."

"No, of course not." Emily chewed on that for a minute. "So you've never lived with your dad?"

"He was always traveling," Jolie said matter-of-factly. "Then after he had his accident, we never saw him. Mom said he wasn't himself and that he needed time to get better. I think he even forgot my birthday that first year."

Emily had read about the accident. In fact, she'd gotten almost obsessive about it. Hollis had been driving when another car ran a stop sign and T-boned him. He'd shattered his hip and the doctors were afraid he might never walk again. Baseball looked like something in the past, but somehow he came back.

That's when they started calling him "Miracle Man McGuire." For a while, it seemed like he'd made a full recovery, but could those injuries have been the reason for his retirement? He wasn't really that old.

Emily glanced at him, and though she couldn't see his eyes behind the sunglasses, she felt him looking back at her. What was he thinking about his daughter befriending Emily the way she was? Was he worried about what she might say?

Or had fame and fortune turned Hollis into the kind of person who didn't care?

"If I tell you a secret, do you promise not to tell my dad?" Jolie looked at Emily, her blue eyes intent.

Emily wanted to say, *"Of course you can trust me,"* but what if Jolie told her something Hollis needed to know?

"I don't know if I can keep secrets from your dad, JoJo."

The girl smiled. "You called me JoJo."

"Should I not?"

"'Course you should. We're friends." Jolie's grin was toothy, and once again Emily was struck by her authenticity. "My secret isn't bad. It's just that I don't think my dad really wanted me in the first place."

Emily's heart wrenched, the pain of that feeling all too familiar.

"Oh, kiddo, I don't think that's true. You heard Mr. Williams—your dad loves you."

Jolie shrugged. "I think if you really love someone, you find every way you can to be with them. That's what Rick told Mom. I heard them talking about it. He wants to adopt me."

Emily glanced at Hollis. Did he know any of this? "Wow, what do you think about that?"

"My dad's a great baseball player," Jolie said. "But he's not a very good dad. Rick said that too. That's also the part you can't tell my dad."

For the rest of the afternoon, those words echoed so loudly in

Emily's mind she could hardly wrap her head around them. She didn't know Hollis anymore, but she never would've guessed he was the kind of guy to not take care of his family. It was the exact opposite of what had been modeled for him.

He had so many people—"his people," as Jimmy had said. Didn't he know how lucky he was?

At the same time, as angry as that made her, didn't he have the right to know if Jolie's stepdad wanted to adopt her?

By late afternoon, the sun had worn everyone out, including Jimmy, who had successfully given them the perfect day out on the water.

They'd motored out around the sound, stopped to admire Brant Point lighthouse, grazed on packed lunches and snacks from Bartlett's Farm, and soaked up every drop of sunlight.

Emily spent most of the day with Jolie, though groups shifted throughout the course of the day, giving her time to catch up with Harper (who was, it turned out, a marine biologist when she wasn't running marathons), visit with Nan, and joke around with Hayes. She even spent a little time conversing with Mr. McGuire, who insisted she call him Jeff.

To which she'd replied, "Okay, Mr. McGuire."

She entertained them with stories of her travels, relishing the way it felt to have their undivided attention.

The only person Emily didn't talk to was Hollis, who stayed a bit removed from the rest of the group pretty much the entire day.

Twice she watched as he awkwardly tried to connect with Jolie, and twice he seemed utterly lost.

But being there, with them, she remembered how it felt to belong. She remembered how it felt to matter. She'd forgotten those feelings for a reason.

I need to protect my heart.

Now, as the boat pulled up to the dock and Hollis jumped out to tie it off, emotions threatened to blow Emily's cover as a free-spirited woman without a care in the world. She hadn't come back here expecting to know anybody, and she certainly hadn't expected to be taken in by Nan and Jeffrey McGuire. They'd always had this way about them—the whole family—of making you feel like you were one of them, no questions asked.

But Emily had gotten used to not being one of anybody. She'd gotten used to being mostly alone, and the way her relationships always ended made the loneliness easier. It wasn't worth the threat of pain, so Emily had surrounded herself with people but never let any of them matter.

The McGuire family didn't fit into that plan and she knew it.

She needed space. She needed to clear her head and remember why she was here. This wasn't a vacation—she had work to do. Besides, the day had shone a light on things about Hollis that had wrung out her insides.

She felt angry with him and angry *for* him at the same time.

Once they'd all unloaded and said good-bye to Jimmy, Emily carried a pile of towels back to Hollis's Jeep.

"I think I'm going to walk," she said as he worked to put everything back in the vehicle.

"Back home?"

Not trusting her voice, Emily nodded.

"That's a long walk. I can take you wherever you need to go." There was that concern lacing his brow again. His eyes held her captive for *one-one-thousand, two-one-thousand, three-one* . . . She looked away.

I don't need you watching out for me.

Emily slung her bag over her shoulder. "Thanks for letting me tag along today."

Jolie wrapped her arms around Emily's midsection and squeezed. "Thanks for telling me about acting. I'm going to google the arts center as soon as I get home and see if they decided to have a show this summer after all."

Hollis's eyes snapped to Emily's. She hoped it was okay she was encouraging Jolie's love of theatre. He quickly looked away, shut the hatch of the Jeep, and faced Emily and Jolie. "You sure you don't need a ride?"

Emily squeezed the handle of her bag, clutching it to her shoulder. "I'm sure."

She needed air. She needed deep breaths. She needed to remember why she was here. And she especially needed to remember that people—particularly the handsome ones—needed to be kept on the outskirts of her heart.

Emily gave another wave to Jolie and started off in the same direction as all the tourists, hoping to get lost in the throng. She passed the shops selling overpriced Nantucket sweatshirts, T-shirts, and hats and went straight up Broad Street. How could she have forgotten? How could she have put this all out of her mind?

She fell in behind a group of tourists, day-trippers who marveled at the cobblestone streets, the brick sidewalks, the assortment of colors popping off of the boutiques and stores along the way. Normally, Emily might've wanted to pass the slow-walking cluster, but today she was quite happy to take her time, to see Nantucket through their eyes.

Maybe they could help her find the beauty she'd long forgotten.

Though, after the day she'd had, that could quite possibly be the worst thing for her.

Her phone buzzed in her purse. She stopped right outside of Mitchell's Book Corner on Main Street and pulled it out, expecting a text from Jolie, but instead found herself staring at an incoming call from her grandmother. She'd been back in Nantucket for a week, and this was the first time her grandmother had called.

Emily didn't want to talk to her. She wasn't ready to disclose her plans about the house, and she definitely didn't want to explain what she'd discovered about the arts center. She didn't want to tell Eliza Ackerman that she'd just spent the day with the McGuire family— *Remember them, Grandma? The people you never thought were good enough to spend time with? Oh, and by the way, did you know Hollis was a baseball superstar? He probably has more money than you!*

Emily sat down on a bench at the corner and dragged in a deep breath. What was she doing here? She could've had someone else handle the repairs and the sale of the house. She could've avoided all of this—whatever this was—and moved right along with her life.

Never mind that her life wasn't moving right along anywhere. Her life was in shambles. Never mind that she had nowhere else to go.

"Miss Ackerman?"

Emily didn't need to turn around to know it was Gladys Middlebury behind her. She recognized the lilt in the older woman's voice. She turned and found Gladys standing behind her, carrying a large purse and wearing the biggest pair of sunglasses Emily had ever seen.

Further inspection told her the sunglasses were actually covering another pair of glasses, and Emily wondered why Gladys didn't break into her substantial bank account to purchase a pair of prescription sunglasses or even try a pair of transition lenses.

Rich people were so odd.

"Good afternoon, Mrs. Middlebury," Emily said.

The older woman walked around to the other side of the bench so Emily could look at her without craning her neck. "I've been thinking about your visit the other day."

Emily didn't respond. It sounded like Gladys was working herself up for something—an apology maybe? Emily had done some searching online and discovered that it had been eight years since they'd had any children's programming at the arts center. Eight years! Knowing how much her grandfather contributed annually, the total of that was quite large. She could probably sue if she wanted to.

Or maybe not. Maybe her grandfather didn't have the right to earmark his donation for anything specific. It didn't matter—she was pretending he did, and Gladys seemed to be going along with it.

"I've talked to the board members—separately, as we haven't been able to have a meeting—but we're in agreement that we need to bring back the children's programs." It sounded like she was speaking through gritted teeth. This was clearly not her plan.

"I think that's a great idea."

"The program was originally cut due to lack of interest by the families and lack of personnel." Gladys removed the dark sunglasses, leaving only her regular glasses on her face. If she hadn't looked so serious, Emily might've laughed.

"Maybe things will be different now?" Emily said. "It's been a lot of years."

"We think with the right leadership, that might be the case," Gladys said. "And we would have to have the right leadership. We don't want just anybody working with our children. The last director we had in there made the kids kiss each other during their auditions for *Beauty and the Beast*."

Emily frowned. "You're kidding."

"She said she needed to 'assess the chemistry between Belle and the Beast.' You can imagine the phone calls we got about that one. They were children! Turns out not everyone who says they're a good director really is." One of Gladys's eyebrows curved upward, and then she seemed to gather her thoughts. "We need someone passionate about the program, Miss Ackerman."

"I agree," Emily said. "And I think you'll be able to find that person if you show them you're willing to place a priority on the children's programming. If the director feels like they're there simply to appease a donor, it'll never work."

"We agree." Gladys's lips drew into a thin line. "And we pledge to give you our full support."

Emily straightened. "Me?"

"Who else?" Gladys lifted her chin. "You're the one who came in ranting about how we needed a children's production—I'd say you displayed passion for it—and I'm told you have Broadway credentials."

Emily raised her hands in front of her. "No way, Mrs. Middlebury. I'm sorry, but I can't—"

"On this short of notice, there's really no other choice. Surely you had children in mind when you told me the kids of Nantucket need this. Think of them."

The image of a smiling Jolie raced through her mind. But no. This wasn't her intention when she marched into the arts center the other day.

"I'm sorry, but I'm here to fix my grandparents' house so I can sell it, and that's going to take up most of my summer."

"Well, thank goodness," Gladys said. "That house has become such an eyesore—you don't know how many times I've—" She shook her head. "Oh, never mind. I don't know what to tell you, Miss Ackerman. We see this as the only option. If you want to have a children's production, you're going to have to be the director." Gladys straightened. "And if you can't make a go of it, then you agree to allow us to spend your grandparents' donations however we see fit."

Emily looked away. This was a terrible plan. She'd never worked with kids. Plus, her one attempt at directing had been a colossal, money-sucking disaster. She'd accepted the fact that she wasn't a teacher—she was a performer. An actor. A pretender. But pretending to know how to direct a show with children? That was a stretch.

And yet, she liked kids. She thought about Jolie and what this could mean for her—and Hollis. It could give them much-needed time together, maybe even mend something that had clearly broken between them.

But she wasn't in Nantucket to mend anything. She was here to do what it took to get her second chance—and then get off this dreaded island as quickly as possible.

"Think about it, Miss Ackerman, and let me know your answer by Monday."

"That's two days," Emily said.

Gladys raised a brow. "We could always leave things as they are and revisit this next summer, assuming your grandfather's estate will still be contributing to the arts center."

Again, Emily thought of Jolie. She might not be here to mend anything, but if she could help, shouldn't she?

"When you find something worth fighting for, fight."

The advice challenged her. Dared her to walk away. But hadn't her mother been talking about something else—equality, justice, something noteworthy?

Surely she hadn't meant a children's theatre. Who fought for a children's theatre?

But what if fighting for it led to another kid's life being changed, the same way hers had been?

As soon as the thought entered her mind, another one bulldozed over it. *What if I fail again?*

She wanted to groan. There was no good answer. She wasn't a teacher. She wasn't even the kind of person most parents would want leading their kids—she was a mess.

"Well?" Gladys's tone radiated impatience.

"I'll think about it," Emily said.

"Very good." Gladys walked across the street, slowly making her way over the uneven cobblestones in her sensible shoes that were probably "good for arthritis."

What would her mother say to all of this if she were here to weigh in on the subject?

Emily didn't have to wonder—she might not have spoken to her mother in eighteen years, but the letters had given her plenty of insight into the kind of person her mom was. Words on paper, frozen in time, gave her a clear snapshot of Isabelle Ackerman, and it was her influence that had turned Emily into the adventure seeker that she was. She lived the life she thought her mother would've wanted for her, the life her mother never got to live.

She'd never paused to wonder what happened if that life suddenly stopped being one she wanted.

To Gladys's proposal, Isabelle would likely say, "Do it, Emily. You'll be wonderful at it, and even if you aren't, you'll have a wild adventure introducing all those kids to the theatre. I can't think of anyone better to teach them—you're so passionate about it."

Emily would argue that she wasn't good with large groups, didn't know the best way to entertain small children, and had too much to do to really give a show her all.

"But what would make your heart happy?" her mother would ask.

Then, sadly, Emily would retreat, because she couldn't remember the last time her heart had been happy.

And that wasn't the kind of thing she could talk about out loud.

~

For when you feel overwhelmed

Dear Emily,

It's no secret I wasn't prepared to be a mother at the age of eighteen. I actually wonder if anyone is ever prepared to be a mother, but I know for certain I was not ready. There was so much I didn't know. There was so much to learn, and sadly, you didn't come with an instruction booklet.

I made a lot of mistakes. One day I was getting ready to leave the house, and as if by magic, your car seat fell off the counter with you strapped in it, landing you upside down (and screaming!) on the kitchen floor.

To this day I have no idea how that happened, only that I never set your car seat on the counter again.

Mistakes are a topic for another letter, but this letter is about that feeling of being overwhelmed—in over your head. We're all there at some point, often daily, like I was in those early years. (Yes, years. Turns out children change as they grow, and there are new challenges like teething or walking or potty training. One day it'll be dating and makeup and boys. I'll probably make mistakes then too.)

I'm always overwhelmed, it seems. But here's what I know for sure: I'm also a lot more capable than I usually think I am. But I have to take each problem one by one. When I pile them all on top of my shoulders at once, that's when I shut down. So whatever the most pressing problem is in that moment, that's what I focus on. Once I've solved that, I move on to the next one. *Obviously this doesn't work with everything—you can't achieve world peace in a day—but the things that affect your daily life, those are things you can take one at a time.*

I don't always agree with your grandparents, but your grandpop always says, "How do you eat an elephant? One bite at a time."

So the next time you feel overwhelmed, just break everything down piece by piece . . . and be sure to chew slowly so you give each one time to digest.

Love,
Mom

CHAPTER 19

Nearly three full days passed before Isabelle could escape long enough to find JD. After humiliating her and carting her off from the beach the night of the Fourth, her parents had grounded her and taken away all privileges for the rest of the summer.

She'd pleaded with them to meet JD, to give him a chance, to take off their blinders and consider that maybe—just maybe—he was a good guy.

"No 'good guy' would encourage our daughter to enter a relationship without telling us," her mom had said.

Now, with her mom at one of her ridiculous luncheons and her dad out on a fishing trip with a business associate who was only in for the day, Isabelle jumped on her bike and raced over to the club, hoping to find JD for a few minutes before she had to hurry back home.

But when she arrived, he was nowhere to be found. Jeb sat at a picnic table outside, eating a hot dog and a bag of chips.

"Isabelle?" He tossed a look over his shoulder as though talking to her could get him in trouble.

"Is he here?"

Jeb stood, moved toward her, and led her toward the staff entrance, away from any watchful eyes, as if her parents had spies all over the island.

Which, to be honest, they probably did.

"Didn't he tell you?" Jeb kept his voice low.

"Tell me what?"

"He was fired two days ago," Jeb said. "He's probably at our house."

"Fired?" Isabelle wanted to cry. "Were my parents behind this?"

Jeb shrugged. "I don't know."

Her parents were most definitely behind this. "Is he okay?"

"He'd be better if he saw you, I think."

Isabelle glanced at her watch. How long would her mother be gone?

She decided she didn't care. She'd risk getting in more trouble if it meant seeing JD.

"Thanks, Jeb," she called out as she rushed back to her bike and then pedaled off toward JD's rental cottage.

She reached the small house, dropped the bike on the ground out front, and knocked on the door.

After a few long seconds, the door opened and JD stood there, looking disheveled but as handsome as ever.

At the sight of her, his eyes brightened. "What are you doing here?" He flung open the screen door and pulled her toward him, kissing her as if it might be the last time, as if he'd been imagining this exact moment for days.

"I had to make sure you were okay," she said.

"But your parents . . . ?"

"They don't know I'm here."

His face fell. Maybe he'd thought—hoped—they'd changed their minds.

She kissed him, inhaling him, realizing in that moment how much she'd missed him, how much she loved him.

"They grounded me," she said, pulling away. "They said I can't see you anymore."

JD raked a hand through his hair. "Then you shouldn't be here."

Tears sprang to her eyes. "You can't mean that."

He pivoted away from her. "I don't want to give them any more reasons to hate me, Bella. I want them to love me—to love us."

She shook her head. "They won't. They never will."

He sat down on the couch and pulled her into his arms. Her heart filled with an unspeakable sadness.

"It isn't right," she finally said.

"But we knew it was like this," he said. "We knew it couldn't last forever."

She swiped a tear as it slid down her cheek. "But why not? Because you aren't rich? That's stupid. This isn't 1810."

He inched back, forcing her gaze. "Look, Bella, I love you. More than anything. And if I can figure out a way for us to be together, I'm going to do it. I promise."

He wiped her tears with his thumbs, then brought his lips to hers, kissing her soft and slow, the way he often did. She savored the moment, silently praying this wouldn't be the last time.

She wrapped her arms around his neck and drew him closer, the anger toward her parents increasing as she thought that she might lose him.

"They can't control me," she said.

"Maybe they can for a little while longer," he said.

"It's not right."

He smiled sadly, pressing his forehead against hers.

She kissed him again. And again. And again, each kiss growing more hurried, more intense.

She didn't know if it was a newfound rebellious streak, anger at her parents, or the fact that she really believed she loved JD more than she'd ever loved anyone before that led to what happened next.

Isabelle pulled the sheets of JD's bed up to her chin and hugged herself as he held her. He kissed her bare shoulders, and she closed her eyes, the memory of what had just happened still fresh in her mind.

Guilt—but not regret—rushed through her. Had they simply been caught up in the moment? Had she been so overcome with her love for him that she failed to keep her wits about her? Or did she have something to prove to parents who were intent on treating her like she was still a child?

She didn't know the answer—she only knew that nothing could be undone.

"Are you okay?" he asked quietly. "You seem upset."

She faced him, and in a flash, her guilt disappeared. She did love JD, no matter what her parents said. "I'm good, but I do have to go." She kissed him again, then gathered her clothes, wishing she could stay with him for the rest of the night instead of going home to the Ackerman prison.

He brushed her hair away from her face and kissed her tenderly. "I love you, Bella."

She smiled. "I love you too."

She might not know when she'd see him again, but she knew that much was true.

CHAPTER 20

MONDAY MORNING, HOLLIS WOKE to the unmistakable sensation of Tilly licking his face. Nothing pulled him from sleep more quickly than her wet, slobbery kisses.

He patted the top of her head and rubbed her ears until finally she was content he was awake enough to take her out.

He pulled on yesterday's T-shirt and followed the dog down the stairs and outside, aware that it was barely light out.

"What are you doing up so early, Tilly?" Hollis grumbled, trailing her down toward the beach. He glanced over at Emily's dark house and wondered if she'd figured out how to sleep indoors.

Tilly took off toward the water. Hollis whistled for her, to no avail. It wasn't like her not to listen—was there an animal down there?

He reluctantly chased her down to the sand, and as he made his way through the grass, he saw Emily standing on the shore, staring out across the water as the sunrise barely peeked over the horizon.

He knew he had only seconds before she noticed them, so he

drank in each one. She stood on the edge of the water wearing white shorts, a long-sleeved, billowy white shirt, and no shoes, and she was the picture of beauty.

Emily didn't even know how beautiful she was. From what he gathered, she'd spent her life flitting from place to place, like a butterfly looking for a safe spot to land. She'd built a wall around herself, and while she was great at pushing everyone away, every time she bristled or closed herself off, it only made him want to know her more.

Tilly reached Emily and nuzzled her hand with her nose. Emily knelt down and rubbed the dog's ears, then looked up and found Hollis staring at her.

Nothing was wrong between them, and yet they were connected by a taut line of tension he couldn't quite figure out. She'd been so short with him after their boat trip, refusing his ride home, that he'd decided to give her space yesterday.

But now here they were, as if the world had thrown them back together. And he couldn't stop thinking of how badly he wanted to touch her skin.

"Hey," he said.

"Hey."

"You're up early."

She gave Tilly another pat. "I like to watch the sunrise."

He should get up early more often. "It's pretty spectacular."

"Are you an early riser?"

He stood next to her and faced the water. "Not so much anymore."

"Since you retired?"

He tossed a sideways glance at her, but she wasn't looking at him. "Hey, are we okay?"

She faced him, her eyes innocent and wide. "What do you mean?"

He looked away. "Things seem . . . strange, I guess."

She shrugged. "I mean, it's weird being back here and not knowing anyone. Plus, I do stupid things like pry into your personal life and try to make you talk about baseball when you don't want to."

"I told you that was no big deal." He bent down and picked up a rock, tossed it in the ocean. "It's just still really hard to talk about." He could feel her eyes on him.

"Because you didn't want to leave?"

Was he really going to admit it out loud? Nobody knew the details of his retirement, but there was still, even after all this time, something about Emily. In some ways, he felt like she was the person who knew him best, though she really didn't know him at all. His eyes found the sand at his feet. "Yeah."

"Was it the accident?"

"Everyone wanted me to be back—my coaches, my teammates . . . me." Man, he hated talking about this. "I wanted it more than everyone."

"But you did come back," she said, hugging her arms around herself as a breeze kicked up off the water.

He glanced at her. "Yeah, I was the Miracle Man."

"It was inspiring," she said.

"It wasn't real." He threw a stick down the shore for Tilly to fetch. "I mean, yeah, I came back, but the doctor told me not to keep playing. I was so stubborn. I didn't listen. I didn't want anyone telling me what I could or couldn't do." Yep. He was saying it all out loud. "I loved that first game back—you wouldn't believe it. The crowd went crazy when I ran on the field."

"I believe it," she said. "I was there."

He looked at her. "What?"

She kept her focus steady on the water. "I was there. I was one of the ones cheering." She glanced up and found his eyes.

"No way." The words escaped, practically under his breath. "Why didn't you come find me?"

She waved him off. "Are you kidding? You were a huge star. I didn't even know if you remembered me."

"Em—" What was he going to say? Truth be told, he didn't know how he would've reacted if he'd seen her at a game. He wasn't his best after the accident, not even after he became the Miracle Man. His last four years in the majors were a blur of pain and medication and physical therapy and bad moods and eventually his being let go by a team he'd dedicated his very best years to.

He'd made his peace with all of it when he got his life back on track, when he started talking to God again. So why was the sting of it all—the shame—still so fresh, even months later? This wasn't a side of himself he wanted to show anyone.

He tried to remember the things he'd learned in the last year, the things Jimmy had helped him realize—that bad choices don't make you a bad person, that God forgave him, that he still had a lot of life to lead.

This second chance with Jolie was, as Jimmy said, a gift from God. "Don't blow it, Mack." It was as if the moment he put his relationship with Jolie back together, he could finally move past the rest of the pain.

There were times he was sure he'd forgiven himself, but recently he was sure forgiveness was the last thing he deserved.

"I wish I'd seen you, is all," he finally said.

"I came to a couple of your games." She studied the water. "Had to see if you lived up to all the hype." Finally she smiled at him.

"And . . . ?"

"In the first game I went to—your first one on some pre–Major League team—you hit a home run on your first at bat." Her grin turned sheepish.

He remembered. First at bat in the farm league and he hit one out of the park. They'd called him up to the show after that. It was one of those memories he'd let go of when he lost everything—it was too painful knowing he'd never feel that way again.

Still, something inside him flip-flopped at the thought of her being there, seeing him at his best, before the accident stole everything from him.

"I wish I would've known you were there," he said.

They were quiet for several seconds, pausing to watch as the sun made its way up a little higher on the horizon. Tilly had lost interest in the stick and was now out chasing the waves, then running back on shore over and over again.

"Secret, secret," she said.

The words stopped time. They were kids again, sharing every thought—even the embarrassing ones, like the time he admitted he wanted to kiss her.

That kiss had been sweet and innocent for both of them. Why couldn't they have stopped right there, in that moment? Why did everything have to change so drastically?

"You know how I feel about this game," he said.

She shrugged. "Secret, secret."

"Who says you get to be the asker?"

"I made up the rules," she said.

"Well, why don't we both do one to make it even?" That was fair, right? Make her squirm so he wasn't the only one in the hot seat.

She paused for a long moment. "You get the next turn. On another day."

He laughed. "I see how it is."

"Fine," she said. "I'll think of one. What do you want to know?"

He stood still for a solid ten seconds, eyes searching hers. "I want to know everything, Emily."

Her expression changed and she shifted where she stood. He shouldn't have said that. It had made her uncomfortable. Never mind that it was true.

"I mean, it's been forever, so we have a lot to catch up on," he said, trying to play it off like it was no big deal.

"Right," she said. "But remember, I don't want to be nosy."

He grinned at her. "Yeah, right."

The heavy cloud of tension dissipated. The darkness gave way to the new morning sun and the moment between them passed.

At his side, she'd gone quiet, and Hollis resisted the urge to take her hand in his, as if that could erase the line of worry across her forehead.

She bumped into him with her shoulder. "Come on, Mack, I know you've got one in there."

He stared at the water for a long moment, then drew in a deep breath. "It wasn't just that I retired," he finally said. "They asked me to leave."

He could feel her eyes on him—attentive, curious. Would he soon see judgment there too?

Sometimes people said it was good to say things aloud, to get them out. This wasn't one of those times. He hated that the words hung there, tarnishing what she thought of him. He'd much rather go on being that baseball hero she'd seen hit the homer that day. The one who made a huge comeback, against all odds.

"Was it your injuries?"

He nodded. He didn't want to talk about it anymore, and yet, this was Emily—his Emily. If there was anyone to tell, it was her. Besides, she was pushy. No way she was going to let him turn quiet now.

"I paid a doctor to clear me." He cast his eyes downward again, this time because the shame of the admission was too heavy to carry.

Emily said nothing.

"He filled my prescriptions and kept me playing, but eventually the damage I was doing became obvious. They started cutting my playing time, little by little, until finally, one day, they said I was done. Said it was for my own safety." He found a stone by his foot, unburied it, and tossed it into the ocean. "I sort of . . . lost myself."

"Is that why you're here?" she asked. "To find yourself again?"

"I don't really know," he said. "I guess I came because I didn't have anywhere else to go."

"I get that."

He shoved his hands in his pockets. "Nobody knows about any of that—not even my family. The pills became more than a crutch." He looked away. How did he admit any of this out loud? Only Jimmy knew the gruesome details of his exit from baseball.

"I was mad, honestly. I didn't live my life the way I should've, but I always believed God wanted the best for me, right? So how could he allow that accident—how could he allow me to lose everything I'd worked for, everything I loved?"

Emily's nod was nearly undetectable. "I've wondered that before too."

Of course she had—she'd lost her mother. By comparison, his grief over a game seemed shallow.

"But Jimmy helped me with that," he added quickly. "Taught me that sometimes you have to lose everything in order to figure out what's really important. Not an easy lesson to learn. Especially because I hadn't put any time into the things that mattered, like Jolie."

She was quiet for several seconds, then finally glanced his way. "I'm sorry, Hollis."

He shrugged as if it meant nothing, when really it meant everything. "It was stupid. I should've listened. I should've been done right after the accident instead of trying to come back and be the hero."

Maybe then he'd have figured out years ago what really mattered. But that's not what he'd done. He'd been so pigheaded, so stubborn, so prideful, that he'd ignored everyone's advice.

And what had the extra time in the majors gotten him? A whole lot of heartache and a hip and leg that would always cause him pain.

"So they asked you to retire?"

He nodded, doing his best not to remember that moment. The results of his random drug test in the hand of his manager. The signed confession of the doctor who'd been fired that morning. All of it was a black mark of shame on an otherwise-shiny record.

"I got to leave with my reputation intact, though," he said.

But what good was a reputation when everything that was important was gone?

She had more questions, he could tell. But that's not how the game worked. She wasn't allowed to probe him—all she could do was let him talk.

And he was done talking. "Anyway, that was a heavy way to start out the morning."

"Maybe, but I'm glad you told me."

He turned slightly to get a better view of her. "You and your stupid game."

Her laugh was barely audible. She faced the water and inhaled the salt air. "It sure is beautiful here."

He took her in, studying her profile. "Sure is."

When she glanced back at him and found him watching her, he imagined it was clear to her that he wasn't talking about the sunrise.

⁓

So many thoughts tumbled around in her head as she stood next to Hollis on the beach. They were in almost the exact same spot they'd been when he'd kissed her for the first (and only) time all those years ago, and he'd just told her something almost no one else knew.

They'd been languishing somewhere out in the strangers-who-used-to-be-friends zone, and now she felt closer to him than she did to just about anyone else in her life.

She wanted to ask more about Jolie. She wanted to know how a father could abandon his daughter—she wanted it out there because maybe it would put things into perspective for him all over again, but more so because it might clear up a few things for her. After all, she'd always wondered how her own father could've abandoned her.

But he'd gone quiet. At least for now.

"That lady from the arts center wants me to head up a children's production," she said, figuring that was a safe topic to discuss on the beach at dawn, watching the sunrise with the handsomest man she'd ever met.

"Yeah?" He angled himself toward her. "You gonna do it?"

She shrugged. "Should I? I mean, I didn't come here to revive a children's theatre."

"No, but you can't hang around the house all summer."

"Why not?" she asked, not letting on that she knew he was right. She was so bored already.

"You'd just be in the way."

She laughed and gave him a shove. "I'll have you know I took set-building classes in college."

"Oh, really? I bet those safety goggles were good and sexy."

She laughed again. "I was actually pretty terrible at it. I just wanted to be onstage."

A thoughtful look washed across his face. "I wish I could've seen you onstage. I bet you were amazing."

She tossed him a glance. "Hardly, but I really did love it for a while."

"You don't anymore?" His eyes were so earnest.

"That's a secret for another day, Mr. McGuire."

He lifted his chin in mock surprise. "Ah, so that's how it's going to be."

She smiled. For a split second, it felt like old times. Maybe old times weren't all bad.

"Come have coffee with me," he said. "Mom will force-feed you waffles and Dad will bore you with the latest news from Wall Street."

She studied Hollis for a few long seconds and realized that if she went with him, her heart would be in danger.

Protect your heart.

"Thanks for the invitation, but I should head in," she said. "Get ready for the crew."

He gave her one quick nod and did a poor job of hiding his disappointment.

He's just a friend, Emily told herself, though a small part of her chose not to listen. The sensible part of her, which didn't often have a say, stepped up and put that small part in its place.

There were far too many question marks where Hollis McGuire was concerned, and while she wanted to, Emily didn't have it in her to hunt down the answers to them all. She was better off keeping their relationship cordial and friendly but emotionally uncomplicated. It's what her mom's letters had said to do—to keep her heart safe. So far that advice had served her well—why mess that up now?

Never mind that his story had tugged at the knot inside her.

None of that mattered. She had a job to do: a house renovation to oversee and a property to unload.

And then she could finally—finally—get on with her life.

CHAPTER 21

A FEW HOURS LATER, and only moments before Jack was supposed to arrive with his crew to get started working on phase one of the home renovation, there was an exuberant knock on the sliding-glass door that led to Emily's patio.

She glanced up from where she stood in the kitchen, pouring herself a third cup of coffee, and saw Jolie's face grinning back at her. She waved the girl in.

"Why didn't you tell me?" Jolie rushed over to where Emily stood.

"Tell you what?" Emily stuck the creamer back in the refrigerator.

"Wait, can I have some?"

"Coffee?" Emily stood with the refrigerator door still open, watching Jolie. "No."

"Why not? Uncle Hayes lets me."

"Does your dad know about that?"

She rolled her eyes. "Like he'd care."

Emily closed the refrigerator door and moved back to the kitchen island, opposite where Jolie stood. "You're pretty mad at him, huh?"

Jolie shrugged. "No, I don't really care if he wants me or not."

Emily could remember saying the same thing. She saw now that it was a defense mechanism—pretending it didn't matter that her dad didn't want her was easier than admitting there was nothing in the world she wanted more than to have a complete family unit.

The unwanted thought startled her. She wasn't pretending when she said it didn't matter whether or not her dad wanted her. She'd decided a long time ago it absolutely did not matter.

So why now, looking at Jolie, did that seem to have changed?

"You know, in some ways, you're pretty lucky." Emily took a box of donuts she'd picked up from a new-to-her place called Wicked Island Bakery and set it on the counter between them.

"Why, because my dad's loaded?"

Emily laughed. "No, because he's here." She opened the box of donuts and inhaled the sweet, sugary smell of fried dough.

Jolie's frown deepened. "Here on the island?"

"Here, with you. I'd give anything to have that with my dad." Emily pushed the donuts toward Jolie, whose eyes lit up.

"I can have one?"

"Of course."

Jolie reached in the box and took a donut, then looked at Emily. "Is your dad dead?" She took a bite of the pastry, then licked the ends of her fingers.

Once again it struck Emily how refreshing it was to talk to someone who said exactly what they were thinking. She hoped age didn't change that about Hollis's daughter, though in her experience, adults weren't usually so forthcoming. "I don't know. I never knew him."

Jolie's face softened and she stopped chewing. "Really?"

"Really."

"I'm sorry, Emily." Again, nothing but sincerity flickered in Jolie's eyes.

The knock at the door drew Emily's attention. She set her coffee mug back down and started toward the entryway. "You never told me what you were so excited about when you first walked in."

"Oh!" Jolie hopped off the stool and followed her. "That you're directing the children's show at the arts center."

Emily spun around. "Who told you that?"

"GrandNan," Jolie said matter-of-factly. "She has friends who know everything about everything—Grandpa called them 'busybodies'—and I guess one of them told her we're getting the kids' show back and it's all because of you!" Jolie's grin could've lit up a moonless night.

"JoJo," Emily said, "nothing's been decided for sure."

Her face fell. "Really? Because I texted my mom to ask if they'd let me stay longer so I can audition. I told her we had a *real-life* Broadway director and everything."

Oh, my. How was Emily supposed to turn down Gladys's offer now? "What did she say?"

"She hasn't responded yet. There's a time difference. But if you don't do the show, no one will, and then I'll never know if I'm any good at acting."

Emily turned back toward the door. "That's not exactly true, JoJo. You'll have lots of chances to see if you're a good actor." She pulled open the front door expecting Jack but found Hollis there instead.

"Oh," Emily said. "Hollis."

"Hey, am I early?"

"Early for what?"

"The renovation."

Emily stared at him. "You're really going to try and help with this?"

"What else do I have to do?"

She leaned closer. "Hang out with your daughter."

Hollis looked past her. "My daughter is already here."

"Fair point."

"Emily bought donuts," Jolie called over her shoulder as she raced back toward the kitchen.

Hollis's face brightened. "Donuts?"

Emily groaned. "You might as well come in since I have a feeling I'm not going to be able to get rid of you."

He stepped inside, and it occurred to her that he hadn't been in the old house since she returned. But then, he rarely came into the house when they were kids either. Unlike the McGuires, who opened their home willingly, fed her whenever they could, and made her feel like a part of the family, Emily's grandmother had strict rules about other kids coming into the house throughout the day.

"I don't want you bringing sand in from outside, Emily," she'd say, "and those McGuire boys can come over, but only if they stay outside in the yard."

It shamed her now to think about how Hollis and his family had been treated when they were kids, and especially that they'd been treated that way by her own family. She wanted no part of that, and her mom hadn't either. In fact, she'd rejected most of what her grand-mother had taught her in favor of the lessons Mom had left behind in her letters. She'd purposed to become the kind of adult who would've made Isabelle Ackerman proud—even if that meant disappointing her grandmother.

"Sorry about the musty smell," she said as she closed the door behind Hollis. "It's been over a week, but I still can't seem to get rid of it."

"New paint will help," he said.

"New everything will help." She started toward the kitchen but stopped short. "Your mom told Jolie I was directing a show at the arts center."

Hollis's face went blank. "I know. Sorry. I tried to explain to them it wasn't official, but you know the Nantucket rumor mill."

Emily did know it—well. Even as a child she'd been aware of the way rumors spread across the island, or at least across her grand-mother's circle of friends.

"So what are you going to do now?" Hollis asked.

"Jolie said she asked her mom if she could stay on the island longer so she could audition."

Hollis shifted.

"Do you want her to stay longer?"

He met her eyes. "Do you even have to ask?"

Emily knew better than to pounce on the Jolie situation in that exact moment, especially after he'd been so open with her earlier that morning on the beach. So why did she hear herself doing exactly that, as if she weren't the one in control of her mouth? "I don't know anything about you and Jolie except what she's told me."

Hollis sighed. "What did she tell you?"

"Dad!" Jolie yelled from the other room. "Donuts!"

"Be right there, JoJo," he called out.

"Forget it." Emily turned to go back to the kitchen, but Hollis grabbed her arm and turned her around.

The connection of his skin on hers sent a shaky shiver down her spine. She glanced at his hand, and he quickly released his grip.

"Sorry," he said. "What did she say?"

Emily narrowed her gaze. "I shouldn't have said anything." *Why is my mouth so big?*

"Well, you did."

She could feel the tension between them returning, and it wasn't the kind that made the air sizzle; it was the kind that balled her stomach into a knot. "I know. I have a knack for sticking my nose where it doesn't belong."

He pulled his baseball cap off and ran a hand through his dark hair. "You won't get an argument from me."

She leveled her gaze at him. "Funny."

"Look, I know you have opinions, but you don't have the whole story," Hollis said.

Emily took a step closer—too close, it turned out, because she could smell whatever man soap he'd used in the shower that morning. "You're right. I do have opinions. And you're also right that I don't have the whole story. The only thing I know for sure is that you have a daughter, and she's a pretty great kid, and she thinks you don't want her here."

Hollis balked, and instantly Emily regretted the words.

This is not your business. Stop talking.

"She said that?" His face fell.

Emily sighed. "I'm sorry, Hollis. I said I wouldn't stick my nose where it doesn't belong, but . . ."

"But you just can't help yourself." He finished her sentence with a dull laugh. "It's fine. I could've guessed."

Emily had already pushed it this far—why stop now? "I don't get it," she said.

He met her eyes.

"I never in a million years would've expected *you* to be the kind of dad who wasn't a part of his daughter's life." He'd opened up that morning on the beach—why did she feel the need to continue to push?

"Like I said, there's a lot you don't understand."

"Then tell me," she said. "Tell me what could possibly have kept you from making sure that little girl knew her dad loved her—no matter what."

He inched back, but only slightly, and his thorough study of her face set something off inside.

She'd not only gotten into his business, but she'd done it with so much gusto there was no denying her issue with him was a personal one. And why? He wasn't her father—she had no right.

And yet, how could she respect a man who treated his daughter the way her father had treated her—with complete indifference?

Ugh, Emily, you were doing so well. Why did you have to go and ruin it?

"I told you what happened to me after the accident," he said quietly.

"But even before that," Emily said. "She said you weren't around much at all."

"You don't know the whole story, Em," he said quietly.

"I know enough."

"Is this about Jolie . . . ?" He paused as if deciding whether or not to continue. "Or you?" His pointed question smacked her in the face.

So this was how it felt to be on the receiving end of bluntness.

The knock on the door did nothing to rattle her. She squared off in front of him, knowing she deserved the discomfort, the turning of the tables—aware that her words had hurt him, though she hadn't intended them to.

"This is about Jolie," she finally said.

His eyebrow hitched—barely noticeable—and she spun around and walked toward the door, her heart racing in her chest with all the pounding of a Nantucket thunderstorm.

"I think it's about you," he said. "Don't put your daddy issues on my daughter, Emily."

She stopped, her hand on the doorknob, her mouth agape, but when she turned around to get the last word in, she found nothing but an empty hallway.

Hollis might've been a sweet kid once upon a time, but he'd grown up to be an obstinate, stubborn man.

She pulled the door open and found Jack standing on the porch, cup of coffee in one hand and a stack of papers in the other.

His sunny smile didn't match her cloudy mood.

"You ready to get started?" he asked.

Yes, I am ready. Let's get this over with so I can hurry up and sell this place and get off this island.

"Let's do it."

CHAPTER 22

THE AIR IN THE COTTAGE was decidedly tense, so Hollis took the long way around the house and out to the backyard. He didn't need Jack Walker to tell him the patio needed to be torn up, and breaking up the old concrete seemed like a good way to expend some unwanted energy.

It had been a long time since anyone had talked to him the way Emily did—even Jimmy hadn't taken those kinds of liberties. Instead, the man had gently led Hollis to the realization that he needed to make things right with Jolie. Emily had all the gentleness of a Mack truck.

And where did she get off? She didn't know a thing about his relationship with his daughter.

Or maybe he was mad because she'd spoken aloud every fear he'd been trying to bury.

He stuck earbuds in his ears and turned his music up—loud—then picked up a sledgehammer and started to break apart the old concrete slab. He'd make this his project so he could stay away from everyone else and stop thinking about his failures as a father.

Of course he wanted Jolie to stay longer. It had been over a week, and he'd made no progress. The girl had such a sweetness about her—with everyone but him. How did he break through that?

His mind spun back to the day Jana called with the news she was pregnant. If he could rewind the clock, he'd return to that moment. He couldn't imagine going back any further because even though he regretted his short-lived nonrelationship with Jana, he didn't regret having Jolie—not for a second.

Had he miscommunicated that? Had his other regrets—the accident, the way he handled his recovery, the loss of his career—somehow told his daughter that *she* was the reason for his pain?

The music blared in his ears, and he swung the hammer furiously. His biceps and shoulders ached, but he kept going, determined to rid the yard of the ugly slab by sheer force. Who needed a jackhammer when he had angst and fury?

Jana had been one of those girls—the kind who appeared as if out of thin air—at the same bar as the team after a game. Hollis had been in a slump, and his mood was sour. In hindsight, he should've headed back to the hotel and gone to bed, but the guys had convinced him to go out.

Enter Jana. Long-legged, curvy, beautiful Jana—who wore too much makeup and had very few ambitions. That night, her only goal had been to land herself in the bed of a pro baseball player, and Hollis was just drunk enough to oblige.

Immediately he regretted sleeping with her. He didn't even know her. The guys called it a "perk" of being a pro athlete, but even at his lowest, Hollis still knew what was right—and spending a night with a complete stranger was the exact opposite of that.

He vowed to do better. It wasn't like Jana had been his first mistake—but weeks later when he found out she was pregnant, he decided to make sure she was his last.

The phone call had come after a game that proved his slump was over. A home run, two doubles, and a game-winning RBI had Hollis walking on air. The team went out to celebrate and Hollis actually had the thought that life couldn't get much better than it was at that moment.

That's when his phone rang. A number he didn't recognize, so he didn't answer. A beep signaled a new voice mail, which he decided to ignore.

The next morning, he woke up with a headache, slightly hungover. The night had gotten away from him as so many of them did. It wasn't until he'd been up for an hour that he remembered the voice mail.

"Hollis, it's Jana—the, uh, girl from the bar in Denver." She sighed. "Do you even remember me? We, uh . . . I mean, I . . ." A pause. "I need you to call me back."

Hollis groaned. He'd heard about girls becoming obsessed with pro athletes—one of his buddies had to file a restraining order on a girl who actually thought they were married—but it had been over a month, almost two, and Jana hadn't done anything to make him think their one-night stand was anything more than that—one night.

She didn't seem like a stalker, and while he'd said he'd call her (and hadn't), she didn't even sound angry in her message.

Maybe she had a disease. Had they used protection? He was usually so careful—and one-night stands weren't his thing—but wouldn't that just be his luck?

He dialed her number and listened as the phone rang, his insides turning over.

"Hey, Hollis," she answered.

"Hey."

"Bet you never thought you'd hear from me again."

He hadn't, but he didn't say so. "What's up?"

"I'm just going to come right out and say it, and I want you to know I don't expect you to do anything."

His stomach lurched, guessing what she was about to say. *Oh no.*

"I'm pregnant."

He rubbed a hand over his messy hair, then covered his face. "You're kidding."

"I wish I was."

He sighed. "And you're sure it's mine?"

The sound she made in response was so slight he almost didn't hear it.

"I'm sorry," he said. "I didn't mean to imply—"

"It's yours," she said coldly.

He stood and walked toward the window.

"You probably want me to get rid of it, but I—"

"No," he said. "I don't want that at all."

"You don't?"

He closed his eyes. This changed everything. And while you'd never know it by the way he was living, he still had a moral compass. "Of course I don't."

"Most guys . . ." She stopped. "I'm just surprised, I guess."

"Is that what you want?"

"No," she said. "I was calling to tell you because you have a right to know, but I'm keeping it. That's not up for debate."

"Good."

"Good."

The pause was every bit as pregnant as Jana, but probably more uncomfortable—at least at this stage.

"So we should maybe . . ." He looked around the stark hotel room, wishing for some flashing sign to tell him exactly what to do next. "Maybe we should get married?"

She laughed. "Seriously?"

"Seriously."

He could just hear the guys now—they'd say she'd trapped him, that he should send her some money and call it done. But those guys didn't grow up with Jeffrey and Nan McGuire for parents. Hollis believed in taking responsibility for his actions, and whether this child could be called a "mistake" or not, sleeping with Jana was, in fact, a mistake.

"I'm not going to marry you, Hollis," Jana said. "I don't even know you. And you don't want to marry me."

He was ashamed to admit the relief he felt at her words.

"I'm just trying to do the right thing here," he said.

"Well, I'm not one of those girls who tries to trap a rich guy into marrying me by getting myself pregnant. The truth is, I've never done anything like that before."

"It's not something I make a habit of either," Hollis said.

"I thought my boyfriend was going to propose to me, but instead he broke up with me. Said he was in love with someone else. We were long distance, so there's no way this baby is his," Jana said. "But I was in a bad place that night."

She wasn't the only one. He'd let that slump rob him of his common sense. Of course this would happen to him now, when he was back on top of his game.

"So what do you need from me?"

"Nothing, Hollis. I know from everything I've read about you that you're a stand-up guy, but you don't owe me anything. You're going to have a kid out here in the world, and I didn't think it was fair to keep that from you. That's the only reason I called."

She was letting him off the hook.

And while there were plenty of guys who would've been perfectly fine with that, Hollis wasn't one of them. A week later, he called Jana back and told her that though they might not be a couple, he still wanted to be a part of his child's life.

And he had been—sort of.

But he should've done better. He should've made JoJo a priority instead of an afterthought once everything else was taken care of.

He'd been so excited when she was born, but it was hard to be there the way he should've been when she didn't live with him. Or maybe that was just another excuse.

Then the accident happened and the only thing that mattered after that was making a comeback. And the only thing that mattered after the comeback was maintaining his career. And keeping his method of doing so hidden from everyone in his life.

It didn't matter that he was moody and distant or even unreachable.

It didn't matter that his daughter was growing up without him. His parents would take Jolie for long weekends, but Hollis spent those weekends in the gym. Jana would send him notes about her school events, but he was always too busy.

And sometimes, as much as he hated to admit it, he was even mean.

Those days were what carved the divide between himself and Jolie. Those days were what made his only child think she was unwanted, unloved.

And that was his fault.

He'd been swinging the sledgehammer with such force, lost in the mire of years gone by, that he didn't see his daughter standing in front of him, waving at him with one hand and holding a tall glass of lemonade in the other.

He tugged the earbuds out and dragged the back of his arm across his forehead, wiping the sweat from one body part to another. "Sorry."

He was breathless, anxious, irritated.

"Emily said I should bring you this," his daughter said. "I guess you've been working like a maniac or something?"

"Is that what she said?"

"Yep." She held the tall glass out toward him, giving it a slight shake, the ice cubes clinking along its side.

"What else did she say?"

"Something about you being as stubborn as you ever were." Jolie shrugged. "Are you two fighting?"

Hollis took the glass and downed half of its contents in one gulp. "No, we're not fighting."

"I'm not a baby, Dad," JoJo said. "I can tell when two people don't like each other." She laughed. "And I thought you were going to try to date her."

"Why is that funny?"

"I don't think she can stand you." Jolie grinned.

Hollis took another drink.

"My mom wants to talk to you," she said. "Before she decides if I can stay another month to do the show."

"Okay. I can call her."

"Are you going to let me stay?"

He glanced at her, saw the pleading behind her eyes and thought about what Emily had said. He should tell Jolie that it was all he wanted—for her to stay the entire summer, to get to know her better, to be what he hadn't been before—a father—but for some reason none of those words came out.

"I'll talk to your mom," he said, finishing the lemonade and extending the glass in her direction.

She reached her hand out to take the glass, her face a mix of sadness and worry. He wanted her to know he'd almost single-handedly brought the children's show back to the arts center. He wanted to tell her he'd done that for her so they could spend more time together. He wanted her to know he was sorry he'd been such a jerk, but explaining all the reasons behind his behavior meant telling Jolie a whole truth he wasn't ready to share.

So instead he chose silence, and he prayed it didn't break her heart.

Jolie turned to go inside, and Hollis picked up the sledgehammer again.

"Hey, JoJo?"

She turned back.

"I really hope she says yes."

His daughter watched him for several seconds; then her face softened ever so slightly. It wasn't a smile, but it wasn't a frown, and it was the first sign of a genuine connection he'd had with her since she arrived on the island. Maybe since long before that.

And he said a silent prayer it wouldn't be the last.

CHAPTER 23

EMILY AVOIDED HOLLIS THE REST OF THE DAY, which wasn't difficult because he'd placed himself out on the patio and had cleared almost the entire concrete slab by himself.

He'd smack the thing with the sledgehammer, break up enough to throw chunks of concrete into a wheelbarrow he must've brought from home, and then haul it off to the place where old concrete went. (A Dumpster? The back of a truck? A black hole somewhere?)

The trouble was, starting around 11 a.m., he did all of his work shirtless. Shirtless! How was she supposed to stay mad at him?

Emily had sworn off men. Too much trouble. Too much risk to the heart. But as she watched Hollis from the kitchen window, she felt her resolve crumbling.

Hollis might be moody and overprotective, but he was also a distractingly good-looking man. His torso and arms were toned the way an athlete's should be, and he'd spent enough time in the sun that his skin had darkened to the perfect shade of bronze.

"I think it's clean."

Emily jumped at the sound of a woman's voice behind her and slammed her hand down on the faucet to turn off the stream that had been running for far longer than it took to wash a glass.

Gladys gave a knowing glance through the window and into the backyard, taking in the view that had been so distracting to Emily that she hadn't heard the old woman enter the room at all.

Gladys stood behind her with a raised brow. Emily set the glass in the sink and grabbed a towel to dry her hands.

"Mrs. Middlebury, what are you doing here?"

"I came for your answer," Gladys said through thin lips.

"Already?"

"It's Monday."

It was, in fact, Monday. Through the window, she spotted Jolie running toward Hollis. The girl had gone home at some point and changed into her polka-dot bathing suit and was no doubt trying to convince her dad to call it a day.

"Miss Ackerman?"

Emily watched the exchange between Hollis and Jolie. The girl's face fell. She hugged her towel to her chest and walked back the way she'd come, clearly deflated.

Emily fought the urge to run out there and give Hollis a piece of her mind.

Are you really this dense? she'd say in her most demanding voice. *Any idiot can see that girl just wants your attention! Do you want her here or not?*

"I don't have all day." Gladys's clipped tone pulled Emily from her imaginary argument.

She inhaled a sharp breath.

JoJo had been so excited that morning when she thought Emily was directing this show. How could she say no?

Once upon a time, she *was* Jolie. Once upon a time, she'd been lost and lonely and wishing for the attention of a father who was as far away as Hollis probably felt from his daughter.

Don't do it, Emily. You're just setting yourself up for another failure. You're not a teacher. You're not a director. You don't even know if you like kids. You have a house to renovate.

She had a plethora of excuses not to do this.

And yet, there were plenty of reasons to jump in, too. Hollis and Jolie's relationship, for one thing. If Jolie was in the show, she'd stay on the island for at least an extra month. Clearly that was time they needed.

"Miss Ackerman?"

Hollis was right: she'd likely be in the way if she hung around the house all summer. What else was she going to do? Go to the beach and lie around?

Why would she do that when she had the option of doing something that mattered to someone?

Something that, once upon a time, had mattered to her.

The pros and cons teeter-tottered in her mind as her gaze settled on Hollis. He might not even know he needed extra time with his daughter, but it was clear to her. She owed him nothing. They weren't attached. Why did he matter so much to her already, after only a few days?

He's always mattered.

She pushed the thoughts aside and faced the old woman who'd ruefully invaded her kitchen. "I'll do it," she said quietly, before she lost her nerve.

"What was that?" Gladys studied her as if expecting Ackerman poise and confidence.

Emily had neither of those things. Not today.

She straightened. "I'll do it."

Gladys gave her one stern nod. "Very good. I'll send over the documents we need. Feel free to stop in to the theatre anytime. We'll have auditions at the end of the week."

Emily's heart sputtered. "The end of the week? That's too soon. I haven't even picked a show."

"I have every confidence in you, as does Mr. McGuire." She inclined her head toward the eating area, where Hollis now stood—skin glistening with sweat, shirt in his hand. "Isn't that right, Mr. McGuire?"

"What are we talking about?" He looked genuinely confused. And also sexy. He looked really sexy.

Get a grip, Emily! It's just a torso. A well-defined, probably rock-hard torso.

"The children's show is back," Gladys said. "I guess you got your way after all."

Emily stopped admiring Hollis's bare chest and frowned. What did she mean?

Gladys gave Hollis a pointed glare before walking out of the room. "See you this weekend, Miss Ackerman," she called as she left.

"What was that about?" Hollis asked, wiping his face with the T-shirt.

"You tell me."

He gave an innocent shrug.

"Did you talk to her about the children's show?" She crossed her arms.

Hollis tucked his T-shirt into his back pocket, answering her question with his silence.

She watched him for several seconds. "I didn't realize it mattered to you."

"It matters to Jolie," he said. "And to you."

"Me?" She laughed. "The program matters, but I didn't want to take it over."

He looked away.

"So you're the one who told her about my experience," Emily said, putting the pieces together. "About Broadway."

"I might've mentioned something."

"You might've?" She took a step toward him, wanting him to feel the full weight of her interrogation.

"I did." An endearing look of guilt made his face resemble a little boy's. It was almost enough to wash away the memory of their argument that morning.

Almost.

"I think you'll be really good at it," he said.

With that, the chip on her shoulder fell.

"You do?"

When Hollis looked at her, he really looked at her. She could see him studying her eyes, her face, all the things she wasn't saying. He nodded. "Don't you?"

She shrugged. "No, actually."

"Really?"

She wouldn't get into all the reasons why not.

"You used to love that place," he said.

"That was a long time ago."

He inched toward her, his movement so slight she almost didn't notice. And yet, with every one of her nerve endings tuned toward him, how could she not?

"Maybe I'm not the only one who got lost along the way?" He reached out and put a hand on her arm.

"I'm not lost." Why she bothered lying to him was a mystery. She could see he didn't buy it.

"You'll be great at this, Em," he said so genuinely she almost believed it.

"We'll see, I guess."

His smile said he had more to say.

"What?"

"They say people don't change, but you've changed. You're different. More cautious or something."

She looked away. He was right. After her giant failure, how could she not be?

"Jolie's going to be happy anyway," she said, desperate to change the subject.

"She'll be over the moon," he agreed.

The tightness between them loosened, though she wished he had a shirt on. It would be so much easier to have a conversation with him if he did.

She walked to the fridge and filled up a glass with ice and lemonade. "I don't get you, Hollis." She handed him the glass.

"What do you mean?" He took a drink.

"You and Jolie."

He sighed. "Maybe we shouldn't talk about this, Emily."

"You obviously did this for her."

"That was one of the reasons."

She didn't want to know the other reasons. Her heart was too tangled up as it was.

"Okay, but why don't you tell her?" she asked, begging her emotions to stay in the game here. "That girl idolizes you, and knowing something like this—it would go a long way."

"Look, I'm really sorry I snapped at you earlier, but Jolie and me—it's complicated. It's not the same as you and your dad."

"No, it's not. Because you're here, right in front of her, but you still seem a world away."

His jaw twitched as if he was chewing on words he wasn't sure he should say aloud.

"You act like this is easy," he said. "I'm making up for a lot of lost time here." Hollis pulled out a chair next to the table and sat. He tugged the shirt over his head—thank goodness. "And I don't . . ."

She walked out from around the island and stood next to the table. "You don't what?"

He shook his head. "It's stupid." He met her eyes, and that's when she saw it—a quiet desperation. "And I don't want to talk about it."

She sat down across from him. "Can I help?"

He folded his hands on the table, the muscle in his jaw twitching around thoughts he kept inside.

"Hollis—"

"I don't deserve a second chance with her." The words were so abrupt they had to be unplanned.

She stilled. "But you've got one."

"I know, but . . ."

"You have to at least try." What she wouldn't have given to know that her dad was trying with her—even if he failed miserably.

"I am trying." He rubbed his temples with both hands, then looked at her again. "Hard. But she hates me, and I don't know how to show her that I'm sorry. You know, I'm not like Hayes. People aren't so easy for me."

No, Hollis didn't need words to attract the people around him. It happened because of those piercing eyes, that smile, the way he could make you feel like you were the only person in the room.

"I think you're wrong," Emily said. "She doesn't hate you. She's just trying to make you work for her affection a little bit."

"No, she hates me. And she should. I screwed everything up." He shook his head. "I don't deserve her forgiveness. I mean, would you forgive me?"

The question caught her off guard.

"If it was your dad, come back after all these years, would you forgive him?"

"That's different," she said. But was it really? Even she had struggled with the similarities.

"How?"

"I'm an adult," she said. "I don't need a father anymore. She's just a kid, and she does."

He turned the glass of lemonade around in a circle. "I don't even know where to start. I don't know what to say to her or how to talk to her. She makes me feel stupid."

"She's a preteen girl. That's what they do." Emily spoke with authority she didn't have. She'd only ever been around a few children in her adult life, and never for long stretches. But she had been a teenage girl. That counted, right? "Tell me how I can help."

"I'm not like you either—I'm not a natural with kids."

She laughed. "A natural? Are you joking? Your daughter is the only kid I've ever liked. Well, with the exception of this boy I met on the ferry ride over here. I'm convinced he and I could be great pals if I ever saw him again."

His face softened, then grew serious. "What do I do?"

"I'm no expert on parenting," she said.

"No, but you have a dad who screwed up." He looked away, frustration obvious on his knit brow.

"I think you're overcomplicating this, Hollis," Emily finally said. "You don't have to have some deep conversation with her."

"I feel like I don't know her."

"Think of how you'd get to know someone new. You wouldn't dive right into their deepest, darkest secrets."

He tossed her a look that instantly lightened the mood. "That's ironic coming from you."

"Okay," she said. "Most people don't get to know other people like that."

His eyes narrowed. "Is deep diving for personal information how you always make new friends?"

No. Her motto was more "Keep everyone at arm's length and you won't get hurt." The less personal information shared, the easier it was to walk away.

"Emily?"

She forced a smile. "You're trying to take a page out of my playbook, aren't you? You're getting awfully pushy."

He shrugged. "Seems only fair for you to know how it feels once in a while."

"What was the question again?" She stood and walked across the kitchen, putting the island between them as if somehow that would protect her.

"Do you force everyone you meet to tell them something personal about themselves? Or is it just me you subject to that unique brand of torture?"

She smiled, though the weight of the moment hung heavy in the air between them. With anyone else, the second the conversation took a personal turn, she deflected. She knew this about herself—she wasn't completely self-unaware.

But with Hollis, she'd lost the desire to pretend. She'd lost the desire to entertain. She didn't want to play the role she'd been playing—she wanted to know everything about him.

And that scared her.

"Actually, no." She tried to sound casual.

"Really?" A cautious smile formed on his lips. "So it's only my secrets you need to know. Interesting."

She rolled her eyes. "I wouldn't read anything into it." She picked up the lemonade pitcher, turned, and opened the refrigerator, thankful for the brief moment to collect herself and for the cool air on her flushed face.

He could easily call her out as the fraud she was, and she'd be helpless to stop him.

Best change the subject.

"You should take Jolie to the beach," she said as she closed the fridge. "Take her paddleboarding or something. Don't worry about the talking. Talking is overrated. If you want her to know you love hanging out with her, then hang out with her."

After a few seconds of mulling the idea over, he said, "You sure you haven't worked with kids before?"

"I can relate to Jolie, I think. You asked what I would do if my dad asked for forgiveness, and the truth is, I don't know. But when I think of what I would've wanted most from him when I was a kid . . ." She studied the outdated popcorn ceiling and made a mental note to tell Jack it had to go. "It wasn't deep conversation, but it would've been nice to know he wanted to spend time with me." She picked up a dish towel and ran it over the counter.

Why did she feel suddenly vulnerable?

"He's the one who missed out, you know," Hollis said.

She felt her insides clench, and she searched her mind for a new topic. To brush it off. To pretend it didn't matter. "Yeah, yeah. I know."

"No, really, Em," he said. "I don't want to make the same mistakes your dad made."

She kept her eyes glued to the counter. "Then don't."

He put a hand over hers, stopped her from moving. "I'm trying."

She froze for several thick seconds, then slipped her hand out and walked over to the sink, not liking the way it felt to be under his microscope. Not liking the fact that she couldn't hide from him.

"Come to the beach with us," he said. "Jolie will love it."

"Thanks, but I'm going to get some work done. Gladys scheduled auditions for Friday."

He nodded, then pushed his glass back across the island. "Thanks for the lemonade."

She smiled. "Are you kidding? Thanks for fixing my patio."

"Oh, I'm not fixing it," he said solemnly. "I just tore it up—you're going to have to figure out how to put it back together."

She threw the dish towel at him, hitting him in the shoulder. "Funny."

"If you change your mind about the beach, the invitation is open."

But Emily wouldn't change her mind. She could feel her heart slipping even now. What she needed was not more time with Hollis. She couldn't let her guard down, not even with him. Especially not with him. The risk far outweighed any potential reward.

Like her mother said, in matters of the heart, caution first.

Caution always first.

CHAPTER 24

TUESDAY MORNING, GLADYS SHOWED EMILY to a small office in the back corner of the theatre's second floor.

"Forgive the mess," she said. "We haven't had anyone in this office in a while."

Emily scanned the room quietly, noting that it was perfectly fine for her needs. A small desk jutted out from one wall, a functional chair positioned behind it. She turned to her left and saw two tall, overflowing bookshelves.

"What's all this?" she asked.

"This shelf is all scripts," Gladys said. "And this one is all memory books from past shows. We had a mom who was really into scrap-booking years ago."

Laura Delancey's mom. Emily remembered. Laura often won the leading role in whatever show they were doing. Her last summer there, Emily had been cast as Fern to Laura's Charlotte in *Charlotte's Web*. After the accident, Emily had left Nantucket before the show date, and she'd always wondered what had happened to her role. Maybe these books would tell her.

"If you need to call out, press nine first. If you need to reach the front desk, press three."

Emily didn't anticipate calling anyone. Her plan had been to make a decision about what show they were doing, choose scenes for the kids to read at the audition, and do some dreaming about the set, the costumes, the details.

Now that she thought about it, it was a lofty plan. She'd be lucky to get the show chosen.

"Okay." Emily sat behind the desk. "I think I have everything I need."

"Very good," Gladys said with a quick nod. "I'm going out for a bit. Good luck." She closed the door behind her as she walked away, the clicking of her thick heels growing more and more faint as the woman left the building.

Emily had just gotten her things situated when there was a knock on the door.

"Come in," she called out.

The door opened and a young woman with dark hair poked her head in. "Look how official you are." She grinned.

"Don't be fooled," Emily said.

"I'm Marisol. I'm your intern–slash–assistant director–slash–professional coffee getter."

"I didn't realize I had one of those."

"I was already interning at the arts center, so Gladys reassigned me to you," Marisol said. "Truthfully, I don't think she knew what to do with me. I'm a theatre major at Boston University, but I'm a lot more interested in writing and directing than I was a few years ago when I thought I wanted to be a star."

Emily forced herself not to tell the girl that writing and directing was a lot harder than it seemed. Instead she smiled and said, "Well, I'm glad to have your help."

"I already started our social media campaign, but the sooner we can land on a show, the better." She handed Emily a stack of binders. "I pulled some scripts for you to consider."

"Thanks, Marisol," Emily said, truly grateful for the girl's thoughtfulness.

"Need anything else?"

"Not right now," Emily said.

"Okay. Everyone else is hard at work, so just holler if you need me. We already have twenty-five kids signed up."

Emily practically gasped. "Really? How? We don't even know what show we're doing."

"People don't care. They just want to be involved," Marisol said. "I've got Hillary organizing auditions." Then, quietly—"It'll keep her from talking your ear off."

Emily laughed. "Great, thank you. I'll let you know if there's anything else."

Marisol nodded and started for the door, but before she walked out, she turned back. "Hey, I'm really glad you're doing this. I think it's going to be so great for these kids. Especially the ones like me, who have trouble fitting in."

There were more years between now and high school for Emily than there were for Marisol, but she still remembered that feeling well. Transitioning away from private on-set tutors back to middle school, then high school had been difficult for Emily. Even harder to navigate without her mom.

For a while, she stayed away from theatre altogether, but in eighth grade, the English teacher asked her to audition for the school's production of *Once Upon a Mattress*.

She'd been cast as Winnifred, the lead, thereby reuniting her with her first love once again.

From then on, the stage became her safe haven. It gave her what she craved—a community, a family, that feeling of belonging.

It stung, knowing she'd lost that now, the one constant in her life. There was no coming back after her dismal failure. Her bad reviews. Her poor judgment. Her lack of talent. Her . . .

Stop, Emily.

"Also, I rewatched a ton of old *Dottie's World* episodes last night," Marisol said.

Emily's heart dropped. Did that mean Marisol had also looked her up online? And if so, did that mean her new intern–slash–assistant director–slash–coffee getter knew about her catastrophic attempt to step out of her lane?

"I just have to say, you rocked those gaucho pants." Marisol laughed.

If she knew about it, she wasn't saying anything. That made Emily love this girl a little.

"That'll be all, Marisol," Emily said in mock annoyance.

"And the butterfly clips all over your hair was quite the style."

Emily shot her a look and the girl ducked out of the office, the closed door doing a poor job of drowning out her laughter. She shook her head, giggling to herself over Marisol's teasing.

Once the office was quiet, Emily found it difficult to concentrate. She leafed through a number of scripts, but her eyes scanned the same pages over and over. She glanced at the bookshelf with the scrapbooks on it.

In eighteen years, she hadn't allowed herself to revisit that summer or those memories, and now here they were, staring her in the face. Not just the scrapbooks, but the house, Hollis, this theatre—all of it. She couldn't get away.

Oddly, she realized, part of her didn't want to run from it. Part of her wanted to remember.

Not the day her grandparents forced her to leave her cast in a lurch, ushering her off the island, heartbroken by the loss of her mother, but the rest of it. Finding her name on the cast list. Going to the first rehearsal. Trying on her costume for the first time. Making new friends.

Emily scanned the spines of the scrapbooks until she found the one for that summer eighteen years ago. She pulled it off the shelf and walked it back to the desk.

Slowly she opened the front cover to reveal the full cast photo and the logo for *Charlotte's Web*. She ran a finger over the smiling faces—so many friends she thought she'd know for the rest of her life, and now she could hardly remember any of their names.

She turned the page and found the header *Rehearsals*.

Page after page of fun rehearsal shots stared back at her. The image of her eleven-year-old self caught in character, frozen in time. Oh, the things she wished she could tell that girl now.

It's about to get really hard for you, little Emily, she'd say, *but hold tight. You'll get to the other side of it someday.*

But was that true? Had she gotten to the other side of it? Or was she still out there, floundering?

She'd found a way to put the past so far out of her mind, she rarely thought of Nantucket or the accident or the way her childhood was stolen from her. But here, in this theatre, looking at these photos—or standing anywhere near Hollis—it all felt so fresh.

It was as if she'd been transported back in time, and now she was stuck there with a broken time machine.

She turned the page, surprised to find a scrapbooked tribute to her mom. The obituary of Isabelle Ackerman had been neatly tacked down next to images of Emily in costume.

A short, handwritten explanation of what had happened had been added to the page.

Our very own Fern (Emily Ackerman) suffered a great tragedy when her mother's car was involved in an accident out on Cliff Road after midnight on July 31.

We were so thankful Emily's injuries were minor, but the loss of her mother led to the loss of our Fern, and with only two weeks until showtime, Jenna Martin stepped into the role.

There was a cutout from the program, a heart drawn around the words *This performance is dedicated to Emily Ackerman with all of our love and prayers.*

Emily stared at the words as a lump formed in her throat. She didn't know they'd dedicated the performance to her. She remembered the flowers they'd sent to the funeral—Emily had taken them home with her. But the rest of this, she'd never seen.

She reread the words Laura's mother had written about the accident. *Great tragedy . . . her mother's car . . . Cliff Road.*

Emily paused. That wasn't right. Her mother's accident had been in 'Sconset, not on Cliff. Laura's mom must've mixed up the neighborhoods. Emily turned the page and found an article that had been clipped from the newspaper,. The headline read *Local Woman Killed in Late-Night Crash*.

Emily's stomach twisted into a tight knot, but she forced herself to scan the words on the yellowing page.

The newspaper reported that Isabelle Ackerman, twenty-nine, and her daughter, Emily, eleven, were rushed to Nantucket Cottage Hospital, where Isabelle was pronounced dead on arrival and Emily was treated overnight and expected to make a full recovery.

Just like that, she was in the backseat of her mother's Buick, trying to get her mom to explain.

"Why are we leaving in the middle of the night?" Emily had asked.

Her mom was uncharacteristically worked up. "Are you buckled?" she'd barked over her shoulder.

"Yes, Mom. What's wrong?"

"I'll explain it all to you once we get there," she'd said.

"Get where?"

"Emily, please." Her mom squinted as the wipers were unable to keep up with the rain covering the windshield. "I can't see anything." She reached behind the seat and stretched a hand toward her daughter.

Emily hesitated.

"Em." Her mom tossed a glance back.

Emily reached up and took her hand.

"You and me, kid," her mom said.

Emily's eleven-year-old mind spun through scenarios of what could've gone wrong between her mom and her grandparents, but she couldn't think of anything that would cause her mom to flee the cottage in the middle of the night.

What happened next was still a blur. It was so dark, and the roads were so slick.

Later, in the hospital, she remembered one of the officers telling Grandma and GrandPop that Isabelle had tried to take a turn at too high a speed and slid into a large beech tree. She'd died instantly, the policeman said, as if that was supposed to comfort them.

The impact had thrown Emily sideways, and she hit her head on the window and was knocked unconscious. She remembered nothing after taking her mother's hand, only waking up in the hospital.

Emily closed her eyes. She hadn't let herself relive that moment in a very long time. For years after the accident, she'd have nightmares where she had to experience those moments over and over again. But she'd found a way to bury them and had been unwilling to dig them up, even for the sake of her craft.

Some memories were best left buried.

She opened her eyes and reread the words on the page.

The single-car crash, which happened just after midnight on Cliff Road near North Liberty Road, resulted in the death of Isabelle Ackerman, daughter of Alan and Eliza Ackerman.

Cliff Road.

Emily couldn't remember where they'd gone. She'd been too upset when they left. She'd been begging her mother to explain, not paying attention to street signs.

But her grandmother had told her the accident was on 'Sconset, at the opposite end of the island. Emily wasn't a mother, but even she knew that wasn't the kind of detail a mother forgets.

So why had Grandma lied about the location of the accident?

Emily ran a finger over the words: *Cliff Road*.

That same curiosity about the past that had led her to open the scrapbook in the first place was back.

"Where were you going that night, Mom?" she whispered. *And why so many secrets?*

The questions nagged, sparking more questions. How was she supposed to walk away from any of this now, without answers to any of them?

She picked up her phone, found her grandma's name in her contacts, and pressed Call.

Grandma answered on the first ring. "Well, finally."

"I know I haven't been around, Grandma. I'm sorry."

"How's the island?"

"It's good," she said.

"You're finding ways to keep busy?"

"Yes, there's plenty to do." She knew Grandma would want details, but she didn't want to share them yet. She didn't want Grandma to know she was directing a show at the arts center or that she'd reconnected with Hollis.

Or that she was having a really, really hard time here.

"Well, I hope you're not doing the work in the house yourself. There's plenty of money to hire it all out. Have you found some good help?"

"Yeah, I have, actually," Emily said. "Actually, Grandma, I have a question for you."

"All right."

Emily took a deep breath and almost chickened out. They didn't talk about the accident. Ever. It was as if the conversation had been marked "off-limits" years ago and everyone obeyed the silent order.

But didn't Emily have a right to know?

"I read an old newspaper article today," she said. "It was about Mom."

She was met with silence on the other end.

"I just wanted to double-check something."

"Emily, some things are better left in the past." Grandma sounded irritated.

"I know, Grandma, but can you just tell me where the accident happened?"

"Where?"

"Like, where on the island?"

Grandma sighed. "I suppose you were bound to ask questions, being back in Nantucket," she said. "She was on her way to 'Sconset. The accident was there."

"But why was she going to 'Sconset?"

"She had a friend who lived over there. Her name was Shae something-or-other. She was a few years older than your mother."

"But why so late at night?" Emily asked. "And why take me with her?"

"Your mother was always impulsive, Emily," she said. "You know this already."

"The article said the accident happened on Cliff Road," Emily said.

A pause went on for several seconds.

"Grandma?"

"That newspaper was notorious for getting details wrong," Grandma said. "They don't have the same quality journalists we have here in Boston. It must've been a mistake. I remember having a whole conversation with the police officer about this. Now, if there's nothing else, I should go. I'm hosting bridge club tonight."

"Right," Emily said.

"Thanks for the call, dear," Grandma said.

"Bye." She hung up the phone, filled with more questions now than she had been before and certain she did not have the whole story about her mother's accident.

And she wondered if she ever would.

CHAPTER 25

HOLLIS FOUND JOLIE sitting on the back deck, scrolling on her phone. She didn't look up when he opened the sliding-glass door or when he sat down in the chair next to her.

Tilly lazed at her feet. Both of them were utterly indifferent to his presence.

Emily was right—he'd been overthinking this. He'd imagined perfect conversations, the exact turn of phrase that would show his daughter he wasn't the jerk she thought he was, but maybe there was no such thing as perfect.

Communicating with Jolie had become more difficult than making contact with a slider, and Hollis knew it was his guilt and not his daughter that was getting in the way.

"Sorry about earlier," he said, breaking the silence.

Jolie didn't respond.

He replayed the moment she came racing toward him in Emily's backyard the day before.

"Dad, do you want to take me to the beach? I want to work on my tan."

"Can't right now, JoJo," he'd said curtly.

"But I'm not a good enough swimmer to go alone," she'd said.

He hadn't even stopped what he was doing long enough to give her the attention she deserved. Not even five minutes of his time. His foul mood had led to another short reply, which led to her walking away without another word.

He was taking out his irritation over his argument with Emily on Jolie, and that wasn't fair. But how did he explain that to her now? How did he explain that one of his oldest friends had walked back into his life and her main observation about him was that he was a bad father?

Emily had a way of saying exactly what she thought, which on normal days he appreciated, but not when her bluntness was directed at him.

But Jolie didn't need to know that.

Maybe he should try it Emily's way. He drew in a breath, aware that a rejection from Jolie would sting worse than any woman who'd ever turned him down. But she was worth the risk.

"Have you ever gone paddleboarding?"

She looked up. She claimed to be scared of the water, but he had a feeling she was a lot more daring than she let on. She shook her head.

He stood and held out a hand to her. She stared at it as if it were something foreign.

"Let's go."

"I'm not sure I want to," she said.

"Come on. I'll teach you."

Reluctantly she put her hand in his and he helped her stand up with a gentle tug. He turned toward the yard, realizing she hadn't immediately let go of his hand, and he imagined this was what it was really like to have a daughter.

When she was younger, Harper had looked at their father like he hung the moon. Hollis would never see that from Jolie.

But that wouldn't stop him from trying to hang it for her.

He retrieved the paddleboards and a life jacket from the shed out back.

The trek down to the beach was a quiet one, but this time, Hollis didn't feel the need to fill the silence. He decided instead to appreciate spending time with his daughter.

After a brief on-land lesson, he convinced Jolie to put the board in the water.

"Just sit on it to start with," he said.

"I don't think I'm going to be very good at this," she said. "What if I fall in?"

"You probably will fall in," Hollis said. "But you've got your life vest, and besides, I'll be here the whole time."

She squinted up at him, the light of the late-afternoon sun bright and full in her eyes. "Promise?" She clung to his gaze, the weight of the question heavy in the air.

"I promise, JoJo," he said quietly, hoping his words were more than empty to her.

She flicked her eyes away from his and stuck the board in the water, working her way onto it. The ocean was calm—thankfully—and she was able to sit without any problem. Hollis stayed close while she worked her way up, but before she stood, a gentle wave knocked her into the water.

Her life vest helped right her, but when she emerged from the water, Jolie was visibly shaken. Hollis reached over and pulled her by the arm back over to the board, draping her arm over it so she could steady herself.

"I told you I wasn't going to be good at this." Jolie pressed her fingers into her eyes, ridding them of salt water.

"It was a great first try," Hollis said.

"I don't want to do this anymore," she snapped.

Hollis wished someone else was there to tell him what to do next. He didn't want Jolie to hate him, so it was tempting to let her throw the board in the shed and go back to her phone. But that's not what he wanted her to learn.

"McGuires never quit," he said.

She glared at him. "I said I don't want to do it."

Hollis pulled himself up on his own paddleboard, straddling it as he turned to face her. "Just get up on it for a minute."

She rolled her eyes.

"Don't worry about standing," he said. "Just sit on it."

Jolie hung in the water for a few seconds before finally heaving herself up. She mirrored Hollis, straddling her board, paddle in hand. "Happy?"

"It's a great start. Maybe you just tried to stand a little too early."

"I'm never going to be able to do it," she said. "I don't know why we're even out here."

"Don't think about standing," he said. "Just enjoy the day. Even if this is all you do, it's progress. I mean, this morning, you couldn't sit on a paddleboard, and last week, you were scared of the water."

She steeled her jaw, a look of defiance crossing her face, but after several minutes, they found a rhythm. She paddled quietly beside him, seemingly content, almost as if she'd forgotten she wanted to stand on the board at all.

"Mom called again," Jolie said.

"And? Is she going to let you stay?"

She was focused on something in the water in front of them—avoiding his eyes. "Said she can't make such a big decision without talking to you."

"I left her a message telling her it was fine with me. Called her right after you told me she wanted to talk to me."

"She wants to make sure," Jolie said. "In case you're just saying it's fine so you don't hurt my feelings."

Hollis studied his daughter. "She said that?"

Jolie's eyes darted to his, then back to the ocean. Jana hadn't said that—Jolie was making her own assumptions.

"I'll call her again when we get back," he said.

"And say what?"

"And say I want you to stay," Hollis said.

Her jaw twitched. After a moment, she said, "Show me again how to stand up on this thing."

He did his best to hide his smile, but for the first time, he saw a little bit of himself in his daughter. She wasn't going to quit. Maybe there was some McGuire fire inside her after all.

He demonstrated again how to stand on the board, then tossed a glance in her direction. "Your turn."

"You make it look easy," she said with a sigh.

"I've been doing it for a lot of years."

Gingerly, she inched her legs behind her, pulling herself onto her knees. She steadied the board as it rocked beneath her.

"Don't rush it," Hollis said. "You're not in a hurry."

She rose up on her knees, waited until she had her balance, and started to stand.

"One foot at a time," Hollis said. "Nice and slow."

As Jolie started to stand, the board wobbled and she quickly went back to her knees to balance herself. And then he saw it—a thin line of fierce determination forming across her forehead.

"You've got this, kiddo," he said quietly, so as not to break her concentration.

After several more seconds, she tried again, this time slower, steadier. Hollis watched as his daughter moved her feet underneath her body until eventually she stood on top of the board. She held her arms out as if she were on a balance beam, rocking back and forth with the water until she captured her balance and stayed completely still.

It took a moment for her to realize it, but when she did, a wave of light came across her face. "I did it!"

"You did it."

She held herself stock-still as the water carried her forward; then she pushed the paddle into the water. The whole time, Hollis stayed right next to her.

Once Jolie got the hang of it, she didn't want to stop. She'd not only conquered a fear today, but she'd pushed herself to do something she didn't even think she could do.

And he'd been there to witness it.

The realization grabbed hold of him. He'd been there.

They stayed on the water for an hour, then made their way back to the shore when Jolie's stomach started growling and their skin started to burn.

On land again, they walked—once more in a comfortable silence—toward home, and Hollis thought about his conversation with Emily. He'd have to thank her for her advice. If it weren't for her words and her willingness to be honest with him, this day never would've happened.

If it weren't for her, he'd probably still be off pouting somewhere.

They found their bags right where they left them, and Hollis fished out his phone while Jolie did the same. She scrolled through text messages, while Hollis turned away, listening as the phone tried to connect him to Jana.

"What are you doing?" Jolie asked.

"Calling your mom," Hollis said.

Jolie looked surprised.

The call went to voice mail. It was probably pointless to leave another message, but he didn't hang up. "She's probably out doing honeymoon stuff," he whispered to Jolie over the sound of her mother's outgoing message.

"Jana, it's Hollis again. Jolie says you want to talk to me before deciding about letting her stay another few weeks—"

The phone beeped and he glanced down to see he had an incoming call from Jana. "Hey," he said once he clicked over. "Sorry if I'm interrupting anything."

He didn't want to think about what he might be interrupting. He'd seen Jana's new husband, and while the man looked nice enough, picturing buttoned-up, borderline-nerdy Rick and bombshell Jana together on their honeymoon was about the last image Hollis wanted in his mind.

"It's fine. We're just heading back down to the beach. Jolie said she wants to stay longer?" Jana sounded incredulous.

"Is that okay?"

"Hollis, what is going on? You can't tell me you really want her there another month."

He glanced at Jolie, whose eyes were intently watching him, then turned and walked a few steps away. "Why is that so hard to believe?"

Jana laughed. "You don't have to pretend, Hollis."

"I'm not pretending. I like having her here. I want her here."

"Let me guess, she's sitting right there and you want to make sure you sound like the good guy."

"I didn't realize there was a good guy in this scenario."

"If I say she can't stay, then I'm the bad guy."

"Then don't say she can't stay."

Another humorless laugh.

"Jana, please. I know I haven't been there for you guys the way I should've been, but she's my daughter."

"I'll think about it," she said. "I have to go."

"Auditions are Friday. Can you decide before then and let us know?"

"Good-bye, Hollis."

He clicked the phone off and waited a few seconds before turning around to see his daughter's sullen face.

"She's not going to let me stay."

"We don't know that."

"I do," Jolie said. "She wants Rick to adopt me."

Hollis's shoulders dropped. "What?"

"He wants to adopt me, and Mom thinks it's the best thing for everyone. She sent me here because she thought if you spent a few weeks with me, it would be easier for you to say yes."

"That can't be true."

"They think I go to sleep a lot earlier than I do," she said.

Hollis moved toward her. "Is that what you want?"

She shrugged without looking at him, plopping down on the sand.

"Well, it's not what I want." He knelt down next to her.

Her eyes, again, found his. "It's not?"

He shook his head. "Not even a little bit."

She sat, unmoving, phone on her lap.

"Let's not think the worst," he said. "I'll keep working on your mom, but in the meantime, I'm starving. Burgers?"

"Yum." She grinned at him, and his heart turned over in his chest. Jolie had smiled—at him.

And it was just about the best thing in the world.

CHAPTER 26

HOLLIS TEXTED EMILY late Tuesday evening.

Thanks for the advice with Jolie. You were right.

I'm always right, Mack, she'd texted back.

And so modest, too.

Are you going to tell me what happened with Jolie or do I have to guess?

Nah, I'd rather tell you in person.

OK. Don't make me wait too long.

Tomorrow. ☺

Sounds good. Good night, Miracle Man.

Night, Em.

Wednesday morning, Emily made a pot of coffee for Jack and his band of merry workers, tucked her laptop, a new notebook, and her phone into a sturdy backpack, and started out the back door toward the shed where the bikes were.

She'd just pulled her mom's bike out when she heard footsteps in the yard behind her. Emily turned to see Hollis, his slow, easy stride bringing him straight toward her. She tried not to stare, but he made looking good seem so easy.

He was clean shaven—something he hadn't been since she'd arrived on the island—and wore a heather-blue T-shirt that pulled across his chest and biceps. His tan seemed to have deepened, and his hazel eyes practically glowed.

"Morning." She smiled as he approached.

"Look at this," he said, shoving his phone at her. "I just got it this morning."

She took the phone and saw the text from Jana.

Fine. She can stay. But you better be taking good care of her.

"She can stay." A quiet excitement filled his voice, but she guessed nobody else in the world would've heard it, he was so subdued.

"She can stay?"

His mouth spread into a slow smile. "I didn't realize how nervous I was that Jana was going to say no until I saw her text come in."

Emily handed the phone back to him. "This is great news, Hollis. I'm so happy for you."

"I owe it to you," he said. "Doing this play—"

"Wait." She cut him off with an upheld hand. "Rule number one—we aren't doing a 'play'; we're doing a musical. It's important for you to understand the difference, especially if you've got a budding actress in your house."

"What's the difference?"

"A play doesn't have music. A musical does."

He grinned. "Doesn't seem too hard to remember."

"You'd be surprised how many people get it wrong." She started walking the bike toward the front of the house.

"Well, whatever it's called," he said, "thanks."

"Are you going to tell me what I was right about?" she asked, referring to the text message from last night. "I mean, what I was right about *this time*."

He bumped his shoulder into hers. "So cocky, this one."

She gave him a shrug in mock confidence. "What can I say? When you got it, you got it."

"Well, in this case, I do owe you. Yesterday was a total success." He smiled. "Took her paddleboarding. Didn't force the conversation. I felt like we really connected." Then he shifted. "She smiled at me, Em."

Slowly her opinion about his parenting changed. She saw in Hollis a man who was desperately trying, nothing like the man who'd abandoned her mom all those years ago as soon as he found out there was a baby coming.

"I told ya," she said, somewhat surprised her advice had merit given the current condition of her life and the lack of successful relationships she'd had over the years.

"She doesn't know yet," he said.

"About staying?"

Hollis nodded. "She was still asleep when I left the house. I'm going to head home and wake her. I just wanted to tell you first."

Something about that stirred Emily's insides. "I'm glad you did."

He glanced at the bike as if noticing it for the first time. "Are you leaving?"

She hitched a thumb over her shoulder. "Jack's already here, so I thought I'd ride into town. Get out of the way. Turns out set-building classes don't exactly prepare you for remodeling a house."

He laughed. It was a nice laugh and one she hadn't heard much since she'd been back.

"So where are you going?"

"To the arts center," she said. "Lots of work to do before auditions."

"So you'll be gone all day?"

"Why, you gonna miss me?"

His eyes sparkled with amusement, but the serious edge in his expression didn't change—and then it did.

"No, just making sure there's no danger of you colliding with the power tools."

She laughed. "Okay, I'll see you later. I'm glad things are going better with JoJo."

He smiled. "Yeah, me too."

She rode off down the driveway, willing away thoughts she didn't want to have. Emily Ackerman was a person without attachments, so how had Hollis and his entire family woven their way back around her heart in such a short time?

She pedaled toward the arts center, forcing herself to take in the beauty of the morning, and once she reached town, she had to ring the bell on the old bike twice to warn people she was coming up behind them.

Each time, the bell reminded her of her mother. Each time, she shook the image of her out of her mind.

She'd spent too much time thinking about her mother already. It hurt.

After all these years, it still hurt. A psychologist would probably say she hadn't properly dealt with her mother's death.

A psychologist would be right.

Emily pulled open the door to the arts center and instantly heard chatter—so much chatter that she wondered if they had an event going on this morning that she wasn't aware of. Could she slip by unnoticed and hide away in her office?

She walked through the lobby and followed the noisy conversation up the stairs with her eyes, realizing that she'd have to pass right through the crowd to get to the office Gladys had given her. Maybe she could find a classroom down the hall to work in—

"Emily?"

She glanced up and found Nan McGuire standing at the center of a large group of women of varying ages.

"Nan?"

Hollis's mother hurried down the stairs, meeting her in the lobby.

"You caught us." Nan tossed a glance upstairs, where the group of women was still visible thanks to the open atrium above where they stood.

"What are you all doing here? Is there some sort of event today?" Emily asked.

"Of course not, silly," Nan said. "We're here for you."

"I don't understand," Emily said.

"Is this her?" Another woman, about the same age as Nan, rushed down the stairs. Well, she more waddled than rushed.

"Emily, this is Pearl Whitmeyer," Nan said. "She's an expert seamstress."

Pearl brightened at the compliment. "I haven't used my sewing machine in a lot of years, but once I start, I know it'll all come back to me."

"And up there is Cheryl Davidson, our marketing expert; Elise Santana, who will handle all your props; and I hear you already met Marisol Duncan—she'll be your right-hand man."

By now, the other women had come downstairs, and each gave Emily a slight wave as Nan introduced them.

"We thought you might need some help, so we assembled a few key people." Nan beamed.

"*We* didn't think anything," Cheryl said. "This was all Nan—and we were happy to pitch in. We think it's wonderful what you're doing for our kids."

"These are just a few volunteers," Nan said. "Once you get your cast put together, we have a plan for mobilizing the parents."

Just like the old days.

Before she knew it, the women had formed a circle around her and the circle started moving, pulling her along like a fish at the center of a school. They were walking through the hallway beside the theatre and back toward the classrooms.

"It's positively wonderful that you decided to stop by," Nan was saying as they all found spots around a table. "I heard you were in yesterday working. Your enthusiasm is contagious."

"Have you picked a show yet, Emily?" Marisol sat right next to her.

"Marisol is the perfect person to assist you, Emily," Nan said. "She's studying theatre in Boston."

"She told me," Emily said. "I'm glad to have her."

"Are you kidding? This will look so good on my résumé," Marisol said. "I watched more *Dottie's World* last night. It was, like, a really big deal back in the day, wasn't it?"

Emily forced a smile. "It was, I guess."

"It's so cool that I actually know Dottie now."

"Really?" Emily felt old.

"Really." Marisol grinned. "I loved the episode where your back-yard turns into outer space and you take the kids on an adventure around the sun. I especially liked how there was a cow in red boots floating around out there."

"The cow who jumped over the moon," Emily said, remembering. "And then apparently spent the rest of her days weightless in outer space."

It felt like a lifetime ago, working in television. A million dreams ago.

"So have you picked a show?" Cheryl repeated. "I can get working on updating the arts center's website and making flyers to take around town, hang in local businesses, drum up excitement for the auditions, and Marisol's already working double time on the social media."

Before she could answer, an inexplicable lump formed at the back of Emily's throat and her eyes clouded over.

She managed to choke out a stifled "Excuse me" as she got up from the table and darted out of the room.

What was wrong with her? She found a restroom and quickly escaped inside and splashed water on her face.

"Get it together, Emily," she said to her reflection.

The door to the bathroom opened and Nan stood there, Hollis-style concern on her face. "You okay?"

She pinched the bridge of her nose. "I'm fine."

"You sure? I didn't mean to upset you by bringing everyone in."

"No," Emily said. "It's not that."

But it was that. It was exactly that. But not for the reasons Nan was thinking. Emily wasn't upset by the fact that these women were here to help—she was moved by it.

Why were they so willing to help her? It was as if they were personally invested in her success, and she didn't want to let any of them down.

What if I fail?

Nan quieted at her side. "It must be hard to be back here after all these years."

And then there was that. Being here. Digging up the past with a trowel when what she needed was an excavator.

She looked away. "A little."

Like her son, Nan seemed to have a sixth sense that made lying to her impossible.

"It's just been a really long time since I had people . . ." She could end the sentence there, but it wasn't the end, was it? *Since I had people who cared about me like this* were the words she decided not to say.

Nan reached over and took Emily's hand. "You have lots of people now, hon."

That stupid lump was back, and Emily wondered if she could swallow it whole.

"God's doing a good job of taking care of you."

Emily didn't bother disagreeing. She didn't want Nan to know how cynical she'd become where God was concerned.

"Now we've got work to do." Nan clapped a hand on her back. "Are you up for this?"

She nodded. "Yes."

"Sure?"

She smiled at Nan. "I'm sure."

Nan squeezed Emily's arm. "Well, if you get overwhelmed, we're all here. You just tell us what you need."

She followed Nan out of the bathroom, bolstering her own resolve with every step. *Okay, Ackerman, you've got a job to do, and these women need a leader.*

The fact that *she* was that leader was still a bit worrisome, but she was determined to make a go of this, if for no other reason than Jolie deserved it.

As they reentered the classroom, the chatter subsided, curious eyes trained on Emily.

"I'm so glad you're all here," Emily said. "I knew I wasn't the only one who wanted to see the children's show return."

"We've just been waiting for the right person," Pearl said.

They were all in front of her, this small army of worker bees, looking at her with kind anticipation, and they were genuinely excited about this project. She hadn't had that for her failed play.

Maybe things would be different this time?

"Okay, ladies." Emily clapped her hands together. "How do you feel about *Alice in Wonderland*?"

~

Emily left the arts center feeling ready and excited for auditions the following day.

Their production of *Alice in Wonderland Jr.* would be a musical adventure with vibrant, colorful costumes and sets, and as long as the kids came out for it, they were ready. Marisol had turned out to be a godsend—not only did she understand theatre; she knew almost everyone on the island. She and the other women Nan had assembled were finding ways to supply everything they needed.

Take that, Gladys. Emily tried not to be smug about their success— they had a long way to go. But knowing they'd already accomplished exactly what Gladys said they couldn't—namely garnering interest from the families—made it difficult.

Those weren't the only goals she had that Gladys found too lofty. She'd been walking through the lobby that afternoon when Emily was explaining her vision to her team.

"I know it may seem ambitious," she'd said, "but I really believe kids will live up to our expectations, so I want to set them high. I want to push them. So when people leave the performance, they cannot believe what they just saw was a *kids' show*."

Gladys had audibly scoffed, drawing everyone's attention away from Emily and onto the old woman.

Gladys waved as if to say, *Don't mind me* but said nothing else as she walked upstairs.

"Well, I think it's a great idea, Emily," Marisol said once Gladys was gone.

"Me too," Pearl agreed.

"You're right," Nan said. "These kids are going to surprise everyone. I just know it."

In a very short time, this show had become important—really important—to Emily. She knew it couldn't erase her past failures, but it was nice to have something to focus on other than that. Other than herself.

Dear Emily,

I've always grown up believing passion was a good thing. "Follow your passion" is the kind of thing I'd like to have cross-stitched on a pillow. If I liked cross-stitched pillows, that is.

I'm all for that. I believe in finding what you're passionate about and pursuing it with everything you've got. Even though you're still young, I see a lot of passion in you. For animals and people and creativity. You've got the same kind of spirit I do, and I love that about you.

But I'll caution you with this . . . Follow your passion, follow your heart, but keep your head in the game too. Take your common sense along with you. Don't let yourself get so wrapped up in passion that you forget you've got a big, beautiful brain in that beautiful head of yours!

Love,
Mom

CHAPTER 27

HOLLIS STOOD OUTSIDE the closed door to the audition room, pacing.

His mom left her spot at the check-in table and walked over to him. "Honey, I think you're making the children nervous."

Hollis glanced at the line of children seated in a row outside the room. They watched him with wide eyes. One little girl looked like she was seconds from bursting into tears.

He heard Jolie's music start inside the room. "I'm so nervous for her."

"She's fine," his mom said. "She's been practicing all week for this."

Didn't he know it. Jolie had decided to accompany herself on the ukulele (he didn't even know she could play a ukulele) in a modern version of "Somewhere over the Rainbow." To date, Hollis was pretty sure he'd heard the song 642 times. He thought she was amazing, had the kind of voice people would like to listen to, but he was her dad. And didn't all dads think their kids were special and talented?

"Come back out to the lobby," his mom said.

He listened for one more second, then followed his mom to the end of the hallway.

"Goodness, Hollis, you're more nervous than she was."

"I know," he said. "I'm more nervous than my first game in the majors."

One of the moms in the waiting area laughed. "Kids'll do that to you."

"Isn't that the truth?" another mom piped up. "I'm always more nervous for things to go well for my kids than for myself."

"Welcome to parenthood," Nan said. "It never goes away. You remember how anxious I always got on your game days, don't you, Hollis?"

He did, in fact. His mother had been his biggest fan. He wondered if there was any truth to what his dad had said—had she really not loved the game? She cheered like she loved it.

Mom smiled and took her seat behind the front table just as the door at the end of the hallway opened and JoJo walked out.

Hollis froze, surveying her expression. At first, she appeared stone-faced, but after she closed the door, her whole face lit up in a bright smile.

She coolly walked down the hallway, straight to Hollis, and whispered, "I think they liked it."

"Are you kidding? I bet they loved it."

She shushed him, tossing a glance at the rest of the auditioners over her shoulder. "Be cool."

"Right." Hollis affected a phony nonchalance. Inside, he was cheering. He was so proud of Jolie for going in there like a pro and singing her guts out. He certainly wouldn't have had the courage to do that.

The door opened again and a dark-haired girl called out the name of the next auditioner. "Marta?"

Marta, it turned out, was the one with the teary eyes, and as soon as her name was called, Marta dissolved into a puddle of tears.

The girl standing at the door glanced at someone inside the room and slid her finger down her cheek to communicate they had tears. Was there protocol for this?

Jolie took a step toward the crying girl, and Hollis nearly melted. His daughter wanted to help this younger child, and knowing that made him love her even more.

But before anyone could reach Marta, Emily appeared in the doorway. She wore a pair of jeans, heeled sandals, a loose turquoise shirt, and a formfitting black blazer with rolled-up sleeves. Her hair was long and wavy, her lips a shade darker than their normal color.

She looked like a knockout.

Emily knelt down in front of the girl and smiled, placing her hands on Marta's.

From where he stood, he couldn't hear what Emily was saying, but he could see Marta nod once, then twice, then one last time, before standing. Emily took Marta's hand and led her into the room.

Before she closed the door behind them, Emily met Hollis's eyes for the briefest moment and smiled.

And for the second time in a span of just a couple minutes, Hollis turned to mush.

It was a side of Emily he'd never seen, and it proved what he'd been thinking all along—there was a lot more of her to discover.

"That was sweet," his mom said over his shoulder. "Emily sure is good with these kids. That's the second one she's talked off the ledge. And earlier she found a way to make that Harris boy behave."

"She told me I had a unique sound," Jolie said.

"Is that good?" Hollis asked, pulling himself out of his Emily-induced trance.

"Sounded like a compliment," Jolie said with a shrug.

"Of course it was a compliment." Nan shuffled through a stack of audition forms. "Who wants to listen to someone who sounds like everyone else?"

They waited through a few more auditions, and Hollis caught another glimpse or two of Emily before he finally felt ready to go.

Jolie beamed. "So . . . ice cream?"

He'd promised her a trip to the Juice Bar, thankful she'd decided not to quit dairy after all. Even though he could've stood there for hours just waiting for another glimpse of Emily, he wasn't about to break his promise to Jolie. "Let's do it."

They waited in line for longer than was humanly decent for a waffle cone, but the second Jolie took her first bite of homemade peppermint stick and he saw her eyes bug out of her head, he knew it was worth it.

Besides, she hadn't stopped talking since they left the arts center. It was as if his daughter had finally come alive, and Hollis knew Emily was at least partially responsible.

If Emily hadn't agreed to do this show, hadn't pushed for it, his time with Jolie would be nearly over. Instead he had the rest of the summer to look forward to.

"What if I don't make it into the show?" Jolie suddenly asked, panic-stricken.

"Don't be ridiculous," Hollis said lightly. "Of course you'll make it."

But his stomach dropped. He hadn't even considered that all the kids might not be cast.

"Why don't we talk about something else?" Hollis said. "Tomorrow you'll know your fate as an actress, but tonight, you've got peppermint stick and your old man."

Jolie took another bite of ice cream. They were walking along the cobblestone streets toward the spot where Hollis had wedged his Wrangler in between two tightly packed cars.

"I don't know what else to talk about," Jolie said. "The show is all I'm thinking about. All the girls in my group said they wanted to be Alice."

"Sure," Hollis said. "Everyone wants to be the lead."

"Not me," she said. "I kind of think it'd be fun to be the Cheshire Cat. Or maybe the Caterpillar."

The caterpillar who was strung out on acid? That sounded like a fun part for his twelve-year-old daughter to play. He laughed silently at his internal dialogue, wishing Emily were here to enjoy his wittiness.

"What's so funny?"

"Huh?"

"You laughed," Jolie said. "You think it's dumb for me to want those parts?"

"What?" Hollis floundered. Hadn't he laughed *silently*? "No, of course not. Honestly I was thinking about Emily."

"Da-ad." Jolie stopped walking.

"Relax," Hollis said. "I thought of something that would've made her laugh, that's all. I think it's awesome you don't want to be the lead."

"Emily told me once that the other parts are sometimes more fun to play. More interesting."

"Is that right?"

"That's what she said. And that was a long time ago, before she even knew she was doing the show, so it wasn't like she was trying to make sure I didn't get my hopes up or anything."

A long time ago. Hollis smiled.

"What?"

He shook his head. "Nothing."

"Why are you smiling?"

"I just think you're really cool."

Her cheeks flushed pink, and even though her face was partially blocked by her ice cream cone, he could tell she was smiling.

∼

In all, Emily and her team sat through eighty-five auditions. Eighty-five kids wanted to be a part of their show, and she was going to find a way to cast every single one of them.

Gladys had said the program had closed due to lack of interest. Again, Emily withheld a satisfied smile at the thought. *Guess we showed you, Gladys.*

Near the end of the last group, a girl about twelve years old had walked in and handed Emily her audition form. As Emily looked it over, her eyes fell to the parents' names, Douglas and Shae Daniels.

Shae.

Not a common name. Was it possible this was the same Shae her mother had been going to see the night she died?

Emily listened as the girl sang a lively rendition of "You're Welcome" from *Moana*, and she instantly thought she'd make a perfect Caterpillar. That role would sing an upbeat version of "Zip-a-Dee-Doo-Dah," and she needed a kid with lots of energy. Shae Daniels's daughter had that in spades.

"Great job, Alyssa," Emily said when the girl finished singing.

"Thanks." Alyssa grinned. "I'm super glad you're doing this. My brothers play baseball, and I need something to do besides sit at the ballpark all summer."

Emily laughed. "Is your mom here with you?"

Alyssa nodded. "She's in the lobby."

"Mind if I meet her quick?"

"Am I in trouble?" Alyssa's eyes went wide.

"Oh no, nothing like that." She stood and followed Alyssa past the last few auditioners and into the lobby, where a tall, dark-headed woman sat reading a novel.

"Mom, I'm done!" Alyssa called out as soon as they rounded the corner.

The woman looked up with a smile. "Great, honey. How'd it go?"

"She did very well," Emily said.

Shae Daniels's eyes landed on Emily. "So glad to hear it."

"Mrs. Daniels," Emily said, "I have a sort of strange question, but did you know my mother—Isabelle Ackerman?"

Shae's eyes darted over to Nan, who was sitting within earshot at the check-in table next to Hillary. "I did, Emily," she said. "Once upon a time, we were very good friends."

Emily felt her breath go shaky. "The night she died—did you talk to her at all? Was she on the way to see you?"

Shae took Emily's hands. "I wish she had been, but no. We'd lost touch a few years before. We'd run into each other occasionally, at the grocery store or down at the beach, but we hadn't been close in some time."

Emily hesitated. "So she wasn't on her way to your house that night?"

Shae shook her head. "No, I lived in the opposite direction in those days. In—"

"'Sconset," Emily cut in.

"Right. And the accident was out on Cliff Road."

Emily's heart dropped. Cliff Road. Just like the article said. The opposite of what her grandma had told her.

"Do you know who she might've been going to see that night?"

"I'm so sorry, Emily, but I don't." She squeezed Emily's hands. "Your mother was a wonderful person. I wish we'd made things right before she passed away. It's one of my greatest regrets."

"Thank you for saying so," Emily said. "Maybe one day you can tell me stories about when you guys were friends. I'd love to know more."

Shae smiled warmly. "I'd be happy to."

CHAPTER 28

~~~

THE NEXT DAY, Jolie sat on the sofa like a hawk on a telephone pole, watching, waiting . . . stalking.

"Jolie, come eat something," Nan said. "You're going to go crazy if you keep staring at your phone."

"GrandNan, I can't eat at a time like this," Jolie said. "What if I didn't make it?"

"Oh, I'm sure you made it," Hollis's dad said. "Emily wouldn't cut you from the show."

"Grandpa." Jolie glared at him. "I don't want to make it because Emily is Dad's friend. I want to make it because I'm *good*."

Hollis stood in the kitchen leaning against the counter, holding a nearly empty mug of coffee.

"Worrying about it isn't going to do anything but ruin your day," his mom said. She looked at Hollis, then motioned toward Jolie with her head, as if he should be the one to comfort her in the midst of her worries.

"When are they going to send the list?" Jolie whined. "It's been literally *hours*."

"They'll send it when it's ready," Hollis said. "Let's try to get your mind off it for a while. We could paddleboard now?"

She shook her head. "I can't do anything until I know my fate."

Mom smiled. "She certainly does have a flair for the dramatic."

Just then, Jolie gasped. "It's here."

Mom set a plate of pancakes on the table and Dad glanced up from the newspaper.

"Well, what are you waiting for?" Hollis asked.

"I'm scared to open it," Jolie said.

"JoJo, you've been waiting literally *hours* for this list. Open it." Hollis set his mug down and walked into the living room, where his daughter held the phone as if it were a ticking bomb.

"Will you look at it?" She extended the phone in his direction.

Hollis stared at the phone, her in-box open on the screen. She wanted him to look for her? The expression on her face squeezed his heart. "Sure."

He sat down next to her and opened the e-mail. "'Dear Brave Auditioners,'" he read.

"Skip that part," Jolie said. "Just find the link to the cast list." She sat cross-legged on the couch, eyes tightly shut, hands folded in front of her as if she were praying. Her lips moved quickly, a slight whisper escaping.

Maybe she *was* praying.

Hollis scrolled down until he found a link that said *Cast List*, clicked on it, and waited for the page to open.

"Well . . . ?"

"It's loading."

"That's what we get when we don't have any Wi-Fi. I have to use data and . . . oh, why is it taking so long?"

The page loaded the words *Congratulations to the Cast of* Alice in Wonderland. He scrolled until he found her name. He looked up at her.

"Jolie?"

"Is it bad? It's okay if it is. As long as I'm in it, I'll be okay. I'm in it, right?"

"It says you're the Queen of Hearts."

"I'm the *Queen of Hearts*?" Jolie snatched the phone out of Hollis's hand and looked at the list as if she couldn't believe it until she read her name for herself. "I'm the Queen of Hearts!"

She ran over and hugged Nan, who said, "Congratulations, JoJo! You must've done very well to get that part!"

Jolie then raced over and kissed Hollis's dad on the cheek and said, "I'm the Queen of Hearts, Grandpa!"

"Is that good?" Hollis's father winked. "Congrats, JoJo!"

Hollis stood, expecting her to run his way next, but instead, she clutched her phone to her chest and closed her eyes. "I've gotta call Mom! She's going to freak!"

She dashed out of the room, leaving him standing there, dumbly.

He glanced at his mom, whose expression told him she'd noticed the way Jolie had passed him over.

"She's just excited," Nan said.

"Yeah, for sure." Hollis waved her off with a forced smile, a fake smile, which he was sure his mom saw right through. "I'm going to head out. I want to get some more work done on Emily's patio."

"Hollis . . ."

But he didn't wait for whatever his mom would say in an attempt to make him feel better. He closed the sliding door behind him and started off toward Emily's house.

He needed a distraction.

Emily's backyard was happy to oblige. Thankfully, Jack's crew seemed focused on the interior of the house, leaving Hollis alone with his thoughts—and his frustrations. He worked nonstop for at least an hour, taking out every last bit of frustration on the dense soil in what had once been the Ackermans' prized rose garden.

He'd overheard Emily mention she wanted to bring it back. If he couldn't get this parenting thing right, maybe he could at least do this one thing for the girl next door.

"You're back."

Hollis squinted up at Emily, who would be blocking the sun if she'd move about a step to her right.

"Yeah, I wanted to get here early because I'm taking Jolie paddle-boarding again just after lunch."

She smiled, and he felt something take hold of him. Something he hadn't felt in a long time.

"You know you don't have to work on my house," Emily said. "I hired a guy."

He stood. "Yeah, I know."

"So why are you here?"

"I came here to tell you thanks," he said.

She grinned. "Jolie?"

He nodded. "She was beside herself when she found out."

"I'm so glad."

Hollis smiled. "You made her whole summer. And mine."

"She texted me a little bit ago," Emily said. "All caps and lots of exclamation points."

Hollis made himself smile, though it reminded him that Jolie hadn't celebrated with him at all. "So what are you going to make me build you?"

"Oh, I've got big plans." She waggled her eyebrows. "We're going to have so much fun."

"I figured."

"Now, why are you really here?" She stuck her hands on her hips and stared him down.

He shrugged. "Making sure everything's okay. Don't like the idea of a bunch of strange guys having access to your house all day."

"Oh, you're being ultra-overprotective, then."

Man, he liked her. She was more than beautiful. She was smart and determined and broken and she had no idea how incredible and rare she was. She lived on purpose—like she used every color in the crayon box. The big box, too, with the built-in sharpener.

"Earth to the Miracle Man." She waved a hand in front of his face.

"Sorry," he said. "Yes, ultra-overprotective. And you can't do anything about it."

She shook her head, and he noticed she had a bag slung over her shoulder.

"You headed to the theatre?" he asked.

She nodded. "I'm nervous."

"About what?"

"Everything," she said.

"That doesn't sound like you."

She shrugged. "Surprise. I'm not as sure of myself as you think."

The words sounded unplanned, and her nervous laugh was a poor cover-up.

"You're going to do amazingly well, Emily," he said. "I'm telling you, you're a natural."

"I'm going to go ahead and pretend I agree." She moved her tote bag from one shoulder to the other. "Fake it till you make it, right?"

"Right." Only he didn't want to fake anything with Emily. He wanted to tell her everything he'd been thinking lately, about Jolie, about baseball, about her.

Mostly about her.

"Don't work too hard," she called over her shoulder.

She walked toward the shed, where her bike was stored. He watched. For several seconds, he watched. She must've sensed it because she turned around and smirked at him. "Slacker!"

He lifted a sweaty arm, waving to let her know he'd taken her point, and forced himself to get back to work.

But that didn't stop him from watching her get on that bike and pedal off in the opposite direction.

He spent most of the morning weeding overgrown flower beds, and by noon, he was ready for a break. He thought back to the way Jolie's eyes had lit like Christmas lights when he asked her yesterday if she wanted to go to the beach later. Had it only been a couple of days ago that his daughter had been a walking riddle he was sure he'd never solve?

Not that he had her all figured out. After all, she was wearing what could only be described as "mom jean shorts," pleated with a high waist that made her backside look a mile long.

Harper had told her how adorable she looked, so Hollis stayed quiet, but the style made no sense to him. He was choosing his battles, and jeans weren't something to argue over. Even if she did look like his mother circa 1981.

He passed through Emily's kitchen and into the living room, which had been emptied of its furniture and was being prepped to have floors sanded and refinished, but he saw no sign of Jack.

Winston "Winny" Peel, one of the workers Jack had hired, walked into the room from the opposite direction.

"Have you seen Jack?" Hollis asked.

"Not lately," Winny said. "Think he was going to do some work upstairs today."

As far as Hollis knew, Jack hadn't assigned anyone else to work upstairs, which was strange because with a couple other guys, they could knock out the bedrooms pretty quickly.

"Did you see this?" Winny stood in front of the fireplace, staring at what appeared to be a collection of keys on the mantel.

"See what?"

Hollis followed Winny's eyes to the keys, but he didn't see the significance.

"What are they?"

"She collects a key from every place she lives," Winny said. "She's been everywhere."

Hollis picked up one of the keys. On the back of it, someone had written the word *Brazil*. "Each key is a different place?"

Winny nodded. "Lots of different countries too. Australia. Spain. Austria. France. Kenya. Costa Rica. Canada. Your girl has seen the world."

Your girl.

He wished.

He picked up another key and studied it. It had been painted turquoise with red polka dots and she'd written *Thailand* on it in white paint.

He wished he'd seen half of these places with her. From the looks of it, she'd traveled all over, like a vagabond—all wings and no roots. It was odd. He'd never thought of Emily as sentimental. If he had to guess, she didn't see herself that way either, but obviously there was some part of her that was looking for something to hold on to. Otherwise, why would she keep these keys as mementos?

Once the house sold, would its key become just another one in her collection? Would she remember it as just another place she'd visited?

"She's pretty amazing," Winny said. "She was telling some of us about this one time she was surfing off the Maldives and the surf turned her upside down. Said she got cracked on the head by her board and went unconscious. She still doesn't know what righted her or how she didn't die. I told her it was probably the Big Guy looking out for her. She didn't like that idea so much."

"Well, you're probably right, Winny," Hollis said, trying not to think about Emily nearly drowning off the coast of some tiny island in the Indian Ocean.

"You gonna make a move on her or what?"

Hollis waved him off. "She's an old friend, Win."

"You can't be friends with a woman like that."

"That right?"

"But if you can get her to fall in love with you . . ." He whistled. "That's a recipe for a happy life." Winston laughed then, a big laugh that crackled and turned into a cough thanks to too many years of smoking cigarettes.

"I'll keep that in mind." Hollis walked out of the living room and into the entryway. On the front table, he spotted the same book that had been on Emily's lap the day he'd found her sleeping on the patio.

This is none of your business.

He thought these words at the very same moment he picked up the book and read the painted words on the front cover.

If for Any Reason

He should put it away. Here he was, worried about Jack's crew having too much access to Emily's privacy, but so far, he was the only one invading it.

This didn't stop him from opening the cover and scanning the first page.

A letter written to Emily in penmanship that could only belong to a woman. His eyes drifted to the bottom of the page, where the words *Love, Mom* were written. Hollis closed the book.

Her mom had written her letters?

He carefully put the book back on the table and walked upstairs. The first room was empty, so he moved down the hall to the next bedroom, where he found Jack, sitting at a desk in the corner, staring at something in his hand. The man didn't stir when Hollis entered the room. It was as if he was in another world.

"Hey," Hollis said.

The look on Jack's face said, *Caught*, and Hollis took a step closer, a poor attempt to make sense of the scene in front of him. As he did, Jack tucked whatever he was holding into his shirt pocket.

"Sorry, Hollis. Going over some figures." He turned away, rubbed his hands over his face and eyes.

"Some figures?" It was an odd place to crunch numbers.

"Uh, yeah, for the remodel."

"Do you have bad news?"

"No, no, not at all. I just get caught up in it sometimes." Jack stood. "How are things going outside? Looked like you were making a lot of progress."

"Yeah, it's fine," Hollis said. "I came up to tell you I'm going to take a few hours off this afternoon to take Jolie to the beach."

"Good," Jack said. "That's a great idea. Spend as much time with your daughter as you can."

Hollis stood in silence, sizing up the man Emily had hired to remodel her house—a man they knew nothing about. A man who was spending hours alone and unchecked in Emily's house.

"What are you working on in here?" Hollis asked. "Emily mentioned the bedrooms were in pretty good shape."

"Oh, they are," Jack said. "I came up here to make a quick phone call and got sidetracked by the figures."

"Maybe I could take a look at them. Do we need to cut down somewhere, make more room in the budget?"

Jack stuck his hands on his hips and affixed a nonchalant expression on his face. "No, it's nothing to worry about. Have a great time at the beach."

Jack left, leaving Hollis alone in the quiet of a bedroom that had once belonged to the most important person in Emily's life.

He walked to the desk and gave it a once-over.

Nothing looked particularly out of place, except for two photographs that seemed to have been pulled off the bulletin board and laid on the desk.

Hollis picked them up. In one, Isabelle held a baby Emily in front of a Christmas tree and in the other, Isabelle and Emily stood side by side on the beach behind the cottage.

Their beach.

Hollis could see two empty spots where the photos had been on the bulletin board. Why would Jack have them out? And what had he stuck in his pocket?

Hollis didn't have a good feeling about this guy.

What if Emily was in danger?

"Dad, where have you been?" Jolie's voice spun him around. "I've been waiting for you."

"Sorry, JoJo. I got distracted."

"Whoa, is this Emily's mom's room?" Jolie walked over to the bulletin board and looked carefully at each photo pinned to it, which gave Hollis a chance to do the same. There was Emily, just as he remembered her, grinning back at him.

"Is this you?" Jolie pulled a photo off the board and showed it to Hollis.

There, captured in grainy, faded color, was an image of him, Emily, and Hayes sitting on the dock, toes touching the water. Their arms were draped around each other, Hayes was missing a few teeth, and Hollis looked, as he generally did in adolescent photos, awkward. Emily was radiant, as she often was in real life. It was like there was a light inside her that glowed a little brighter than everyone else's.

She commanded a room. She turned heads. She made people happy to be alive.

And yet, thinking about her now, he knew something had happened to dim that light. Oh, she still played the part beautifully, but Emily—his Emily—was more cautious, more withdrawn. Unhappy, maybe?

Did she have anyone to talk to? Was he the only person in her life who could sense her discontent?

"Is it?" Jolie nudged him with her shoulder. For a moment, he'd forgotten she'd asked a question.

"Yeah, me and Uncle Hayes," he said.

"You guys were so young."

"About your age, I think."

"Emily's beautiful," Jolie said.

And this time it didn't sound like a trap, so Hollis had no problem uttering a thoughtful "She sure is."

Beautiful and broken, like so many people. And all he wanted to do was help put her back together.

CHAPTER 29

EMILY WAS SCHEDULED TO SPEND all of Sunday at the arts center with her team. Nothing about those hours felt like work. She was supposed to be the one casting the vision, but she found their excitement infectious.

When she left that morning, she was surprised to see Jack's work truck pull up.

"You work on Sundays?"

"Tight schedule," he said. "Besides, you're working, aren't ya?"

She smiled, apologized that there was no coffee made, and then got on her way.

That night, Emily arrived home after most of the workers had gone but found Jack standing in the center of what she thought had been her kitchen but was now mostly an unrecognizable shell of a room. The cabinets had been torn out, the appliances were gone, and the flooring had been ripped up.

They'd gutted it in a matter of hours.

"Wow," she said, dropping her bag on the floor just outside the kitchen door. "You guys were busy today."

"We got a lot done."

"New cabinets and appliances will go a long way in here," Emily said. "Though I'm not sure how I'll function without a kitchen."

"That's why God invented carryout."

"I guess." She walked over to the wall she'd instructed them to remove. Knocking it down would open up the lower level, and Emily had no doubt an open floor plan was just what the old cottage needed. "The wall is still here."

"I was waiting for you," Jack said. "You sure you want to tear it out?"

She faced him. "Do you think I shouldn't?"

"Would it matter if I did?"

She shrugged. "Not really."

He laughed. "That's what I thought."

He'd picked up on her decisiveness. Good. While she'd been vague at the onset, she'd come up with a pretty good plan for the renovations, feeding them to Jack one room at a time.

To his credit, the man had taken her changes and suggestions in stride.

"What can I say? When you know, you know." She smiled.

For a split second, Jack froze. "Right," he said after several seconds. "When you know, you know." He bent over and picked up a giant hammer-looking thing and held it out to her.

She stared at it. "What's that?"

"It's a sledgehammer."

"What would you like me to do with it?"

"Thought you might want to do the honors." He nodded toward the wall.

She laughed. "You want me to hit the wall?"

"No," he said. "I want you to demolish the wall."

Emily finally reached out and took the hammer. "This is heavy."

He only shrugged.

"How am I supposed to demolish the wall if I can't even lift this thing? Maybe you should do it." She tried to hand the hammer back to Jack, but he took a step away, hands up as if in surrender.

"You know," Jack said with a sheepish grin, "this is a great way to let off steam."

"You think I need to let off steam?"

He shrugged again. "You seem a little stressed out."

A little anxious. A little neurotic. A little of a lot of things.

She thought of her professional disaster—of how it was highly unlikely she'd ever recover from it. Of how she didn't have the energy to try. Of how Gladys didn't believe in her even now, and of how she couldn't really blame the old woman.

She didn't believe in herself either.

Never mind that the auditions had gone well, that the cast was solid, that she'd spent the day researching costumes and sets and props, creating giant vision boards to hang in the rehearsal space.

That feeling of accomplishment was so short-lived in the shadow of such a giant mistake.

Would she ever feel confident again?

Yeah, she needed to let off steam. Demolishing a wall wasn't something she'd tried before. What could it hurt? "What do I do?"

"Just hit it," Jack said. "As hard as you can."

"As hard as I can?"

"As hard as you can." Jack chuckled. "Here, maybe this will help." He walked over to his tool bag, pulled out a can of black spray paint, shook it, then painted a giant X on the wall.

Emily imagined it was the face of the reviewer who'd given her play the worst of all the bad reviews. She turned sideways, heaved the sledgehammer up over her shoulder, and hauled it into the wall with as much muscle as she could muster.

The hammer got stuck smack in the middle of the X, and she didn't have the strength to pull it out. "At least I have good aim."

Jack laughed, reached over, and tugged until the hammer came out.

"Now do it again."

The impact had jarred her to the core, and she wasn't sure she had the strength to do it again.

"Come on, Muscles. If you can demo a room, you can do anything."

"Ha." Emily wasn't so sure. Could demolishing a room help her put up a show in a matter of weeks? Could it erase the mistakes of her past? Could it help her get through the rest of this summer without too much pain?

She picked up the sledgehammer again and assumed the position.

"Maybe swing from your legs, use them like you would if you were lifting a heavy box."

"I don't lift heavy boxes," Emily said with a smile. She heaved the hammer back and slammed it into the wall again, and again her insides were shaken like beans in a pair of maracas.

Without a word, she yanked it from the wall and did it over and over until the hammer broke through the other side of the wall.

She gasped. "I did it!"

"You did it," Jack said.

"I need to get to the gym," she said, out of breath.

Jack grinned.

Emily looked at the giant hole in the wall. "That was fun."

"Well, then, keep going."

Despite her initial concerns, Jack was a nice guy. Not a serial killer at all. It occurred to her that she still knew almost nothing about him.

"Is this really the way you wanted to spend your summer?" she asked as she picked the hammer up again.

"Beats sitting around," he said.

"But sitting around on the beach? Does it really beat that?"

He laughed. "I'm not a do-nothing kind of guy. I like to keep busy."

"I get that." But she didn't—not really. She thought about her long days before she moved back to New York to mount her play. She'd lived off her trust fund and contributed nothing at all to the world in those days, and she'd been perfectly content to do so.

Somehow, Jack's way seemed better. Working at the arts center had already shown her the benefits of having something to do. But it was more than that, wasn't it? Those moments where ideas were firing back and forth across the table with her team—they ignited something inside her. Gave her a purpose.

For the first time in a long time, she felt like what she did mattered, and that feeling far outweighed anything she'd ever done for herself. And to be honest, she'd mounted that New York play for herself. She'd done it because she wanted to prove she could, because she wanted to be a star.

And look what had happened.

"You just had auditions, right?" Jack asked.

She was midswing, and his question caught her so off guard she lost her momentum. "You know about that?"

He sat down on a stool across the room and shrugged. "I hear things working here all day every day."

"Right," she said.

"Plus, people around town talk."

She wondered who it was that Jack talked to when he wasn't working on her house. Did he have friends? How did he spend his time?

"Do you have a family?" she asked, then swung the hammer into a different part of the wall.

"I do," he said. "Well, I did."

She glanced at him.

"Divorced. Two boys. They're spending the summer with their mom."

"Do you live near them?"

"Yeah, we see each other a lot. They're planning to spend a week here with me in August."

"That's so nice," she said. "It's good you make time for them." She purposefully kept the sadness out of her voice.

"What about you? Do you see your family often?"

She hit the wall—hard. "It's just me and my grandma now. GrandPop passed away last month."

"I'm sorry to hear it."

She never knew how to respond when people apologized for her grandpa's death. Or her mother's. *Thanks* felt so out of place, so instead, she changed the subject. "And I never knew my father. He must've been one of those guys who wasn't cut out for fatherhood or something."

"Your mom never told you who he was?"

She shook her head and drew the hammer back. Jack was right— this was great for getting out your frustrations. She just didn't know she was going to tap into a whole new set of frustrations while she was doing it.

"Wow," he said quietly. "And your grandparents didn't tell you either?"

"My grandma said she didn't know who the guy was," she said. "Whoever he was, he broke my mom's heart enough to turn her off of love for the rest of her life. She never got married and told me if I was smart, I never would either."

Jack crossed his arms over his chest. "Not sure that's the best advice."

She shrugged and set the heavy hammer down, stretching out her arms. "I get her point. If you open yourself up to someone, you inevitably get hurt."

"But if you stay closed off, you miss out on everything love has to offer."

"My mother would disagree with you," she said with a wry smile.

"How do you know?"

"She told me," she said.

"Weren't you a little young to be talking about love before your mom died?"

She eyed him for a moment. Jack had been divorced—he was fooling himself if he thought love was anything more than a farce. And as usual, she wanted to prove her point.

"She didn't tell me that before she died. She told me after."

Jack's face turned mysterious. "Like a séance?"

Emily laughed. "No." She walked into the entryway and retrieved the book of letters from the table. She'd taken to placing it on the table by the front door whenever she wasn't carrying it in her oversize bag. It seemed to be a good spot for a book that meant so much, like a place of honor or something.

When she returned, she handed the book over. "After she died, we went back to our apartment and packed up all my things, and we found this."

Jack flipped through the pages carefully. "She wrote you letters?"

"For all the big moments in my life. Key things, you know, like—"

"'When you feel left out.' 'When you feel misunderstood.'" He read as he flipped the pages.

She put her hand down on the book to stop him from turning the next page. "That's one of my favorites."

He read the words her mother had written on the envelope holding the letter safe. "'When you make a mistake—a big one.'"

She reached over and took the letter out. "'I'm not talking about wearing a pair of jeans that are out of style—I'm talking about the kind of mistakes you don't bounce right back from. I don't want you to be afraid of taking risks because you're afraid of messing up. Messing up is a part of life. In some ways, I guess getting pregnant was a big mistake, but that mistake brought me the biggest blessing of my life.'" She paused, then realized Jack probably didn't want to hear her silly letter. "Anyway, that's how I know what my mom thinks about love. And everything else."

She glanced up and found Jack watching her, and while he wore a quiet smile, his eyes looked glassy.

Maybe he was thinking about the mistakes he'd made. Maybe they were still fresh, like hers.

It was odd that as much as she took Mom's letters to heart, this one hadn't quite gotten through. At least not enough for her to move past the regret and the shame of her colossal failure.

"So you don't think your mom would've changed her mind? Met someone else or maybe even reconnected with your dad?"

Emily shook her head. "Definitely not. I mean, maybe she would've met someone else, but she never would've reconnected with my dad. He left her when he found out she was pregnant. Didn't want her. Didn't want me. He broke her heart in so many pieces, nobody could've put it back together."

She hugged the book to her chest. "So when she said, 'Be cautious with your heart,' she knew what she was talking about."

"That why you're still single?"

She laughed and set the book aside. "Probably. That and the fact that I don't stay in any one place long enough to have a relationship with anyone."

"On purpose?"

She picked up the sledgehammer. "Definitely on purpose."

"What about Hollis?" Jack asked.

"Hollis McGuire?" Emily moved to the other end of the wall and squared off in front of it.

"Don't know many guys named Hollis."

"It's a family name." She laughed. "Hollis and I are just friends."

"But you could be more," he said. "I've seen the way he looks at you when you're not watching."

"Is that right?" She smacked the hammer into the wall, suddenly uncomfortable with where the perfectly pleasant conversation had gone. "How's that?"

"Like he's not being cautious with his heart."

Emily hit the wall again. "I think you're mistaken, Jack. Hollis McGuire will only ever see me as a buddy."

Even as she said it, she knew it wasn't true. There had been moments between her and Hollis—moments filled with possibility, with heat. Surely she wasn't the only one who felt it.

"Well, I'm going to pray you find someone who makes you willing to throw caution to the wind."

She turned away, not wanting that prayer out there, just in case God really was listening. The last thing she needed was someone to make her lose her common sense in the name of love.

Jack continued, "And that he's the kind of guy who will have the good sense to hold on to your heart and protect it like it's a treasure to be kept."

She looked at him.

"I wish I'd had that kind of sense when I was younger," he said. "I had something perfect and wonderful and I blew it."

"Your wife?"

He inhaled a slow breath, then looked away.

"Maybe it's not too late," Emily said. "Maybe you can still get her back?"

Jack met her eyes, his face drawn with sadness. "Sadly, that's not possible."

"Why not?" Emily asked, knowing she was being nosy but not feeling even a little bit sorry for it.

But Jack wasn't so forthcoming. "I should get this out to the Dumpster." He moved toward the debris on the ground.

"Seriously?" She laughed. "I just told you my whole life's story, and you're bailing at my first question."

He picked up a large pile of plaster and tossed her an amused smile. "It's been nice chatting with you, Miss Ackerman."

She shook her head. "Turnabout is *not* fair play, Mr. Walker." She pounded another hole in the wall. "But thanks for teaching me how to knock down a wall."

"Of course." He walked out of the room toward the front door, leaving Emily to contemplate the oddity of having a heart-to-heart with her contractor, but feeling like when this whole remodel was over, she'd have a big dinner party and Jack would be on the guest list.

CHAPTER 30

Even under her parents' very watchful eyes, Isabelle found ways to see JD. She'd sneak out at night after her mom and dad had gone to bed, race down to the beach, and find him there, waiting.

She'd find reasons to visit the yacht club, where he was now working as a waiter, and they'd steal kisses in the staff locker room when no one was watching.

Their relationship turned innocent again, as if they'd never slept together. As if that was a mistake, and while it couldn't be remedied, Isabelle didn't believe JD had any intention of taking advantage of her. If she were to explain the situation to a friend, she would've said they were caught up in the moment or they thought they might never see each other again.

It didn't make it right, and it didn't take away the fleeting bits of shame that found their way into her mind, but going back to the way they'd been before was comforting. JD felt, in every way, like a part of her. He allowed her to be more herself than anyone else.

With him, she felt like she was home. And the days when she couldn't be home were hard.

It was strange, not doing exactly what was expected of her. Strange and . . . exhilarating.

Until it wasn't.

Until the day she had to go to the clinic for an antibiotic and ended up getting tested for mono.

"Miss Ackerman, your blood test turned up something interesting," the doctor said.

"I'm not dying, am I?" Isabelle half laughed.

Dr. Solstrom's smile looked forced. The man had been treating her for years. He was her "summer doctor," as her mother said.

"No, nothing like that," the doctor said. "Isabelle, when was your last period?"

Isabelle didn't keep track of these things. She should probably, but she didn't. She tried to think back and drew a blank.

He sat down on his rolling stool and looked her in the eyes. "Is there a chance you might be pregnant?"

Isabelle's face turned hot. Though her mother was sitting in the waiting room, she still felt like she should whisper and almost asked the doctor to do the same. She swore her mother could hear through cement walls.

"I don't think so," she said. Her mind spun back to the day she found out JD had been fired, the day she'd gone to see him, the day they'd slept together. "Oh no."

The doctor let out a slight sigh and pushed back on his stool. "Should we talk about your options?"

Isabelle covered her face with her hands. "No, I know my options, but thank you."

He patted her on the shoulder. "It's going to be okay."

Easy for him to say. He wasn't seventeen, pregnant, and the daughter of Alan and Eliza Ackerman.

"Do you have to tell my mom?"

The doctor inhaled, then sighed again. "I should."

"No," she said. "I should."

"Do you want me to have the nurse get her from the waiting room?"

Isabelle shook her head, suddenly overcome with the need to see JD. "I have to go, Dr. Solstrom, but thanks."

"Isabelle, you need to talk to your parents—sooner rather than later," he said. "Or I'll have to."

She nodded. "I will, but there's something I need to do first."

She raced out, trying not to look as terrified as she felt, and found her mom in the waiting room. It was a miracle Eliza hadn't come into the exam room with her in the first place, but after Isabelle said she could hardly get in trouble in the doctor's office and could her mother at least let her do this one thing on her own, the woman finally relented.

Thank goodness she had.

"Everything okay?" her mom asked as Isabelle approached.

"Yep. All good."

"Well, do you have mono?"

"No," she said. "I guess I just need more sleep."

Her mother laser-focused her gaze on her daughter. "Maybe I should go talk to the doctor, Isabelle."

"Mom, I promise there's absolutely nothing you can do," Isabelle said. "Maybe I'll go home and take a nap on the beach."

Her mother held her position for several seconds, then finally shook her head. "Well, all right, let's go."

Half an hour later, Isabelle was dressed in her bathing suit, carrying a beach bag and looking every bit like a person who was going to spend the day lying in the sun.

"Is it okay if I head down toward Lydia's beach?" Isabelle asked.

Her mom gave her a sideways glance.

"Mom, please," Isabelle said. "I've basically been a prisoner all summer. Haven't I proven that I can be trusted?"

The words practically smacked her in the face. *What a liar!*

But how was she supposed to escape her mother's watchful eye? She absolutely had to see JD.

"Isabelle, if I find out you're deceiving me again—"

"I'm not, Mom. I swear."

"I have a meeting at the arts center, but I will know if you're lying. I have friends everywhere."

No, Mother, only in the places where rich people go.

Isabelle hurried off on her bike, praying her mom didn't find out the truth about where she was headed and then quickly realizing the irony. Once her mother found out the truth about her condition, a bike ride to the yacht club would be a most welcome deception.

She rushed toward the staff entrance, dropping her bike on the lawn out front and running inside.

JD would likely be in the restaurant, waiting tables, and she didn't want to get him in trouble—but was that as important as what she needed to tell him?

She stood off to the side near a doorway and tried to remain inconspicuous. Finally—finally—JD looked her way, his expression running a wide range until finally it landed on the right one: concern.

She motioned for him to meet her in the staff area, and she walked into the employee locker room and waited for him.

A few minutes later, he came through the door. She raced into his arms, clinging to him as if she had to hold tightly or she might not survive.

And she might not.

"Bella, what's going on? Are you okay?"

"I need to talk to you," she said.

He opened the door to the men's changing room and peered inside. "There's no one in here."

She followed him in and paced back and forth as he sat on one of the benches.

"Okay, Isabelle, you're freaking me out."

"I don't even know how to say this."

"What is it? Are you sick? Are your parents leaving early? It can't be that bad. Just tell me."

She faced him. "JD, I'm pregnant."

There. It was out. Unable to be taken back. And now she'd deal with the aftermath as best she could.

"You're what?"

She felt a lump swell in her throat. "Pregnant." The word came out in a whisper.

He stood up in front of her and stopped her from moving. "But we only—"

"Did it once? Yeah, I know."

He looked stunned. Or maybe terrified. Or completely freaked out. Or all of the above. Exactly the way she felt.

"I guess once really is all it takes."

"Okay," he said. "First of all, are you okay?"

"My parents are going to kill me." Her voice broke and she started to cry, falling into his arms again. He held her and they cried together because what else did two kids do when they found out news like this?

She pulled away. "I'm scared, JD."

He ran his hand through his hair and met her eyes. "Okay, but you're not alone. I'm not going anywhere. Maybe . . ." He seemed to be searching his mind, but what possible solution would he find? "Maybe we get married. You move to Boston and go to school there?"

"And you finish college with a wife and a baby?"

"For you, I'd do that," he said. "It's not perfect, but it's what we've got. We could get a little apartment, and I'll get another job. Or I'll quit school and work full-time. Whatever it takes, Bella. I'll do whatever it takes."

The tears started again. Listening to him, she knew it was crazy. She knew the plan wouldn't work. She knew there were a million reasons they couldn't get married and play house, and yet she found herself wanting exactly that. Never mind that it would be a while before she'd travel the world. Never mind that it wasn't exactly what she'd planned. They'd be together, and that mattered more than anything else, right?

"We'll figure it out, okay?" He pulled her into him again and held her while she cried, kissing the top of her head protectively. "It's going to be okay."

And for some reason—maybe naiveté—she believed him.

CHAPTER 31

HOLLIS DIDN'T MEAN TO EAVESDROP.

He stood in the entryway of the cottage, having opened the door right in the middle of Emily pounding a hammer into the wall. At first he was going to rush in, make sure she was okay, but then the pounding stopped and the conversation started.

She wasn't alone.

Emily had always been the kind of person to share her thoughts freely. She'd always been open, saying pretty much whatever came to her mind.

But he also thought (hoped?) she was only that way with him.

He should've interrupted right away, made his presence known, but then Jack mentioned his name, and what was he going to do? Barge in and contradict him? Tell him he was wrong—Hollis didn't look at Emily *that way*—and she was right not to get involved with anyone?

Especially Hollis.

Like Jolie said—Hollis ruined things.

So why did the words *"Hollis and I are just friends"* sting the way they did?

Now, standing just outside the kitchen, he heard Jack say something about the Dumpster, so he slipped back onto the front porch, where he could confront the man without Emily overhearing.

He waited for Jack to step out of the house and into the sticky summer night as the sun dipped low in the sky.

The load of debris from the house came out of the door first, positioned on Jack's shoulder, and Hollis knew Jack couldn't see him standing off to the side. The older man walked down the stairs and over to the Dumpster, tossed the garbage away, then glanced to where Hollis stood.

"Hey, Hollis," he said, unruffled by his presence. "Emily's inside. She's demo'ing the wall in the kitchen. It already looks better."

Hollis glared. "Don't do that."

Jack's eyebrow twitched upward. "Sorry?"

"What's your deal here, Jack?"

The older man straightened. "I'm not sure I follow."

"First I catch you looking through the desk in Isabelle's room; now you're here having a conversation with Emily like you're a long-lost family friend or something. Why do you care so much about her personal life if you're just here to remodel the house?"

Jack locked onto his glare and didn't back down. "I don't do this for a living, Hollis. I like to know the people I'm working with."

"For."

"Sorry?"

"You work *for* her."

"And she's a great young woman."

"The kind of woman you want to know better?" He eyed Jack for a long moment. "She's too young for you, man. You need to keep a healthy distance from her or we're going to have a problem."

"You've got the wrong idea here, Hollis," Jack said.

"What kind of idea should I have, then, *Jack*?"

"None," Jack said. "I'm just here to do a job, to turn this house into exactly what Emily wants it to be."

"Right," Hollis said. "You'd be smart to remember that."

Jack didn't argue. Instead, he gave Hollis one stern nod, then walked to his truck, got inside, and drove off.

Whoever this guy was, Hollis didn't trust him.

And he didn't like the way Jack's conversation with Emily seemed to be on repeat in his mind.

"Be cautious with your heart."

It was a directive her mother had given her, which meant his old friend would only ever be a friend. And while he knew that was best, he also hated knowing it. Yes, he wanted to keep his promise to Jolie—had to, really, if he had any hope of winning her over. But Emily—she'd woven her way into the underside of his heart, the deep parts that most people couldn't reach.

He shook the thought aside and walked back into the house, closing the door behind him.

"Jack, look," Emily called out from the kitchen. "Look how much bigger the house seems now."

Hollis walked into the kitchen and stopped at the sight of her, hair pulled up in a messy bun on the top of her head, wild strands falling around her face. She wore a pair of cutoff jean shorts and a red tank top, a navy-blue plaid shirt tied around her waist. In her hands, a sledgehammer.

And she looked adorable. More than adorable, in fact. She looked gorgeous.

For a split second, they stood there, not saying a word. The air between them sizzled and he imagined all the things he'd like to do if circumstances were different.

He wouldn't say a word. He'd walk straight to her, back her up against the wall, and kiss her until neither of them could see straight.

Desire coursed through his veins, spiking his heart rate, impossible to ignore.

Finally she let the top of the hammer fall loose to the ground. "Hey."

"Hey." He begged his pulse to slow down. Willed his mind to stop running off without his permission. Remembered there would be repercussions if he acted on the things he was thinking.

Remembered he ruined things.

"What are you doing here? Where's Jack?"

"He had to go," Hollis said. "Need help?"

He counted off the seconds in his head as she watched him, their eyes connected as if they were something more than *just friends*. This was doing nothing to steady his breathing.

"Uh, sure," she said.

He walked over to where she stood and brushed past her as he began to create a pile out of the massive mess she'd made tearing down the wall.

A heavy tension hovered in the air between them as he worked, and he searched his mind for something—anything—to say to make it disappear.

"You're a messy worker," he finally said.

He wouldn't be winning any awards for excellent conversation starters, but it was the first thing that came to his mind. And it was followed by her glorious laugh, which was enough to keep him from feeling stupid—and enough to cut the tension out of the room.

They worked in amicable silence for several minutes while Hollis made trips to the Dumpster and she continued to pound on the wall.

"You seem to have a knack for destroying things," he joked. "Remind me not to get on your bad side."

"It's very therapeutic. You should try it."

He glanced at her, and she held the hammer out in his direction. "Are you tired?" he asked.

"Actually, yes, and starving."

He took the hammer from her and handed her his phone. "Order a pizza. You've put in more than a full day."

"But there's still a little more wall to knock out," she said.

"I'll get it."

She sighed the words "My hero" and grinned at him.

He turned away to hide his smile, but man, he loved being around her. He told Emily to go figure out what Jack did with her plates as he finished knocking out the wall, then carried the debris to the Dumpster.

He'd just about finished when the pizza guy showed up in the driveway. He paid for the food, then returned to the kitchen carrying the box, but the room was empty.

"Em?"

"Outside," she called.

He followed her voice to the patio, which, in spite of still being torn up, looked cozy under the moonlight with two flickering candles on the table. Emily lounged in one of the chairs, feet up on another one.

"My shoulders are killing me from that hammer," she said. "Will you rub them? I know it's annoying, but I can feel the knot right . . . here." She stuck her hand where her neck and shoulder met.

Hollis set the pizza on the table, then moved over behind Emily and rested his hands on her shoulders. She picked one of his hands up and pressed it down on her shoulder where she did, indeed, have a healthy knot forming. "Feel that?"

"Yeah, it's tight," he said.

He stared at the back of her neck, and it stared back, bare, like a welcome invitation.

"I don't really know what I'm doing, you know," he said.

"You've never given any of your girlfriends a back rub before?"

He chose to laugh instead of respond. He didn't know how to tell her he hadn't seriously dated many women. He'd had a few relationships, but none were noteworthy. His longest was with a woman named Cherise, a flight attendant and maybe the only person he knew who traveled more than he did. They'd only been together a year, but he knew at the beginning it wasn't going to last—he was just too . . . *something* . . . to end it. He kept thinking maybe he'd feel differently the next time he saw her.

He never did.

He looked at his hands resting on Emily's neck. She was perfectly relaxed, but he was a rigid mess.

He moved the strands of hair that had fallen from her elastic out of the way, and let his hands linger there for a moment, the skin of her neck enticing him. That's when his mind started to play tricks on him, flashing images of *what could happen* without permission, like a slide show he shouldn't be watching.

He imagined leaning down, letting his lips graze the side of her neck, moving over to her shoulder and back up again—he'd inhale the scent of her while he left a trail of kisses all along her collarbone.

"Hollis?" She twisted and looked up at him.

"Sorry," he said. He forced himself to concentrate on the knot in her right shoulder instead of thoughts that could get him in trouble.

"What do you think of Jack?" she asked as he rubbed.

How was he supposed to form sentences as his hands made contact with her skin, as he became acutely aware of how soft it was? "Uh, I'm not sure. Why?"

"I think he's a really nice guy," Emily said. "I think he wishes he could get back together with his ex-wife."

"What makes you say that?"

She let her head fall to one side and stayed silent for a long moment. "Something he said tonight. I think he regrets getting divorced."

"I think you should be careful with that guy, Emily," Hollis said.

She straightened. "What do you mean?"

He stopped rubbing her shoulders for a split second and drew in a breath. How to say it without alarming her or sounding like a jealous loser?

"Well, what do we really know about him?"

Emily went back to her relaxed posture, and Hollis pressed his fingers into the backs of her shoulders. "I don't know," she said. "How much do we really know about anybody?"

"Well, I know plenty about you."

She laughed. "You think you do."

He pulled his hands away and sat down next to her. Her hand went immediately to her shoulder and started rubbing.

"Maybe you need a massage," Hollis said. "Don't women love massages?"

Emily stared at him. "First of all, I think that's mildly sexist, and second of all, they cost a fortune."

Hollis leaned back in his chair. "Since when does that matter?"

Her face went blank for a split second, and then she recovered (or tried to) with a quick shrug. "I'm just trying not to spend money frivolously. Besides, you did a great job on my shoulders. It doesn't hurt at all anymore."

He could see she was lying, though he had no idea why. He opened the box of pizza and breathed in the smell of garlicky sauce, cheese, and delicious baked dough. He dished up two pieces for her, then two for himself, leaned back in his chair, and forced her to meet his gaze.

"Secret, secret," he said.

Emily groaned. "Oh no."

"Oh yes." He grinned. He'd been saving his turn for a time when he actually had something worth asking, and now he had it.

"Fine." Emily took a bite. "What do you want to know?"

He swallowed his pizza, took a swig of water, then drew in a breath as if prolonging her torture was a game he enjoyed very much. Then he met her eyes. "Why does it matter how expensive a massage is when I know you have a substantial trust fund that was meant to carry you through your golden years with enough left over for your children's children?"

She set her plate down on the table. "Do you need more water?"

"Emily."

Now he knew there was more to her frugality than simple frugality. And she had to know there was no point in lying to him about it for another second because he'd call her out on it and this was her stupid game to begin with.

"This game is dumb," she said.

He laughed. "I told you that years ago, though it is the only reason I ever got to kiss you, so I guess I can't hate it too much."

She found his eyes, and he smiled at her. Sometimes Hollis said things he shouldn't, and he almost always regretted it—but not this time.

She averted her gaze. "I don't want to talk about it."

He took another bite. When she finally looked at him, he shot her a "too bad" kind of look, not unlike the one she gave him when he didn't want to talk about retiring from baseball. She obviously remembered the same moment because she quietly looked away.

"It's a long story," she said. "But I'm basically broke."

Hollis straightened. "What do you mean 'broke'?"

"I mean I have no money, broke." She leaned back in her chair, acting nonchalant and *Emily*-ish, as usual. Inside, she had to be freaking out, didn't she?

"What happened?"

She took a quick drink, set her water down, and went back to leaning in the chair. She glanced up at the sky and ran her hands over her forehead. Even without a stitch of makeup left on her face, with her hair all messy and unkempt, and wearing dirty clothes, Emily still looked beautiful in the moonlight.

Just friends. Just friends. Just friends.

The words raced through his mind purposefully, an important (if unwanted) reminder.

She pinched the bridge of her nose in that endearing way she did when they were kids. "I guess the short story is—"

"I don't want the short story," Hollis interrupted.

"Trust me, you do."

He shook his head. "That's not how this game works."

"Well, whoever made up the rules was not thinking clearly," she shot back. She picked up her pizza crust, stared at it, then dropped it back onto the plate.

"I travel a lot."

"Yeah, I saw your collection of keys."

"Really?" She glanced at him.

"Winny showed them to me," he said. "He said you keep one from every place you've lived?"

She nodded. "Yeah, I don't know why."

"Take a little piece of each place with you, I guess? It makes sense."

She shrugged. "It's not cheap, traveling like I do."

"I know," he said, starting to sense she was procrastinating. He'd traveled at least a little bit, enough to know it wasn't cheap, though he'd never paid a dime for his accommodations. "You know whatever happened, you can tell me."

Her eyes found his for the briefest second, and he could see they were filled with tears. Knowing Emily, though, she'd refuse to let them fall. "It's just . . ." She sighed.

"Emily?" Hollis set his plate down. "You don't have to tell me. Forget it. I'll ask you something else. What's the best country you've ever visited? Or what's the craziest food you've ever eaten?"

She hugged her knees to her chest, wrapping her arms around her legs. "No, maybe it'll be good for me. I kind of want to tell you about it."

His heart flip-flopped.

"I'd just finished working on a tour, living in Australia, having the time of my life, when I got this crazy idea that I could . . ." She looked away. "That I could launch my own show."

"Like onstage?"

She nodded.

"What's so crazy about that?"

"Well, it's crazy when it's a dismal flop," she said.

His lip twitched. "I'm sure it wasn't that bad."

She raised her eyebrows. "No, it was."

He didn't say anything.

"It probably all sounds silly to a professional athlete, but that show was my shot to become something more than a former child star, and I failed. If I'd been smart, I would've workshopped it in a tiny venue that cost next to nothing, but I had to go all in. I thought I knew so much when really I was nothing more than a giant failure."

"Don't say that," Hollis said.

"Oh, I don't have to. The critics said it for me. The thing was, after traveling all my life and only working when I felt like it, I blew through a lot of money. I made a couple of bad investments, but I really thought this one was going to be solid. I thought *I* was going to be solid."

"You had a project that maybe didn't do as well as you wanted it to, but that doesn't make you a failure."

"It does, though," Emily said. "I'm not even sure I'm qualified to be directing a children's show. The critics were right—I should've kept the play in my desk drawer and never been stupid enough, arrogant enough, to think it needed an audience."

"They said that?"

She nodded sadly.

"Well, critics don't know everything," he said.

"They know enough." She looked away. "I just wanted something of my own, I guess. Something I was good at." She turned back and met his eyes. "Do you think less of me now?"

"What? Why would I?"

"Because unlike you, I am not a huge, crazy success. I am a person who peaked at age eleven. The end."

"Maybe you need to redefine success."

She crumpled her napkin into a ball and tossed it onto her plate.

Hollis took another slice of pizza from the box. "So that's why you're here this summer."

"It's my second chance." She turned to look at the house, lights filtering from the kitchen windows and spilling out onto the patio. "My second-chance house in Nantucket, of all places."

"I'm really sorry, Emily," he said.

"Yeah, me too." She swiped at her cheek, and for a split second he thought maybe one tear had actually escaped.

"Right," he said. "And now you have a job at the arts center, so off you go."

She laughed. "I'm not even sure that pays."

"It pays," he said.

"How would you know?"

He shrugged. "I'm a well-connected guy."

She stared at him for a few long seconds. "It was you, wasn't it?"

"What was me?"

"Who sent me all those people to help with the show." She sat up straighter. "I thought it was your mom, but it wasn't. It was you."

He set his plate down. "I plead the Fifth."

She shook her head, a smile playing at the corners of her lips. "You're something else, Hollis, you know that?"

"I do, in fact, know that," he said. "I also know that I better get going. But we should do this again."

"The dinner or the humiliating conversation?"

He narrowed his eyes on her. "You're not really humiliated telling me this stuff, are you? After what I told you?"

She shrugged. "A little. I mean, you've had a big, wonderful life, Hollis."

He held her gaze. "But I don't have any of that anymore—does that make my life less important somehow?"

"No, of course not."

Sometimes he wasn't so sure.

"Dinner tomorrow on me. You'll have the first rehearsal under your belt, and you can tell me all about it."

She shot him a look. "Okay, but this time, you're back in the hot seat."

"That's fair," he said, realizing he didn't mind telling Emily his secrets.

He stood, gathered the plates and the pizza box, and waited while Emily picked up both of their glasses of water.

He followed her inside, but before she opened the door, she turned to him. "Thanks for listening."

His gaze dipped ever so slightly from her eyes to her lips and back again. "Of course. Anytime."

She inched up on her tiptoes and kissed his cheek, sending the smell of something vanilla and intoxicating straight to his nostrils. He was thankful his hands were full; otherwise, he might not have been able to keep them to himself.

She turned, opened the screen door, and went inside. He followed, warning bells going off in the back of his mind. *Get in, drop the stuff, get out.* That's all he could do right now.

He couldn't linger. He couldn't be around her any longer without breaking his promise to Jolie. Tomorrow he'd come prepared with a healthy dose of willpower, but tonight he was all tapped out.

"I'm kind of nervous for tomorrow," Emily said as they made their way into the gutted kitchen.

"You're going to do awesome," Hollis said. "Maybe this is the thing you've been hoping to find."

She laughed. "Working with kids on an island thirty miles from civilization? I doubt it."

They entered the room and Emily came to a stop so quickly, he almost ran into her.

Turned out, he didn't need willpower after all.

Standing in front of the spot where the wall used to be was an older version of the woman he remembered from so many years ago.

Eliza Ackerman, dressed in a slick black pantsuit and heels and wearing a horrified expression.

"Hi, Grandma," Emily said weakly. "I made a few changes to the house."

❧

Dear Emily,

Let's talk about your grandparents for a minute. As you know, I haven't always had a perfect relationship with them, but when it mattered, they've been there for me. They've helped me support you and still get an education. They made sure we've had everything we could ever need or want. However rebellious I was against their seemingly rigid rules as a teenager, I've learned something as I've gotten older.

Grandma and GrandPop come from a different time. They see the world differently. In fact, their world isn't exactly "the real world." That's what happens when you've got a lot of money. I've never loved money. I've never cared about it. Someone once told me that was because I had it.

Maybe they were right.

Regardless . . . (Notice I didn't say "irregardless." Since we're chatting like this, I want to make it very clear that "irregardless" is not a word. Got it? Anyway . . .) Regardless, I've come to appreciate my parents, and I hope you will too. I want you to have a good relationship with them. They may not always have the best way of going about things, but they do always have good intentions, and I really believe they'll always be there for you— no matter what.

Will they make you feel like a walking disaster? Maybe. But in spite of that, there is still a lot of love.

I just thought you should know.

Love,
Mom

CHAPTER 32

EMILY STOOD AWKWARDLY IN THE DOORWAY of the kitchen. She still held two plastic cups, and she stared into the room imagining how awful it looked to her grandmother. After all, her job wasn't to demolish the house; it was to make it better—and right now, it looked a whole lot worse than it had when she arrived.

"I must say, Emily, this was not what I was expecting." Grandma waved a hand toward the wall.

"I was thinking it would open up the lower level, let in more light, make it more conducive to family functions—that sort of thing."

She could hear herself floundering. She sounded like an idiot. Suddenly all of her plans for the house felt misguided and silly.

And she'd been so sure before.

"Is my room still intact, or did you knock down walls upstairs too?" Grandma's smile was terse.

"It's still intact. We'll be painting it, though. I already picked out the colors—you can see the swatches taped to the wall."

Grandma raised an eyebrow, looking at Hollis as if seeing him for the first time. "I didn't realize you had a . . . *friend* on the island."

One thing Grandma was never quiet about was her disapproval of Emily's boyfriends. There hadn't been a single one Grandma had liked, unless you counted William Justus (Emily didn't), the grandson of a wealthy couple who ran in the same social circles they did. Grandma decided he was a perfect match for Emily in the tenth grade and tried to set them up on numerous occasions.

Sadly, Emily didn't take to William, a sensible boy Grandma hoped would talk Emily out of traveling the world. She still hadn't decided if it was William's body odor or his lack of manners that turned her against him permanently, but regardless, she and her grandmother had different ideas about who would make a good match for Emily.

"You remember Hollis, Grandma. His family always rented the cottage next door," Emily said. "They own it now."

She threw that last bit in there as if owning the cottage made Hollis more respectable. *Not just a renter anymore, Grandma. An owner.* But she didn't want to cater to her grandmother's snobbery. She silently told herself to knock it off.

"Good evening, Mrs. Ackerman," Hollis said like the perfect gentleman he was.

Grandma gave him a nod. "Hello."

"Hollis played professional baseball," Emily heard herself saying, as though she needed to give her grandmother a reason other than *sheer goodness* to accept this man in her home. Of all the people she'd known in her life, Hollis needed the least amount of talking up. He was genuinely kind and good all on his own.

But those things rarely mattered to Grandma.

She was doing it again. Presenting her choices with a spit shine so Grandma would approve. *Stop defending yourself. Stop apologizing for who you are.*

"I'm tired," Grandma said abruptly. "I'm going to sleep. We'll talk about the house in the morning."

And just like that, Eliza Ackerman walked out of the room, leaving Emily to wonder when exactly the other shoe would drop.

She turned to Hollis, wide-eyed.

"Did you know she was coming?" he asked.

Emily shook her head, then spoke quietly, just in case Grandma was outside the room listening (because there was a very good chance she was outside the room listening). "I had no idea. I've mostly avoided her calls, but when I talked to her the other day, she didn't say a word."

"Why have you avoided her calls?" Hollis whispered back.

Emily took a step closer to him, which she quickly realized was a mistake. He smelled like heaven—or some kind of woodsy aftershave, though those two things might be identical. He looked at her with those crazy beautiful hazel eyes and not a speck of judgment, even after she'd confessed everything.

Why was she surprised? She should've known Hollis was safe. He'd never done anything but try to protect her.

Like the time he punched a day-tripper in the face because he didn't like the way the kid talked to her.

He had bright-red hair, pale skin, and freckles all over his face and arms. Hollis, Hayes, and Emily were minding their own business down at the beach and this "punk kid," as Hollis called him, started making chicken noises as they walked by. At first, the trio thought the kid was just goofing off, but then he and his buddies walked by again and the boy clucked at them and started flapping his arms like a chicken.

Hollis, Hayes, and Emily stopped, looked at each other, then back at the kid, whose friends had fallen in behind him. "Those are some sweet chicken legs, girlie."

The boys laughed, and Emily shrank under the weight of the insult. Skinny and boyish had been her curse, though she'd never much cared until that moment.

Emily stuck her hands on her hips and drilled a glare straight into the boy's face. "At least I'm not an ugly ginger!"

"Maybe you're not a ginger, but you're still ugly," the boy said, laughing.

Emily felt her stomach knot. She stepped toward the kid—confident she could punch him square in the jaw and make him look like a fool in front of his friends. But Hollis moved in front of her, hand held out to prevent her from going any closer.

"You wanna say that again?" he challenged.

Emily had to admit her kindhearted friend did "threatening" very well.

The boy, shrimpy compared to Hollis, cringed ever so slightly, then jutted his chin out and puffed up his chest. "Which part? The part about her having chicken legs or the part about her being ugly?"

Hollis took a step closer. "You should walk away."

Again, the boy straightened and advanced toward Hollis.

"Barry, let's go," one of the friends said. "You're gonna get creamed."

But Barry wasn't a good listener. Instead, he squared off with Hollis and said in a squeaky, annoying voice, "Chicken lover."

Hollis responded with a fist in Barry's face—punched him right in the nose. Barry's head shot backward as he stumbled a few steps, struggling to keep his balance.

Seconds later, a man down the beach hollered, "Hey!" and came running toward them.

Barry practically growled at Hollis, and Emily grabbed his hand. "Let's go!"

"You should learn to watch your mouth," Hollis said to Barry, whose nose was covered in blood.

"Come on, Hollis," Emily said as the man drew closer, but her friend didn't appear to be in much of a hurry. Finally he started off toward the street, away from the beach, the day-trippers, and the bleeding boy with a big mouth.

It was years ago, but that fire for keeping her safe was still going strong. She'd seen it so many times since she'd come back to the island. Hollis might not say much, but he was fiercely loyal, and though they'd only recently become reacquainted, she was sure that he'd stand in front of a bus for her.

She didn't know anyone else in the world who would do that—not even her grandmother.

"Grandma can be difficult," Emily said.

Hollis laughed.

"I know that's an understatement." She tossed the cups in the garbage can and stuck the leftover pizza box in the nearly empty refrigerator, which had been relocated to the dining room. She returned to the kitchen and found Hollis watching her.

"You haven't told her about the money yet, have you?"

Emily shook her head. "You're the only person in the world who knows what a loser I am."

"You're not a loser," he said matter-of-factly. Then, "You know she's going to find out."

"I don't want to think about that. I have to figure out what I'm going to do with her all day long tomorrow to keep her out of Jack's way."

Hollis nodded. "Well, I'll be back in the morning. Maybe I can help."

"Okay." She forced herself to smile at him.

"Okay."

It was almost like he was stalling, like he wasn't quite ready to leave. But he had to leave. She needed him to leave. Because if he stayed here, in her house, with *that* face and *those* eyes, she might do or say something she would very much regret.

Like kiss him. Like cross right over the line of friendship and straight into the black hole of *unidentified relationships*.

Her eyes scanned his face, lingering on soft, full lips, noticing a slight scar just above his mouth on the right side.

She reached over and touched it. "What happened there?"

"Got hit in the face with a line drive," he said, not shrinking from her touch.

"Ouch," she said.

"Four stitches. Missed two games because of that."

"How old were you?"

"Thirteen."

The summer after she left the island. She used to love cheering for his Little League team. The whole family, Emily and her mom included, would pile onto the bleachers and do their very best to embarrass Hollis.

How many games had he played without her in the stands?

She'd missed out on so much of him, and standing there now, only a foot separating their bodies, she realized she didn't want to miss out on another single minute of his life.

But as soon as the thought entered her mind, she pulled her hand back and turned away. This was the exact way hearts were injured. Fantasy had never gotten anyone anywhere. And just because Hollis felt protective of her, that didn't mean he wouldn't hurt her.

"I should head to bed," she said. "Long day tomorrow."

"Right." Hollis clapped his hands together and pulled his baseball hat down a little tighter on his head. "I'll see you bright and early. I think they're laying the flagstone tomorrow. Thought I'd see if I could help."

She smiled. Jack almost never let Hollis help anymore because Emily told him not to. She wasn't going to let Hollis do the work without getting paid—and she knew he'd never accept payment. Plus, he needed to spend his days with Jolie. "See you tomorrow."

"Night, Emily." He brushed past her, and she instinctively turned toward him on his way out the door, leaving her alone as the words *I can do hard things* floated through her subconscious, as if somehow her brain knew putting thoughts of Hollis out of her mind was going to be a challenge.

And unfortunately, she wasn't sure she was up for it.

CHAPTER 33

EMILY SET HER ALARM EARLY, wanting to be downstairs before her grandma and Jack and his crew.

But the night didn't go as planned. She'd lain in bed thinking about Hollis and his catastrophically kissable lips for far longer than she wanted to admit and sleep hadn't met her until somewhere around 2 a.m.

It wasn't only Hollis that kept her awake. It was knowing her grandmother was there. It was suddenly doubting every decision she'd made from paint colors to tiles to knocking out the kitchen wall. It was feeling like a liar for not being straight with her about the play and her money.

And it was the lips.

As a result, she slept right through her alarm and now found herself rushing to shower, dress, and get downstairs to make coffee before Grandma woke up.

But as soon as she exited the bathroom, she saw Grandma's bedroom door was open, the paint swatches Jack had taped to the wall gone.

She reached the end of the stairway just as Jack's pickup truck pulled into the driveway. How was she going to get her grandmother out of their hair for the day?

She stifled a groan. What if her grandmother stayed the rest of the summer?

"Grandma?"

She walked through the house, the smell of coffee tattling on her grandmother's presence but doing nothing to lead Emily to her.

"Grandma?" She stood in the center of the empty kitchen, silently praying Jack could pick up the pace and put the house back together even more quickly now that Eliza Ackerman had descended upon them.

"Why are you shouting?" Grandma's voice came from outside.

Emily walked out to the still-torn-up patio and found her grandmother sitting in one of the chairs, holding a newspaper and a cup of coffee.

"Sorry," Emily said. "I didn't know where you were." Emily took a seat next to her.

"There's coffee," Grandma said, then added dryly, "In the living room."

Emily heard the words as they were intended—a dig. "I know it looks like a mess right now, but trust me, it's going to look amazing when we're all done."

Grandma raised a brow but didn't respond.

"I didn't know you were coming," Emily said. "You didn't mention it the other day."

"I thought I'd surprise you." The older woman stared out across the backyard, which also looked like a bit of a disaster now that Emily considered it.

"Things are busy here," Emily said. "I've been helping with the house and—"

"Spending time with that McGuire boy," Grandma cut in.

"I was going to say working down at the arts center," Emily said, ignoring her grandmother's condescending tone.

Grandma looked at her. "The arts center?"

Emily nodded. "I'm directing the children's production."

Grandma's eyebrows rainbowed over surprised eyes. "You're *directing* it?"

Emily thought she heard pride in her grandma's voice. Was it possible she was finally making a decision the older woman approved of?

"How did that happen?" Grandma asked.

"It's a long story," Emily said.

"Do you have somewhere to be?"

"No . . . well, yes, actually. The first rehearsal is today."

"Emily!" Jolie's sweet voice preceded her sweet face into the backyard. She came around the side of the house carrying a Nantucket Bake Shop box, Tilly close on her heels. "Emily! I can't wait for rehearsal! I've got the best song in the whole show."

Emily stole a peek at her grandmother. The woman wore a familiar what-is-the-meaning-of-this? expression.

Jolie stopped chattering as soon as she saw Emily wasn't alone. "Oh, sorry." She handed over the box. "These are from GrandNan. Or Dad. I'm not sure who."

Hollis had probably gotten up at dawn, gone to the bakery, and sent his daughter back with breakfast for her now that he knew she was practically a pauper. It was so thoughtful. It was so *Hollis*.

It was friendly. That's what it was. That's what he was. A friend. *Focus.*

"Jolie, this is my grandma. Grandma, this is Hollis's daughter, Jolie."

Jolie stuck her hand out in Grandma's direction, and the older woman shook it pointedly. "I didn't know Hollis was married."

"Oh, he's not," Jolie said. "My mom's on her honeymoon with a doctor named Rick. They're in Hawaii. That's why I'm here with my dad."

"I see," Grandma said.

"JoJo, why don't you take these donuts inside and see if any of the guys are hungry?"

"Don't you want one?" she asked.

Emily peeked inside the box, the smell of fried dough wafting to her nostrils and making her mouth water. "Does this long john have filling?"

Jolie nodded.

"Save me that one."

"You got it." The girl ran inside.

"I'm betting that Hollis McGuire is full of secrets," Grandma said.

"Jolie isn't really a secret, Grandma," Emily said.

"Is he divorced?"

Emily's stomach twisted itself into a tight knot. She did not want to debate Hollis's morals with this woman. She knew where it would lead. Grandma seemed not to have grace for people's mistakes, something Emily had always struggled with. And to be honest, she didn't feel like defending Hollis today. She shouldn't have to.

If Jolie was a mistake, then so was Emily. Was that how her grandma felt about her after all this time?

"He's had an amazing life," Emily said.

"I know all about his baseball career," Grandma said. "Your grandfather became quite a fan."

"Me too," Emily said. "He was an incredible athlete."

"Indeed."

"He's a good man, Grandma."

Grandma sipped her coffee. "Are you two . . . ?"

"We're friends." Emily filled in the blank of her grandmother's question. "He's been really good to me since I got back."

"Fine."

Emily hated that word. *Fine.* Her mother had hated it too.

My mother loves to end conversations with one dreaded word: "Fine." It's her way of expressing her disapproval without coming right out and saying what she's thinking. Her way of getting the last word in without saying anything about what she actually thinks. I promise you I'll never "Fine" you. And don't you "Fine" me either. We're going to finish our conversations, you and I. Got it, kid?

"Do you want me to tell you the plans for the house?"

"Can you start with the color you've picked for my bedroom?"

"It's sort of a dusty-blue color," Emily said.

"It's gray."

"But it's neutral, and whoever buys the house will likely want something neutral."

Grandma's lips pulled into a taut line. "So you're selling it, then?"

Emily squirmed. She needed caffeine. Or a sedative. One of the two. "Yes, I think that's the most practical thing, don't you?"

Grandma's shrug was barely noticeable. "I want to honor your grandfather's wishes."

Emily inhaled. Prayed she stayed calm. "That doesn't answer my question."

"He wanted you to decide what happened to the cottage, so I'm going to stay out of it." Grandma almost looked pained saying it.

"Really?"

"Though I don't know why you had to knock the whole wall out."

Ah. Grandma's version of "staying out of it" meant interjecting her opinion in swift barbs that would make Emily question every one of her decisions.

"Would you like to join me at the arts center?"

Grandma bristled. "No, I've arranged to spend my days volunteering at the hospital and catching up with old friends."

Emily tried not to let her relief show. Knowing that Grandma wouldn't be hanging around the house all day every day was something of a blessing.

Just then the sliding-glass door opened again, and Emily turned, expecting JoJo, but instead found Jack standing there, carrying a clipboard. "Morning."

Grandma turned in the direction of his voice, then froze the second she set eyes on Emily's contractor.

"Grandma, this is Jack Walker. He's the man with the plan." Emily stood and smiled at Jack, whose smile had faded. He was probably worried Grandma was going to get involved and make him start all over, and rightfully so. Emily was worried about that herself.

Grandma set her mug on the table and stood, her face puckered in familiar disapproval, mixed with a drop of something Emily couldn't pinpoint.

"Actually," Jack said, "we've met."

Emily glanced at her grandmother. "Oh, really? Did you know each other years ago?"

"Something like that," Jack said, eyes holding steady on her grandmother.

"I'm sorry," Grandma said. "I'm having trouble placing you."

It was standard you-aren't-important-enough-for-me-to-remember talk for her grandmother, and Emily did her best not to roll her eyes.

"Oh, wait. You worked at the country club," Grandma said. "Am I right? You were one of Alan's caddies." Her glower faded into a brusque and short-lived smile.

Jack watched Grandma, and for a long moment, it was as if the two were communicating via telepathy. Emily's eyes darted back and forth between the two of them, but the moment was interrupted by the sound of someone in the yard behind them.

She turned and saw Hollis, looking especially gorgeous in the early morning light. How could a man make cargo shorts and a T-shirt look so good? Was it the ball cap? The aviators? The biceps?

Definitely the biceps.

"Morning," he said. "I've got a load of flagstone and I'm ready to build a patio. Hayes is on his way over to help me."

The tension in the air hung like a thick rain cloud, about to burst.

"Well, I'm meeting a friend in town to do some shopping," Grandma finally said, breaking herself away from her pointed stare.

"Yep," Jack said. "And I've got to get going on the kitchen."

Grandma brushed past Jack, and the man waited a pregnant pause before heading in after her.

Emily looked at Hollis.

He frowned. "What was that about?"

She looked back at the spaces the two had vacated. "I have no idea."

CHAPTER 34

THE USUAL LITANY OF NEGATIVE SELF-TALK raced through Emily's mind as she stood in the office at the arts center just half an hour before rehearsal was scheduled to begin.

You're going to make a fool of yourself.

You don't really know what you're doing.

You're never going to connect with these kids.

She'd begged the voice in her head to shut up the entire ride over that morning, but so far it wasn't listening.

She needed to stay busy. Get focused. Take control of her thoughts.

She left the office and found Marisol and some of the other team leaders in the auditorium. They'd already figured out their plan for the day, decided which room would be for costume fittings, which would be for music, which would be for dance, and which would be for blocking. They were ready.

She was ready.

They were about to welcome a new generation of kids to their first-ever Ackerman Arts Center children's theatre production.

The thought made Emily squeamish and excited at the same time.

Marisol, perky like a cheerleader with the kind of personality that had no problem making a fool of herself, welcomed the kids with high fives and smiles. Emily used to have that same personality—life of the party—but that was before she screwed everything up.

Now she felt unable to do anything.

Nan caught her eye from across the room. She gave her a thumbs-up with a questioning look, as if to ask if she was okay.

Emily nodded, though her stomach turned.

Nan made her way through the growing crowd of chatty children and stood next to Emily. "Overwhelmed?"

"Terrified."

She put an arm around Emily's shoulders. "You've got this, kiddo. Believe me, you've got this."

"You sound so sure," Emily said.

Nan smiled, her whole face radiating motherhood. "I saw you at auditions. You have nothing to worry about."

Emily gave her one firm nod, then moved down to the front of the stage.

Kids had filled the auditorium seats, giggling and talking and being kids. She looked over to the house-right side and saw Jolie sitting on the end of a row next to Shae Daniels's daughter, Alyssa. Already they looked like fast friends.

Jolie lifted her hand to wave at Emily, who gave her a wink and a smile.

"You ready for this, boss?" Marisol asked, joining her on the stage.

"Ready or not," Emily said.

She lifted her hands and clapped four times, then motioned for the kids to echo. They caught on immediately. She responded with another series of claps, this time a quicker rhythm. They repeated what she'd done and she did one more, finishing with a long "Shhhh."

The kids followed suit and—surprisingly—quieted down.

She had their undivided attention—now what?

She smiled. "Congratulations to everyone in this room! You made it into the cast of *Alice in Wonderland*!"

A series of loud cheers rang out.

Emily started by laying down the ground rules, explaining her expectations, and casting the vision for the show. Next, she introduced everyone in the cast by the role they would play, happy to hear the cheers of support for the kids in the lead roles. She knew she'd likely have some sour grapes to contend with (every show had them) but overall, these kids seemed like they were here to have fun.

They spent the morning doing a read-through of the script. They listened to the songs and explained what each group was doing and when. Halfway through, they stopped and played an icebreaker game, and then Emily split all the kids up into pairs—one older with one younger.

"Everyone gets a 'big' or a 'little,'" she said. "And this is your buddy for the whole show. You can send each other notes of encouragement, ask each other questions if you're unsure about something, and basically just watch out for each other. If you're a big, we're expecting you to act like a good role model for your little and all the other littles. This is important—you have to remember, someone is always looking up to you."

She found Jolie's eyes squarely focused on her.

Someone is always looking up to you.

She'd be smart to remember that herself. These ideas had come pouring out of her in their planning meetings, but even she wasn't sure where they'd come from. This hadn't been modeled for her, but every time she thought about standing up in front of a group of kids, of leading them, it became increasingly more important that she didn't muck it up.

By lunchtime, Emily expected to feel exhausted, but she was surprisingly energized.

"That was so fun," Marisol said, cracking open a lunch box. She took out a sandwich and bit into it.

"Is that peanut butter and jelly?"

Marisol grinned. "Jealous?"

Emily laughed. "Someday that white bread will catch up to you." Emily pulled her salad from her bag and opened the container. Her eyes scanned the room and fell on a little boy, about nine, who was sitting off to the side by himself, quietly eating his lunch. The boy looked around, wide-eyed panic on his face.

"Which one is that?" Emily asked. "Colin?"

Marisol followed her gaze to the dark-headed, pale-skinned boy. "Aww. Yes, that's Colin."

As far as she could tell, he was the only one sitting alone. Emily took her salad and walked over to the boy. "Hey, Colin. Can I sit by you?"

He looked up at her, eyes still wide. He nodded.

"Did you have a fun morning?" She ate a forkful of her salad.

Colin gave a halfhearted shrug.

"I noticed you're sitting over here all by yourself."

"Yeah." He stuck a Cheeto in his mouth.

"Do you like to be by yourself? Because that's super cool if you do, but if you'd rather be with some friends, I bet you could find a few here." She scanned the large, open room. Kids sat at tables, in circles on the floor; some even stood while they ate. Mostly they talked really loudly and laughed a lot.

But not Colin. He ate another Cheeto. "Nobody asked me to sit with them."

Her heart stuttered for a split second, and she wished just one other kid would notice him over here by himself. "Did you ask anyone to sit with you?"

He looked down, his face forlorn, and shook his head.

"Hm," she said. "You know, sometimes I think we have to put ourselves out there."

"Out where?" His face twisted like it was the weirdest thing he'd ever heard.

She motioned out across the wide-open room. "Out there. With the other kids."

"But what if they don't like me?"

Emily shrugged, swallowed her bite, and looked at him. "Not everyone is going to like you, kid. But you'll never know if you don't take a chance to get to know them."

Colin looked skeptical.

"Come on, little man. You can do it."

It struck Emily that she had no idea where this advice was coming from. The words she lived by would suggest Colin was safer over here in the corner, eating his turkey sandwich by himself.

"Be cautious with your heart."

And yet, looking at him, Emily only felt sad that this was the choice he'd made—to be alone—when he could be a part of this incredible group of friends.

Slowly he packed his plastic baggies back into his lunch box.

Emily pointed over to a small group of boys and girls about Colin's age. "Why don't you go sit right over there in that circle?" She prayed she wasn't steering him in the wrong direction. She prayed he was welcomed with smiles and giggles and kindness. She prayed he fit in.

Had she been praying those same things for herself?

He stood, and Emily handed him his lunch box. "I'm not sure about this."

She smiled at him. "If it all goes bonkers, you can come right back here with me."

He sighed. "Okay."

Colin approached the small circle. When he reached them, two of the kids turned their attention to him.

"Hi," he said.

One of the little girls, Brooklyn, looked up at him and gave him a crooked, gap-toothed smile. She scooted over and moved the elements of her lunch out of the way so Colin could sit down.

He looked over his shoulder at Emily, who was inexplicably choked up. She gave him a thumbs-up and watched as he sat down in the group.

Moments later, he was laughing and smiling right along with the other kids.

Emily picked up her salad and walked back to where Marisol was standing.

"Good job, boss," she said.

And Emily took the compliment, because for the first time in . . . maybe ever, she felt like she *had* done a good job.

And she decided it was the kind of feeling she could get used to.

CHAPTER 35

MID-AUGUST 1989

JD was standing on the deck of one of the yachts, cleaning it after it had been returned by a weekend renter, when he spotted Alan and Eliza Ackerman near the club.

His heart dropped.

He hadn't spoken to Isabelle in two days, and they'd agreed to talk to her parents together, but nothing about their being here appeared to be coincidence.

One of the other guys threw a wadded-up towel at JD, who forced a laugh as if pretend nonchalance could substitute for the real thing. He picked up the towel and tossed it back just as Isabelle's parents reached the edge of the dock.

They didn't say a word. Instead, they stared him down as if he knew why they were there, which, of course, he did.

"Can we help you?" another worker named Shane asked the couple, whose focus never wavered.

"I think they're here for me," JD said.

COURTNEY WALSH

"Oh." Shane nodded.

"I'll be right back." He stepped off the boat and onto the dock, moving away from where his coworkers continued to clean. He could feel Alan and Eliza following him, and before he faced them, he drew in a deep breath, exhaling as he turned around.

"Do you have any idea what you've done?" Eliza spat.

"I talked to Isabelle a couple days ago," he said.

"So you do know," she said.

"I'm sorry. We never meant for this to happen."

Alan's face changed. "I bet you didn't, but you did mean to take advantage of our daughter."

"I didn't, sir," JD said. "I love her."

Eliza's laugh mocked him. "Well, now I know where she got that ridiculous idea. Do you really think you have what it takes to provide a good life for our daughter—and now, for a child?"

"I'd do anything for Isabelle."

They exchanged a tense glance.

"If you want to do what's best for Isabelle, then you'll leave her alone," Alan said.

"Sir?"

"Son, our daughter is used to a certain way of life. She's come to expect certain things. Things you won't be able to provide. Pile onto that a baby, and you're looking at a recipe for disaster."

"You want to get rid of me?"

Eliza straightened. "We want what you want—the best for our daughter and for our grandchild. Surely you want that too."

"Of course I do."

"*We* can give them a good life," she said. "We can make sure every need is met."

JD didn't look away.

"We have to think logically here, son." Alan again, calling him "son," which was really starting to wear on JD's nerves. "The best thing for both of them—for all of you—would be for you to walk away."

"That way, you could finish school without the added pressure

273

of a family. You don't want to drop out now, do you, when you're halfway through?"

"There might be a way for me to keep up with my classes and still work full-time," he said.

"Doing what? Waiting tables? Cleaning yachts?" Eliza's superiority also grated on his nerves.

"If that's what it takes."

"That's not a life," Eliza said. "Not for our daughter, anyway."

JD looked away, pretending to be engrossed in a seagull in the distance. "We don't care about that stuff."

"You think you don't," Eliza said. "She thinks she doesn't. But as soon as it gets hard and she doesn't have instant access to whatever she wants, reality will set in."

JD shifted. "And if I don't leave her?"

Alan straightened, gave his pants a tug, and let out a sigh. "Well, then you'll be forcing our hand, son."

"Forcing your hand?"

Eliza leveled her gaze at him. "If you choose to go through with this ludicrous plan to marry Isabelle, or even try to continue a relationship with her, we will be forced to cut her off completely."

His stomach dropped. "You would do that?"

She shrugged. "We would have to. We can't stamp our approval on this kind of scandal, and sending our daughter to live with a boy she hardly knows so they can 'play house' in some tiny, roach-infested apartment in the city is not an option."

"I would never let her live in a roach-infested apartment."

"As if you would have a choice." She pressed her thin lips together, still maintaining her you're-not-good-enough-to-be-in-my-presence attitude. How Isabelle had grown so down-to-earth was a mystery, but it made him love her even more.

And that was the whole story, wasn't it? He loved her. He loved her so much that what her parents said began to make sense.

"I know you want to be with Isabelle, and the two of you think you're in love, but trust me, you throw a baby in the mix, add adult responsibilities, and you're looking at a recipe for disaster." Eliza knew she'd won. He could see it on her face.

"If you really love her, son, then do the right thing—the unselfish thing." Alan clapped a hand on his shoulder. "Maybe we could even help you with some of your college bills. Get you into some special programs, the kind that guarantee job placement after graduation."

JD's face fell. He loved Isabelle too much to make her leave the life she'd known for an unknown life with him. Sure, the romance of it was exciting, but her parents were right—much as he hated to admit it.

He wasn't good enough for Isabelle. He never had been.

"I don't want your money, sir," JD finally said. "Or your charity."

"Don't look at it that way," he said. "It's an offer to help the father of our grandchild."

"It's a bribe to get me out of your lives."

"Son, you deserve every possible chance to be a success. With a few phone calls, I can ensure that happens."

"But only if I walk away from Isabelle."

"And that means you walk away for good," Eliza interjected. "You don't tell her about this conversation and you move on. That's the only way this will work."

JD didn't like this—not one bit. It meant walking away without a word of good-bye. It meant letting Isabelle think he was running, that he never loved her. It meant not being a part of his child's life.

But was staying a better option? Staying meant Isabelle lost everything—all the money she was entitled to, not to mention real estate and investments and whatever else rich people passed down to their children. He couldn't rob her of that. He couldn't rob his child of that. They deserved it.

"Fine. I'll go—for her sake and not because you told me to. If she finds out what you've done, it will break her heart."

"Then let's all pray she never finds out," Eliza said.

~

Isabelle hadn't heard from JD in five full days. Her parents had discovered the truth thanks to a phone call from the doctor, and she'd been on house arrest ever since.

And she was getting stir-crazy.

Finally her parents went out with friends, warning her that if she left, there would be consequences. Those consequences felt like nothing compared to the pain of not seeing JD, so after about twenty minutes, Isabelle rode her bike to his aunt's cottage and pounded on the door.

The memory of what had happened there only weeks before came flooding back. She regretted her rash decision to sleep with JD, more so now than ever. And yet she didn't regret loving him. He made her feel like she had a voice and like that voice mattered.

The door opened and Jeb stared through the screen. "Isabelle, hey."

"Hey, is JD here?"

Jeb frowned. "Didn't he tell you?"

"Tell me what?"

Jeb swallowed, clearly uncomfortable, and Isabelle's heart sank.

"Tell me what?"

"He left."

"Okay, is he at work? In town? Where?"

"No, he left the island. He already went back to school." Jeb opened the screen door. "I'm sorry, Isabelle. I thought for sure he would've told you."

She chewed her bottom lip to keep from crying. "Did he leave a number or anything?"

Jeb shook his head. "No, he didn't have it when he left, but listen, when I get back to school, I can make sure he looks you up. Wanna leave me your home number?"

Did she? What good would that do? JD had left without so much as a word. No good-bye. Nothing. Their plan to get married and figure out how to raise a child together suddenly felt so juvenile, so ridiculous. *She* felt so juvenile and ridiculous.

"No thanks, Jeb," she choked out. "I'll see ya."

She raced off, aware that he called after her twice, but she didn't turn around. She pedaled back to her house, cursing the day she ever met JD and wondering how on earth she was going to move forward without him.

CHAPTER 36

EMILY SAT ON THE BEACH as the sky darkened. She'd bypassed the house (and her grandmother), stopping by the shed to grab a blanket, then heading straight to the water. She'd taken her shoes off and now burrowed her toes in the sand until the warmth of the top layer turned cool.

The unmistakable jingling of Tilly's tags signaled the dog's arrival, and Emily expected Jolie to come bounding down to the beach full of energy after their first rehearsal earlier that day.

From the second Jolie had opened her mouth to sing her audition song, Emily had been impressed with her. She'd played it completely cool and didn't give the girl any special treatment, but truth be told, Hollis's daughter was a natural. She'd been relieved. What if Jolie had been terrible? She almost laughed at the thought of *that* awkward conversation, but she was mostly relieved she didn't have to have it.

Tilly ran straight up to her and plopped herself down in the sand, rolling over so Emily could rub her belly. "You silly dog."

"You made it."

She didn't need to turn around to know it was Hollis, not his daughter, accompanying the Lab. Her heart skittered, missing two beats: *Hol-lis*.

She drew in a deep breath.

He sat down on her blanket and set a Bartlett's bag between them. "Hungry?"

"You brought dinner?"

"I said I would," Hollis said. "It's nothing fancy." He pulled two sandwiches from the bag. "Chicken salad or turkey?"

"Chicken salad." She reached over and took the sandwich. "Thanks for this."

"I can't let you starve."

"Now that you know how poor I am?" She laughed. It was nice to laugh about it—made the tragedy less . . . tragic.

He gave her a look. "Yeah, you're downright destitute up there in that big cottage overlooking the ocean."

She smiled, thankful for the dose of perspective. *Things could be so much worse.*

They ate in silence for a few seconds, and then he shifted, angling himself so he faced her. "So how was it?"

She was wondering when he'd ask about the rehearsal. He'd hovered for longer than he needed to when he dropped Jolie off. It was adorable, if she was honest, watching him fuss over his daughter.

Before he left, Hollis caught her eye and mouthed the words *You okay?* She'd nodded and wished for an ice pack to take down the swelling in her heart.

She wasn't used to having someone check up on her. And it wasn't only Hollis. On audition day, Nan had stayed from start to finish, welcoming young performers, quelling their nerves and putting parents' minds at ease. The woman also brought homemade brownies in for Emily and the rest of the team sitting through the auditions and replenished their water bottles twice.

Today, she'd shown up to help in the costume room and checked on Emily three times after giving her the prerehearsal pep talk she needed. "Just want to be sure you don't need anything."

And as much as she'd tried to fight it, Emily found herself feeling like she belonged. Or at least like she could belong if she let herself.

She swallowed a bite of delicious chicken salad sandwich and met Hollis's eyes. "Honestly? It was amazing." She couldn't have kept the smile off her face if she tried.

"Yeah?" He set his sandwich down. "You liked it?"

"I mean, yeah," she said. "The kids are all so brave. We played improv games at the end, and it was inspiring, watching them get up there and do things most adults wouldn't have the guts to do. They're fearless, you know?"

"Like you?"

Emily laughed. "Not so much these days."

Maybe she'd been fearless once upon a time, but she'd suffered enough heartache to pull back on her reins and slow her down.

"Come on, you're out there living a crazy life, meeting new people on a never-ending rotation—that alone makes you fearless. It's hard for a lot of people to go to places they've never gone before and jump right into the culture. I mean, what's the longest you've spent in any one place?"

"Maybe a year. A little less."

His eyes widened. "See? Fearless."

Emily took another bite, chewed it slowly, and pondered his comment. "That's never felt fearless to me."

"Skydiving? Surfing during a tropical storm? Did those things feel fearless?"

She shrugged. "I never really felt like I had the choice to be scared about those things."

He watched her—too carefully. "What do you mean?"

How much did she tell him? He already knew about her professional failure—did she have to tell all of her secrets? She met his eyes and heard herself start talking, as if she had no choice in the matter at all. A part of her wanted Hollis to know her stories, even the ones that made her feel naked and vulnerable.

Maybe especially those.

"After the accident, my grandparents took me back to the apartment where Mom and I were living to pack up our things, and that's when I found this book of letters from her." She explained the book and the letters inside.

"I've seen the book," he said.

"Yeah, I carry it in my bag most days." Emily stared out across the ocean. "Makes her feel close."

Hollis's silence felt more like an encouragement to continue than disinterest, so she rummaged through the big bag at her side, pulled the book out, and flipped through until she found the letter titled "On Dreams."

"There are a lot of letters that have stuck with me, but this one especially," she said. She handed him the book so he could read the words she'd committed to memory so many years ago.

Dear Emily,

When it comes to dreams, there's only one way to do it—big. I have big dreams of traveling overseas, and not with my parents. Their version of Europe is much different from mine. I want to see the people and eat the food and experience the culture without all the luxuries Eliza Ackerman insists on.

There's something wildly wonderful about this planet, and I want to see it all: to take grand adventures, learn about culture, and gain a whole new perspective on how big this world really is.

It's a dream worth having, don't you think?

Life should be lived to the fullest, to the utmost, to the overflowing brim, and every dream of your heart should be seized with unwavering excitement.

That's what I pray for you. Wild adventures. Crazy stories. Big dreams. When they grab on to your heart . . . follow them.

You deserve a big, full life.

Love,
Mom

Hollis met her eyes. "So you live this wild life for your mom?"

"Yeah," Emily said. "Well, no. I mean, I love it. I love traveling and seeing the world. I've had this big, grand life—I live out of suitcases and stay in hotels all over the world. Who wouldn't want that life?"

"I wouldn't."

"You wouldn't?"

"I've had it," Hollis said. "It's not what I want—not anymore."

She eyed him thoughtfully. "So what do you want?"

He shrugged. "Something simple. Small town. Nice house. White picket fence. A couple of kids, maybe another dog. Summers in Nantucket. Family dinners and cookouts, coaching Little League and all kinds of kids running around . . . Don't need much more than that." He paused. "Probably sounds boring to you." He popped a cracker topped with cheese in his mouth.

"Actually, it sounds kind of perfect."

Their eyes met, and he scanned her face, reading through to what she wasn't saying the way only he bothered to do. "Yeah?"

She sighed. "Truthfully, I've grown a little weary of all the roaming around. But there are still so many countries left to see."

"Do you feel like you have to keep going?"

"Well, yeah," she said. "You read the letter."

"I did," he said. "Did you?"

She frowned. "Hollis, I have it memorized. It's all I have left of her."

"Right, but she didn't say you had to follow *her* dream. She said you had to follow yours."

Emily glanced down at the letter, its words racing through her mind.

That's what I pray for you. Wild adventures. Crazy stories. Big dreams. When they grab on to your heart . . . follow them.

"She wanted this for me—a big life, full of adventure."

"But she didn't say what constitutes a big, adventurous life. You get to decide that for yourself."

Emily shook her head. "No, she wanted me to travel, see the world."

"*She* wanted to travel and see the world. You can't feel tied to a dream that was never yours to begin with."

"No, it was," Emily said. "It *is* my dream." A panic rose up inside her that she didn't recognize. Why was she getting so worked up over this? Why did it matter?

Her heart sputtered.

Because if what Hollis was saying was true, she'd misinterpreted her mother's words. And if she'd misinterpreted her mother's words, that changed everything—every single thing in her life.

She'd lived by the rules outlined in that book. She'd been so careful to turn into the woman her mother would've wanted her to be.

Had she misunderstood everything?

"Emily." He reached across the blanket and took her hand. "It's okay to want a simple life."

"No," she said. "It's not what I want."

"I've seen you, Em. Not just today, but at auditions, with that little girl . . ."

She pulled her hand from his and hugged her knees to her chest. The little girl—Marta—had been one of five she'd talked off the ledge, and each time she made a connection, each time the child faced their fears, Emily had beamed with pride, as if she could take part in their victory.

She hadn't told a soul how any of that made her feel. How did Hollis know?

"The way you rushed in, calmed her right down—the way you instantly connected with Jolie . . ." Hollis regarded her for a moment. "You've got a gift, Emily."

She waved him off, along with thoughts of Colin, thankful Hollis couldn't add him to his arsenal of proof. "Your right arm is a gift. That was just—" What? What was it? Certainly not a *gift*.

"You can downplay it all you want, Em, but not everyone can do what you did in there. I sure couldn't." He took his sandwich wrapper and balled it up, then put it back in the bag. "You have the right to your own dreams. Don't you think that's what your mom would want for you?"

Was it? She didn't know. For the first time ever, she doubted that she knew her mother's wishes, wishes she'd originally thought had been crystal clear. She didn't like it.

But she couldn't deny how much she'd loved running rehearsal today. She loved the thought of helping these kids tap into their creativity, of giving them a safe space to fail gloriously and without judgment, just as she'd been given that so many years ago. She'd already imagined their curtain call, the way that post-show adrenaline would kick in and bring with it so much unfiltered *joy*. She wanted that for each one of these kids.

She'd even entertained the idea of *next summer's show*, something she most definitely would not be involved with, but still there it was.

And somehow it all made the failures in her past feel a lot farther away, almost like they didn't matter so much anymore.

"What are you thinking about?" he asked.

Emily looked away. She couldn't say. She couldn't admit that there was a chance Hollis was right.

Never mind that his words had spoken to the deepest part of her soul. His dream for simplicity—it stirred something inside her. He'd described a life she'd always coveted and never had. A life she never would have.

And considering even for a moment that maybe, just maybe, she had a purpose on this planet—a purpose that amounted to more than flitting around from place to place with a bottomless trust fund to back her up . . . She couldn't say what that did to her insides.

What if she was made for more? Emily, the girl whose father didn't want her? The girl who'd screwed up more times than she could count? The girl who wouldn't let anyone get close to her because she had to protect her heart?

Could that girl have something to offer?

She desperately wanted to believe it, but if she did, she'd be setting herself up for a heartache greater than any she'd suffered before.

She wasn't the small-town, picket-fence kind of girl. She was consumed with wanderlust—it was who she'd always been, and a few words from a handsome baseball player wouldn't change that.

No matter how much she wished they could.

"I should go." Abrupt, yes, but she needed a clean getaway.

He watched her as she packed up her garbage, sticking it all back in the bag. "Did I upset you?"

Was it that obvious? She thought she was a better actor than that.

"No, of course not," she said. "I just remembered my grandma is here, and I probably need to face her sooner rather than later."

Liar. Liar. Liar.

"Okay," Hollis said. "So we'll talk about sets tomorrow?"

She grinned. "I'm not sure you're ready for what I have planned."

He groaned, but she could tell he was joking. They started walking toward the path that led back to the houses.

"Picture a giant tree with a slide coming out of it and a swing and all kinds of color."

He stopped walking and stared at her. "Is this a ploy to get me away from your home renovations?"

She shrugged. "Is it working?"

"Maybe," Hollis said. "I've never built a tree before."

"It'll be fun."

"With you involved, Emily," he said, "I have no doubt."

And the compliment wormed its way past her outer layer and straight to her heart, leaving her (not for the first time since she'd arrived on the island) a little worried that where Hollis McGuire was concerned, a strong resolve was a thing of the past.

CHAPTER 37

THE DAYS WENT ON, and at some point, Hollis realized he wasn't missing baseball as much as he used to. He worked in the scene shop during rehearsals, stealing glimpses of Emily while she stepped into a role she seemed born to play.

They spent their days off on the beach with Jolie or working on the sets alongside a small crew of volunteers. Even Jack showed up once or twice to help.

And Emily seemed to be warming up to his family, spending more nights around their dinner table than alone in that big, empty house.

Hollis wouldn't have wanted it any other way.

By the Fourth of July, Jack had made great progress on Emily's house, all under Hollis's watchful eye. He couldn't pinpoint why, but he still didn't fully trust the man.

The entire family, Emily included, spent the holiday moving from one event to the next. The parade, sack races on Children's Beach, a lobster boil in the McGuires' backyard followed up by fireworks—the kind that made Hollis wish he had the courage to tell Emily exactly how he felt.

Nearly every night over the past few weeks, he'd found Emily sitting outside on the beach just after sunset. Sometimes they talked. Sometimes they sat in silence. He didn't really care what they did as long as he was with her. It had become something of a ritual—one he was starting to love.

It had gotten to the point where he practically relied on this time to help him relax before going to sleep—or maybe he simply liked falling asleep with the memories of her laugh fresh in his mind.

She asked questions about life in professional baseball and even dared to bring up the offers he'd gotten to become a commentator, a previously sore subject for him.

Since the first time she mentioned it, he'd had a few conversations with the network, and while he hadn't told Emily yet, he had an interview scheduled in a few weeks.

Maybe there was more for him to do than just be a former professional ballplayer. Same way there was more for Emily to do than just be a former childhood star whose adult career didn't work out the way she'd planned.

He hadn't realized that parallel between their two lives until now.

Their conversations always made their way around to the show, too, something she loved to talk about, something he loved to listen to her talk about. She came alive with ideas and stories about the kids. And while her big imagination meant a lot of work for his sets team, he didn't even care. He got to spend time with Jolie, spend time with Emily, and be a part of her realizing she was born to do exactly what she was doing right now.

Sometimes he wondered if she saw it yet—and if not, how long would it take to sink into her stubborn head?

Now, just a week before *Alice* would open, he awoke with a fresh to-do list. He and Emily were meeting that morning to look over a handful of last-minute set-building questions. He hurried to get ready and made his way across the lawn to her cottage.

The front door was unlocked, so Hollis let himself in. Before he could call out to Emily, he heard a conversation happening somewhere in the house.

He listened from the entryway for a few seconds, deciphering both Jack's and Eliza's tense voices coming from the living room.

He should leave. Or announce his presence somehow. How many conversations was he going to eavesdrop on?

But curiosity got the better of him. He'd have to repent for this later.

"I'm sorry you don't approve, but *Emily* hired me to do this job, and I'm going to see it through to the end," Jack said.

"Emily might think she's in charge here, Jack, but we both know whose name is on the deed to this house," Eliza fired back.

"She said Alan wanted her to decide what to do with this place." Jack spoke about Alan Ackerman as if he knew the man. There was a familiarity in the way he said his name.

"What are you even doing here?" Eliza asked.

"Alan wanted me to come, Eliza," he said.

"That's a lie."

Hollis leaned in closer. He'd been suspicious of Jack from the start, but he'd only been thinking of the man's intentions toward Emily. What kind of connection did Jack Walker have to her grandfather?

Hollis leaned into the doorway until he caught sight of Jack, facing off against Eliza the way only the bravest of men would do. He had to give the guy credit for that.

"We don't have to be enemies," Jack said.

"Well, we certainly aren't friends."

"But maybe we could be. Don't you think she would've wanted it that way?" Jack reached into his shirt pocket and pulled out something that looked like a photograph folded in half.

Eliza stiffened. "What's this?"

"Just look at it."

She glared at him. Whatever the relationship was between the two of them, it wasn't a good one. Slowly Emily's grandmother unfolded the photo. One look at it, and her face went pale. "Where did you get this?"

He took the photo from her and stuck it back in his pocket. "I found it upstairs."

Was that what he was looking at the day Hollis caught him in there snooping around?

"You had no right."

"Maybe not, but Emily does." Jack stood his ground.

"You can't show this to her. Think about what that would do to her."

"If you'll excuse me, Eliza, I have work to do."

Hollis felt his shoulders slump. He didn't know exactly what was going on, but he had the gnawing feeling that Emily was about to have her heart broken all over again.

Just when he'd started to sort of accept Jack might not be as bad a guy as he'd originally feared.

Jack stormed out of the living room—thankfully not in his direction—leaving Eliza, dumbfounded, with a concerned expression on her face.

The front door opened and Emily appeared, holding a box of Wicked Island Bakery donuts and four to-go cups of coffee.

"Hollis?"

He glanced over and saw Eliza's eyes snap toward him. *Caught.*

"Hey, Emily," he said.

"What are you doing?"

He forced a smile. "Waiting for you."

Eliza moved to the entryway, looking none too pleased.

"Good morning, Grandma," Emily said.

"Good morning," Eliza said. Her face was pulled tight as she looked at Hollis. "Mr. McGuire. Apparently we no longer knock before entering someone else's house."

Hollis's gaze fell to the floor.

"I got you coffee, Grandma." Emily held up the tray of drinks. "Your name is on that one there." She motioned with her head.

"I already had my coffee," her grandma said. "But thank you. Mr.

McGuire, could I have a word with you in the kitchen please? Or what used to be the kitchen."

Emily regarded her grandmother for a long moment. "Why do you need to have a word with Hollis?"

"Don't be nosy, dear." Eliza walked toward the kitchen, leaving Hollis standing there, under Emily's watchful gaze.

"What's this about?" Emily whispered.

"No idea," Hollis said. "But I better go."

Emily widened her eyes. "I'll take this stuff to Jack and come back to save you."

He smiled. He'd have a million conversations with Eliza Ackerman if it meant being saved by her granddaughter.

Eliza stood at the sliding door, staring out across the backyard. She held her shoulders straight, arms crossed over her chest, and she didn't turn to acknowledge him.

"It's not polite to listen in on other people's conversations," she said.

"I'd just come in, Mrs. Ackerman." Was it a lie? The conversation had been fast-paced, and he really had only been standing there for a minute.

"How much did you hear?"

"Not much—"

"Jack threatening me?"

"I don't trust him, ma'am."

"Well, that makes two of us." She turned to him now as if she'd found an ally, and a sickening feeling washed over him. "Of all the people Emily could've hired for this job," she muttered.

"How do you know him?" Hollis asked.

She regarded him for a moment, then flicked her hand in the air as if deciding to keep her ally at arm's length. "He used to hang around here years ago. He and Alan had a sort of altercation at the golf club one summer. Alan got him fired—but rightfully so. You don't mouth off to members when you're just a caddie."

"Seems like water under the bridge," Hollis said, knowing by what he'd overheard that it absolutely was not. He wanted to ask about the photo. He wanted to ask why it would be upsetting to Emily and why Eliza didn't want her to see it. But doing that would reveal just how much he had overheard.

"Could you do me a favor and not mention any of this to Emily?" Eliza asked. "I'd like to discuss it with her myself."

"I think maybe Emily should know your concerns about the man she's hired," Hollis said. "Especially if she's going to have to make a change."

"You let me worry about that. It's a family matter, really." Her smile looked forced, but she'd made her point—he wasn't a part of the family. "And maybe, while you're working around here, you can keep an eye on Mr. Walker?" Eliza's penciled-in eyebrows elevated over her eyes. "If you see anything out of the ordinary, anything suspicious, you can let me know?"

Why did it feel like he was conspiring with Eliza against Emily? Why did it all feel horribly wrong?

"Hollis? You ready to talk sets?" Emily had entered the kitchen, and Hollis wondered if she'd eavesdropped the same way he had. Eliza was talking so quietly, he doubted Emily could've heard anything, but she would definitely ask him questions.

What was he going to say? He couldn't lie to her. He wouldn't.

And yet, for some reason, he had a feeling he needed to find out for himself who Jack really was and what he was doing here before alerting Emily. No matter how many times Eliza told him to butt out, even *she* couldn't stop him from asking his own questions if it meant making sure Emily wasn't in any danger.

The only problem was, he had a feeling that if he started digging, he wasn't going to like what he found.

CHAPTER 38

$\sim\sim\sim$

EMILY WATCHED HER GRANDMOTHER exchange a tense look with Hollis before heading out for another morning of shopping with an old friend.

"What on earth was that about?" she asked, expecting Hollis to tell her how pushy her grandmother was.

Instead, he half laughed and waved a hand in the air dismissively. "She was asking about the crew, the kind of job they're doing, that sort of thing."

Emily groaned. "She doesn't think I can handle this job. She's checking up on me. That's probably why she's here."

Hollis flashed her a smile. "What do you expect? She's used to calling all the shots."

Jack poked his head in from the hallway. "We're good on paint colors for the bedrooms, right?"

Emily spun around. "Oh, there you are! I got you coffee." She'd gone looking for him but ended up dropping the donuts with his crew chief, a younger guy named Marcus.

Jack moved a few steps in, took the cup from her, inhaled, and drank. "How'd you know I needed this today?"

"I'm just that good." She grinned.

He left, and she turned to find Hollis wearing a scowl. An actual scowl. Had everyone gone mad overnight? "Whoa," she said. "What is that look for?"

Hollis shifted, changing his expression. "No coffee for me?"

She tilted her head to the side and drank him in. He looked exquisite this morning in a pair of jeans, work boots, and a blue T-shirt with the Colorado flag on it.

"You feeling left out?" she mocked.

His smile made her heart sputter.

"Of course I got you coffee." She handed over a cup, and when he took it, his fingers brushed over hers for a brief second, sending a shiver straight down her spine.

Oh, please, she thought. *Get a grip. You sound like one of those stupid girls who live for a look or a word or a touch from a good-looking guy. That is not who you are, Emily Ackerman.*

Although . . . what she wouldn't give for a look, a word, or another touch from Hollis McGuire. . . .

This was not good. If he'd never made that speech about wanting a simple life—with kids and Little League and a picket fence—she'd be perfectly fine right now.

But he had made that speech. And many more just like it. And those speeches kept her awake at night, daydreaming about the possibility of throwing caution to the wind.

Because as much as she didn't want to admit it, it spoke to the deepest part of her soul. It made her think—as impractical as it was—that she might want those things too. And she'd never wanted those things, not really. At least not in the aching sort of way she wanted them now.

"No donut?" he asked after taking a sip.

She smacked his arm. "You're the worst."

Their familiarity had grown. In some ways, it was just like old times. But every now and then, she'd catch him looking at her—at rehearsal as he worked or on the beach during one of their late-night chats—and nothing felt like old times.

It felt new and fresh and exciting.

And scary.

IF FOR ANY REASON

She'd spent the better part of the summer with Hollis and Jolie and the rest of their family, and she was feeling more and more like a person who belonged.

It sometimes startled her, the depth with which she felt it. She loved them. Not just Hollis, but all of them.

How would she ever leave Nantucket now? Now that she knew how this felt, the pain of letting it go would break her heart.

He smiled. "You look lost."

She pushed the thoughts away and found his eyes, ever intent and kind and laser-focused on her. "No," she said. "I'm anything but that."

~

Forty-eight hours had passed since Hollis's uncomfortable conversation with Eliza. He'd spent most of that time avoiding the topic, thankful that Emily seemed to forget the awkward exchange completely. She had other things on her mind: namely, the show.

He spent as much time as possible at the theatre, and he was about 95 percent sure he'd fallen completely in love with Emily.

Exactly what he'd promised JoJo he wouldn't do.

He'd done a good job so far of keeping his feelings to himself, but that had gotten more difficult as the days went on.

Twice that day during rehearsal he'd nearly hurt himself working on the set (once with a chop saw and once with a nail gun) because he'd gotten distracted by something Emily was doing.

Or maybe he'd just gotten distracted by Emily. Her hair. Her eyes. Her smile. Her easy way of drawing people in. She'd always thrived as the center of attention, and now, seeing how the kids gravitated to her . . . well, it was hard not to be completely mesmerized.

Did she see it yet? She was a natural at this. The way she welcomed the kids, the way she made sure no one ate lunch alone, even the way she sat with them through meals, listening to their crazy stories and answering all their questions about Broadway and acting and traveling the world.

Whether she knew it or not, he wasn't the only one who'd fallen head over heels for her.

And if he had to guess, she'd fallen for those kids, too.

He and Jolie walked into the rehearsal space, and his daughter took off toward a group of girls about her age. She'd made fast friends with Alyssa, the girl playing the Caterpillar, and the two had been nearly inseparable since rehearsals began. It was exactly what Hollis had prayed for—that his daughter would find her place here, that she would fall in love with Nantucket. If that all happened, then maybe she'd even realize she loved him a little bit too.

"Hollis!"

He turned toward Emily's voice and found her rushing toward him, panic on her face. "What's wrong?"

"I forgot my script at home, and I can't leave. We need to get started, but all my blocking is written in that script."

"I'll run and get it. Just tell me where it is."

"It's a blue binder in my room." She stumbled over her words. "The guest room. The one at the very back of the house."

She was sleeping in the guest room?

"I'm guessing on the desk in the corner or maybe on the bed."

"Okay. Will you be all right without it at the start?"

"Yes. We have a few other things we need to do before we jump in, and I can play a game or two."

"I'll hurry," he said, heading toward the door.

"Hollis?" she called out.

He turned to face her.

"Thanks."

The you-just-saved-me expression on her face was one he'd tuck inside his pocket and save for a rainy day. The way it felt to help her, to do any small thing to make her day better—yep, he was a goner.

He raced down to the parking lot, hopped in his Jeep, and sped back to Emily's house. When he arrived, he saw the crew dispersed around the yard.

He walked up the stairs to the porch and in the front door, not bothering to knock because Eliza's car was gone and no one else would pay attention. He went straight upstairs, down the hallway, and pushed open the door to the guest room.

Instantly, he was struck by her unmistakable scent—vanilla with something else mixed in. Coconut, maybe? He'd inhaled it enough times to recognize it immediately. He couldn't pinpoint when it had happened—the moment he crossed out of his safe "friend zone" and began entertaining other thoughts about Emily. It was almost as if he'd been unaware it was happening at all. Or maybe he'd simply been in denial. Because he was pretty sure it started the moment he thought he spotted her getting off the ferry her first day back.

Now here he was, standing in her bedroom, ignoring what she sent him here to do and picturing the way she spent her nights. Did she sleep all under the covers or did she leave one leg out? Did she close the curtains or let the moonlight fill the room? Did she get lonely or sad or have trouble falling asleep?

He wanted to know these things—all of them.

"Hollis?"

He turned and found Jack standing in the doorway of the guest room.

"Do you need something?"

The way Jack asked the question, as if he were the one who could help him, bothered Hollis. "Uh, no. Emily needs something."

Hollis glanced down and saw the turquoise binder on the end of Emily's unmade bed. A binder he could've grabbed without lingering over the way the room looked and smelled.

He picked it up.

"Just making sure," Jack said. "Do you have a second? Thought I'd show you the progress they made in the backyard. I have a feeling she's not going to want to sell this place once we're done."

It was too much to hope for. Hollis was pretty sure nothing was going to change her mind on the house.

"Sure," he said, though he really didn't have a minute. Emily needed him back.

And yet, this could be the in with Jack he'd been waiting for. He followed the man down the stairs, through the house, and out back. As expected, the crew had done a stellar job with the landscaping. The flagstone patio was only one of an endless number of things they'd done in the yard. They'd added sprays of colorful flowers and bushes and giant pots of greenery that would likely blossom later in the season. They'd trimmed trees, pulled more weeds, added mulch—basically, they'd made everything presentable again.

Even Gladys Middlebury would approve.

"Think she'll like it?" Jack asked. He was staring out across the yard, and Hollis took a moment to study Jack's profile. The curve of his nose, the high cheekbones, even the skin tone was remarkably similar—why had he never seen it before? The resemblance was unmistakable.

Jack looked at him, expectancy on his face, and only then did Hollis realize he hadn't answered the man's question.

"Yeah," he said. "I think she'll love it. You guys did a great job."

"Well, thanks for your help with it," Jack said.

"What were you doing looking around in Isabelle's room that day?" Hollis asked.

Jack went back to staring at the yard.

"I heard you and Eliza talking last week," Hollis said. "She doesn't like you—why?"

"It's a long story," Jack said, facing him.

"Do you have any intention of telling Emily that story? Don't you think she deserves the truth?"

"The truth about what?"

"About who you are," Hollis said.

Jack turned away.

"I've been trying to figure out your game this whole time."

"My game?"

"Yeah. Something never added up. I can't believe I didn't see it before. How Eliza can't stand to have you around, how you seem to know the family as more than just someone who caddied for Alan back in the day, how you sort of look like Emily—the parts of her that don't look like her mom. It's been staring me in the face this whole time."

Jack dragged a hand over his face, the whiskers of his unshaven chin scratching against it. "I'm going to tell her. I just . . . I don't know how she'll react."

Hollis could feel his stomach twist into a tight ball. "Oh, you don't know how she'll react to meeting the father who never wanted her? Do you know her mom left her a letter basically warning her to never fall in love because you good and broke her heart like you did?"

Jack sighed. "There's a lot to this that you don't understand."

"I have a daughter," Hollis said. "I understand."

Regret rolled around inside his belly. He had a daughter he'd basically abandoned—did he have any right to lecture this guy for making the same mistakes he'd made?

"Then you know how important it is that I get this right," Jack said. "I came here because Alan asked me to. And because I finally felt like I could."

"What are you talking about?"

"Isabelle's dad sent me a letter," Jack said. "Or I guess his lawyer did—after Alan died. In it, he told me he was leaving her the house and to keep checking on it because he knew she'd come back here."

"Why would he do that?"

"It doesn't matter," Jack said. "But he did. And I watched and waited until finally I got word she was back. This is my only chance to get to know my own daughter. Do you know how long I've waited for this?"

Hollis shook his head. "This isn't fair to Emily."

"Hollis, please." Jack reached inside his front shirt pocket and took out the folded photograph. "I was crazy about Isabelle. We were crazy about each other." He handed over the photo. Hollis opened it and the image of Emily's parents, younger, eyes sparkling with laughter, stared back at Hollis.

"I saw her that night—the night of the accident. For the first time in years. It was one of those crazy coincidences—the first summer I'd come back to the island. I'd only been divorced a few months, and I don't know—maybe part of me was hoping to run into her. I saw her at the Chicken Box of all places. Just walked in and saw her standing there looking like she did all those years before. It was like time stopped."

Hollis knew that feeling. He'd had it himself at the ferry landing the day Emily returned.

"She smacked me." Jack laughed. "She smacked me hard."

Hollis didn't say anything, though his pulse was racing with Emily's frantic energy. He needed to get back, but how did he walk away now? When Jack was finally giving answers?

"I explained things to her, after she finally settled down. Told her I'd finally made something of myself." He sighed. "Told her I never stopped loving her. After a lot of explaining, by some miracle, she agreed to try again." Jack raked a hand through his hair.

Hollis's heart dropped.

"She died on her way to my place."

"Jack, I'm sorry," Hollis said. "And I do feel for you, but the only thing I really care about is Emily. And I have a hard time believing her mom magically forgave you for leaving like you did."

"You don't know the whole story," Jack said. "And I'm going to tell Emily everything, but I just need a little more time."

"This is going to break her heart."

"Don't you think I know that?" Jack asked. "Why do you think I haven't said anything yet?" He took the photo back, folded it up carefully, and slid it inside his pocket.

"I really messed up," Jack said.

"You really missed out," Hollis said. "She's the most amazing woman I've ever met, and you missed all that—why? What reason could you possibly have to miss out on her?"

Jack fixed his eyes on Hollis. "You love her."

Hollis looked away.

"I mean, how could you not? She's full of life, just like Isabelle.

She's infectious. You can see why I don't want to say anything—if she's angry, she could walk out of my life forever."

"Why now? After all she's been through, why didn't you come back years ago when she really needed you?"

Jack shoved his hands in his pockets. "She didn't need me. Not back then. I did what I thought was best for my daughter."

"And lying to her now—that's what you think is best for her?"

"I'm not lying, Hollis," Jack said, then thoughtfully, "I'm just trying to find the words."

"You've had weeks to find the words."

"You have to let me tell her." Jack squared off in front of him. "Please."

Hollis shook his head. It was bad enough feeling like he was conspiring with Eliza, but her request paled in comparison to what Jack was asking. He couldn't lie to Emily—he wouldn't.

"Maybe the way I handled this wasn't the right way," Jack said. "But you have to understand, everything I've done I've done because I believed it was in Emily's best interest."

Hollis looked away. "I'm having trouble seeing it that way."

"I just need time," Jack said. "Please."

Hollis sighed. "What you're asking me to do . . . it means every time I'm with her and I don't tell her, I'm lying to her." Hollis rubbed the knot that had formed at the back of his neck. "Knowing how I feel about her, how can you ask me to do that?"

"I know you don't believe it, but I'm not the bad guy you think I am. And I'm gonna tell her everything—I need to figure out what to say. I need to figure out how to make her not hate me. Please, Hollis, it's what I came here to do."

"I'm not keeping your secret for very much longer, Jack," Hollis said. "So you better figure it out fast."

"I understand," Jack said.

Hollis gave Jack one last pointed glare, then turned and walked away, wishing like crazy that Emily hadn't forgotten her script at home.

CHAPTER 39

~~~

WITH JUST A FEW MORE REHEARSALS before opening night, Emily had some tightening to do. The show was mostly in good shape, with the music, blocking, and almost all of the choreography taught. But there were a few things that needed tweaking, and today, she would tweak.

As the director, it was her job to not only cast the vision for the whole show (costumes, sets, props, etc.) but also to work with the kids on their interpretation of the scenes.

Before auditions, she was certain she wouldn't be successful at this. Even today, sitting in a chair as the kids filed into the room, she still felt that way, and she'd been doing it for weeks.

Get it together, Emily.

The show was so close to ready—why were her nerves back?

Maybe because this one scene was giving them trouble, and she knew it was up to her to fix it.

Marisol must've sensed her hesitation that morning during their icebreaker game because she walked over to Emily and said, "What's the matter?"

Emily forced a smile. "Nothing."

"You look green."

"I think I'm starting to get nervous," she said. "We're opening two days from now."

"Don't be nervous," Marisol said cheerfully. "We've got this."

"And I have to fix that scene today—the Caterpillar one."

Her assistant groaned. "That scene is not good."

Emily widened her eyes. "I know."

"Well, you'll fix it. You're like a master magician."

Emily wasn't so sure.

"Besides," Marisol said, "the show is in great shape otherwise."

It was. And yet, some days, Emily found herself waiting for the whole thing to fall apart, like a supersize game of Jenga. Had she forgotten something important? Something that would make or break this production? What if she let everyone down?

"I still don't really feel like a director," she said. "I was always a performer."

Marisol put a hand on Emily's shoulder. "These are kids, Em. No matter what, you know a lot more than they do. Just talk to them the way you wish your directors would've talked to you."

Emily nodded. Marisol was right. So far, nobody knew she was a fraud.

"Where are we starting, Miss Emily?" Alyssa Daniels asked. The girl had a powerhouse voice, but she'd been struggling with the acting side of her part. Emily saw it with several of the kids, actually. Good voices could carry them to a certain point, but if she wanted the show to be truly excellent, she needed to teach them about becoming the character.

And she felt wholly unqualified. The last time she'd tried to help anyone "become a character," she'd gotten publicly torn to shreds.

She reminded herself this was different. And like Marisol said, no matter what, she did know more about theatre than the kids did.

Even Bethany Thompkins, whose mother was very clear at auditions that her daughter was a musical prodigy and should be treated as such.

"You're going to want her as Alice, of course," Mrs. Thompkins had said. "She was accepted to Boston's prestigious Little Voices program and has been singing with a private instructor for five years now." The woman nodded at Emily as if she'd just issued a directive.

Bethany was eleven years old and did, in fact, have a beautiful voice. If they had been casting an opera. Emily spent a good deal of time at the piano with her, trying to find a way to make her sound more current, but five years with a private voice instructor had drilled a very particular sound into the girl.

Mrs. Thompkins had many thoughts about Bethany's role in the ensemble, and she hadn't kept them to herself.

"Apparently, Bethany's mom is telling the other parents you're unqualified and don't know what you're doing." Marisol had laughed as if it were the most ridiculous thing in the world, but the barb cut Emily like a deep wound that had been there for a long time and had never healed.

Now, as she stood in front of a handful of her leads, her confidence level dipped.

I can do hard things.

She never thought that would include directing a group of kids. How had she gotten here?

All right. Enough.

Emily cleared her throat. "Okay, let's run the scene."

In front of her, Alyssa and a blonde girl named Madison, who was playing Alice, stood with their scripts in hand.

"Got your pencils?"

They each held up their freshly sharpened number twos—one of Emily's rules: show up ready to work, with a pencil, and write down everything you need to know.

Maybe to some people, the scene wouldn't matter much, but to Emily, it set the stage for "Zip-a-Dee-Doo-Dah," which immediately followed. She saw no point in having a showstopper that slogged onto the stage with a boring or poorly acted scene before it.

IF FOR ANY REASON

And watching Alyssa and Madison up until this point, it was clear that was what she was going to get unless she jumped in.

"Alyssa, do you know what a beatnik is?"

Alyssa scrunched her face and shook her head.

Emily stood in front of her, changed her stance, and said one of the lines as if she were a 1950s poet with a set of bongo drums.

Alyssa laughed.

"The Caterpillar is the coolest character in the show."

The girl beamed. "Really?"

"Oh yeah. She's got this certain vibe, like someone who knows she's cool. Everything is 'Ya dig?' and 'Are you pickin' up what I'm puttin' down?'" Emily said that last part in a character voice.

Alyssa smiled. "You want me to talk like that?"

"Not exactly," Emily said. "I want you to make it your own. Think of the coolest person you know."

Alyssa started to speak, but Emily cut her off with an upheld hand.

"Don't tell me who it is. Just think about them for a minute. How do they talk? How do they move? What is it that makes them so cool?"

Alyssa closed her eyes, then nodded.

"Now I want you to try the scene again and think of that person the whole time. And keep that one word in your mind—*cool*."

Alyssa's face grew serious, but she nodded again as if to let Emily know she was up for the task.

Within seconds, Emily saw the difference. The kind of change she wouldn't have believed if she hadn't seen it with her own eyes. Alyssa's dull monotone had been replaced with a character, one that would most certainly work for their Caterpillar.

They finished the scene and Madison grinned at Alyssa. "You did so good!"

Alyssa looked at Emily. "Was it okay?"

Emily had inexplicable tears in her eyes.

Alyssa's face fell. "Oh no, was it bad?"

Emily shook her head, a nervous laugh flowing out. "No, no. It was so good. *You* were good, Alyssa." She opened her arms and the girl raced in for a hug. "Now, just remember that next time we do the scene, okay?"

"You got it, Miss E.," Alyssa said in her beatnik voice. "I'm pickin' up what you're puttin' down."

Emily laughed. "Good job. Let's run the scene one more time to get it in your head."

She watched as the whole scene sprang to life as if it had been injected with a healthy dose of energy. As if what she'd done had made a difference.

They were getting it. Alyssa was getting it. Because of *her*.

Emily watched, certain there was undeniable pride on her face, and when they finished, she cheered.

"I'm so proud of you guys," she said. "Really good job. Now go find Miss Marisol so you can work on your song."

The girls ran out, but seconds later, Alyssa darted back in. "Miss Emily?"

"Yes?"

"Thanks."

"Just doing my job, kiddo."

"No, I mean thanks for directing the show."

Emily smiled. "You're welcome."

"This is my favorite summer on the island ever, and I got a new best friend because of it." She wrapped her arms around Emily's midsection and squeezed.

"It might be my favorite summer on the island too, Alyssa."

The girl looked up without letting go. "I hope so."

CHAPTER 40

AFTER REHEARSAL, EMILY SAT in the center of the stage, letting her mind wander as she painted a set piece in the silence of the empty space. Typically, these work sessions were filled with other people—parents, cast members, Marisol—but today it was only her and Hollis.

She wanted everything to be perfect, including the tiniest set details, even if it meant working on them herself.

With Jack and his crew handling the house restoration, she had all the time in the world to think of ways to make the show a success—and thankfully, she had people to help bring her ideas to life.

And maybe that was it. The key to a successful production. She'd tried to make her first attempt happen by herself. She had no one to bounce ideas off of. No one to steer her in a different direction or come up with a different way to do things. No one to help take her ideas and make them reality.

Maybe the trick was relying on other people.

Something Emily didn't do well.

She had a bad case of *I can do it myself*, and look where that had gotten her. She was trying to do better.

Was that why she'd asked Marisol to go to the library and look up information on her mother's accident? Or had she done that because she was scared of what she might find?

She'd been putting it off for weeks, but there it was, gnawing at the back of her mind. Every time she saw her grandmother, she almost asked the million questions running through her mind—but something always stopped her.

Maybe some things were better left in the past. Some secrets better buried.

Still. The obituary. The holes in her grandmother's story. The confirmation from Shae Daniels that the accident had, in fact, happened on Cliff Road. All of it raised more questions than Emily knew how to process.

And despite her best efforts, she couldn't shake any of it.

What if Marisol returned with information Emily was better off not knowing? What if her mother had been involved in something unseemly and her grandmother was trying to protect Emily's memory of her?

But no. Not Isabelle. She'd grown up so quickly out of necessity, because of Emily. She wasn't the type to put herself or her daughter in danger.

Emily didn't like thinking about it, so until this point, she hadn't. She'd done a great job putting it all out of her mind. Why were these things nagging her now?

"Penny for your thoughts?" Hollis must've come in through the scene shop. She'd been too lost in her thoughts to hear him. He sat down next to her. He'd become a permanent fixture around the theatre over the last several weeks. It had been nice having him there with her. Whenever he was around, she felt invincible, as if all the things he believed about her might actually be true.

And like maybe she wasn't a complete failure after all.

She held a paintbrush loaded with brown paint, which she'd been applying to the canvas they'd stretched over chicken wire to create the giant tree. They'd use something called Good Stuff to create texture, and she'd paint it various shades of brown to give the trunk dimension.

"You look pensive," Hollis said. "It's making me nervous."

Emily smiled. She hadn't told Hollis anything about the mysteries surrounding her mother's death. She hadn't told anyone because if she said it all aloud, that made it true, and while she was curious, she wasn't sure her heart could handle another break.

What if what she uncovered left her wounded again?

"Do you think it's better to know the truth even if it'll hurt?"

Hollis's face dropped. "What do you mean?"

She hesitated at first but decided to tell him the whole story, even without the prompting of their silly childhood game. She started with Gladys's comment that her mother and grandparents had a rocky relationship. She covered Cliff Road, Shae Daniels, and her grandmother's lie.

"What do you think the truth is?" Hollis asked when she finished unloading all the thoughts she'd bottled up.

She shrugged. "I'm not sure. I just keep wondering why Grandma would lie. Why say Mom's accident was in 'Sconset if it was on Cliff Road? Who lived on Cliff Road? Where was my mother going that night and why did she take me with her? Why not come back and get me in the morning?"

"Emily, are you sure you want to go digging around?"

She shook her head. "No, I'm not. That's why I asked if it was better to know the truth even if it hurt."

Hollis reached over and took her hand. "I'm not sure how to answer that, but I know that I'd do just about anything to keep you from getting hurt."

Emily's heart fluttered. Like an actual butterfly, only a big one, something genetically altered. She'd been immune to these kinds of girlie proclivities for so many years—was this what it was like to fall in love?

The thought startled her. Love? And not the kind you felt for your friends and family, but romantic, head-over-heels love?

She looked up at him and saw the concern that laced his brow.

These weeks spent with Hollis had been the best weeks of her life, but having someone else to think about, to consider—was she ready for that?

"I think I want to know the truth," she said. "I want to know what happened the night my mother died."

It would be like picking at a loose thread, not knowing when everything would unravel—but she was ready. She needed to know.

Hollis held her gaze for several seconds before asking, "Then how can I help?"

She looked into those earnest, kind eyes and smiled. "I'm not sure yet, but when I figure it out, I'll let you know."

He nodded. "Did I already tell you I'm glad you came back this summer?"

She raised an eyebrow. "You did."

He let go of her hand, and she could feel a weight in the air between them. It was too heavy—if she wasn't careful, she would buckle underneath it.

Without thinking, she took her paintbrush and poked him in the chest with it, leaving a brown mark on his faded-red T-shirt.

She laughed, then hopped up, as if that could protect her from his impending revenge.

Hollis flinched, then laughed, eyes wide. He jumped to his feet and grabbed a paint roller from a bucket of purple paint, stretching it out toward her and rolling a trail of purple right down her side.

She dunked her brush in the bucket again and came out with another threatening glob. He ran to the other side of the stage and she followed him, wielding her brush like a sword.

When she lunged for him, he grabbed her arm, pulling her closer, focused on disarming her of her weapon. But one moment of nearness and the heaviness in the air returned. A brief laugh escaped without her permission and she found herself pressed against him, arm limp and eyes fixed on his.

He stared down at her, the lazy smile on his face melting.

Use caution! Protect your heart!

The words rang like an alarm in her mind, but she swatted them away. She didn't want to be practical. Just for a moment, she wanted to get lost in the scent of him. She wanted to embrace the falling.

"Emily." He whispered her name, his voice husky.

Her empty hand found its way to his back, taut with muscles she didn't even know existed. She let it rest there, still holding on to his gaze and aware that his grasp on her arm had gone soft.

Her heart sputtered as Hollis searched her eyes for permission she was absolutely certain she gave.

Kiss me. Kiss me. Kiss me.

As if he heard her silent plea, he wrapped an arm around her waist, drawing her closer until their lips met. Unlike their first kiss, Hollis wasn't tentative or shy, and he didn't taste like cherry Popsicles.

Emily sank into him, dropping the paintbrush so she could wrap both arms around his muscled torso. His kiss made her toes curl, made every worry she'd been holding on to disappear. Heck, for a minute, it even made her forget her own name.

His lips moved steadily over hers and she inhaled every second of him, greedy for more.

Finally she pulled away, expecting the feeling of dread to follow—but it didn't. She didn't regret kissing him. She didn't regret sharing the deepest parts of herself with him, despite the warning bells she'd shoved aside.

"Was that okay?" His eyes studied her.

Wordless, she nodded.

"Good, because I've wanted to do that for weeks."

"What took you so long?" She smiled, arms still wrapped around him.

"I promised Jolie we were just friends." He looked at her. "But that's not how I feel. At all."

"Me neither," she said.

"Does that scare you?"

"Maybe, but I think the scarier thing is imagining my life without you in it."

He took her face in his hands and traced her cheekbones with his thumbs. "Don't imagine that. It'll never happen."

She inhaled him as he kissed her again.

I love you. I love you. I love you. The words raced through her mind as she gave in to another kiss, drawing him closer. But she didn't dare say them aloud.

He pulled away. "I have to talk to Jolie. I have to tell her about all of this."

"Are you sure?" Emily asked.

"Yes," he said. "And until then, we have to be friends."

"You mean the kind of friends who don't kiss?" She smiled up at him.

He took a step back, then laughed. "You're going to make this impossible for me, aren't you?"

"Depends on how long you wait to tell her." She pressed her lips together, the taste of him still on her mouth. "I think you probably shouldn't wait very long."

He drew in a deep breath, hands up in front of him in mock surrender. "Go easy on me, Ackerman. I've got no willpower when it comes to you."

She slid her hand up the side of his arm. He closed his eyes at her touch, then came toward her and with one swift movement drew her close for another mind-bending kiss.

She gave in to it immediately, letting herself relax in his embrace.

At the sound of voices in the hallway, she tore herself away from him and picked up the paintbrush. She turned away from Hollis, her adrenaline racing.

"Emily!"

It was Marisol, and she was doing that I-have-lots-of-energy-because-I'm-still-in-college kind of thing she did when she stumbled upon something fun or exciting.

"Hey, hottie Hollis," Marisol said as she passed by.

Emily couldn't be sure, but she thought it was possible Hollis's cheeks were flushed. Her eyes darted to his for a split second and unlike him, she hid her smile.

This man. She couldn't have stopped loving him now if she tried.

Every warning bell that had sounded at the back of her mind had been silenced by the sheer hope that maybe, just maybe, she was meant to have a life she'd never even dared to dream of. The one he described that night on the beach. Was there room for her in that simple life he craved?

"What happened in here? Are you painting with toddlers?" Marisol looked at the trail of purple paint down Emily's side.

"Something like that."

Marisol shrugged, then turned her attention back to the papers in her hand. "I made copies of the newspaper like you asked," Marisol said. "Let me know if you need anything else. I'm headed back to the costume shop—they had a question about the Mad Hatter's costume."

"Thanks, Marisol," Emily said.

Hollis turned toward her. "What's that?"

"The newspaper from the week my mom died," Emily said. "As much as a part of me doesn't want to know any of this, I feel like it might be time. I've put it off long enough. If I'm going to confront my grandmother, I need some evidence to back me up."

"Evidence of what?"

"Her lies." Emily glanced at the stack of papers in her hand. *Here goes nothing.*

The color copies were surprisingly clear. Emily skipped over the obituary, flipping through the typical boring local news articles until she found one on the front page from August 4. Her mother's funeral had been held in Boston, where the family plot was located, but it looked like someone from the Nantucket newspaper had made the trip. There were photos of the mourners at the cemetery, along with a brief write-up about the event, as if it were a high society function.

Emily's stomach turned as she spotted her eleven-year-old self in one of the close-up shots. "Someone took pictures at my mother's funeral?"

Hollis looked over her shoulder. "Kind of tacky if you ask me."

"Very tacky," Emily agreed. She scanned the photo, the familiar faces of her grandparents, old friends, people from a life that felt so far away now.

"I'm sorry we weren't there," Hollis said. "We should've been. My dad was just starting a new job, and he couldn't ask for any time off."

"Don't give that a second thought."

"I wanted to be there, Emily," he said. "I tried to make sure you were okay."

"Kind of hard for a kid to do that on his own," she said, letting him off the hook. No sense in him beating himself up over something that was not only out of his control but also nearly two decades old.

Her eyes returned to the photo. She scanned the mourners one more time when a familiar form caught her attention. Back by the trees, behind the family and friends standing in rows beside the grave was a man, alone.

"Hollis?" Emily said, pointing. "That's Jack."

Hollis leaned in closer to see. "How can you tell?"

"He still stands like that," Emily said. "When he's supervising his crew. He sort of hunches over. But also look at his face. He's younger, but that's definitely Jack."

Hollis looked over the photo again but said nothing.

"Why was Jack Walker at my mom's funeral?" Emily said. "And why was he standing off to the back by himself? It's weird, right?"

Hollis stared at her for a few seconds, a blank look on his face. "I guess you could ask him?"

"Yeah," she said. "I guess I will."

CHAPTER 41

AFTER HIS CONVERSATION WITH EMILY, Hollis made his way to the lobby of the arts center, where he paced back and forth, waiting for her to gather her things so they could go to her house and confront Jack Walker.

But Hollis already knew what the man would say. And he had a feeling he knew how Emily would respond. And he wasn't sure of his place in any of it.

It was too much to hope for, that they would be able to spend time together, just the two of them, without all of this getting in the way.

Not to mention he had a daughter to talk to. He'd broken his promise to Jolie, something he'd sworn he wouldn't do. And as much as it would hurt, he knew that if Jolie felt the same way she did about him and Emily at the beginning of the summer, he'd let Emily go. It would be the hardest thing in the world, but he'd do it.

Please don't let it come to that, God.

Emily walked out of the auditorium toward him, somehow making paint-splattered look adorable, but he could see a tight line of worry across her forehead. She wouldn't rest until she put the pieces of this puzzle together. And while he didn't have all the answers, he did have one—and it was a big one.

Shouldn't he tell her what he knew?

He remembered his conversation with Jack. He'd promised the man, father to father, he'd let him tell her himself. It wasn't Hollis's place. No matter how much he wanted it to be. But it had been two days, and Jack still hadn't said anything.

"Hey, why don't you go find Jolie?" Emily said. "And I'll go find Jack."

Hollis paused. "You don't want me to come with you?"

She hitched her backpack onto her shoulder. "I think I should do this on my own, but I'll call you as soon as I know anything."

He nodded.

"Go convince your daughter that you and I could be really, really good for each other."

He smiled. "Is that what you think?"

She shrugged, looking uncharacteristically shy for a split second. "Is that what *you* think?"

"No, Em, that's what I know," he said. "There's not a single doubt in my mind."

Her mouth twisted as she attempted—and failed—not to smile.

"Look," he said. "I know you're scared, but I'm not going to hurt you."

She looked at him, her eyes full and wide. "You promise, Hollis?"

He touched her face. "I promise."

"Because I don't think I could handle it," she said. "Not after letting myself imagine that small-town, white-picket-fence life you talked about."

"Oh yeah?" He grinned. "I didn't think you were a picket-fence kind of girl."

"Surprise." She smiled back at him. "Call me after you talk to JoJo."

315

"Call me after you talk to Jack."

She nodded.

He looked around to make sure they were alone, then leaned down and placed a gentle kiss on her lips. When he pulled away, her eyes were still closed. "I'll see you later."

She opened her eyes, pressed her lips together, and nodded again.

As he watched her walk away, he said a silent prayer for her, that God would protect her heart no matter what secrets she uncovered. Then he said another prayer that his daughter would be more open-minded than she was at first.

When he reached the house, he found his mom sitting on the back deck, Tilly at her feet.

"Where's JoJo?" he asked.

"Down by the water with Harper," his mom said. She looked over her magazine at Hollis. "What's wrong with you?"

Was it obvious? How was it possible to feel complete joy and complete fear at the same time?

"I just need to talk to her," Hollis said.

Nan straightened. "Is everything okay? Are Jana and Rick okay?"

"Everything's fine," Hollis said. "They're coming here for the show. I just got a text from Jana this morning."

His mom put her magazine down. "But that's not why you have those frown lines on your face."

He sat down on the love seat across from her. "No."

"So what is it?"

"Emily," he said simply.

"What's wrong with Emily?"

"Nothing's wrong with her," Hollis said, staring out across the yard to the ocean. "I'm in love with her."

"Oh, is that all?" Nan returned to her magazine.

"Is that all?" Hollis shot his mom a look.

"Everyone else has known this for weeks, Hollis," she said, not looking up. "I'm just glad you've finally figured it out for yourself. We were about to stage an intervention."

Hollis sighed. "What do I do about it?"

His mom's forehead creased in surprise. "You don't know this by now?"

"I mean because of Jolie."

"Jolie loves Emily."

"But she made me promise I wouldn't. She said if I dated Emily, I'd ruin it for her."

Nan half laughed. "She's twelve, honey."

"And?"

"A twelve-year-old doesn't get to decide these things for her father. What if God put you and Emily together?"

"I think he might've." Hollis spotted Jolie walking toward them through the sea grass. "I've never felt like this about anyone."

His mom smiled. "It's what we've been praying for you, Hollis."

"But I owe Jolie, Mom," Hollis said. "And if she's still against it, that means something."

"Give her a chance to get her head around it," Nan said. "Maybe it's less important to her now."

Jolie raced toward them, Harper close behind.

"Your girl is killing it out there on the paddleboard," Harper said as she followed JoJo up the stairs.

"She had an awesome teacher." Hollis tried to sound lighthearted in spite of the tight ball of dread turning over in his stomach.

"How was rehearsal this morning?" Hollis asked, handing Jolie a towel.

Jolie grinned. "Like you don't know. I saw you in the wings watching."

"I'm just proud of ya, kiddo."

"Kiddo." She rolled her eyes. "That's such a babyish thing to call me, Dad."

His eyes darted to his mom, who watched him with a little too much interest. "Harper, help me with dinner."

Harper mock-saluted their mother. "Aye, aye. Your grandma is a slave driver, JoJo," she said. "Don't let anyone tell you different."

Jolie plopped down in Nan's vacated seat and picked up her phone.

"Jolie," Hollis said. "Can we talk for a minute?"

She didn't move, but her eyes popped up to his. "Why? What's wrong?"

"Nothing's wrong," he said. "At least I hope nothing's wrong."

She set her phone down on the table and wrapped the towel around herself more tightly. "Is this about Rick? Are you going to let him adopt me?"

Hollis's fingers turned cold. "What? No. Why? Is that what you want?"

JoJo looked away.

Oh no. Was that what she wanted?

"Jolie?"

She shook her head.

"No?"

She found his eyes again. "No."

"Okay, good."

She smiled that crooked smile at him.

His heart leapt. *No.* Jolie didn't want Rick to adopt her. She wanted Hollis. Would she still after what he was about to tell her?

Suddenly it seemed like terrible timing, but not telling her meant sneaking around or not seeing Emily, and he didn't like either of those options.

"So what did you want to talk about?" she asked, picking her phone back up.

"Well, do you remember at the beginning of summer when you first met Emily?"

"Sure," Jolie said. "I loved that day."

"Me too," Hollis said, trying to keep his smile in check. No sense getting all dopey.

"Dad, is this about you and Emily?" She leaned forward, elbows on her knees.

He wanted to look away, but he didn't. "It is."

"You love her, huh?"

Hollis sputtered. "What?"

"I heard Uncle Hayes and Aunt Harper talking about it. Uncle Hayes said, 'He'll never do anything about it,' and Aunt Harper said, 'If he loves her as much as I think he does, he will.' And I said, 'Why?' and Aunt Harper said, 'Because when you love someone as much as your dad loves Emily, you can't keep it inside. If you do, you'll explode.' Or implode. I think she said 'implode.' Is that a word?"

So they'd all been talking about his feelings for Emily. He didn't know whether to be irritated or thankful because it seemed his siblings had unknowingly broken the ice for him with Jolie.

Hollis sighed.

"It's okay if you love her, Dad," Jolie said.

He found her eyes. "It is?"

"Yeah. I think she loves you too."

"Did Harper tell you that?"

Jolie shook her head. "No, I told myself that."

"Oh, really?"

"Sometimes I see her looking at you," Jolie said. "And the way you guys are always out on the beach at night."

"You know about that?"

"I'm almost a teenager, Dad," she said incredulously. "I'm not stupid."

He laughed softly. "Oh, I know you're not."

"Good, because if I'm going to live with you in the summers, it's important that we make that really clear. I don't want you thinking I'm a little kid anymore. No more of this 'kiddo' stuff."

He watched her as she tapped around on her phone for a long moment. Finally she glanced up at him and smiled.

"You're going to live with me in the summers?"

Her eyes darted back to her phone. "If you'll let me?"

He heard the question in her voice, and he wanted to figure out the very best way to reassure her that this was exactly what he'd wanted all along.

"Jolie," he said, "that would make me the happiest guy in the world."

"Good. It would've been embarrassing if you said no."

He laughed. "So you're really okay about Emily?"

"I guess," Jolie said. "I mean, Aunt Harper said I really shouldn't be selfish about this and that it had been a long time since you've been happy and don't I want you to be happy? I told her of course I want you to be happy, and she said, 'Emily makes him happy, JoJo.' And she does, huh?"

"She really does."

"Fine," she said. "But don't screw it up."

"I'll do my best."

She nodded. "Good. I'm hungry."

"Me too." He got to his feet. "Let's go see what GrandNan has for us tonight."

"Lobster rolls, I think." She stood.

"You hope." He gave one of her braids a soft tug. "And, Jolie?"

She looked at him.

"I love you."

Emily's heart raced as she made her way up the driveway toward the house. She'd planned to confront her grandmother with what she'd found in the newspaper—proof that her mother's accident had happened on Cliff Road—but that didn't seem important anymore, not with a photo that put Jack Walker at her mother's funeral.

In Boston.

Hadn't he only known *of* her mother? Did he leave the island to go to a funeral in Boston for an acquaintance? That didn't make sense.

Emily passed Marcus on her way to the front porch. "Hey, do you know where Jack is?"

"You didn't hear?" Marcus asked.

"Hear what?"

"Your grandma fired him, Emily," Marcus said. "He's gone."

"What? She can't do that," Emily said, knowing full well that she absolutely could. Eliza Ackerman could take control of this project anytime she wanted to. The fact that she hadn't done so before now was the real surprise.

"Said she hired a new guy and he'd be here tomorrow."

Emily's heart lurched. "You can't be serious."

"'Fraid so."

"So he's just gone?"

"Went home about an hour ago," Marcus said. "We weren't sure if we should keep working."

"Yes," Emily said. "Keep working. I'm going to go get Jack."

"What about your grandmother?"

Emily groaned. "I don't know yet, but I'll figure it out. And no matter what, I'll make sure your entire crew is paid for today."

"And we should come back tomorrow?"

"Yes," Emily said resolutely. "For sure."

Marcus nodded. "You're good people, Emily."

"I try." She smiled despite her frustration. "Do you know Jack's address?"

"No, but he's out on Cliff Road, near the bike path, I think," Marcus said.

"Cliff Road?" Emily's heart fell.

"Said the place had sentimental value." Marcus shrugged. "I don't know. The guy's always talking about the old days. I can find the address and text it to you. I was out there not long ago."

"Cliff Road."

"You okay?"

"Yeah, I'll be fine." She hoped that was true. "Text me the address. That would be helpful."

"You got it, boss."

Biking to Cliff Road would take too long, but she didn't have her own car. She looked at her grandmother's Lexus in the driveway. She raced inside, found the key fob in a small dish on the entryway table, and took it without a word.

"Grandma, you owe me this much," she said under her breath.

The drive to Cliff Road filled her with anxiety. She told herself there were a lot of houses in that area. She told herself there could've been countless explanations for all the coincidences she'd uncovered. She told herself that Jack Walker was nothing more than a contractor who'd known her mom once upon a time.

But she didn't believe a single word she told herself.

She glanced at Marcus's text and found the address where Jack Walker was staying. How long had it been since he was on the island?

The image of his photo—sullen at her mother's graveside service—floated through her mind.

If she hadn't been driving, she would've closed her eyes, feeling every bit of the magnitude of the situation, the summer, the questions. But the worst part was feeling like nobody was being honest with her. Nobody was being genuine.

Nobody smiled with their eyes.

Mom had taught her to value honesty above just about everything else, and nobody in her life seemed to feel the same way. Not her grandma, not Jack . . . She stopped. But that wasn't true, was it? Because she had Hollis.

Hollis was genuine and honest and good. And in spite of all this, when she thought about him, she smiled.

Her GPS told her that her destination was on the left, but she didn't slow down fast enough, so she drove right past it. Maybe that was a sign she should keep driving?

No. She wanted to learn—no matter what it was—everything she didn't know about the night her mother died.

And the only way to find out was to start asking hard questions.

To start doing hard things.

She'd spent so many years running away, convinced it was what her mother wanted for her—to live a life full of travel where she jumped around and never got close to anybody.

But she was tired. She didn't want to run anymore. She wanted to settle down. To plant roots.

Did asking hard questions guarantee she could do that?

She'd turned around and now pulled into the driveway of a small cottage. With gray wooden shingles and white trim, it looked like the majority of the houses on the island. The landscaping was immaculate but not flashy. Nothing about the little house was flashy.

The door was a deep peacock blue and the name on the mailbox said *Walker*.

Her journey had brought her here, with a fistful of questions and the resolve to hear the answers.

She pulled the photocopied article from her bag and looked at it again.

"Okay, Jack Walker," she said aloud. "Time to start talking."

But Emily sat behind the wheel of her grandmother's posh car, staring at the cottage. It was as if a weighted barbell had just been laid across her chest, making it hard to breathe, let alone move.

She thought about her time here, about Hollis, about how he continued to try and do better in spite of his mistakes. He hadn't quit on Jolie after his life fell apart, and he'd messed up—really messed up.

Emily had messed up too. Her whole life had been a series of small disasters and bad choices, starting with turning away from God.

She reached across the seat and found the book inside her bag. She pulled it out and opened it.

Dear Emily,

Faith is kind of a tough subject for me. It's hard to explain all the things I feel about God. Mostly I feel like he's been this true, unconditional friend who's never turned his back on me even when I've made giant mistakes.

I don't want to force my faith on you. I believe everyone has to find their own way when it comes to God, but at the same time, I want you to know it's important. When things fall apart, it's crucial to have hope that there is a way to put them back together.

Faith brings that to you.

And the way to have faith is to trust what God's said. I always thought it was crazy that God promises so many things to us. (It's in the Bible. Someday the Bible won't be super boring, I promise.) He promises he'll never leave us, and I have to say, when your world feels like it's crumbling, that's a really important promise to hold on to.

As you grow up and get older, and probably every time something bad happens, you may want to blame God—you might get mad at him, and that's okay. Tell him how you feel. I promise he can take it.

But I've learned that in those hard times, if you can hold on to him instead of pushing him away, it makes you stronger and more fearless than you ever thought you could be.

I hope you pray. A lot. I hope you go for long walks and hash out your feelings with Jesus. I hope you hold on to what you know in your deepest soul to be true—that he loves you, that he's got a plan for you, that you are fearfully and wonderfully made.

And that he's right there for you, no matter what.

Love,
Mom

The words stared at her—Mom's handwriting, an instant source of comfort. She'd all but forgotten this letter. She was surprised she hadn't torn it out and thrown it away.

She was angry with God, and she had been for a lot of years. She blamed him for her mother's death because who else was there to blame?

Now, sitting in this car, staring at this house, holding this article, she faced an unknown future—one she wasn't sure she wanted.

But if what her mother said was true, God wasn't unknown. He was proven. He made promises and he kept them.

Then why didn't you keep my mother safe?

The words hit her square in the chest.

He was God. Couldn't he have made it so the car hadn't started and they'd never left the cottage in the rain that night? Couldn't he have stopped the car from hitting that tree? Couldn't he have kept her mother's heart beating?

If he could do anything, why hadn't he done that? Why hadn't he saved the one person who meant more to her than anyone else in the world? Why had he left her so alone?

"I'm mad at you," she said out loud to the empty car. "I'm mad that you took her from me. She was the only one I had, and you took her. Why?"

Tears welled in her eyes, but she pressed her fists into them, refusing to cry. She stared at the words on the page, wishing her mom were here. Wishing she could ask for clarification, not only on this letter, but on so many of them.

Having her words was wonderful, but what if Emily misinterpreted them? What if she didn't understand?

She looked back up at the house. "Okay, God. If you're really here, then can you find a way to keep whatever is about to happen from breaking my heart?"

She waited for a few seconds as if she might actually get an answer, which, of course, she didn't. She exited the car, and crushed shells crunched underneath her feet. She walked to the door, pausing for a brief moment for a little self pep talk.

She inhaled a deep breath. She'd regret it if she didn't at least try to piece this all together. She'd spend her whole life curious, and she already knew how that felt.

No. It was time. No more running.

She knocked on the front door before she lost her nerve.

Seconds later, it opened to reveal Jack standing on the other side. "Emily."

"Hey," she said. "May I come in?"

He opened the door wider and took a step back to make room for her to enter the cottage.

"Nice place," she said. And she meant it. The cottage was cozy and charming and so very different from her grandparents' house. It had a homey feel, like walking into a hug the second you entered.

"It's actually my aunt's," he said. "But she lets us use it sometimes. I think she's going to sell it, though, so this might be my last summer here."

Emily chewed the inside of her lip. "Look, Jack, Marcus told me about my grandmother."

"Is that why you're here?"

"Partly," she said. "I'm going to talk to her. The job's almost finished, so it makes no sense to fire you now, especially since she doesn't have a reason."

He half shrugged. "I'm sure she has her reasons." He led her into the kitchen. "Would you like something to drink?"

"Water, if it's okay," she said. Her throat had turned to sandpaper and her mouth was like cotton. Not a great combination for someone who needed to be able to speak.

Jack pulled a glass from the cupboard, filled it from the filtered water in the refrigerator door, and slid it across the island toward her. She took a drink, then followed him to the living room.

"I'm going to get you your job back," she said.

"I hope so. I'd really like to see it through. I don't like to leave things unfinished."

A brief lull stunted the conversation.

"How many years have you been coming here?" she asked.

"I've stayed here off and on over the years since I was a kid," Jack said. "The summers I spent on the island, I spent them here."

"So you would've maybe been here eighteen years ago?" She began rummaging through her purse.

Jack held her gaze. "Emily—"

She produced the folded sheet of paper and handed it over.

"What's this?" he asked.

"An article about my mom's funeral."

His face went pale.

"You implied that the two of you didn't know each other."

Jack didn't respond.

"If you didn't know her, then why would you travel to Boston for her funeral? You've never lived in Boston, right?"

"No, I never have." He stared at the image on the photocopy before handing it back to her.

"It's kind of strange," she said. "Do you make a habit of attending funerals of people you admired from a distance?"

"I asked Hollis to let me talk to you about this myself."

Emily's heart dropped. "Hollis?"

Jack shot her a look.

"What does Hollis have to do with this?" *Please say nothing. Please say you misspoke.*

"Nothing," Jack said.

But she could see it wasn't nothing. Anyone could've seen it. "Talk to me about what?"

"I was going to tell you, Emily," he said. "I just didn't know how."

"Tell me what? That you knew my mother?"

A part of her knew what he was about to say, but that part was silenced by the part that didn't think she could handle it. It took everything she had not to run from the house, get back in the car, and drive straight to the ferry and off the island—for good.

So much for not breaking her heart.

So much for believing God was really going to be there for her this time.

CHAPTER 42

SHE STOOD IN JACK'S LIVING ROOM, the realization of what he'd just said fresh in the air between them.

"What did you say?" She studied him. He didn't flinch. Instead, he held her gaze as if it were a life preserver and he were a man bobbing in choppy seas.

"It's me, Emily," he said. "I'm your father."

Emily's pulse quickened. Jack Walker—the only contractor who'd answered her ad, the man who taught her how to use a sledgehammer, the man who'd been in her house practically every day she'd been on Nantucket—wasn't just an acquaintance of her mother's. He was so much more.

He was the man who'd broken Isabelle's heart. He was the man who'd found out about Emily and taken off right afterward. He was the one who'd abandoned her, without ever giving her a chance to prove to him that she was good enough to be loved.

She turned away.

"Look, I know this is a lot to take in."

"Why didn't you tell me?" she said quietly. "That very first day you showed up? Why did you keep it a secret?"

Jack sighed, then slid onto the sofa. "I came here for one reason, Emily—to get to know you. To see what kind of person you've become. And I was afraid if you knew who I was . . ."

She glanced at him, and while she didn't want to feel pity for this man who'd hurt her simply by not being a part of her life, she did. Because the look on his face made his pain obvious.

"I was afraid you wouldn't have spoken to me at all."

Emily scuffed her shoe against the wood floors of the small cottage. They needed to be refinished. It was a task that would be easy for Jack, and yet it went undone, likely because he'd spent so much time working on her cottage.

"Shouldn't you have given me a chance?" she asked, not letting on that Jack had a point. If she'd opened the door that first day and he'd told her this, she would've slammed the door in his face. She would've kicked him out, gotten back on the ferry, and traveled as far away from Nantucket as she could. It was smart, his hanging around, being charming, making her like him.

Yet it felt like she'd been played. How could she have been so foolish?

"Maybe," he said. "Maybe I should've been straight with you from the start, but, Emily, I knew what you probably thought of me—"

"How?" She spun around to face him. "How could you possibly know anything about me at all?"

Her eyes had clouded over. *Traitors!* She squeezed the bridge of her nose to keep from crying.

Was it possible his lie by omission had actually been good for her?

No. A lie was still a lie. And after all these years, that was his choice—to lie.

"Just tell me one thing," Emily said.

"Anything, Emily."

"Did you even love her?"

The noise the man made was hard to describe. Not a scoff, but almost, and one that seemed to happen to him, like he wasn't quite in control of himself. The almost scoff seemed to say, *How can you even ask me that?*

And yet, how could she not?

Jack leaned forward, forearms on his knees, hands folded in front of him, eyes on the rug under his work boots. "I've never loved anyone like I loved Isabelle."

"Then how could you leave?" Emily heard her volume climbing, and she warned herself to keep her emotions in check.

"Guard your heart."

"I didn't want to," he said.

She inched back. "That's a lie."

"It's not." He looked at her now. "I—it's complicated."

"It doesn't seem complicated to me," she said. "Either you wanted us or you didn't. You left, so you obviously didn't want us."

"Emily, it's not that simple," he said, eyes still fixed on her.

"Then explain, Jack," she spat. "Now's your chance. Tell me what happened."

His gaze hung on hers as an old clock on the mantel behind her ticked off the seconds. His eyes seemed to replay a years-old memory. He had answers to questions she'd always asked. He knew what had really happened that night. He knew why her mother had rushed out the way she did. He might even know what Isabelle and Emily's grandparents had been fighting about.

But when he looked away, Emily feared Jack, just like Grandma, wasn't going to share any of what he knew with her.

"Some things are better left in the past," Jack said. "Just know that I didn't want to go. I didn't want to leave Isabelle—or you. I wanted to know you, to raise you, but I . . ."

"You what?"

"I wanted you to have a good life."

"And you couldn't have given that to me? A life with both of my parents—wouldn't that have been enough?"

COURTNEY WALSH

He shrugged, his eyes red. "Would it?"

"Of course," Emily whispered. "That was all I ever wanted." And it was. She hadn't realized it until she said the words, but it was the truest truth she'd ever spoken aloud.

Jack raked a hand through his hair. "I wanted you to have the kind of life I'd only ever dreamed of. Your grandparents gave that to you. They made sure you had everything you ever needed."

Emily narrowed her gaze. "But they didn't."

He met her eyes.

"Because what I needed were my parents."

"No, you needed to be taken care of," Jack said. "You needed a home and stability and the best education. You deserved those things."

"Who told you that?" Emily asked. "Who told you *that* was more important than having a parent?"

Jack looked away.

There was still so much he wasn't saying. What would it take to get him to be straight with her?

"Was my mom on her way to see you that night?"

Jack maintained his floor-bound gaze as he slowly nodded. "I was going to meet you that night."

Emily wiped a tear that had slipped down her cheek. "So after the accident . . . ?"

"I felt like it was my fault she was gone," he said. "That you'd really hate me now. I didn't deserve any piece of her then, especially not one as beautiful and kind and good as you."

Emily's hands turned to fists at her sides. "You should've tried harder, Jack." She started for the door, but before she reached it, he stood.

"Wait," he said.

She stopped but didn't turn toward him.

"I found this," he said. "In your mom's room. It's the only one there is, and I thought you might want it."

331

Slowly she faced him and saw he was holding a small photograph out toward her. She took it. The faded image of her mother and a much-younger Jack stared back at her.

"I loved her more than anything," Jack said. "I'm sorry I ever let her go."

Emily willed herself not to crumple the photo and throw it at Jack. Instead, she dropped it on the floor, then turned and walked out of the cottage, slamming the door behind her as she did.

CHAPTER 43

EMILY PULLED THE LEXUS into the circular drive in front of her grand-parents' cottage, mind spinning.

"Am I supposed to believe you were there for all that?" she said aloud. "What happened to you never leaving me? What happened to you being there when I need you? Where are you *now*?"

If she'd been angry with God before, her feelings had only intensi-fied after discovering a piece of the truth. When would she find out the rest? When would she ever have all the pieces to make sense of everything that had happened?

Jack said he hadn't wanted to leave, so why did he? It made no sense.

"Why is everyone lying to me?" A tear escaped, and she angrily wiped it away. She parked the car and drew in a deep breath.

Hollis stood on the porch, leaning against the post and looking painfully handsome. More than that, though, he looked kind. It was obvious from Jack's comments that Hollis had found out the truth about who the man was—but Emily had to believe he had a reason for keeping it a secret.

And now, simply by meeting his eyes as she turned the engine off, she could see he was worried.

She wanted to collapse in his arms, to draw her strength from him, to finally let herself cry. But she wouldn't, of course. She was stronger than that.

He met her in the driveway, next to the car, and without saying a word, he pulled her into a protective hug. "Are you okay?"

Emily didn't want to think about the way any of this made her feel. Thanks to this house in Nantucket, everything—everything—had been dredged to the surface again. How did she get away from it all?

She shrugged softly, aware that her tears were getting his T-shirt wet. Maybe she wasn't as strong as she thought. "How long have you known?"

Hollis pulled away and looked at her. "Not long, but you have to believe I wanted to tell you. I told Jack I wasn't going to keep this secret for very long—it was killing me. But he really wanted to tell you himself, in his own way."

Emily searched Hollis's eyes for any sign of insincerity. She found none. He would never intentionally hurt her, would he? Still, his keeping this from her stung.

She started toward the backyard. She wanted to drink in the ocean, to be reminded how big this world was. It made her problems feel a little smaller, a little less significant.

He fell into step at her side.

"How did you find out?" she asked.

Hollis sighed. "You know I never really trusted the guy."

She nodded.

"I guess I finally put it together. I overheard him talking with your grandma."

A breeze kicked up, blowing her hair over her eyes. She tucked it behind her ears and looked at him. "What did they say?"

Hollis reached for her hand. She slipped it inside his, loving the way it made her feel, then worrying she loved it too much.

"I didn't hear everything," he said. "Just enough to gather that your grandma didn't like him. I'd seen Jack in your mother's room really early on. He was sitting at the desk, looking at something. He seemed sad. But then, all of the sudden, there was something about him that reminded me of you—I guess it all clicked."

She looked away. "He found a photograph of himself and my mom. Said it was the only one they'd ever taken. My mom must've hidden it in her room somewhere, and during the renovations, he unearthed it. He tried to give it to me."

"You didn't take it?"

Emily shook her head. "How could I?"

"Look, Emily, I know you've got a lot of mixed feelings about him, but I really believe he thought he was doing what was best for you."

Emily pulled her hand from his. "How? How is leaving your daughter to grow up without a father 'what's best'?"

Hollis was quiet for a moment, likely thinking of Jolie, of his own mistakes. "I'm just saying, maybe you should give the guy a second chance?"

Emily stopped walking. They'd reached the edge of the beach, and the sand stretched out in front of them. "Why would I do that, Hollis? He had so many chances over the years to reach out to me. He could've come to the hospital after my mom died. He could've seen me at the funeral—he was obviously there. He could've come to my grandparents anytime and said, 'Hey, I want to be in her life.' But he didn't. He stayed away."

"Do you know that for sure?"

She looked up at him. "What do you mean?"

"I mean, what if he did come to your grandparents?"

"You think they knew?"

Hollis shrugged. "I don't know, but there's history there, Em. Your grandma must have a reason not to like him."

She shook her head. "No, that would be too cruel, even for her."

After a pause, Hollis said, "Then maybe he had another reason for staying away."

Emily took a step back. "I can't believe it. You're siding with him."

Hollis moved toward her, but she turned away. "I'm not siding with anyone. I'm just saying, I talked to the guy, Em. He seems sincere. He seems like a dad who screwed up and just wants a chance to make things right."

She spun around. "And you know all about that, don't you? You let Jana raise Jolie like she was a single mother, sending money as if money was what either of them really needed."

"Emily, don't."

"But here you are, wanting a second chance, and because you're Hollis McGuire, you get it. You've got that girl wrapped around your finger now—but what happens when you let her down again? What then?"

"I'm not going to let her down again," he said.

"You don't know that," Emily said. "That's what people do. They hurt each other."

Hollis's face fell. "I know you're upset, Emily."

"No, you think because Jack Walker showed up to renovate my house that means he's somehow ready to be my dad. Well, guess what, I don't need a dad anymore. I don't need anyone."

"So, what, you're just going to run away?" Hollis leveled her gaze. "Because that's what you do, isn't it? You run."

"Like you did with Jolie?" Her tone had turned bitter. She didn't like it, but she didn't know how to control it—it was as if her emotions had taken over, leaving all sense of logic and kindness somewhere in the dust.

He looked wounded, but only for a moment. He drew in a breath and let it out gently. "You've never stayed anywhere more than a year," Hollis said. "You've never had a meaningful relationship with anyone, Emily. When things get hard, you run away. But the hard stuff is necessary to get to the good stuff. Don't you get that?"

"And suddenly you're an expert on relationships," she said with a dry laugh. "You spend a couple of weeks with your daughter and you think everything is just fine now."

"No, I don't," Hollis said. "I've got a lot of work to do—you don't think I know that?"

"Do you?"

"Of course I do. And Jack does too. He screwed up, but maybe there was something else that happened. Maybe there was an explanation—shouldn't you at least hear him out?"

"I tried! He barely told me anything."

Hollis pushed his hand through his hair and turned away.

She didn't want to think about it. She didn't want to think about going through the hard stuff—she just wanted it all to go away. She wanted him to go away.

"I know this is hard," Hollis said. "But hard isn't always bad. It can be life-changing if you let it."

"I suppose you're going to talk to me about God and how much he loves me? How he's here for me when things are tough?"

He kept his eyes intent on her. "I wasn't going to, but I believe those things."

"Well, I don't," Emily said. "I tried asking God to help, and this is what happened."

"Then maybe it was time for you to find out," he said. "Maybe you needed this information to move forward."

"This is exactly why I keep everyone at arm's length. This right here."

"Why? Because it's messy? Because it makes you feel something?" Hollis forced her gaze. "What's wrong with feeling something? It means you're alive."

She looked away.

"I know that book of letters means everything to you, but, Emily, have you ever stopped to think maybe your mom didn't have all the answers?"

Emily wrapped her arms around herself. *No.* He didn't get to talk about the letters. She willed herself to stop listening, but he didn't stop talking, and no amount of wishing it would make him leave.

"She was young. She hadn't even had time to change her mind

about anything she'd written. Do you really want to live your whole life based on the advice of a twenty-five-year-old?"

"She was the only person who ever really loved me."

"That's not true," Hollis said. "And all that stuff she said about love—it's wrong, Emily."

A sob grabbed hold of her throat and squeezed. She choked it back, turned away. She didn't want to talk about this anymore.

"She said use caution. She said be careful. She said don't risk your heart." He walked around her, placed his hands on her arms, and forced her to face him. "That's no way to live. That's no way to love. I don't want to be cautious. I want to jump in headfirst. I want to give you every single part of myself—no questions. And when it gets hard, I want to go through it—together. I want to be here with you while you sort this all out. I'm not going anywhere."

She shook her head. She didn't need Hollis or anyone else. She didn't need pity and she didn't need help. She needed to get as far away from all of this as she could. "You just don't get it, do you? You don't get it because you're just like him."

Hollis pulled away. "What?"

"The only difference is you had everything—you were rich and famous and everyone liked you—but you still didn't have time for your own daughter."

"I explained that to you, Emily."

"I know what you said," she said. "You were messed up. You had issues. As if that can explain away a father not being there for his only child. As if there's ever a reason to let months of a kid's life pass without seeing them."

"It was more complicated than that."

"No wonder you side with Jack. No wonder you want me to give him a second chance. Because if I don't, it makes you feel like you don't deserve one with Jolie. And you know what? Maybe you don't."

Hollis's shoulders slumped. She'd wounded him for real this time. No amount of redirecting his emotion would bring him back. She'd been here before. She'd gotten too close, and this was the only way to put the necessary distance between her and the man she thought she loved. This was the only way to protect her own heart.

He found her eyes. "Emily, what do you really want? Not your mom, not your grandma—you."

She held on to his wounded eyes for many more seconds than she should've, the images of the life he'd spelled out for her playing on a continuous loop through her mind.

I want to belong.

But she didn't. And she wouldn't. Not with Hollis or anyone else. She couldn't face the fact that none of this made sense to her or that nothing was what it had seemed.

"Good-bye, Hollis," she said, and then she turned and walked away.

~

Hollis watched as Emily made her way back toward the cottage. Going after her now would be a mistake, and besides, he'd run out of words to say. Did she really believe those things about him? He drew in a deep breath, saying a silent prayer that somehow God would change her heart. She was injured—he understood that—but he didn't want to lose her. Were his mistakes too painful for her to forgive? Too much of a reminder of the way her own father had treated her?

He turned and took a step toward his cottage when he saw Jolie, standing off to the side. She glared at him.

"Hey, JoJo."

Her face crumpled. "See? I knew you'd ruin everything!"

She raced off toward the house, Tilly following close on her heels, leaving Hollis standing on the empty beach with nothing but a sick feeling in his stomach.

CHAPTER 44

Isabelle didn't get out much anymore. She'd accepted life as a single mother, rarely dated, and had mostly given up on her dreams of traveling the world. Sure, she'd been overseas with her parents and with Emily, but it wasn't the dream she'd had in mind all those years ago.

Those years when she'd been young and foolish and momentarily impulsive.

And while she wouldn't trade her daughter for anything, there was, of course, a part of her that wondered how different her life would be if she hadn't gotten pregnant so young, if she hadn't lost JD so abruptly, if she hadn't settled right back into what was expected of her, gone to school, and immediately begun working at one of her father's companies.

Maybe it was the weight of these thoughts that caused her to agree to a night out with three friends she'd known for years. They were young moms now, and they all complained about how they never had time for themselves. The plan was to take a whole night and not think or talk about children.

But that plan quickly went awry.

Sitting at a table at the Chicken Box, Isabelle listened to all three of her friends drone on about diapers and teething and not sleeping through the night. She quickly lost interest, people watching at the cramped bar, which was unlike any of the places she usually frequented.

This place was unpretentious and down-to-earth, like JD's friends had been all those years ago. It was hard to be on the island without thinking of him. Hard to look at Emily and not see the resemblance.

Her eyes scanned the crowd, drifting from a group playing darts to a handful of people playing pool and then over to the dance floor, where two drunk women were making complete fools of themselves.

"I should probably get home," she said absently.

"Are you crazy, Isabelle?" her friend Janet squawked. "It's only eleven."

Still, Isabelle was tired. She stood. "I have an early morning."

Rebecca grimaced. "Doing what?"

"My daughter has rehearsal for *Charlotte's Web*. You better all get tickets or I'll consider it a personal insult." She picked up her purse with a smile.

A voice behind her stopped her before she could turn to go. "Bella?"

Rebecca, Janet, and their other friend Dawn all looked past Isabelle, to the voice. A voice she hadn't heard in twelve years but would never forget.

She spun around and found a rugged, slightly older-looking JD staring at her.

"I thought that was you." He smiled at her.

She smacked him—hard—across the face.

He grabbed her by the wrist and held her still as she steadied her breathing, eyes locked on to his.

"I *hoped* it was you." He brought her hand to his lips and kissed it, lingering as the seconds ticked by and her resolve crumbled.

Even after all these years—even after what he'd done—he still cast a spell over her with one single glance.

She pulled her hand from his, hitched her purse over her shoulder, and pushed her way through the crowd. She didn't get more than a few feet when she felt his hand around her arm. She tried to pull away, but his grip was too tight—too tight and yet still gentle, as if he wanted her to know he would never hurt her.

But he had, hadn't he? He'd hurt her worse than any physical pain ever could.

She spun around. "What are you doing?"

"I need to talk to you," he said. "Can we go outside where it's quiet?"

She hesitated.

"Just for a minute, Bella. Please."

In seconds she was seventeen again, standing in front of JD, wondering what it would be like if he was her "forever."

His touch. His kiss. His eyes. They were all so familiar, and yet she had no right to any of them.

"I don't have anything to say to you, JD." She pushed her way through the crowd, wishing she could disappear. He followed her outside, and once they were away from the noise, the music, the people, she finally exhaled.

Only then did she remember she hadn't driven herself there. It had been Janet's idea to come to the bar and Dawn's idea to take a cab.

She turned to face him. "What are you doing?"

"Trying to talk to you," he said.

"I don't want to talk to you. I don't ever want to see you again."

"I know you're mad."

"You think?"

"Let me explain."

"Are you crazy?" She sounded frantic, and his calm tone only made her more so.

"I didn't want to leave you back then," he said. "It was the last thing in the world I wanted, but it's taken me this long to make something of myself, to grow up."

"What are you talking about?"

"Think about it, Bella," he said. "If we'd stayed together, what kind of life would you have had? We would've struggled for everything, and you deserve so much more than that. Our daughter deserves more than that."

"Oh, so you do know we have a daughter," she spat.

"Yeah," he said sadly. "I know about Emily."

Isabelle shook her head. "Why did you leave without a single word? One day you're talking about getting married, and the next you've vanished."

He took a step toward her. "I guess I just realized I wasn't what you needed. So I left. I left and I tried everything to forget you. I even got married."

"You're married?"

"Not anymore. It wasn't right, and I tried, but . . ." He shrugged.

"But what?"

"She wasn't you." He rubbed a hand over his face. "I messed up, and I've spent a lot of years working to turn myself into the person you deserved. It's like that goal has been there at the back of my mind this whole time."

"What do you mean? Like, a person with money?"

He nodded. "I did that, Isabelle. I can take care of you now, and Emily. I mean, if you'll have me."

"You've got to be kidding me." She turned and walked a few steps away from him. Why hadn't she driven herself tonight?

"I know it's a long shot, Bella, but let me prove myself to you."

"No," she said. "I can't believe you think any of that matters to me." She faced him. "You really never knew me at all."

He pressed his lips together and drew in a deep breath. "I did know you, Isabelle. Better than anyone else. I loved you—I still do. But you can't tell me we would've made it with no money. We were kids."

"But at least we would've been together," she said. "And that would've been enough for me."

"You say that, but you don't know!"

"I do know!" she fired back.

"How? How do you know that it would've been enough?"

"Because I loved you, JD." They were face-to-face now, only a foot between them, and he'd captured every ounce of her attention.

"We would've made it," she whispered. "I had my trust fund. I had money."

His face fell, and he pulled his hand away. "You have it because I left."

She searched his eyes. What was he saying?

Seeing the confusion on her face, he drew in another shaky breath, then exhaled slowly. "I didn't want to tell you this—not ever."

"Tell me what?"

"The real reason I left."

After hearing his story, the way her parents bullied him into believing he wasn't good enough for her or Emily, everything began to make sense. Why he left the way he did. Why he never looked them up. Why her parents moved to North Carolina only months after they returned from Nantucket the summer she got pregnant, making it impossible for JD to find them.

"I never wanted to leave you, Bella," he said. "I just didn't think I could give you the life you deserved, and I didn't want to be the reason you lost everything. You and Emily deserved to have everything— this was the only way I could make sure you did."

She held on to his gaze, unable—or unwilling—to look away.

A mix of anger and sadness and regret and hurt all wound itself into a tight ball in her belly.

"You actually did love me?" The words sounded pathetic and weak, even to her, but she needed to know the truth. After twelve years of lies, she needed the truth.

He took her face in his hands the way he had so many times before, so many years ago, and took a step closer to her. He used his thumbs to catch her tears, wiping her cheeks dry; then gently, he kissed her forehead, then one cheek, then the other. "I never stopped."

She brought her eyes to his, searching for a reason to run.

She found none, only that same genuine love she'd always found when she looked at him.

"I'll do anything I can to prove myself to you," he said. "And if I'm not too late, I wondered if maybe we could start over?"

She covered his hands, still holding her face, with hers and closed her eyes.

"I promise I won't make the same mistake twice, Isabelle. If you let me, I'll love you for the rest of my life."

She opened her eyes, locked on to his, and nodded.

"Yeah?" His mouth spread into a slow grin.

She nodded again as he brought his lips to hers and kissed her with a pent-up passion that hadn't been unlocked in twelve years.

"I want you to meet her," she said, pulling away. "I want her to meet you."

"That would make me the happiest person on the planet."

Another kiss—then another—and she felt his arms around her in a way she sometimes dreamed of late at night.

Was this really happening?

"I'll go home and get her, but I want to talk to my parents first."

He let his forehead rest on hers. "I can come with you."

"No," she said. "I've got to do this on my own. But after I do, we can be together, and this time, nobody else is going to get in the middle of it."

He smiled as she removed herself from his embrace.

"Where will you be?"

"My aunt's cottage," he said. "Cliff Road."

Her breath caught in her throat. "Our cottage?"

His eyes found hers again. "Our cottage."

She stood on her tiptoes and kissed him again, this time slowly, deliberately, and without the rush of the past. "I love you, JD Walker," she whispered.

"I love you too."

And as she got in the cab to take her back to her parents' house, back to Emily, her heart leapt at the idea that finally—finally—she might get her happily ever after.

CHAPTER 45

EMILY TRUDGED BACK UP TO THE HOUSE, so angry with Hollis she wondered for a fleeting moment how it would feel to punch him. It was a ridiculous notion considering he likely had rock-hard abs that would do more damage to her fist than to him, but still, she wondered. She'd expected him to be on her side, but then that would've made him feel bad about his own mistakes, wouldn't it?

Of course he'd side with Jack. He *was* Jack.

The thought sent her stomach roiling. Coming back to Nantucket had been the worst mistake she'd ever made, and she'd made a lot.

She plowed through the yard and into the house through the sliding-glass door. She closed the door behind her and walked into the kitchen, where she found her grandmother standing, stick straight like a beauty queen.

She'd never made sense of her grandmother. They were from two different worlds—she'd spent so much of her life trying to reconcile the person she thought her mother wanted her to be with the person her grandmother was actively trying to turn her into.

Emily froze, and her grandmother gave her a long, pointed look. Sure, she'd borrowed the car without asking, but Grandma had fired Jack without asking. Grandma had refused to fill in any of the blank spaces in Emily's story. Grandma had answers where Emily only had questions.

Emily hung on to the older woman's gaze, mustered every ounce of courage she could find, and jutted out her chin. "Why didn't you tell me?"

Her grandma's already-straight shoulders stiffened. "Tell you what?"

"About Jack."

Grandma pressed her thin lips together until they disappeared. "I'm sorry, Emily. I know you wanted to handle this remodel all on your own, but I had to intervene when I saw some of the mistakes you were making."

"That's not what I'm talking about."

Eliza quirked an eyebrow ever so slightly.

"Don't you think you owe me an explanation? Don't I at least deserve that?"

"I haven't the foggiest idea what you're talking about," Grandma said.

Emily moved to one side of the large island Jack had built for the center of the kitchen. He'd installed a beautiful granite countertop on the white base, which was filled with drawers and cabinets and meant to store dish towels, mixing bowls, and serving dishes. He'd done a beautiful job—even Grandma had to admit that.

"Why didn't you tell me he's my father?"

Grandma's eyes darted to Emily's. "What did you just say?"

"You can stop pretending now, Grandma," Emily said. "I know the truth. I talked to Jack."

"And he told you this?"

"I found this." Emily pulled the copy of the newspaper article from her pocket and handed it to her grandma over the kitchen island.

Grandma took the paper gingerly and gave it a once-over as if she knew exactly what it was. "What's this got to do with anything?"

"He was there," Emily said. "At Mom's funeral."

Grandma looked again, squinting this time.

Emily reached over and pointed to the blurry image of a younger Jack Walker.

Grandma's brow puckered. "Oh, how can you tell?"

"It's him, Grandma. He didn't deny it."

Grandma gestured as if to flick an imaginary bug away. "That man is nothing but trouble. Always has been, always will be."

"You knew this whole time," Emily said, the realization of it washing over her with so much force it almost knocked her down. "Why would you keep this from me?"

"What did Jack tell you?"

"Nothing," Emily said. "He wouldn't tell me anything."

Grandma tried to hide the look of surprise on her face, but Emily saw it clearly. What did Grandma think Jack told her?

"So *you* need to tell me, Grandma," Emily said. "It's been eighteen years, more if you count all the years before Mom died. Something happened, and I want to know what it was."

Grandma walked toward the sink and stared out the window toward the ocean. With her back to Emily, she looked slight and angular, all jagged edges—not a single soft line on her body.

"Jack Walker showed up in Nantucket the year before your mother's senior year of high school. He was trouble right from the start—anyone could see it." She didn't turn around as she spoke.

Because he wasn't rich, like the rest of you? Because he was like Hollis?

Emily resisted the urge to say the words racing through her mind, choosing instead to drop onto a stool next to the island. Were they finally going to talk about this? After all this time, was Emily finally going to get answers?

"Your mother had never defied us before, but she became the definition of rebellious after she met Jack. We found out about their little fling and we tried to put an end to it—your grandfather even went to his boss at the club—" She stopped abruptly as if thinking better of continuing.

"Did GrandPop get Jack fired?"

Eliza crossed her arms over her chest and faced Emily, that all-knowing, holier-than-thou expression on her face. "He simply pointed out some of the issues he'd had with Jack on the course."

"He got him fired," Emily said.

"Jack was no saint, Emily," Grandma said. "Don't go making your grandfather into the villain here."

Emily drew in a deep breath and willed herself to stay quiet—at least for now.

"It didn't matter anyway," Grandma said. "He found another job almost immediately, working at the yacht club."

Good for Jack, Emily thought.

"And your mother refused to stop seeing him. 'I love him,' she said, as if she had any idea what love was." Grandma waved her hand in the air. "We did everything we could think of to keep the two of them apart, and when she turned up pregnant, it was obvious we were right. That boy and all his raging hormones pressured Isabelle into sleeping with him, and her whole life—everything we'd planned for her—it was all ruined."

Emily's shoulders sank. *Ruined.*

"Oh, don't look like that," Grandma said. "You know I don't mean anything negative. You, of course, were a gift—and one we'd never give back—but the circumstances of your birth were less than ideal. That's just a fact."

Emily looked away, and she did her very best not to let herself cry. *Ruined.*

Had she ruined her mother's life? Was that why she'd worked so hard to make it up to her? The traveling, the adventure, living out her dreams—had she been trying to pay for the sin of being born?

"Anyway, Jack found out about the pregnancy and he was gone a few days later," she scoffed as if to dismiss him even now.

Emily eyed her grandmother. The woman had always been proud. She loved a good debate, prided herself on winning. She'd always had an air about her that made other people feel they weren't quite up to her standards, Emily included. Grandma's face puckered, and her expression turned sour.

"There's more to that story, though, isn't there, Grandma?" Emily wouldn't leave this room until she had answers, and the same old story wasn't what she was looking for.

"What do you want me to say, Emily?"

"I want to know the truth," she said. "All of it."

Grandma drew in a terse breath and let it out as a heavy sigh. "What do you want to know? Did we do everything in our power to make sure you had the very best life you possibly could? Of course we did, and I'd do it again in a heartbeat."

Emily narrowed her gaze on her grandmother. "You'd do what again?"

Emily had never seen her grandmother flustered until that exact moment. She looked—for the first time Emily could remember—like a woman who didn't know what to say. Like a woman who'd run out of sentences to deflect and detract from the truth. She looked like she'd been caught.

"Your mother was so young, Emily," Grandma said after several long seconds. "She was young and foolish, and she thought she loved that boy."

Emily resisted the urge to interrupt.

"After she found out she was pregnant, Isabelle had a grand delusion that she was going to marry this boy—this *golf caddie*."

She said the words as if they were a swear.

"We knew it wouldn't do," Eliza said. "We knew there was no way Jack Walker could provide for our daughter. Isabelle was going to college. She was a star student. She was an Ackerman."

"And Jack Walker was a poor kid from the wrong side of the tracks."

"Oh, I know how it sounds," Grandma said. "It sounds cliché. It sounds like a story you've heard over and over in the movies, but it was true. That boy wasn't good enough for Isabelle, and he certainly wasn't good enough for you."

Grandma's lips drew into a tight, thin line.

"So what did you do?"

She shrugged, her face innocent. "I did what any sane mother would've done. I laid out the options for Jack."

"The options?"

"We went to see Jack Walker at the yacht club. He was out in the back laughing it up with his buddies as if he didn't have a care in the world. As if his actions hadn't caused irreparable damage."

"Did he know my mom was pregnant?"

"Of course he knew," Eliza said. "Who do you think put those ridiculous ideas of getting married and living in some tiny apartment in Boston in her head?"

Emily shook her head. "I didn't know about those ridiculous ideas."

"Well, your mother wouldn't listen to reason. She was dead set on playing house with the poor kid she met on Nantucket. We all know how that would've ended."

"So you went to see him . . ."

"And we made it plain. We simply showed him the truth of the situation."

"Which was?"

"That we could provide a life for the two of you that he never could."

"So you told him he wasn't good enough for her."

"Not just her," Eliza said. "You too."

Emily didn't know what to say. She had no words. Her grandmother was completely unapologetic for her actions, as if they were perfectly justified.

"It's kind of hard to believe he would've walked away without a fight," Emily said. "I mean, if they were so crazy about each other."

"Well, once Alan told him we'd cut her off if they went through with their ridiculous plan, Jack saw the error of his ways."

Emily's stomach twisted into a tight knot. "He told him what?"

"Don't be so surprised," Eliza said. "We simply explained that if he stayed in our daughter's life, we would no longer support her. That's what being an adult is, after all. Did he really want to be the reason Isabelle lost her trust fund and everything else she stood to inherit? That was enough to make him walk away."

"Because you made him think he couldn't take care of us," Emily said. "You made him believe that your way of life was the only way for us to be happy."

"I wasn't wrong," Grandma said.

"Did my mother know you did this?"

Emily watched as her grandmother wrapped her arms around herself as if she suddenly needed protection. For the first time since they started their conversation, Eliza looked slightly sad.

"I'm tired, Emily," Grandma said. "Let's finish talking about this tomorrow."

"No." Emily stood. "She didn't know my father loved her. She thought he left her because of me. I've spent my whole life believing that I was the reason she never got her happy ending."

"Emily, none of this had anything to do with you," Eliza said.

"How can you say that?" Emily raised her voice. "This whole thing happened because of me."

"That's not true."

"Did she find out what you did, Grandma?"

Her grandmother sighed. "Not at first. But that summer, the summer she died—Jack came back. I guess they ran into each other, and he told her everything. Made us out to be the bad guys, of course."

"That's what you were arguing about that night."

Eliza nodded. "She was so angry with us, and as usual, she wouldn't listen to reason. I don't know how much you remember, but your mother was hysterical. It was embarrassing, really."

Embarrassing to whom?

"Grandma, her whole world came crashing down that night," Emily said, putting the pieces together.

"But everything we did we did for you—for both of you. You must see that. You had a wonderful life because of us."

"But she didn't even get to make the choice for herself. You made it for her."

"Oh, Emily, please. Someday when you have a child, you'll understand. Kids don't know what they want. They don't know what's best for them."

Emily shifted. "Losing Jack broke my mom's heart, Grandma. *You* broke her heart. I don't think she ever recovered from that."

"Well, she would've if she'd been alive long enough. Time passes and makes things so clear, Emily. She would've seen the woman you've grown into and she would've known that was because your grandfather and I were in your lives. You've never wanted for anything."

But that didn't mean she was happy. She'd had things. She'd had a hefty bank account and vacations and culture. She'd grown up in a house fit for a princess. And yet she had wanted for something. For someone. For love. She'd wanted to belong. She'd wanted what Hollis described—a simple life with kids and a dog and a little house that could only be described as "cozy."

She wanted a family.

Sadness filled Emily's heart, not only for the love her mother lost, but for the years she'd spent believing her father didn't want her. And also—surprisingly—for her grandmother, a woman who had no idea that love was often far more important than *things*. To Grandma, life was about status and money and power and what everyone else thought of you.

It was as if the older woman had never considered there might be more to life than this.

Grandma pivoted in a circle and wrung her hands. "I stand by what we did. It was the best choice for you and your mother. Can you imagine being raised by Jack Walker?"

Maybe Mom would still be here today.

The thought entered Emily's mind without permission, and she did her best to shove it aside, though the effects of it lingered. She didn't want to blame anyone else for Mom's death, but a case could be made that her grandparents' actions had directly led to the events of that night.

How could she ever forgive them?

"I could just throttle your grandfather," Grandma said.

"GrandPop? Why?"

The older woman groaned. "He's the reason Jack Walker is here at all. Your grandfather, in all his wisdom, had a letter sent to the man after he died. Apologized for the way we treated him, as if we were the ones in the wrong. Apparently your grandfather grew soft in his old age."

"I don't understand."

"He told Jack he was leaving the house to you, that if Jack was receiving the letter, Alan had passed away and he should pay attention to Nantucket because that's where you'd be."

"He wanted me to meet him . . . ," Emily said, her voice barely a whisper.

"Yes," Grandma said. "It would seem so. Never mind that I'm the one left to pick up the pieces of this disaster he set in motion."

Emily watched as her grandmother walked over to a brand-new cabinet, pulled out a glass, filled it with water, and took a drink. It all seemed methodical, as if Grandma was waiting for Emily to magically understand her point of view. But that wasn't going to happen. The woman had been lying to Emily her entire life, and now, looking back on the night her mother died, it was hard not to blame her.

Suddenly the air grew thin and Emily found it hard to breathe. The realizations in front of her were too many.

Everything she'd believed had been a lie. And she'd never felt more alone in her life.

CHAPTER 46

EMILY STOOD IN LINE, ferry ticket in her hand, refusing to look back at the island. Instead, she focused on the large boat in front of her as passengers spilled out into the street.

She told herself this wasn't running. This was self-preservation. She told herself Hollis was all wrong about her, and it was time to start over and put Nantucket behind her for good.

She told herself those things, but they didn't help. Everything inside her ached for the life she'd almost had here on the island. It ached for Marisol and Nan and the other volunteers. For the kids she'd taught and grown to love. She'd wanted to stay in their lives. She ached for Hollis and his promise of simplicity.

She ached to belong.

And she was angry that she'd let herself believe that she did.

Of course she didn't belong here. Why would she delude herself into thinking she did? She'd lost sight of her original plan—get in, renovate the house, and get out.

If she'd just stayed on task, if she hadn't let herself get pulled into Hollis's world, if she hadn't let Nan's kindness or Jolie's sweetness convince her she was a part of their family, everything would be fine right now.

As much as she wanted to blame Hollis for that, it was her own fault. It was as if she kept searching for the same thing in the wrong places and always she ended up with a broken heart.

This pain was much deeper than a failed play or a restless spirit, and it was about more than discovering what she had about her father, about her mother, about her grandparents.

Truth be told, she was most devastated to lose Hollis all over again.

She quietly swiped a tear as it slid down her cheek. As she did, she felt a tug on her arm.

"Emily?"

She turned and found Jolie standing behind her, suddenly mortified that she'd left the girl without so much as a good-bye. How selfish had she been? Jolie had done nothing wrong, and yet the thought of losing her was too much for Emily to process.

And so she'd left.

She'd run.

The realization nearly crushed her. Maybe Hollis *was* right.

Emily forced a smile. "Hey, JoJo."

"Are you leaving?"

She drew in a deep breath. "I am."

"What about the show? It's so soon."

I'm the worst. I can't do hard things. I don't deserve any of this. I need to get out of here.

"I spoke with Marisol. She's going to get you guys through the last few rehearsals. You're ready, though—more than ready. You guys are going to be amazing."

"But you're not going to be there to see it?"

Emily looked away, and the line started to move toward the ferry. "I don't think I will be, JoJo. I'm sorry."

"Is this about my dad?"

Jolie had been worried about this exact thing happening. Emily couldn't make Hollis out to be the bad guy, not when there were so many other things that had led her to make this choice.

"No. Not really, anyway." Emily tried to find words. "I mean, there's a lot going on right now."

The girl's face fell. "No one ever tells me the truth. Everyone thinks I'm too young."

Emily knew how that felt. "Some things are just hard to explain."

"I knew he would ruin it. Because of him you're leaving, and the show won't be as good without you."

"That's not true."

"But I won't see you again," the girl said, her eyes filling with tears.

Emily stepped out of line and pulled Jolie into a hug. "That's not true either. Plus, you have my number, so you can text me anytime."

Jolie's arms were wrapped tightly around Emily's waist. "It's not the same."

"We'll stay in touch, I promise." But even as she said the words, she wondered how it would be possible. How could she keep anyone in her life without being reminded of what she'd lost?

Jolie stepped away and looked at Emily. "Do you love my dad?"

Emily was surprised by her forwardness, though she wasn't sure why. Jolie had never been one to beat around the bush. "I might."

"Then how can you leave?"

"It's complicated, JoJo."

"He said that too. But I think he loves you, and he doesn't want you to go."

"No," Emily said. "I'm pretty sure after the things I said to him, he probably can't wait to get rid of me."

Jolie reached into her small backpack and removed a white envelope. "He doesn't know I took this. I don't think he was planning to send it or anything, but I thought you should have it."

"What is it?"

"You'll see." Jolie took a step back, and Emily realized the rest of the line had boarded the ferry.

"I should go," she said.

Jolie threw her arms around Emily again and squeezed—hard. "I'll miss you."

"I'll miss you too, JoJo." The lump in her throat almost made speaking impossible.

Emily pulled away, then headed up the ramp. When she reached the top, she turned and waved at the girl, who waved back. Then Emily wiped her cheeks dry.

Leaving was the right thing to do, so why did it hurt so much?

She tucked the envelope in her purse and made her way inside, positioning herself at the center of the boat and trying not to remember Andrew and his little red-and-yellow backpack. Her first day back on the island had only been a couple of months ago, and yet so much had changed—she'd changed.

And yes, a part of her had wanted to believe it was all real, but none of it was. It was only a way to help her learn the truth, that people couldn't be trusted.

Her head spun with conflicting emotions. She was angry with Jack for not coming forward sooner, too angry to consider giving him a second chance. She was sad about losing Hollis, though she knew it was safer this way. She was furious with her grandparents for keeping the truth from her, for interfering the way they did in her parents' relationship. Her head was filled with more what-if questions than she knew how to manage.

What if her parents had gotten married?

What if her grandparents had stayed out of it all?

What if they'd told her mother the truth from the beginning?

What if Isabelle had gotten her happily ever after?

She reached inside her bag and found the book of letters, her only connection to her mom. She pulled out the letter that explicitly told her to be careful when it came to love and she reread the words, words she'd practically memorized.

Dear Emily,

In matters of the heart, I've learned one very important lesson: be cautious. You don't want to go around giving your heart to just anyone, and even if you do let yourself fall head over heels for some guy, remember there's still the great probability he's going to hurt you. Statistically, most relationships end, so you'd be smart to be very careful.

None of this "reckless abandon" stuff. It'll just get you into trouble.

Hollis didn't believe any of that. He'd flat-out said her mother was wrong. And Emily could admit he'd almost convinced her—his words had made love sound like something different, like something worth risking her heart for.

But she knew better.

She watched as the boat moved away from the dock. She stood and walked toward the window, trying not to replay every memory she'd had that summer and failing miserably.

It was as if every happy moment had stuck itself on a continuous loop in her mind.

She slid into a seat near the window, still watching as the island grew smaller and smaller behind them.

"That's what you do, isn't it? You run."

Hollis's words ripped through her mind, an unwanted memory.

She wasn't running. She was making a conscious decision. She'd decided she didn't want to risk the heartache. That wasn't the same thing.

She leaned her head against the window and closed her eyes, wishing she could fall asleep, but instead lingered on what she'd learned about her parents and her grandparents.

Jack and Isabelle had fallen in love—a hormonally driven kind of love, but love nonetheless. Her mother had approached it the way she'd cautioned Emily not to—with reckless abandon. Nothing had held her back. And while she'd made mistakes, Emily had to believe her mother loved Jack, more than she'd ever loved anyone before.

Then Mom's parents interfered, split the couple up, broke Isabelle's heart.

Isabelle wrote that letter through her pain, a warning to Emily—a warning she herself hadn't exactly heeded as well as she should've.

Hollis said her mother was wrong.

Emily sat with that for a long moment. Would Isabelle have thrown that letter away if she'd lived a few more years? Her thoughts turned to the night her mother died. She'd run into Jack in town, and he must've told her the truth. He must've explained he didn't want to leave, but he'd been convinced it was the best thing for Isabelle and Emily. Convinced by her parents.

Isabelle was furious. She was angry. She was on her way to Cliff Road.

Jack lived on Cliff Road.

Isabelle was going to Jack. After everything that happened, she was going to give him another chance. She was going to introduce him to his daughter.

Isabelle loved him even after everything they'd been through.

Emily opened her eyes but saw nothing. Instead she wrapped her mind around the realization she'd just had.

Her mother was throwing caution to the wind. Her mother was diving in headfirst. Her mother was going against her own advice in hopes that her relationship with Jack could be rekindled.

Her mother was choosing love.

Emily blinked back fresh tears. If only she'd gotten the chance. If only Jack had gotten the chance. For the briefest moment, she lost sight of her own pain and felt very deeply the pain her parents must've felt having realized the time they'd lost. She felt Jack's pain when he discovered Isabelle was gone, that he would never be able to make things right with her.

Hollis had asked what Emily wanted—not what her mom had wanted or what her grandmother wanted, but what *she* wanted.

And she hadn't been able to answer because the truth was, what she wanted conflicted with what she thought she *should* want.

She wanted to feel the same way she'd felt all those years ago before her mom had died, like she belonged to somebody. But giving yourself to somebody else was a giant risk, and Emily wasn't sure she could take it.

Pain squeezed her from the inside. But she already had taken it, hadn't she? With Hollis, with Jolie, with every single kid who was a part of the show she was directing?

Emily loved those people—they gave her a sense of purpose. Instead of only living for herself and her so-called dreams, she was discovering that she could play an active part in other people's lives, and she'd never felt that way before.

She'd never felt so fulfilled.

She remembered the way it felt to hug Marta at auditions and tell her she could do this. The way it felt to watch Alyssa and Jolie giggling together, possible friends for life. The way it felt when the kids listened to her advice and became stronger performers because of it. The way it felt to know that she helped create a safe place for them to stretch their creative wings, to find friends, to do things they maybe didn't believe they could do.

But it was a mirage. A fairy tale. And now she was eleven years old all over again, pulling away from Nantucket with nothing.

She'd lost it all.

She reached inside her bag and took out the envelope Jolie had given her.

Against her better judgment, she opened it and unfolded the sheet of paper inside.

Emily,

You just left me standing on the beach, but I already know you're leaving. I said a lot of things I regret, and I'm sorry. You didn't deserve to feel like I wasn't on your side. The truth is, Jack and I aren't so different—you were right. And I hate to think that you see in me the same things you see in him, things that have hurt you for so many years.

I guess I just want you to know that I love you, and I never wanted to hurt you. Actually, I've only ever wanted to protect you from getting hurt, so this is hard—seeing the pain in your eyes was hard.

I want you to do what you need to do, but I also want you to know that I'm here. I couldn't move on at this point if I tried.

Whatever you need—I'll give it to you. I'll leave you alone. I'll get in your business. I'll listen to you and wipe your tears when you cry. I want to help you figure all of this out if you'll let me.

Nobody's ever challenged me the way you do or made me feel the way you do. After I lost baseball, I thought I'd lost everything. But this summer made me realize there is so much more in life—you and Jolie and building a home.

Because yeah, I've turned into a sappy loser, and it's all your fault.

I'm here, Emily. Always.

I love you.

Hollis

She stared at his name for several seconds, then reread the words he'd written. It was a rare peek inside what he was really thinking, words he most likely would've never said aloud.

She ran her finger over his handwritten *I love you*, her heart conflicted at the words.

He could love her, but that didn't mean he wouldn't hurt her.

She folded the letter up and tucked it inside her purse, replaying the words she'd said to him the last time they'd spoken.

Her words were mean and full of anger, and he'd written these kind things immediately after she'd treated him so poorly?

She didn't deserve his kindness. She didn't deserve his love.

But he was giving it to her. Freely. No strings. Like a gentleman, he said he'd give her what she needed, whether it was a shoulder to cry on or space, with no thought to his own needs.

The realization shamed her. It was a pure example of unconditional love, something she'd only ever felt from her mother. Something she'd given up on ever feeling again.

But then, wasn't it just an example of the way God loved her? How many times had she gotten angry with him? How many times had she said terrible, awful things to him? And yet, as far as she could tell, he was still there, loving her.

And she didn't deserve it. But she needed it.

She glanced out the window, aching for a view of the island and wondering why she'd gotten on the ferry at all.

It was time to stop running. It was time to actually step up and do hard things.

But she had no idea where she'd find the courage to begin.

~

Dear Mom,

It's funny in all this time, I've never written you back. I suppose it seemed crazy because, you know, you're gone.

But today, sitting in a hotel in Cape Cod, contemplating the mess I've made of things, I realized it was time. Time for me to let you go.

I was trying to hold on to you so tightly that I didn't realize there was a whole life out there that I wasn't living. My life.

I never stopped to ask myself what I really wanted or who I wanted to spend time with. I did the things I thought I was supposed to do instead. And some things that turned out to be huge mistakes.

It all caught up with me, though, and I've realized lately that I only get one life, and it would be wrong not to figure out what I'm supposed to do with it. And for the first time, the only one I want helping me make that decision is God.

Surprising, right? I thought he'd abandoned me, but it seems maybe he was there all along—maybe it was time for me to deal with this pain so I could move forward.

Your letters sometimes talked about God, about faith, about how he's there whenever I'm ready. And I thought my mistakes negated all of that. I thought all the ways I messed up meant that I was not worthy of that kind of love.

But then . . . Hollis. He showed me what that kind of love looks like.

You remember Hollis, right? You always said he'd be a heartbreaker, and you weren't wrong.

But he hasn't broken my heart. In fact, I have a feeling if I give it to him, he'll protect it like it's a priceless treasure. He'll take good care of it, I think. I know it won't be perfect, of course, and it's risky—loving someone else. But I think it's also risky not to at least try. Because I don't want to get to the end of my life and regret that I never let myself be loved.

Hollis recently did something so unselfish that I realized what it means to be loved even when you don't deserve it. I guess a part of me has always felt undeserving. I felt responsible for everything that happened. I ruined everything, so of course I would live the life I thought you wanted me to. I owed it to you.

But I finally see that the only life you want me to live is the one uniquely designed for me.

I'm going to do that now. I'll make mistakes. I might stumble into some trouble or feel pain once in a while—but that's just it—I'll finally feel alive. Because life isn't only about the good things. It's about the roller coaster of emotions. It's about diving in headfirst even when you're scared.

It's about finding the place where you belong and then holding on with both hands.

And it's especially about working through the hard to get to the beautiful.

So here's to a beautiful life, Mom. Lived in your honor but in my own way.

I will always cherish the words you left behind, and I pray I'll make you proud. But it's time to stop running now, and it's time to forgive and move on.

All my love,
Emily

CHAPTER 47

HOLLIS STOOD BACKSTAGE, listening to the sound of indistinct chatter filling the auditorium.

Jolie appeared at his side, dressed in her red-and-gold Queen of Hearts costume. Her hair was pulled back in a tight bun, her face painted white with a tiny heart drawn at the center of her lips. She pulled back the curtain ever so slightly and looked out at the audience. "Is she here?"

Hollis leaned in closer, making Jolie's sight line his own. "Your mom? Yeah, she's right there, with Rick."

The two lovebirds had arrived earlier that day. They'd checked into a bed-and-breakfast and, having been instantly charmed with Nantucket, decided to turn their weekend into a week.

Apparently the honeymoon wasn't over. Hollis cringed a little at the thought.

"Not Mom," Jolie said. "Emily."

Hollis stepped back. "JoJo, you know she's gone. You saw her leave."

"Yeah," Jolie said, letting the curtain fall closed. "But she won't let us go on without her, right?"

Hollis wished it were true. What he wouldn't give for the chance to make things right with Emily. They'd left things so undone.

"Plus I gave her your letter."

"You what?" Hollis spun toward her.

"The one you left on your dresser," Jolie said.

"Did you read it?"

"Who do you think I am?" Jolie asked. "Of course not."

"Jolie, that was private," Hollis said. "If I'd wanted her to read it, I would've given it to her myself."

"But you did want her to read it, Dad. Otherwise you wouldn't have written it." Jolie glanced at the table next to him. "And you think she's coming too. Otherwise you wouldn't have bought two bouquets of flowers."

Hollis followed her gaze to the table, where, sure enough, there were two bouquets wrapped in brown paper. This kid was too smart for her own good.

"You weren't supposed to see that until after the show."

"Yeah, yeah," Jolie said. "You're not very good at keeping secrets."

He wished that were true. Maybe if he'd been straight with Emily about who Jack was as soon as he found out, things would be different now.

But that's not why they'd argued. She wasn't mad he didn't tell her the truth; she was mad he'd defended her father. Why had he done that? Because he was worried he was just like Jack?

It was selfish. It wasn't what she needed, and he knew it.

At least he knew it now.

"You need to go get ready," Hollis said. "I think Marisol is going to want the cast together for a preshow pep talk."

"I don't care about a pep talk unless it comes from Emily."

"Jolie, don't be like that," Hollis said. "Be respectful. And go with your cast."

She pouted. "Fine. Are you going to your seat now?"

"Yes," he said. "I'll be right in the front. You won't be able to miss me or your crazy family."

A slow grin spread across her face.

He might've lost Emily, but at least JoJo had forgiven him. Oh, she'd given him the silent treatment for a full twenty-four hours, but she'd eventually forgiven him.

"I know it wasn't all your fault that Emily left," she'd said. "And I know that you love her, so you're sad too."

Hollis hadn't been able to respond. The lump in his throat was too big to swallow.

He *was* sad.

But as the seconds ticked by and the time to raise the curtain drew closer, he'd all but lost hope.

Emily was gone. Just like when they were kids.

And this time, he wasn't sure he'd ever recover.

⁓

Emily stared at the building where she'd spent so many hours preparing for her production of *Alice in Wonderland*.

She'd tucked the letter she wrote to her mother into the back of the book with all the other letters and then put the whole thing in the bottom of her suitcase. She didn't have it with her now. She was on her own.

And she wasn't so sure she could follow through with her plan to walk in that door.

She'd abandoned Jolie and the rest of the cast when they needed her most. How could she have done that?

And would they ever forgive her?

Before she lost her nerve, she walked into the back of the theatre and found herself in the scene shop in the middle of a flurry of activity. At the sound of the door, everything in motion stopped and pairs of eyes turned her way.

Marisol was standing on a poorly built wooden box, the entire cast in a semicircle around her.

"Emily, thank goodness," Marisol said, hopping down. The girl hugged Emily tightly. "I knew you'd be back," she whispered. "Your cast is ready for their opening night chat."

Emily pulled away and looked at all the kids, fully dressed in their costumes with their hair and makeup done just the way Emily had instructed. Seeing them made her want to cry.

She might've missed a crucial rehearsal, but the work had been almost done before she left. Marisol likely had a few fires to put out, but most of the hard stuff had been finished.

It didn't excuse her leaving, however. That had been a poor choice, and she regretted it. Running was no longer the answer.

Time to grow up. Time to do hard things.

She stood on the box Marisol had just vacated and scanned the crowd until she found Jolie. She'd expected the girl to be angry with her, but she met Emily's eyes with a smile.

Kids were so forgiving. Was it too much to hope they all felt that way? Was it too much to hope that Hollis did too?

"I want to start by telling you all how sorry I am I wasn't here for dress rehearsal," she said. "I had some things come up and I had to leave." She glanced at Jolie, who gave her a soft nod. "But I knew I couldn't miss tonight. Your opening night." She paused, eyes moving from child to child. In their faces she saw a mix of emotions—nervousness and excitement and a little bit of admiration, which she definitely didn't deserve.

"I wanted to let you all know how proud I am of you. Getting up onstage is hard. It takes so much courage. Sometimes we can get so nervous or worried about something because it isn't easy, and that can make us miss out on the good stuff. You have to go through the hard stuff to get to the good stuff."

She smiled. "Right now, you might be feeling nervous, and that's hard . . . but tonight, when the show is over, you're going to have a healthy dose of good stuff. Because you conquered your fears. Because you did hard things. Because you worked for something and it was worth it. So go out there and do your very best, and above all—" she paused, making sure she had everyone's attention—"have fun!"

The kids cheered and the excited chatter she'd interrupted when she walked in picked up again.

"Places!" Marisol called out. "Places for the top of the show!"

The kids raced by, some stopping to give Emily a quick hug, bouncing around like pinballs in a machine.

She stepped off of the wooden box and found Jolie standing in front of her.

"I'm sorry I left, JoJo," Emily said. "It was a mistake."

Jolie smiled. "I forgive you. And I'm super glad you came back. I'm gonna knock your socks off."

Emily pulled the girl into a hug. "I know you are. Now, go get in your spot for the top of the show."

She ran off, leaving Emily standing in the scene shop alone but feeling anything but lonely.

CHAPTER 48

EMILY STOOD BACKSTAGE, watching her kids perform the scenes they'd worked so hard to perfect. As was typical with live theatre, not everything went as they'd planned. The Mad Hatter lost his microphone halfway through the show, and the girl playing Small Alice forgot some of her lines. But none of that mattered. These were her kids, and they were doing what she'd taught them to do.

The sense of pride she felt the moment the final curtain went down wasn't something she'd ever experienced before. The applause wasn't for her, and she preferred it that way. The audience cheered for children she'd grown to love. She'd gotten to be at the helm of this ship, and in the process, she'd discovered something that mattered more than herself.

She watched as the kids stepped forward for their bows, and she stood in the wings, applauding. The only thing that would've made it better would've been standing down in the front, directly in front of the cast, so they could see how proud she was of what they'd done.

As the song ended and the crowd died down, Marisol stepped out onstage with a microphone. She stood in front of the rows of kids, center stage, and waited until the audience was quiet. They'd taken their seats again and now gave Emily's young assistant their full attention.

"As most of you know, this show wouldn't have been possible without the hard work of one very special person," Marisol said.

Emily's stomach churned. *No, no, no.* She didn't want them to pull her out on the stage. She took a step back as Marisol turned toward her.

"She doesn't want us to fuss over her, but I'm fussing anyway because she deserves it. Emily Ackerman, can you come out here so we can thank you properly?"

Emily shook her head.

"Come on, Emily!" Marisol raised her eyebrows expectantly as she gestured for Emily to join her on the stage. The cast began applauding and cheering, coaxing her from her spot in the shadows.

Slowly, unsteadily, she began to walk onstage. The spotlight hit her as she did, making it nearly impossible to see beyond what was right in front of her. But as she met Marisol front and center, she looked down and found Hollis's eyes. He sat right in the front row, next to his parents and siblings, the exact same spot her mother and grandparents had sat when she was a kid.

Did he know how foolish she felt? Did he know how sorry she was? Did he care?

He watched her for a few seconds until finally his mouth spread into a smile. Then he stood up and applauded, that same look of pride in his eyes that she'd seen in the faces of her family all those years ago.

And that's the moment it hit her. The thing she'd been searching for, the thing she wanted most of all, was a home.

And Hollis was it.

Hollis was *home* to her.

His parents, Hayes, and Harper had all joined him in his standing ovation, followed by the rest of the audience, and while Emily was grateful for their appreciation, the truth was, it was them who'd given something to her.

Marisol handed her the microphone. "Go on, boss. Say something."

The crowd settled, then quieted, everyone waiting for Emily to share something profound.

"Thank you, everyone, for being here tonight. We appreciate your support so much. You know, I've spent a lot of years of my life searching for a place where I could put down roots. I've never found it until this summer when I came here. The way you all jumped on board with this crazy idea to bring back the children's show, the way you've donated time and talent to making the show a success, the way you've accepted me and made me feel like a part of your family—" She glanced at Hollis, then at Nan, then the rest of his family, and she found herself unable to continue until she swallowed the lump in her throat.

"Well, you'll never know how much it's meant to me. I've learned so much over the last two months. Most importantly, I've learned that sometimes your failures can lead right to your purpose. Thank you for letting your kids spend their summer with me. It's truly been one of the best summers of my life."

Hollis gave her a slight nod as she handed the microphone back to Marisol and left the stage.

Seconds later, he was at her side, standing in the wings as the kids took one final bow.

He had every right to be furious with her. She'd been rude and hurtful. But she saw nothing but kindness in his eyes.

"It's good to see you."

She looked away. "I don't deserve any of this." She motioned toward the stage, where the curtain had fallen and the kids were now cheering and celebrating. A little girl ran over to Emily and threw her arms around her waist.

"I love you, Miss Emily," she said.

Emily hugged back, but the girl was gone before she could respond. She found Hollis watching her. He walked over to a table off to the side, picked up a bouquet of flowers, and handed them to her.

"They're wildflowers." Just like the ones he'd given her when they were kids.

"Probably should've gotten you something a little more grown-up, huh?"

"Are you kidding? They're perfect." She stuck her nose in the bouquet and inhaled. "But you didn't even know I would be here."

"No, but I was hoping you would be," he said with a grin. "I know how much you love these kids."

She smiled, looking at her kids rushing around, celebrating their job well done.

"That's true," she said. "But not just them."

He met her eyes.

"I'm sorry, Hollis," she said.

"Forgotten."

"No, I owe you a real apology."

"You don't owe me anything, Emily, and you never will." He took her hand and stepped toward her. Her eyes clouded over as his words made their way to her heart.

"I read your letter," she said.

Hollis groaned. "You weren't supposed to. Jolie shouldn't have given that to you. It was stupid to write it."

"No, it wasn't. I loved it."

He looked embarrassed for a split second, but his goodness was all she could see. That letter had moved things around inside of her. Did he know how much his words had meant?

Could she learn to love without condition? Could she learn to forgive—even the people who'd hurt her so wholly the wounds were still fresh and painful? She didn't know, but she wanted to try. She wanted to stay. She wanted to stop running.

She wanted to chip away at what was hard in order to get to what was beautiful.

She even thought maybe she wanted to give God a second chance. She'd seen the good in all that had happened that summer. Was it possible he knew what he was doing after all?

"There you two are!" It was Nan, and she was beaming. "Oh, Emily, you did a fantastic job with this show. We've already bought our tickets for the rest of the weekend. You are truly gifted. I don't know many people who can pull what you do out of these kids."

Emily smiled, the memory of her directing debut (or debacle) fading further and further away.

"It's true," Jeffrey said, joining them. "That's a gift."

"Thank you both," Emily said. "I really love working with them."

"So you'll do next summer's show?"

Emily turned and found Jolie standing behind her, a small crowd of other cast members around her.

"I think we should do *Annie*," one of them said.

"Or maybe *The Wizard of Oz*," another one said.

"You're coming back, right, Miss Emily?"

She opened her arms and the five of them moved in for a big group hug. "I wouldn't miss it for the world."

~

Hollis stood in the lobby, watching as Jolie moved from friend to friend, hugging and laughing and congratulating each one as if it were the last time she'd see them. As if they weren't doing this twice again tomorrow.

The twenty-four hours that Emily had been gone had felt like an eternity. She hadn't responded to his texts or voice messages, and it was a clear indication that he didn't want to live his life without her. Yep, he was that guy—the one the guys in the locker room would've relentlessly teased. And he didn't care. He loved her.

Maybe a part of him had always loved her.

"I have to hand it to you, Hollis. You really surprised me." Jana had found his hiding spot off to the side.

"How's that?"

Jana cocked her head to one side and squinted her eyes. "Something's just different about you, and it shows."

He looked away. He didn't want credit for finally doing the right thing. God had worked him over—he should get the credit.

"I know you regret a lot of things, Hollis, but we're doing well, and Jolie's doing awesome, and you did a good job with her this summer."

He met her eyes. "Yeah?"

She nodded. "Honestly, I thought you'd be handing her back to us ready to sign those adoption papers."

He shook his head. "That's not gonna happen."

Jana smiled. "I'm actually glad to hear it."

Rick appeared next to her and wrapped an arm around her waist. "Great show, huh? Our girl did good."

Our girl?

Hollis glanced at Jana, who widened her eyes as if to say, *Don't make a thing of it.* And he decided not to, no matter how annoying Rick was. Maybe they could all claim a piece of Jolie. Maybe he was okay with that now because he had his piece firmly tucked close to his heart.

Emily appeared across the lobby, and he could tell she was looking for someone. He didn't dare hope it was him.

Okay, maybe he hoped. Maybe he wanted to believe that he'd always be on the receiving end of her expectant expression. And he wanted to believe he'd never let her down.

Jana must've followed his gaze to Emily because she nudged him with her shoulder, then waggled her eyebrows at him. "You've got it bad, Mack."

Hollis returned his gaze to the girl next door who'd stolen his heart. "Yeah, I do." He smiled just as her eyes found him.

She waved, then made her way through the crowd toward him.

With her at his side, suddenly he felt complete, like he could climb mountains. She made him feel strong. She made him want to be a better man.

He loved her for that.

But mostly he just loved her for her. He loved the times when he found a crack in her confident exterior. He loved that she had no idea how beautiful she was. He loved the way she loved his daughter. And he loved this journey she was on—this journey of uncovering the past so she could forgive and move on. He'd been on that journey, so maybe he could help her.

"You must be Jana," Emily said. "Jolie showed me pictures of your wedding. It was beautiful." She radiated authenticity—another thing he loved about her.

"Thanks." Jana smiled. "It was a perfect day."

"The show was really fun," Rick said.

"Yeah, the kids are pretty amazing." Emily's eyes were bright. She looked happy.

"So's their director," Hollis said quietly.

She found his eyes, and a smile skittered across her lips.

"Thanks for teaching Jolie," Jana said. "It's all she talks about. She's already looking forward to next summer."

"She's a great kid," Emily said. "Really, I have her to thank for helping me remember why I loved the stage in the first place."

"We should go shopping or something while I'm here," Jana said, turning Emily into one of her girlfriends.

Emily glanced at Hollis, then back to Jana. "I'd love that."

"Great," Jana said. "We're going to head out. Hollis, tell Jolie we'll see her in the morning."

"You got it."

They disappeared, leaving Hollis wishing the rest of the crowd would do the same so he'd have Emily all to himself.

The thought was fleeting because seconds later, Eliza Ackerman exited the auditorium and made a beeline straight for them.

Emily's face turned pale. "I had no idea she was here."

"I should go."

She reached out and grabbed his hand. "Please don't."

The simple gesture made him feel wanted. She'd given him permission, not to protect her, but to stand beside her, even though this could be a potentially difficult confrontation.

She was letting him in, and that knowledge settled in a warm spot inside his belly.

⁓

Emily wasn't prepared to see her grandmother. She hadn't come back to the island for Eliza Ackerman—where the older woman was concerned, Emily still had a lot of mixed emotions. Actually, her emotions weren't mixed; they simply weren't kind.

She'd prayed about her grandma while she was away. She found herself unmoved. She'd keep praying, but how would that help her right now?

"Maybe she's here to say she's sorry?" Hollis whispered as Grandma approached.

But Emily knew better. Emily knew that Eliza Ackerman didn't apologize to anyone. Ever. Besides, her grandma didn't regret what she'd done. Nothing would change that.

Grandma stood in front of her now, chin jutted upward as if she needed to look down her nose on the rest of them. "I thought you might come back."

Emily inhaled slowly. "I came back for the kids." *And for Hollis.*

But she wouldn't say that. She wouldn't let her grandmother in on the part of her life that brought her joy. Grandma had lost the right to know her most personal thoughts.

"They did a lovely job," Grandma said.

"Yes, they did," Emily agreed.

"I'm glad you're here." Grandma began rummaging through her purse until she found a small key ring with two silver keys on it. "I thought you should have these."

Emily held her breath as her grandma pressed the keys into her hand. "What are they?"

"They're my keys to the house," Grandma said. "It's your house now, so I don't really need them."

Emily watched as Eliza looked away, plastering a smile on her face as she waved to Gladys Middlebury and another older woman.

"You don't have to do that, Grandma," Emily said.

Eliza brought her eyes back to Emily's. "It's what your grandfather wanted." She reached out and took Emily's hands. "And what I want. You deserve it, and you've done a lovely job with the renovations so far."

"Really?" Why her grandmother's approval still bolstered her confidence, Emily wasn't sure.

"Really. And I hope one day you can come to understand that everything I did I did because I thought it was what was best for you and for your mother."

It wasn't an apology—Emily knew that was too much to hope for—but it was an indication that her grandmother wanted things to be right between them. She just didn't want to admit any wrongdoing on her own part.

Emily didn't have forgiveness to offer her—not yet. But maybe one day she would. She hoped she would. She'd have to work on it, to pray about it, because it wasn't going to magically appear.

As if her grandmother read her mind, the older woman took a step back, dropped Emily's hands, and straightened.

"I'm heading out tonight," she said. "The house is all yours."

"Thank you," Emily said.

Grandma looked at Hollis. "You take good care of her."

Hollis tightened his hand around Emily's. "I plan to."

His touch was familiar, and yet it still sent her insides swirling. She knew now that relationships weren't easy—they were messy and challenging and filled with emotions, but for the first time in her life she wanted to brave those things in order to see what was on the other side.

Was she scared? Yes. But Hollis was worth it. *They* were worth it.

Grandma gave a pointed nod, then walked off. Emily wondered when she would see her again. It could be months. It could be never.

She stood in her spot for a long moment, then glanced at Hollis, whose eyebrows shot up as if to ask a question.

"I'll be right back," she said.

The crowd had only slightly thinned out, so it was a struggle to make her way through the lobby and to the front door, but she pushed on until she did, muttering, "Excuse me" on a continuous loop. She shoved the door open and walked out onto the street, where she spotted her grandmother hurrying toward the parking lot.

She jogged toward the older woman. "Grandma?"

Her grandmother turned around just as Emily reached her. Emily wasn't prepared to see her grandmother's tearstained face, a rare, jarring sight.

Grandma sniffled, then looked away, wiping her cheeks dry as discreetly as she could. Turns out it wasn't very discreet at all. Grandma had been found out.

The woman did have a soul.

Emily stared at her grandmother for several seconds, then remembered she was the one who chased after her. What did she say?

"I don't know if I'll ever understand what you did, Grandma," she finally said. "I can find a lot of issues with your thinking."

Grandma didn't respond.

"But I do believe you had good intentions. Misguided though they were. Mom told me you always wanted what was best for me. I believe her." Emily reached out and took her grandmother's hand. She didn't feel a magical jolt of peace that took her anger away. She didn't feel a change in her emotion at all—in fact, she was still angry. But she didn't want to let her grandmother leave the island thinking they weren't on speaking terms.

She'd forgive her, in time and without an apology, but for today she'd just say good-bye.

"I'm proud of you, Emily," Grandma said.

The words hit Emily square in the chest. Nobody had said that to her since her mother died.

"And your grandfather was proud of you too." She squeezed Emily's hands, then smiled at her. "I've got to go."

Emily nodded. She would've said something, but she couldn't speak around the lump in her throat.

Instead, she watched as her grandmother made her way to the parking lot, got in the Lexus, and drove away.

Help me forgive her, Lord.

She'd pray it every day if she had to, and she might, because she didn't much feel like forgiving her right now.

Emily turned back and looked at the theatre. Through the front doors, she could see the crowd of people still gathered in the lobby. Costumed kids wove their way through a sea of adults and every single one seemed to have a cheerful expression on their face.

She'd helped create that happiness.

That thought made her smile.

And while she'd spent so much of her life as a loner, with acquaintances scattered all over the world and no real friends to speak of, she now felt exactly the opposite.

She was home.

CHAPTER 49

EMILY HADN'T INTENDED to be the last one to leave the theatre, but here she was, standing on the stage in the darkened space, the rest of the building empty.

Hollis appeared in the wing, illuminated only by the ghost light she'd dragged onto the stage and plugged in. The faint cloud of light from the single bulb attached to the top of a pole did very little to brighten the shadowed areas around her and nothing to light the seats in the auditorium.

"Why's it called a ghost light?" Hollis asked, standing in front of her, only the skinny light between them.

"It's supposed to keep away ghosts," Emily said with a smile. "Don't you know theatres are haunted?"

Hollis's face was barely lit enough to make out his features, but she thought maybe his eyebrows shot up as he said, "Is that right?"

"Actually, I have to leave it here so nobody accidentally walks off the stage in the dark."

Hollis grabbed her shirt and used it to tug her toward him. "That makes a little more sense."

She put her hands on his chest and inhaled the masculine scent of him. He didn't wear cologne, but the lingering smell of whatever soap he used was distinctly *Hollis*, and it was a smell she'd grown to love.

He brushed her hair back and studied her face, and surprisingly, she didn't shrink under the weight of his attention. Instead she met his eyes, then let her gaze fall to his lips, his strong jawline, then back to his crisp hazel eyes.

"I'm proud of you," Hollis said.

Two in one night? After years of making no one proud, it was turning out to be a banner day.

"You're a natural at this, you know?" he continued. "It was fun to watch."

"I'm surprised how much I loved it."

He leaned closer and let his lips graze hers, softly, gently, not really a kiss so much as an exploration, as if he wanted to uncover every part of her one second at a time.

"The cast is meeting down at the beach for a bonfire," she said.

"I know. My parents took Jolie."

"Do you want to go?"

He shrugged. "A case could be made for staying here."

"Or having our own picnic on the beach?"

"Or that."

She inched up on her tiptoes and brought her mouth back to his. She tried to memorize the movement of his lips, the way they felt on hers, the way his muscles felt underneath her hands, the way she wanted that moment to go on forever.

His arms slid around her waist, drawing her closer, deepening the kiss.

She abruptly pulled away and searched his eyes. "I'm still a little scared, Hollis. What if this ends?"

He kissed her again; then, slowly, he knelt down in front of her, picked up her left hand, and smiled.

"I've made a lot of mistakes in my life, but loving you is the best thing I've ever done. I've always known when it came time for me to settle down, it would be forever. I don't want you worrying that this is only temporary or that I'm going to hurt you. I'm not. The only thing I'm going to do is love you forever, if you'll let me."

Emily's eyes widened. "Hollis, what are you saying?"

He reached into his pocket and pulled out a tiny blue box. "I'm saying I want you to marry me. I'm saying this isn't going to be perfect. We're going to hit hard times. I don't even have a job right now—"

Emily laughed as her eyes clouded over with tears of happiness.

"But we'll figure it out together. We'll muddle our way through the hard stuff until it turns into something else, until it becomes our story."

"Hollis, I don't know what to say."

"You belong with me, Em. I hope you'll say yes."

She scanned his eyes, his face, looking for a reason to run, but there wasn't one there. There was only love.

She belonged with him. With Jolie. With Nan and Jeffrey. She belonged on Nantucket or in Boston or wherever life took them. She *belonged*.

And that was a beautiful feeling.

She slid to her knees and squared her gaze with his, then took his face in her hands, his slight stubble rough to the touch. "Of course, yes. There's nothing in the world I want more than to marry you."

"Well, thank goodness," he said. "You had me worried for a second."

She laughed, then fell into his arms, relishing his kiss, as the ghost light flickered and her heart latched on to the promise of a future.

~

Hollis pulled into the circle drive in front of the Ackerman cottage, and Emily turned over the keys in her hands. Her grandmother had officially relinquished control, which meant this house was all hers. For real this time.

"You gonna add those to the rest of your keys?" he asked.

Emily nodded. "Sort of appropriate, don't you think? That these keys will be the end of my collection? I mean, that part of my life is over."

He looked at her. "You're not sad about that, are you?"

She smiled. "Not even a little."

"Good."

"I want to go in and change; then I can meet you down on the beach if that's okay?"

Hollis leaned over and kissed her forehead, then grazed her nose, settling fully on her lips. Seconds later and she was lost in it.

Good night, this man knew how to kiss.

He pulled back, then picked up her hand and kissed the ring he'd slid onto her finger.

Emily had never been one to wear a lot of jewelry, and Hollis must've known it. It was as if this ring had been made for her unique personality. A simple white-gold band with a large round diamond, encircled by a ring of smaller diamonds, it was beautiful without being flashy, and she loved the way it looked on her hand.

"I'll meet you down there," she said.

He nodded as she leaned over for one more kiss, then got out of his Jeep and started up the walk toward the house.

Grandma must've left some lights on because the entryway and living room lights both shone through the windows into the yard outside.

She pushed the door open and walked inside. She inhaled the smell of fresh paint, then took a moment to admire the work they'd done over the last couple of months.

When she'd arrived, the house had been an empty box of tormenting memories. Now, it had become something else entirely—it had become a place where she'd figured out who she was. The house had been instrumental in giving her a purpose, in showing her that there was a lot of life left to live, and she wanted to live it well.

She was proud of what they'd accomplished, though she was more eager than ever to get it finished, which presented a strange conundrum. Did she call Jack and ask him to come back? He knew the plans; he had a crew.

Or did she find someone else to do the last of the work—someone less complicated?

Emily startled at the sound of movement in the kitchen. Maybe Hollis had come in through the back door? But she hadn't heard the door, only the sound of someone rummaging around.

Against her better judgment, she walked through the entryway and toward the doorway that led to the kitchen, surprised when she spotted a familiar silhouette.

Jack.

She watched as he ran a rag over the freshly installed sliding-glass door, unaware that he wasn't alone.

She wasn't prepared to speak to him. She didn't know how she felt or what she thought or what she wanted to say, but here he was, the father she'd always imagined and also the father she'd never imagined.

She cleared her throat and he stopped midswipe as his head snapped in her direction. "Emily?"

"Hi."

"I thought you were gone." He dropped his arm to his side and faced her.

"I came back." She watched him shift his weight from one foot to the other. "What are you doing here?"

Jack tucked the rag into his back pocket. "Your grandmother called me to come back and finish the remodel. As of about five minutes ago, I think I'm officially done."

Emily couldn't hide her surprise. "My grandma called you?"

"Shocker, right?"

"Huge shocker."

"She said she still doesn't like me, but she knew it was important to you that I finish the job."

Emily smiled, mostly because that sounded like Grandma and also because she wasn't sure what to say.

"Have you talked to her?"

"Just for a minute after the show," she said.

"I wanted to come to the show," Jack said. "I wasn't sure if I'd be welcome."

She smiled—from the heart this time. "Come tomorrow."

"Yeah?"

Emily nodded.

"Emily, I—"

Her upheld hand cut him off. "Listen, I don't have anything figured out right now, Jack. Nothing makes sense to me, but I've thought a lot about it since I left your house that day, and I'd like to get to know you if you'll let me."

Jack's entire face brightened. "Yeah?"

"Yeah."

"That'd be . . . It'd be really great."

"So maybe we can get coffee tomorrow?"

"That sounds good." Jack crossed his arms over his chest. "I'll pick you up at seven."

Emily groaned. "Let's make it seven thirty?"

Jack laughed. "All right. I'll see you then."

Emily saw him to the door, then went upstairs to change out of her dress and into a pair of jean shorts and a T-shirt.

She found her flip-flops, packed a bag in the kitchen, then trudged down to the beach, where Hollis sat on a blanket, stoking a fire in a small charcoal grill.

"Did you bring s'mores stuff?" he called out as soon as she stepped onto the sand.

She held up the bag. "Dinner of champions."

He stood, took the bag from her, and waited until she sat, then covered her in a plaid blanket.

"Thanks," she said.

In the distance, she saw a young family walking toward them. It was rare to see other people on this stretch of beach, but as they approached, realization set in and she smiled.

"What is it?" Hollis asked, following her gaze to a young boy darting down the beach in their direction.

"Just an old friend." She stood and walked toward the water, eyes on the little guy, who seemed to be chasing the waves back out to sea. He hadn't noticed her yet, but when he brought his eyes away from the ocean and found her standing there, recognition spread across his face.

"Hey! It's you!" he said.

"Hi, Andrew." She grinned.

"You did that *Alice in Wonderland* play."

She decided not to correct him. He had plenty of years to learn proper theatre terminology. "I did. Did you see it?"

Andrew nodded enthusiastically. "It was so good. I loved the part where the queen yelled." He took a step closer. "Kenton loved it too," he whispered.

She winked at him. "I'm so glad." She reached into her pocket and pulled out the smooth white stone he'd given her on the ferry ride over—a ferry ride, it turned out, that would change her life. She'd kept it with her like a touchstone all these weeks.

Maybe she was more sentimental than she thought.

"Look," she said, showing him the stone.

His eyes brightened. "You still have it!"

"Yep. It's one of my most prized possessions."

Andrew's parents caught up to him. They exchanged pleasantries, and Emily invited him to participate in one of her shows when he was old enough, which, it turned out, would be a couple of years.

"Have a good rest of the summer, Andrew," Emily said as they continued on down the beach.

He giggled and waved, then went back to chasing the water.

She turned back to Hollis, who put an arm around her. "Does that mean you'll be here in three years when that kid is old enough to do a show?"

"I hope so."

They sat on the beach—their beach—roasting marshmallows and

making s'mores. Every once in a while, she'd steal a glimpse of him, his face only dimly lit by the fire.

Hollis was good and kind and everything she ever could've dreamed of in a man. Why God had brought them back together now, she didn't understand, but she was so grateful he had.

It was strange to think about God that way after years of ignoring him, but she'd made a sort of peace with him here. It was as if her eyes had been opened to the fact that life wouldn't be perfect, that bad things would happen, but that God was still good. No matter what.

Maybe God brought her back to help her move forward. Maybe he had more for her than the vagabond life of wanderlust she'd been living.

Emily glanced at Hollis and realized there was no "maybe" about it. The thought filled her with gratitude.

The waves lapped the shore, and Emily dug her toes into the cool sand.

"What will you do with the house now that it's done?" Hollis asked after Emily's update about running into Jack inside.

She looked back up at the cottage, focusing on the light coming from her second-story window.

"Well," she said, "I've been thinking a lot about that."

"You want to keep it, don't you?"

She shook her head. "Actually, I want to sell it."

He regarded her thoughtfully. "Really? You know you don't have to worry about the money anymore, Em. I'm going to take really good care of you."

She scrunched her nose. "Your job pays well, huh?"

He laughed. "I'm going to find a great job."

"I don't doubt it."

"It just might not pay as much as we're used to."

"No?"

He drew in a breath. "I think I want to coach."

Her eyes widened. "Really?"

"What can I say? You've inspired me."

She smiled. "You'll be so great at that."

"Well, I'll talk to you before I apply anywhere. I don't want to move you to Alaska or something."

"What's wrong with Alaska?"

He rolled his eyes. "I forgot. You've lived everywhere."

"So I can be happy anywhere," she said. "Except Florida. Too muggy."

He laughed. "Man, I love you."

She startled at his words, the way he seemed unable to contain them. She'd never been loved so well in her life. She decided she liked it. She decided it was exactly what she'd been missing.

He grinned at her. "If you sell the house, will we stay at my family's cottage when we come back to Nantucket? You know you're committed to doing the show next summer."

"I've been thinking about that, too," she said. "And I think we need our own place. Small. Cozy. White picket fence."

"Yeah?"

She nodded. "I'm ready for a simple life, Hollis. And as long as I get to spend it with you, I'll be the happiest woman in the world."

He stood, walked around the fire between them, and knelt down in front of her. "Then prepare to be happy, Emily Ackerman. Because I'm never going to let you go."

She closed her eyes, the warmth of the fire doing nothing to compete with the warmth of her flushed cheeks as she gave in to his knee-buckling kiss.

MORE GREAT ROMANCES BY
COURTNEY WALSH

TURN THE
PAGE FOR
A PREVIEW

CHAPTER

1

HE SHOULDN'T BE HERE.

A diner in some little tourist town in Michigan was no place for Grady Benson, but here he was. From the second he walked in the door, it was clear he'd made a mistake. Eyes found and followed him all the way to this table, conspicuously located at the center of the space.

A girl with glasses and wild, curly hair rushed over and set a glass of water in front of him.

If he had to guess, he'd say tourist season was over and this place was filled with locals. He didn't even catch the name of the diner when he walked in, but when Wild Hair handed him the menu, he read *Hazel's Kitchen: Harbor Pointe, Michigan* on the cover and figured that's where he was.

Where he definitely should not be.

So much for staying under the radar.

"Did you see the sign on your way in? It had all the specials written on it." Wild Hair wore a name tag that read *Betsy*. Now that he looked at her, she was cute, in a small-town, innocent sort of way. Not like the girls he was used to dating. They were anything but innocent.

"I didn't." He opened the menu and kept his head down, but the whispers started despite his best efforts to disappear. Apparently Harbor Pointe had noticed him.

"Can I just get a cheeseburger with everything, fries, and a chocolate milk shake?"

Betsy's eyes went wide. "Are you sure that's a good idea?"

He glanced up at her, and she quickly swiped the menu out of his hand.

"I'm sorry. I shouldn't have said that."

"What do you think I should eat?" he asked.

She looked away, visibly ruffled. "Grilled chicken with a big plate of roasted vegetables and a glass of water?" There was a question in her voice.

He pretended to think it over for a few seconds but shook his head. "I'll stick with the cheeseburger."

She scribbled something on her notepad, then scurried away like a mouse. Grady sat for a few long minutes, feeling too big for the chair she'd put him in. He pulled his phone out of his pocket and opened Twitter.

Grady Benson needs to learn the art of knowing when to quit.

Benson chokes again. Time to hang up the skis, buddy.

Kiss the Olympics good-bye, GB. You'll be lucky to land a job training little kids with a run like that. #crashandburn

He clicked the screen off and flicked it on the table with a clunk.

The race in Vermont would follow him all the way to Colorado with Twitter comments echoing in his head. He should've just gotten on a plane like everyone else. A solo road trip to clear his head suddenly seemed like a ridiculous idea.

Betsy returned with his milk shake, half of it in a tall glass with whipped cream and a cherry on top, the other half still in the metal mixing container. He ate healthy most of the time—it was one of the few rules he actually followed—but he didn't feel like making wise choices right now.

He wanted to do whatever he wanted to do.

Grady glanced up as the door opened and a pretty blonde woman walked in. She wore ripped jeans rolled at the ankles, slouchy and a little too big for her, along with a gray T-shirt underneath an Army-green jacket that cinched in at the waist. Like him, she looked out of place, like she didn't belong here, but judging by the welcome she received when she walked in the door, she absolutely did.

He couldn't tell, but it seemed the crowd at the front of the diner was congratulating her about something. Not his business. He went back to his milk shake, and a few seconds later his food arrived.

Betsy stood beside the table for an awkward beat. "Need anything else?" she finally asked.

"I'm good, I think," he said. "Thanks."

She nodded, then skittered away, leaving him to eat in peace. He took a bite of his burger and washed it down with a swig of the shake. While so many of the people around him still seemed on high alert that he was sitting there, several had gone back to their own meals, their own food, their own company.

"Hey, aren't you Grady Benson?"

Grady turned in the direction of the voice and found a booth of three guys, early twenties, off to his left. He swallowed his bite and gave them a nod.

"I remember watching you at the last Olympics, man," one of the guys said. "Tough loss."

"He didn't lose, you idiot; he came in fourth," another guy said.

He didn't need the reminder. The first guy was right. He'd lost. Fourth place had never been good enough, not when he was favored to win the gold. Not when he only had himself to blame.

"Don't beat yourself up, man. Hard to come back after something like that."

"I'm fine." Grady set his burger down.

The guy laughed. "Dude, you're done."

"Jimmy," one of the other guys warned.

Grady gritted his teeth.

Jimmy laughed again. "What? You saw what happened in Vermont. He didn't even finish. Washed-up at thirty, that's gotta suck."

He should stand up and walk away. He should pay the waitress, get in his SUV, and keep driving to Colorado, where he could get ready for the next race. He should . . . but he didn't.

He'd been listening to commentators talk about his skiing, his messy technique, his disregard for the rules for years—but now they'd started using terms like *washed-up* and *retirement*, and whenever he heard them, something inside him snapped.

Grady turned toward the table. "You got a problem with me?"

Jimmy's expression turned smug. "I'm just not a fan, is all. You're not as great as you think you are."

Grady reminded himself he didn't know this guy, didn't care what he thought. And yet something about Jimmy was really getting under his skin. He looked around for Betsy so he could get his check and leave.

But Jimmy didn't let up. "We all watched the races the other day. Guy choked. He choked, man."

"Dude, shut up," his friend said.

"Supposed to be the fastest guy on the slopes, but my aunt Frieda could've skied better than him. In her sleep."

"You don't even have an aunt Frieda." The other guy sounded as irritated with his friend as Grady was. Grady's knuckles had gone white around the edge of the table.

"Heard he got his girlfriend pregnant and then tried to pay her to keep quiet. Not like he's got a squeaky-clean image to protect or anything."

That was it. How that lie had ever picked up steam, Grady didn't know, but he was sick of hearing it. Grady spun out of his chair and lunged at Jimmy, pulling him out of the booth by his jacket. A plate crashed to the floor, but Grady barely noticed.

Jimmy tried to fight him off, but he was several inches shorter and not half as strong as Grady. Still, he managed to squirm from Grady's grasp, falling into a table and knocking over more dishes.

The guy didn't know when to quit. He smirked at Grady. "I forgot you've got a temper, too. Is that why nobody wants you on the team?"

Who did this punk kid think he was? Grady didn't hold back as he hauled off and punched Jimmy square in the jaw. Jimmy's body shot backward into a wall of framed photos, which shattered when they hit the floor.

Grady stepped back to catch his breath when out of nowhere, Jimmy lunged toward him, catching him off guard and ramming Grady's body into the long counter on the other side of the diner. He was scrappy, Grady would give him that, but this kid didn't have nearly the fighting experience Grady did. He'd grown up fighting. He practically enjoyed it. He knew how to handle himself.

Grady wrestled him to the ground, his only focus to keep him there. Jimmy yanked himself from Grady's grasp and landed a punch across his left eye. Anger welled up inside him as the sting of pain zipped through his body. Grady's mind spun; long-buried grief demanded to be felt. He had Jimmy's comments to thank for that.

Washed-up at thirty.

Injuries beyond repair.

Sloppy technique.

Embarrassed. Frustrated. Ashamed.

Someone grabbed him from behind and pulled him off Jimmy. Only then did Grady realize he'd unleashed the full force of his rage on the man, who now lay beneath him, bloody and moaning.

He shrugged from the grasp of the person who'd pulled him away and wiped his face on his sleeve. He scanned the diner and found pairs of eyes darting away from him. All but one. The blonde's. She stood off to the side, unmoving, watching him.

He looked away.

He didn't need to be judged by Little Miss Goody Two-shoes.

Jimmy's friends pulled him to his feet as two officers in uniform yanked the front door open. Grady glanced at Betsy, who wouldn't meet his eyes. He should apologize. He'd made a huge mess of the place. Tables were overturned, at least one of them broken. The glass from the shattered picture frames crunched underneath his feet, and there was at least one place where they'd put a hole in the wall. Oh no, make it two.

He didn't even remember doing that.

Before he could say anything to the wild-haired waitress (or anyone else), one of the cops—an older man with a wrinkled face—grabbed him by the arm. "You'll have to come with me, son."

The other officer did the same to Jimmy, who immediately launched into his side of the story, spouting about how Grady "freaked out for no reason" and "I'm the victim here, man."

Grady let the older cop lead him through the small crowd, avoiding the stares of the people who'd just witnessed yet another of his colossal mistakes. The blonde stood near the door, arms crossed over her chest. She said nothing, but her eyes never left his as the officer pushed him through the door and into the street.

"Do I need to cuff you, or have you calmed down?" the cop asked.

"You don't need to cuff me," Grady said, wishing he'd never stopped in this ridiculous town in the first place. What was it that made him pull off at the Harbor Pointe exit? He wasn't particularly hungry—he was just tired of driving. He should've kept going. If only he could rewind the last hour.

Who was he kidding? He'd have to rewind a lot further back than that to undo the mess he'd made.

The second officer was shoving Jimmy into the back of a squad car parked at the curb.

"Look, Officer—" Grady turned toward the older man—"I'm sorry I lost my temper back there. I'll pay for the damages to the diner."

"I'm sure you will." He opened the other back door of the car and motioned for Grady to get in.

"There's really no need for this," Grady said. "I screwed up. I get it. But I'm fine now, and I'll make it right."

399

"Well, your version of 'making it right' might not be the judge's version of 'making it right.'" He eyed Grady. "There's still time for the cuffs."

Grady let out a stream of hot air, anger prickling the back of his neck as he leaned down and got into the car. Jimmy sat on the opposite side, sulking. At least he'd shut up. For now, anyway.

Through the windows of Hazel's Kitchen, Grady saw the people who'd witnessed the fight picking up overturned tables and chairs and sweeping broken plates into a dustpan. What a mess he'd made.

The main stretch of Harbor Pointe was made up of cotton candy–colored buildings neatly stacked together on either side of the street. As they drove, he saw a bakery, a flower shop, a couple more diners, antique stores. Old-fashioned lampposts shone on alternating sides of the street, casting a warm yellow hue over the brick road in front of them.

They drove in silence for several seconds until finally the older officer turned around and looked at Grady.

"I know you're not from here. What kind of beef could you possibly have with Jimmy?"

"He's crazy," Jimmy said.

"I'm not talking to you," the cop said.

"No beef. Just don't like people with smart mouths."

The cop laughed. "That I understand."

"It's not funny, Sheriff," Jimmy protested. "I'm pressing charges. Assault and battery. And I want a lawyer because I didn't do anything here." Jimmy was still riled up, and normally Grady would be too, but he'd been here before. He knew exactly what would happen next. He'd be arrested. Booked. Pay a fine and be on his way.

Though, sadly, this time, he wasn't even sure where he was on his way to.

A NOTE FROM THE AUTHOR

IT'S AMAZING TO ME to think about the journey I've been on as I wrote this book. When I first started brainstorming the idea for *If for Any Reason*, I had no clue what was about to happen. You see, it seemed like a charming plan to write a book full of letters from a mother to a daughter. Who could've guessed that as I was writing it, my own daughter would be diagnosed with thyroid cancer, sending me on the kind of journey no mother ever really wants to take.

I admit I didn't pick up this manuscript for a full month, maybe even two, after Sophia's diagnosis. It was too hard to write these letters—letters full of wisdom from a mother to a daughter. How I wanted to impart wisdom to my own girl, but I simply felt unworthy. I didn't know how to help her deal with the kind of diagnosis nobody ever wants to get, especially at the age of seventeen.

But as is always the case, the writing helped me through. It seems I'm unable to think or feel anything unless I'm processing it through the written word.

More than once, this book had me in tears as I contemplated the lessons and thoughts and dreams and ideas I most wanted to communicate to my own daughter. More than once I had to delete letters simply because they made no sense in Emily's story . . . because they were written to be a part of mine.

I suppose you could say that this book has become tremendously important to me, carrying me through the most difficult season of my life thus far. It accompanied me on that journey, helped me weather that storm, gave me a much-needed distraction, and inadvertently reminded me how very precious life is—not because of what we do or what we own but because of the people who make every day so much richer.

I'm so thankful for Vanessa Reyes, a scrapbooker who, years ago, created a small album full of letters for her daughters—letters that would serve as their connection to her *if for any reason* she was no longer there. It stuck with me and inspired me to write my own letters and, eventually, this novel.

I sincerely hope you enjoyed Emily and Hollis's story, and I would *love* to know what you thought of it. I truly love to hear from my readers, especially when I get to know you a little better! I invite you to stay in touch by signing up for my newsletter on my website, www.courtneywalshwrites.com, or by dropping me a line via e-mail: courtney@courtneywalshwrites.com.

With love and gratitude to you,
Courtney

ACKNOWLEDGMENTS

TO ADAM. Always and forever. Me + You. We've been through the wringer, haven't we? And yet here we are, still standing. I know I wouldn't be if it weren't for you. Thanks for believing in me and for telling me it was going to be okay . . . even though there were moments neither of us knew that for sure. You are my favorite.

Sophia. In awe of your strength and your vulnerability. You are truly one of a kind. Thanks for pointing out my gray hairs and keeping me on my toes.

Ethan. Your kindness inspires me as much as your hard work motivates me. I'm so glad I get to be your mom.

Sam. I'm so thankful for all the ways you make me laugh. Someday maybe you can thank me in one of your books. ;)

Natalie, Tonia, Chamara, and Tenille. The way you blessed us during such a difficult time in our lives will never be forgotten. I'm so very grateful.

My parents, Bob and Cindy Fassler. So grateful for your love and wisdom in my life.

Stephanie Broene. I was thinking just this morning about how much I love our chats. Thank you for helping me make my stories better, stronger, more realistic. And especially for believing in the words God's put in my heart.

Danika King. You make every story better, and I am so blessed to work with you. Thank you for being such a gift.

Carrie Erikson. I'm not sure there will ever be a truer friend.

To everyone who supported us during Sophia's diagnosis, surgery, and treatment. There are so many people who helped carry this burden, and we are indebted to all of you. I've never felt an outpouring of love like that, and while the circumstances were not ideal, there were many sweet and unexpected gifts along the way—this was one of them.

To Katie Ganshert, Becky Wade, and Melissa Tagg. Sweet writer friends who put up with my lamenting right around the middle of every book. What would I do without you? I'm so thankful for the hours we spend talking writing, publishing, and life. God's given me such gifts in each of you.

To Natasha Kern, my agent. Thank you for challenging me to be better and write stronger. I am so thankful for your wisdom on this journey.

To Deb Raney. Always my mentor and always my friend. For all you've done to help me understand story, I am grateful.

To the entire team at Tyndale. I know how very blessed I am to work with the best of the best. Thank you for allowing me to be a part of your family.

To my Studio kids and families. Thank you for making my "day job" so much fun. Every single one of you is an inspiration to me—an example of bravery. Some days we need that a little more than others.

And especially to you, my readers. I hope you know how special you are. I hope you know that your kind words (either directly to me or via a review or social media) are so greatly appreciated. I hope you know that these stories are my way of sharing my heart with you, and I am so grateful to have that opportunity. You mean the world to me.

DISCUSSION QUESTIONS

1. When Emily arrives on Nantucket at the beginning of the story, she's trying to recover from a significant professional failure. Hollis is also faced with the premature end of his baseball career. Have you ever had to deal with unexpected setbacks like Emily and Hollis do? How did you respond?

2. Hollis longs to connect with his daughter, Jolie, but at first he has no idea where to start. Why is it so difficult for him to relate to her? What are some things Hollis does to demonstrate his love for Jolie, and what impact does this have on their relationship?

3. One of Emily's life philosophies is "You have to go through the hard stuff to get to the good stuff." How does this play out in her story? Can you think of any "good stuff" in your life that resulted from going through challenging times?

4. For much of her life, Emily has unquestioningly followed the advice in her mom's letters. In what ways does Isabelle's advice benefit her, and how does it hold her back? How does Emily's perspective on the letters change throughout the story?

5. Isabelle's parents insist that she conform to their standards of success and decorum, but she has different ideas for how

her life should go. How can parents guide and instruct their children while still allowing them to become their own people? How should older children respond when they feel unfairly constrained by their parents?

6. Emily must choose between taking the risk of loving others and shutting them out or running away. What does this choice look like in her relationship with Hollis? With Jolie? With her grandmother? Why does it often feel so risky to love others and let them love you?

7. Hollis credits his friend Jimmy with encouraging and supporting him after his injury and setting an example of faith in God. "When it came to his faith, Jimmy approached things his own way. God wasn't something far-off in the sky that couldn't be grasped or understood—to Jimmy, he was as real as Hollis and the other guys he called friends." Can you think of a friend or family member in your own life who has played a role like this for you? What would it look like for you to be this sort of friend to someone else?

8. Jack edges his way into Emily's life by signing on as a contractor for her home renovation. Do you think he went about this the right way, or would you have advised him to be more straightforward in connecting with her? How would you describe Jack and Emily's relationship by the end of the story? How are they able to move toward reconciliation in spite of the mistakes of Jack's past?

9. Emily discovers a passion for working with kids: her love for youth theatre grows over the course of the summer. What about this vocation is so rewarding to Emily? If you could transform one of your passions into a career, what would it be?

10. In Emily's letter to her mom, she writes, "I thought [God had] abandoned me, but it seems maybe he was there all

along—maybe it was time for me to deal with this pain so I could move forward." How does Emily arrive at this place of renewed faith and determination to move forward? Looking back over your life, can you identify a painful situation where God was at work, even if you couldn't see him there at the time?

11. Nantucket serves as a vacation destination for several generations of the Ackerman family. Does your family have a favorite spot to vacation, now or when you were a child? What are some of your favorite—or least favorite!—memories from that place?

12. At the end of the story, Hollis and Emily discuss possibilities for their future together. How do you imagine their lives unfolding beyond the final page of the book?

ABOUT THE AUTHOR

COURTNEY WALSH is the author of *Just Look Up*, *Just Let Go*, *Paper Hearts*, *Change of Heart*, and the Sweethaven series. Her debut novel, *A Sweethaven Summer*, was a *New York Times* and *USA Today* e-book bestseller and a Carol Award finalist in the debut author category. In addition, she has written two craft books and several full-length musicals. Courtney lives with her husband and three children in Illinois, where she is also an artist, theatre director, and playwright.

Visit her online at www.courtneywalshwrites.com.